SECRETS OF THE VOID

II

ALSO BY EMMA HAMM

Deep Waters
Whispers of the Deep
Song of the Abyss
Echoes of the Tide
Call of the Fathoms

Kingdom Below
A Darkness So Sweet
A Light So Blinding
A Spark So Bright

Seven Deadly Demons
The Demon Court
The Demon Crown
The Demon Prince
The Demon Mark

and many more...

Emma Hamm

Copyright © Emma Hamm 2025

All rights reserved. This book or parts thereof may not be reproduced in any form, stored in any retrieval system, or transmitted in any form by any means—electronic, mechanical, photocopy, recording, or otherwise—without prior written permission of the publisher, except as provided by United States of America copyright law. For permission requests, write to the publisher, at "Attention: Permissions Coordinator," at the address below.

Visit author online at www.emmahamm.com

Cover Design by Giulia Soeima
Interior Artwork by Chuck Monty

This book is a work of fiction. Any references to historical events, real people, or real places are used fictitiously. Other names, characters, places, and events are products of the author's imagination, and any resemblance to actual events or places or persons, living or dead, is entirely coincidental.

For all you monster fuckers out there.
I finally gave you your tentacles.

Chapter 1

Proteus had long been asleep.

But no longer.

He could feel himself coming back to life, piece by piece. First it was his gills. The fluttering, thin membranes against his neck filtered in seawater that he hadn't tasted in centuries. So many flavors danced through his mind. The sweetness of oysters and clams that were just outside of his prison. The saltiness of the sea itself. Brine from hundreds of years of brewing in the deepest depths of the sea. It was as it always had been, and yet, somehow more.

It was fresher than he remembered. The sea itself had come back alive in the long years he'd been imprisoned. This place, this ocean, had once been filled with tragedy. It had tasted like oil and blood when he'd first been locked away. Now, it tasted as it always should have. As he remembered it from when he had first been created.

Then his claws flexed. His hands had always given him away as something "other." Inhuman, certainly, but not one of the People of Water either. They were larger than they should be, with an extra joint that made his fingers even more elongated. The claws that tipped them were poisonous, if he remembered correctly.

He still dreamt of the time when he had first been created. He had gone to the People of Water, a messenger from the depths itself, and they had been terrified of him. They had feared his massive claws, his strange body. His odd appearance proved that he was like them, but not close enough.

The memory flared an age old anger that had once nearly burned him alive. His chest heated, and rage flowed all the way down into his tail. Slowly, piece by piece, anger heated his blood and made him glow.

The light that illuminated his prison didn't come from his skin. The People of Water glowed through tiny, bioluminescent dots that emerged from the depths of their skin. They were stars in his sea, sparkling with beauty and grace that very few could ever mimic. But Proteus? It was not his skin that glowed.

It was his bones.

His ribs illuminated first. Each of them warming, blinking, one by one, the light spearing through the thin flesh of his chest. He knew if he looked down, he would see the shadows of his dual hearts and the four lungs that dotted down his massive torso. And then it continued, light sparking down his spine and traveling into his tail where all the dozens of bones made up the massive length. He was so brilliant that he could suddenly see his tight prison in stark relief. Every detail. And the lack of anything in this coffin but him.

He'd been trapped here so many years ago, he couldn't even remember how long he'd been waiting. There was no way to tell how many days had passed, or how many years. Only that time had seemed to pass so slowly that his mind had eventually snapped. He'd given up even trying to think about where he was or how long it had been.

Proteus had passed into a meditative state that had given him some peace of mind.

Plotting what he would do when he finally escaped this prison was the only thing that had kept him sane. And oh, he had plans.

He had great and wondrous plans.

Flexing the fins along the side of his tail, he moved his palms so that they were pressed against the cold metal that surrounded him. All those years ago, he'd been locked in here by his own people. The People of Water, who were meant to worship him, had deemed him too dangerous, but they were willing to keep him alive in hopes of stealing his gifts.

For the first hundred years, they had still come to worship him. They begged and pleaded for him to see into their futures, but also into the minds of those who would harm them. They had used him as an oracle, locked where they could use him as they pleased, and he was so bored he would do nearly anything he was asked.

Until they petitioned the ancients, begging for more than just a limited existence and a need to rattle his cage for prophetic truths. Soon enough, there was an entire subspecies of their kind that could see the future. But they would never know what he knew. They would never see as far into the future, nor would they experience the depth of his power. They had not lived during the time he had. They did not know the secrets he knew.

What had awakened him this time? The last time had been a depthstrider who had dared come speak with an ancient being. He had told the priest what he wanted to hear, but also added in a flavor of fun to the mix. He did not care why that depthstrider had been so desperate, but Proteus was so bored in his prison.

Playing with them had once been his favorite past time. He hadn't done so in a very, very long time. Let the male see his dead wife. Let him dream of a future with a human at his side. It was possible after all.

And it brought Proteus one step closer to being released from this hellish place.

He listened intently, waiting for a voice that might have woken him from his slumber. No voice came, though. There was only the faint sound of scratching on the outside of this locked prison.

No one knew how to open it. He'd had many people try over the centuries. Many People of Water were easy to trick. They listened to who they believed was once a god, and he had been, so they did whatever he said when they found him. But they had all failed. Each and every one of them until he was certain the locking mechanism required something else.

The tiny sounds could easily be just another crab. They had driven him mad years ago; hearing the sounds of their claws scraping above him had made him want to tear out his ears. It was a uniquely grating sound, and it made him want to scream every time he heard it. Years ago, there had been hundreds that clambered all over his prison. More and more of them, each of them devouring parts of his mind as he was forced to endure their movements.

Even the thought made him want to tear at his prison again. Attacking the coffin would only lead to broken claws and his own blood, but sometimes it helped ease the anger. Proteus was the teeth and claws of the ancients. He was the creature who was made to terrify the world when they could not leave the depths. His creators had been very explicit about what he was to become.

He would guard the sea against all those who would stand against the ancients. He would ensure the oceans remained under the ancients' control, as it always should have been and as it always would be.

He had a feeling that had changed since he'd been locked away.

Agitation grew in his chest as it hadn't for many, many years. He usually knew how to keep himself calm. Getting angry in a place like this only served to make his life more miserable. But he was angry. He was furious at all those who thought he could be contained, and he was furious with the ancients for leaving him here. Worst of all, Proteus was offended by the very world for throwing him into this prison and never once giving him a chance to fight back.

He deserved to be free. He deserved to be out in the waves.

Another tap. Another long scrape of what sounded like a claw, and then...

Light.

It wasn't coming from him, and then there was water. More seawater that wasn't burdened by the bitter bite of the metal that surrounded him. He could actually breathe it in without wincing. There was life that came with that.

Reaching with his fingers that were still pressed down against his sides, Proteus felt for the tiny gap that had suddenly appeared around the lid of his prison. The coffin they had placed him in was always upright, but his arms were pinned to his sides. If he moved his fingers just right, he could slide his claws out into the open sea.

It was the closest he'd been to freedom in so many years. His heart thundered in his chest. His bones glowed even brighter with hope and excitement.

Whoever this was, he was going to gift them whatever they wanted for solving a lock that had kept him imprisoned for this long. He would heap gold upon them. Raid every wreck that still languished at the bottom of the ocean to give them jewels, crowns, and coin.

Just a bit more, that's all he needed. Just a little more and then he would be free. He would be able to push the lid of the coffin off, and he would burst forth from this prison forever. They would never be able to put him back in here. He would make sure of that.

And then he looked to the right, at that small splinter of light, and saw the legs of a crab through it. Not entirely a crab, though. Those legs were made out of metal. They had seen better days, rusted as they were, but they were still legs.

Then antennae that were made of metal peered through the gap. There had once been screens at the end of them that likely were meant to look like eyes, but now only one still worked, and it blinked on and off rapidly.

"There you are," the voice emitted from whatever strange droid had found him. "I've been looking for centuries for this tomb. Do you know how hard it was to find without a tracker?"

"Open it."

"It's mostly rusted shut now. But considering the size of you, if you give it a good push, it should move. The silt has grown up from the bottom, or you've been sinking into it. You're almost level with the sea floor."

He didn't care. Coiling his tail underneath him, he slammed his body against the door. Over and over again. Every strike made the metal move just a bit more. The sea rushed in to meet him, and he had been thirsty for such a long time. The seal of his prison hadn't let him enjoy the best part of his world, and then…

Suddenly he was free.

The door burst open, and he rushed out into the ocean. It didn't matter where he was or what surrounded him. For the first time in centuries, he could swim.

Proteus flexed his tail and shot off into the darkness. It mattered little what might be out there. If there was a megalodon waiting for him, or a leviathan itself, he would battle it until the bitter end because none of it mattered. He was free. He was finally, wonderfully, breathlessly free.

His gills flared wide, and his lights illuminated even more of his skeletal form. The beast of the ocean, the terror of the waves, the firstborn son had returned, and he would make sure that the sea itself knew.

Spiraling through the water, he moved with a speed that would have shocked any who could see him. He remembered people being terrified of how quickly he could move because certainly he was too big to be able to do so. But he had more than just his own magic.

Reaching out into the sea itself, he felt her. The goddess who had given him life, the one who had gifted the ancients the power to create a being all on their own. The sea goddess welcomed him back into her embrace, and then he turned his head up into the current that flowed around him, and he roared.

The sound vibrated through the ocean around him. The water seemed to bubble, turning into steam with the centuries of rage that poured off of him and made the very sea boil with his anger. He was furious with all those who tried to trap him. Enraged that the sea had allowed it. So angry that all he wanted to do was destroy everything that stood in his way and only remake it once he was ready to do so.

They would all feel the wrath of the first son.

But the cold touch of the sea reminded him that it had been some time since any of the People of Water even remembered his existence. He was, without a doubt, a foreign creature to them now. They didn't even have stories about him. The depthstrider, who should have known who Proteus was, hadn't even guessed at what he might have found.

Time had worn away their terror of him. He had faded into myth, and then nothing at all. No one remembered who he was now, and he was going to have to change that.

Turning his glare in the direction he'd come, Proteus headed back toward the cage that had trapped him. How he knew where it was, he did not understand. He only knew that the sea guided him where he needed to turn, and he trusted it implicitly.

She, the goddess who had gifted them all life, was the only one who had never betrayed him. She had never forgotten he was in there, always sending him little gifts even while he remained rotting. Food had never fully eased his hunger, but she had ensured that he was still alive.

Breathing out, he finally found the tomb where they had kept him. It was a coffin. They'd carved his face on the outside, or something of that likeness. But it had long ago been worn away by the currents and creatures who had tracked paths across it. Even now, he could see the barnacles that had grown all over him, and how far he had indeed sunk into the silt at the bottom of the sea floor.

How deep was he? His gills were working harder than he remembered, but he also hadn't been alive in quite some time. It would make sense that his body didn't quite remember how to have this much fresh seawater to breathe.

"You look better already," a voice came again.

This time he was certain it was the small metal crab that was currently frozen on top of his tomb. The creature was made entirely out of rusted metal, and the reddish color was so prominent on its shell that he might have thought it was a real crab.

"What are you?" he asked.

Proteus swam close enough to grab the little beast by a leg and dangled it from his clawed hands. It was so small he could have crushed it in his massive grip.

The legs wildly struck out at him. "Put me down!"

"No. What are you?" Before it could argue, he snapped his jaws at it. "I don't enjoy waiting. You will tell me what you are, or I will rip out all your circuits."

For good measure, he stretched his jaw as he had not been able to do for such a long time. Proteus was not one of the People of Water, and his body showed the differences. He felt his jaw snapping, popping and then finally it opened as it was always meant to do. It split along his cheeks, likely spilling even more light into the water as the bones of his jaw cracked in half. And then it kept splitting, a line carving out his throat, the twin pieces of his jaw falling open to reveal more teeth that stretched down his neck and into the wide open maw he revealed.

The droid squeaked. "I am Pilot! I was sent to release you."

"What took you so long?"

It scrambled still, the legs still moving erratically. "I was only awakened a hundred years ago, and the ocean is rather large. I did not know where they had moved your tomb, and like I said, there's no tracker on you."

"Why were you programmed to awaken only a hundred years ago?"

"That was the appropriate time to... to..." Pilot stopped moving and then said, "I don't know. You were supposed to do the rest, I think."

With his mouth still split wide, he grinned. "Then I will do whatever I want."

Chapter 2

The droid directed him through the sea to a place he had never been. Or at least, he had no memory of it. Proteus had seen many things in the years he had been alive, so he was surprised that there were still places in this water that he did not know about. The droid surprised him often, though.

He swam past ancient shipwrecks and signs of battle. This area had apparently seen much of the war between humans and the People of Water. He had known it would happen long before the world had been destroyed. Perhaps that had even been part of why they had locked him up.

Proteus hadn't asked. He'd been too busy fighting against them, snarling that they would not put him in that damned coffin and weld him inside of it. The complicated locking system was one he still saw when he closed his eyes. All the pieces and parts that he'd destroyed year after year from the inside. He'd even bitten some of that metal off, taking hundreds of years to tear at it with his teeth that would always grow back. And still, the mechanism did not break.

Shaking himself free from the memories, he stared at a massive ship with masts so tall that it was clear it was very old. "How is that still here?" he muttered as they swam by it.

The droid in his hand wriggled. "Time is not the same in this place. I have only been here once before, when I was looking for you, and it is not the same as the rest of the world. This is an odd pocket of the ocean. A place outside of time."

He could feel it. The strangeness in the water. The odd glide of sensation against his skin that wasn't entirely water. He had seen the People of Water create a slick oil that oozed over their skin, allowing them to slip away from predators. The water here felt almost like that. Thick and hard to breathe.

Still, he took a deep breath of it, forcing the ooze through his gills, and moved farther into the depths.

The droid pointed him in certain directions, but it never said much until he finally saw where they were headed. The shadow looming in the sea before them was somewhat of a facility he recognized. Back in the days before they had imprisoned him, Proteus had worked on many creations. This strange box may have been one of them.

"The humans were the ones who wanted to wake me?" he asked, confusion turning his words a little guttural.

"Yes."

"Why?"

"I do not know. They wanted you to see what had happened in your absence, though. And they want you to be the person to take control of the sea once again." The droid clicked its legs against his hand to get his attention. "We go there."

The metallic box was similar to how he remembered the research facilities. The floating building was tethered to the ground by massive anchors. Very out of place for where it was at these depths. But considering it hadn't imploded, he could only imagine that it was built to withstand time. Unless, of course, this place helped keep it whole as well.

He swam closer, surveying to see if there was any glass on the exterior he could peer through. But there wasn't. It was just a box. A large box. He imagined there were many rooms within, but he couldn't get a glimpse of what the humans had hidden inside.

"This looks like a trap," he snarled.

"It is not."

"How do I know I can even trust you? You are merely the droid who released me."

"The only thing that has done so in centuries," Pilot reminded him. "You were requested to be released for a reason. I cannot tell you what the reason is, or why they want you alive. The only answers you will get are inside that building."

He didn't like it. He didn't trust the humans any more than he trusted the People of Water. But he did want answers.

Proteus flexed the muscles in his tail. He needed to feed before he could fight anything off. They had passed by a few whales that would have done, but the orcas would put up a fight he knew he couldn't win right now. He'd have to find a decaying carcass and devour that whole to feed himself well enough.

That would be another day, though. Today, he would find out why he had been released.

He swam beneath the building, his heart already thundering in his chest. Metal screeched above his head as a panel slid open and revealed an entrance to the room within. There was only a meager light coming from above his head, but considering the flickering, he had a feeling it would take a little while for the power system to turn on. Once that did, he would have to squint his eyes to see through the glare.

Humans had always loved their blinding white lights.

It wasn't the first time Proteus had been inside a research facility. There was a time long ago when he had been inside many of them. Humans and the undine, as they called them, had never gotten along. Thus, their interactions had always been secret. But that didn't mean there had never been interactions between the two.

He remembered a scientist back then, a young man who had been so thrilled to be going against his government and even the world. He'd had so much money he didn't know what to do with it, other than indulge his own strange need to disregard what others wanted. That man had been certain he could use the undine to his advantage. The People of Water disregarded his attempts at contacting them. They'd seen him only as a human who was just like all the others, and unworthy of any conversation.

Proteus had seen otherwise.

He heaved himself out of the water, splashing liquid up and into the room that had been prepared ahead of time. The humans knew anyone entering would bring water with them, whether that person was human or undine.

The drainage system on the floor awakened. It turned on loudly, sucking up the seawater that would damage the electronics that covered the walls from floor to ceiling. The wall to his right was all screens. They were flickering on one by one, but it was taking much longer than it should have. Another wall was mostly panels, but he knew those would be good for summoning droids. Then there was a table against the back corner, but it wasn't really a table. The strange humming noise coming out of it was his first clue, and then clanking noise as the generator was turned on. He'd wondered how there was power down here. Apparently, the humans had created a generator that could run with water after all.

This was a research lab, no question about it. But what he didn't understand was why this would be the place the droid was directed to bring him. There was no reason for him to be here.

"You summoned me," he said, his deep voice echoing throughout the room. "Now what do you want with me?"

A few more lights flickered on at the sound of his voice. He dropped the droid, which immediately scuttled over to a control panel. The crab-like being connected to the main screen with an electrical cord that extended out of its stomach.

"Pilot, connecting. Package acquired."

Package? He was no package. He was a god of the sea who demanded to be treated with respect. How dare this droid refer to him as a package? He would crush it into oblivion.

A panel in the center of the floor flickered with light, and suddenly a hologram stood before him. It was the same man he remembered from long ago, although significantly older. The very wealthy man had thought money could control the world around him, and who had been very, very wrong in that thought process.

"Proteus!" the hologram said, a little too excited even though he had recorded this two hundred years prior. The man had always been oddly energetic and excitable. "I had hoped we would meet each other again under better circumstances, but I suppose that is what time does to a mortal body. I wasn't so lucky as to be in the early proceedings of the Longevity project, but the more I find out about it, the less I wish to be involved. Anyway. You're here because I want you to continue our work."

"Our work?" Proteus muttered, drawing his tail into the room to allow the door to seal. "We were never working together."

"But first, let me catch you up on a few things. The droid that awakened you is one of thousands I created just for this moment. They have all been keeping an eye on the world for you. Recording it. Readying themselves to provide all the details you will need in a very short amount of time. You've been asleep for a long time and… well, I don't imagine you'll want to spend the next few hundred years hearing what happened in your absence." The man pinched his fingers together as though to emphasize how short a time it had been, but then stretched his hand wide to indicate how long he'd been away.

He didn't need a reminder.

Baring his teeth in a snarl, Proteus looked over at Pilot, who was still plugged into the center console. "How long has it been?"

"Um..."

"How. Long." Proteus ground the words out, tired of this droid already. It shouldn't be able to argue with him, or stall providing information. The entire reason for its existence was to take orders and do what it was told. How someone had programmed it otherwise was a mystery to him.

"Nearly four hundred years, give or take. It's hard to go back that far and determine just how long it has been, and how long it's been since you were... you know." It lifted a metal arm and waved it in the air. "Only two hundred years of information is stored in this room, though. Essentially all the history after the fall of the humans. Are you ready?"

"Ready for what?" he grumbled. The hologram of the man was frozen in place, blinking on and off.

It gave him a few moments to look at the man he had worked with over four hundred years ago. Even in this glimpse, he was older. Proteus remembered him with wild, curly black hair. Not the curls that were rather limp with gray streaks running through them. His face was thinner too. More hollow when it had been plump. He hadn't been remarkably tall or short, nor notably handsome or strong. This was a man who could walk through a crowd and no one would remember he had been there.

That had been his superpower. No one had ever questioned a man like him, who was so hellbent on destroying the world.

"Show me," Proteus snarled.

All the screens on the wall burst to life at once. There were thirty of them, each depicting many scenes of what he had missed.

"I have been assured that your ability to absorb knowledge is renowned," Pilot said, its voice floating around him like some kind of omnipotent being. "Thirty screens shouldn't be too much for you, is it?"

"No," he muttered, his gaze already flicking between each screen. "Track my eye movements. Once I have seen enough, change the screen."

"Understood."

And so he remained there for days on end, watching what had happened to the world he'd left behind.

He knew the humans had been bloodthirsty, but he hadn't thought they would destroy their own planet with such ease. There was a sadness to it that he hadn't expected to feel. The ocean had endured, as it always did. But it enraged him to watch the lands above that he had always been so enthralled with slowly disappearing. The storms that brewed killed so many. The wildfires ate and consumed until there was little left. What had once been lush and green turned barren and ashen.

The world was no longer what he remembered, and he watched it all happen far too fast. Then the humans had come into the sea, and he watched the wars start. He watched as the People of Water fought to maintain what was theirs, to control the destruction of the ocean that happened. It infuriated him to no end to watch them slowly, bitterly, unendingly losing.

Where was their drive to fight? How had they been beaten so thoroughly? They were creations of the sea herself, beings who had endured for centuries on end. They should not have failed.

But then he watched the People of Water regroup, gather together. He watched the humans patch themselves back up, even after losing cities. The need for life flowed through all of them, no matter how hard it became. They weren't all that different from each other.

He watched love bloom while battles were won and lost. He watched people become new beings and new lifeforms, all in the need for progress.

And at the end of it all, he knew what he had to do.

"I do not wish to work with the same people I worked with before," he murmured. "But I do know what our path must be next."

"Oh good," Pilot said. "I was worried you wouldn't understand the message."

There was much he had to plan to do this, though. The world above had been destroyed, and there was little room for what he wanted. But he would see the humans removed from the oceans once and for all. They had tried working together. They had tried to collaborate, but it always ended in bloodshed. Now, he would separate them for good.

"How do the People of Water refer to the land now?" he asked.

"Above."

He tsked. "Of course it was would be that simplistic. And what is the state of the land?"

"Not good."

"Clarify."

The droid unplugged itself and hopped down onto the floor. "I would suggest that the land is likely beyond saving at this point. There are still pockets of land that support some life forms, but there are not many. The airborne droids that were assigned to the surface have all long since died. Access to sunlight is no longer consistent enough to power them, and without solar energy, they are unfortunately incapable of continuing their work."

"So we will have to see it for ourselves then. I find it hard to believe that all life forms were wiped out. And even more than that, I remember the resilience of the human spirit. We will discover what has happened Above." He slapped his tail against the metal. "This will work. But I will need someone more talented than you to help me. There are many places that a droid simply cannot reach."

"No one is alive who would be able to help. They are all long dead."

"Tau?"

"Destroyed when you helped the depthstrider."

Ah, now he remembered. That was why he had helped the depthstrider as well. He had prophesied that Tau would be destroyed and that it needed to be for the betterment of the world. But why...

Then he remembered. "I made a deal with that depthstrider. A gift to the ocean. What was that?"

The sea itself had told him to make that bargain. He needed to swim in this direction, or the future would never be right. He needed whatever sacrifice the depthstrider had been willing to make.

"A pod," the droid replied. "There was a pod dropped into the sea, and it was supposed to be a gift for you. I do not know where it landed, though."

He hummed low in his chest, the rumbling sound igniting the lights of his ribs. "Then I suspect we need to go find it."

21

Chapter 3

The sea guided him to where his sacrifice had fallen into the void. He knew where to find it, even without her help. The goddess always wanted to make things easier for him, however, and he took her advice with all the pleasure of one who could still speak with a being like her.

She gave him the peace of mind to know that the gift left for him by that depthstrider would be helpful. He could feel it in his bones. But for some reason, the sea hid what it was from his mind.

How strange. He wasn't used to her hiding anything. This time, however, she merely allowed him to continue through the water until he was over an abyss. Deep and narrow, a canyon carved into the earth, disappearing beneath him. It was unlucky for any gift to end up all the way down there.

How could anything survive that fall? Frowning, he darted into the crevice, deeper and deeper toward the core of the sea.

It was warmer in these waters. Not the frigid wasteland where he had seen even ice growing on the ocean floor, no matter how much salt prevented its growth. He was used to the ache and bite of cold, not the blast of heat that warmed his gills and threatened to sear his already worn fins.

Here was undiscovered by most, if not all beings in these waters. There was nowhere for them to escape if a predator followed them. No hidden crevices where they could hide. No comfort they would be able to find until they came close enough to the core.

Light bloomed from deep volcanic vents. Lava bubbled up from them often, giving a strange texture to the ground when it erupted and cooled, leaving a rippling wave of hard stone that guided him closer and closer to the strange object waiting for him.

A metal tube rested luckily on a cooled mound of lava, rather similar in appearance to the coffin he had once been trapped in. The light of the crimson flow turned it red in his vision, reflecting the light from its metal surface until it almost appeared to glow. This was not just a gift. It was far more than that.

He swam up to the edge, uncaring that the water here was so hot it made the scales on his tail ache. It didn't matter. This tube was strangely impervious even to the lava that heated the metal. Though it was warm, and he could see areas that had finally succumbed to the heat and started to melt, the entire coffin was largely intact.

Even stranger, he could see that the front of it was clear. It was foggy though, textured on the glass, so it was hard for him to peer within it.

He was not going to pick up a molten metal tube without knowing what the depthstrider had gifted him. He refused. Any of this could be a trap, and he would not be attacked when he had just awoken.

Planting his massive hand on the clear surface, he marveled at the sight of his massive claws. A light turned on within the tube the moment he touched it and dragged his hand down the glass, and the silhouette of his unusually built, dark hand tipped in deadly talons dragged across the face of the woman inside.

Her face was smooth and unblemished, perfect skin as though she'd never had a moment outside of that coffin to contaminate the body within it. Her dark black hair smoothed away from her face, not a single strand out of place, even though she must have had quite the tumble through the water to get here. She had clearly never seen the sun in her life, and he wondered if she'd remain so pale if she had seen it before.

Humans were rarely interesting to him, and this one was only interesting because of her circumstance. She shouldn't have been stuck in that glass coffin any more than he should have been stuck. And he supposed he had been asking for someone to help him. All he had to do was wake her up, terrify her into agreeing to do whatever he said, and then move forward with his plan. This time with an accomplice.

Time would tell if it was a good plan or not. She certainly wasn't going to like it, no matter what he asked her to do.

While he stared down at her moon-shaped face, a small metal leg shifted a strand of her hair back in place. So the pod was what had kept her alive this long, and what was keeping her safe. The metal appendage then turned toward the glass, and fogged it from the inside this time. The frosted glass made it almost impossible for him to see the woman within.

"Curious," he muttered as he leaned down and heaved the molten metal into his arms. "We'll have to see what else is inside you."

It was heavy, but not so heavy that he could not carry it. Proteus took his time speeding back to the hidden place where Pilot had brought him. He needed the sea to cool the metal before he picked it up. But perhaps the heat was the last of his worries as he risked a human seeing the facility. It could all go very wrong, and then there would be blood all over that clean facility. A tragedy, really.

Besides, he didn't think rushing would make any difference to the woman in the pod. She had been sealed in there for a while now. Unlike him, she did not appear to be awake.

The strange square floating in the middle of the ocean awaited him just as before, with four anchors on each side. Speeding underneath it, he impatiently waited for the hatch to open before throwing her coffin up into the room and following behind her.

The echoing clang of metal striking metal made his ears ring. He flopped into the room at the same time the sound echoed, and immediately his tail coiled. He hated loud noises. Always had, even when he was a child.

And once the echo stopped, all he could hear was a high-pitched shriek that still made the entire room far too loud and far too small at the same time. Wincing, he glanced up to see the sound was coming from Pilot. That little droid screamed in terror, and the entire room had to suffer with the sound until Proteus shouted back, "Droid, enough!"

Ah, blissful silence.

Finally, he could relax. The droid stopped screaming, no one moved in the room, and Proteus could think again.

Hauling himself up the side of the coffin he'd brought back with him, he was pleased to see the temperature change had made the mist bead up and drip away, revealing her pretty face. It was so strange to look down at her and see a person. Alive, but not quite.

Her chest rose and fell. Now, in the light of the room, he could see that she was wearing a strange, skin-tight suit. It was molded to her form, clinging to hills and valleys. Her body barely even cast a shadow considering all the light that reflected from within her chamber and within the room they were in. His eyes were nearly blinded by all that light.

"What is it?" Pilot asked, climbing up the side to stand on the glass and peer down at her with those strange, flickering eyes.

"The gift the depthstrider gave me," he replied, disgusted by the lack of help that had been provided. "It is useless. A pod like this could only mean she's been in stasis for a very long time."

Pilot had already extended the tentacle from his belly and plugged into the pod. The flashing lights on top of the pod stilled, and suddenly the clear section was a screen. Proteus couldn't read any of the words flying across it, but they were mostly zeros and ones, something he assumed droids were fluent in.

"Oh," Pilot said. Then again, but more drawn out, "Oh."

"What is it?"

"Still learning."

The little droid muttered "oh," about thirty more times before it unplugged itself and turned those elongated eyes to him. "This is a clone. In Tau, there were many of them used to keep the Originals alive. But after Tau fell, most of them were brought to the other cities to start their new lives. Some were to remain frozen, like this one, as they would overrun the cities with their numbers. But it was also thought to be kinder to not have clones of the same person running around in the same area. Mentally, they weren't sure that the clones would do well with that."

"Or anyone else in the city," Proteus murmured as he looked her over.

He had seen all of this on the screens while Pilot had shared with him the last two hundred years. But it didn't explain why the depthstrider had given him one, or why the sea had seemed so pleased that he had.

He was disappointed. The clones were empty vessels. Shells of people who had no memory or personality. They were children who had been allowed to grow adult bodies without ever actually developing.

"Useless," he muttered, turning away from the pod. "I do not need a servant who has never been awake. This is not helpful at all."

"But this one has been awakened," Pilot said, and then started tapping on the glass to activate some message. "Look for yourself."

Proteus leaned over to read the logs that were actually legible this time and realized, yes. This one had been awakened. Many times, in fact. He could see there were almost a hundred logs of this pod having been opened and the person within it awakened.

Knowing humans, if it had been logged that many times, then she had been awakened at least double that.

"Why would they have done that?" he murmured.

Pilot tapped a few more times on some of the messages and then there it was. An explanation. He wasn't very quick at reading the human language—it had been centuries since he'd even tried—but it came back to him fast enough.

Not only had this woman been awakened for a few days at a time, it appeared... "She's been... downloaded? What does that mean?"

"It means they were using a simulated environment to teach her," Pilot replied. Even the droid seemed confused. "Apparently they were creating a space where she could exist and learn and... well, frankly, mature. All in her mind. She was a real person, wandering through a fake world, until whoever had these codes woke her up."

"Who had the codes?"

"I don't know."

So she had been learning as if she were awake. Growing and doing who knows what in that simulated environment. That was a lot of time for any one person to have been groomed into a weapon, or even worse that he couldn't imagine. The people in Tau weren't known for being kind to the clones. Her kind were used for all sorts of things, from what he had watched on the personal surveillance from the city itself. He wondered what this one had been used for.

"Find out who it was," he said as he slunk back toward the open hatch. "I need to feed."

He wouldn't waste any more time on a fictional woman he would never understand. This clone was a person; that much was clear from her logs, but he had no idea what kind of person she was.

That's why he had a droid.

Proteus followed the whims of the sea then, floating through the waters and finding a recently deceased whale. Quite a few predators were already there, but they saw the size of him and felt the energy of hatred that poured off of him, and they didn't bother him all that much. One of the bigger sharks shoved him when he started to feast, but when Proteus turned toward it with the gaping maw of his mouth fully revealed, the beast slunk away.

A shame, really. He could have used a fight.

But the salty blubber eased the hunger that had been gnawing at him. He devoured pieces of the whale, consuming them until his gullet was so full he could feel his belly extend. And then he felt his strength return.

The power he had been missing flexed throughout his entire form and... yes. He was back to himself. He could feel the sea bending to his will now. He could feel the muscles that were always so strong filling back out. He could go for months without eating now.

Endless.

Enduring.

The kind of creature that was almost impossible to kill.

Grinning perhaps a little too wide, he returned to the box in the sea that kept his captive. Soon enough, he would enact his plan. Soon enough, he would discover what this woman knew and what she had been trained to do.

He slipped inside and approached the coffin, where Pilot had plugged himself in again. "What did you discover?" he asked.

"One of the Originals had woken her many, many times. It's not entirely a good finding, but the man was a very remarkable scientist. He downloaded technical skills into her mind. She's particularly good at computer science and mathematics, although most of what she has learned will not be helpful here. She is used to much newer technologies than what will be required to connect us with Above."

"But the understanding of such things will not be beyond her?"

"Doubtful. She would be useful enough to do what you need." Pilot hesitated though. He could hear there were more words in that response that the droid wasn't telling him.

"And?"

"And..." It seemed to pause even more for dramatic effect. "If you'd like, we can wake her now."

So easy.

It was going to be almost too easy to wake the creature who would help him for ages to come. The creature who, for all intents and purposes, would become his slave and do his bidding no matter what he ordered her to do.

He leaned over the coffin, staring down at her serene features where she rested. She had no idea what monster she would wake up to. "What about our language?"

"I've already taken the time to download it. The software on this pod is significantly advanced. It only took the better part of an hour while you were gone for it to affix new protocol in her mind. No need for a translation device." Pilot quieted before muttering, "The ethical concerns about this machine are endless."

"When was the last time she was conscious?"

"Two years ago. Her Original had her working in the lab with the other clones. He was... experimenting upon them."

"How so?"

Why was it the droid seemed uncomfortable telling him? "They had many People of Water that they were testing, and he wanted to determine whether or not he could combine the species' DNA. She was helping him splice gills into human subjects and trying to make it so they could breathe underwater. They all drowned. She had to watch many versions of her own clones... drown."

He hated humans like that man. It was why he had hated the wealthy one who had built this place too. Proteus had no reason to be loyal to any of them, but his choices now were his.

Again, he smoothed his clawed hand over the image of her face, his hand shaking with the need to crush in her skull and rid the scourge of her species from this planet.

"Wake her," he snarled. "And we'll see what she has to say for herself."

Chapter 4

In her dreams, she was a real person.

Ellie had been pulled out of her stasis so many times, it was hard to guess what was real and what wasn't. But here, in this dream world, she was always treated like a real, living being. Like she wasn't a clone of the person who had come before her.

That's how she always knew the difference. It was easy to guess when she was awake and when she wasn't by the programming around her.

The people here smiled when she walked through the halls. They laughed at her jokes, waved at her when she meandered past them. They wished her to have a good day every single time they saw her. Sometimes they even brought her little gifts. Today it was a fresh apple from the gardens of Tau.

She wasn't even sure if the real Tau had apples. Or gardens. But here, where everything was perfect and nothing ever went wrong, she knew that there were apples.

Biting into the crisp flesh, she headed toward the lab to continue her experiments. This simulation was so powerful, she was actually doing real work. It was recorded by the pod that she was in, or at least, so he said.

Malcolm Maximus Cornwall. He was the scientist who woke her every few months or so, and the one who had taught her everything she knew. He'd even built the program she was currently living in. Absolutely everything had been designed by his hand. So she had him to thank when she got into her cozy bed, when she marveled at the beautiful wallpaper in the room she worked in, or when she had a crisp apple like the one she held in her hand.

As she turned the pale white corner that led to the labs, an unsettling thought bothered her.

She'd never eaten an apple. She had no idea if what she tasted now was actually what an apple was like, or if it was very different in the real world. Thoughts like that bothered her sometimes. Malcolm would tell her that was entirely natural, and she shouldn't let it bother her too much. After all, it wasn't likely that she would ever bite into a real apple. She might as well enjoy this one.

She entered the lab, and a very handsome man spun around in his chair. He had always been her counterpart. In the simulation, his name was Romeo Steel. In the real world, his name was Steve, and he was not anywhere near as handsome as this.

He'd programmed himself to have a strong jaw and plush lips. His eyes sparkled with mischief no matter what he was doing, and his shoulders were broad and square. Muscles packed onto his form, almost ridiculous in their quantity. He pointed them out to her often, but she didn't look at him that much.

Because Ellie knew what he really looked like. And it wasn't anything like this at all.

Steve was a very scrawny white man who was severely balding at a very young age. He'd always wanted to be tall and strong, and was absolutely incapable of convincing himself to work out in the real world. He lived in this simulation almost as much as she did.

"You're finally here! I was wondering when you'd show up." He grinned at her, trying to flirt like he always did.

He said the same thing every single morning. No matter what time she arrived, Steve tried to make her feel like she was late. It didn't make any sense whatsoever, considering time didn't matter here. She wasn't alive. She wasn't dead. She was just here to learn and develop and grow all the things that Malcolm wanted her to grow.

Why? She had no idea. Whenever they woke her, she was tested. Over and over again. They made her code things, write different scripts, see if she could compete with the droids as they spewed out binary code for her to decipher. A hundred things they had her try to figure out, but none of it ever linked together.

She didn't know why he was trying to teach her these things. Only that she had mastered Python when she was five years old in her reality. Of course, her body was that of a grown woman. It had been difficult for her the first few times she'd been woken up. And then he'd built the simulation, and it was even stranger.

She wasn't a child anymore, but she'd never been a child to begin with. She'd had to learn that other people weren't the same as her, and that clones weren't really people, anyway.

She was a doll. Something for him to insert knowledge into and bring back to life whenever he wanted to play.

The room was cold and clean. Malcolm liked things to be just right, and he'd designed this room to have no distractions. There was a panel in front of her, along with a keyboard to type whatever she needed, and then a wall of screens. She could watch a great manner of things there. All of her lessons took place in this room, as she learned theoretical knowledge that she only rarely put into practice. The white walls, white floor, and stark fluorescent lights always grated on her, though.

"I'm not late, and you know it," she muttered before heading to her table. "What are we focusing on today?"

"Genetics. Today is all about learning how splicing genetics between humans and undine affects the average body."

Ellie frowned. Hadn't she already learned that? When Romeo leaned forward and pressed a button, she was certain that they had in fact gone over this lesson before. The screens were full of the same content that she'd gone through just last week.

"Romeo?" she asked. "We've already had this lesson."

"No, we haven't. Every day brings new knowledge, unless we're continuing a study that we did throughout the week. This week is a new week, you know that." He leaned back in his chair and pulled out a newspaper.

That was where the algorithm ended. He stayed frozen like that while she flicked through all the things she was supposed to learn. It was exactly the same routine every single day.

The only way she could wake him up was if she had a question. Then, he would turn back on again. Alive suddenly to answer whatever she wanted to know.

The real Romeo didn't know the answer to almost any of her questions. He just stared at her blankly when she was awake. His stare made her uncomfortable.

So she didn't ask him any questions. Instead, she just started staring at the same genetic code she had stared at last week. The more she looked, the more certain she was that it was exactly the same. There were no differences. She'd been doing this kind of testing day in and day out, and this was the same thing she'd already learned.

Come to think of it, she'd been doing a lot of similar things lately. Her lessons seemed longer. She had told Romeo that she had already done lessons like this a few times, or that she was ready to move on but then couldn't for some reason. He drew out the lessons, but his programming didn't allow him to lie, so she now realized maybe he had been repeating days because... he had to.

She leaned back in her chair, ignoring the squeaky wheel that was literally programmed to distract her.

The lunch had been the same every day as well. Usually, she had a variety of fake food, their simulation was meant to keep her spirits high, given the circumstances of her life. But the lunch had been exactly the same. Almost as though it couldn't change.

No, that wasn't possible. There was absolutely nothing wrong with her programming or the simulation that she lived in. Tau was doing fine in the real world, and she was just paranoid. After all, Ellie was locked up in here by herself day in and day out. A girl was bound to get uncomfortable.

Still, her gaze went to the ceiling as though she could see the real world somewhere way above herself. What was going on up there, though? She hadn't heard from Malcolm in a while. He was predictable. Like clockwork, every two months he would pull her out of sleep and test her again. He was trying to create the perfect specimen, she assumed. Or maybe he liked toying with her. Whatever his reasoning, she just liked being alive for a few moments.

Using real lungs.

Smelling real scents.

Experiencing the world as a real person would experience it was a rare and wondrous treat every time she got to do it. He didn't know the gift he bestowed upon her, or he was very aware of it and thought she should be more grateful than she was. It depended on the day.

Sighing, she continued memorizing the same gene sequence that she had last week until she was certain she could recite it in her sleep. Memorization had always been easy for her. Malcolm said that was because her Original was a woman of impressive knowledge. Her brain worked differently from other people.

She'd tried to scan her own brain once. Malcolm had left her alone in the lab for a few hours when she'd actually been awake, and she wanted to see if there really was more brain activity in there than the average person.

He'd found her almost halfway through the test, and he'd been so furious. "You are wasting resources for what?" he'd snapped at her, ripping electrodes off her head so quickly he tore hair out with them. "You aren't capable of even reading these results! You aren't here, Ellie. You're just a copy of her."

That was the day he'd sat her down and explained to her that she wasn't a real person. He could dispose of her so easily, and no one would even care. Her death wouldn't even make people angry, and she had to remember that. There were hundreds of creations just like her. Dolls to be woken whenever someone wanted to play.

Leaning back in her chair, she spun around to face Romeo. "I have a question."

He immediately came back to life, but this time there was a strange glitch in him. He flickered a bit, and then one of his eyes started looking in the wrong direction. "I have an answer. What's your question, Ellie?"

She was so put off by his eye that she completely forgot what she wanted to ask. "Romeo... What's wrong with your eye?"

"Nothing can be wrong with my eye. Please state your question, or I will go back to reading my newspaper."

Steve never read anything. She wasn't even sure he could actually read. "I wanted to know what's happening in Tau. I haven't heard from Malcolm in a while, and I'd like confirmation that everything is all right in the real world."

Then, something even stranger happened. The same side of his face with the wandering eye started to droop. His mouth pulled down, like wax melting off a skeleton beneath. Then his head started tipping to the left as well, but his voice never changed. "Everything is fine in Tau. I would have been informed if there was anything wrong."

"I think there's something wrong with you," she whispered as she slowly stood. "Maybe we should reboot the simulation. Can you do that?"

Her chair disappeared. The one she had been sitting in was suddenly gone. And then all the screens flickered on and off, each of them showing a city on fire. Tau flooding. Bodies floating in the water and blood turning the ocean red until it was all she could see. Death. Destruction. Danger.

"Nothing is wrong," he said again, his body limp and slowly sliding onto the floor. "There is no reason to be alarmed. I am certain the system would reboot on its own if there were something... wr... wrong..."

Everything went dark.

It only did this when she was waking up. There was no world for a little while. Just her, locked in her head and the body that wouldn't wake until her pod let her. It was a terrifying silence that she had never grown used to.

Was this what all the other clones lived in? Were they also aware, stuck in their own heads as they wasted away into madness because no one allowed them to even open their eyes?

Panic started to set in. She could feel her heart thundering in her chest, racing as though it might be able to flee out of her body and leave the rest of her behind. It didn't want to be here either. It didn't want to suffer in the darkness and silence and pray that someone might find them.

A sharp prick hit the side of her neck. The only time that happened was when she was indeed waking up. Which meant all of that had been a nightmare. She would request that Malcolm allow her to look at the pod, because something had clearly gone wrong with the programming. Or perhaps this was all a test. Perhaps he wanted to see what she would do when she was afraid.

He was always testing her. That could definitely be the explanation.

Maybe clone bodies reacted differently under pressure, and he wanted to see how high her cortisol levels went. Or maybe there was an algorithm update that needed to happen, and he hadn't realized that doing it before she was awake would cause such nightmarish reactions within the programming.

So many explanations raced to the front of her mind because if she didn't explain it, then it was simply a cruel man wanting to hurt her.

She wouldn't even entertain the possibility that something might actually be wrong. She couldn't think that the images she had seen on those screens were real. That people were dead and that Tau... Tau was no more.

Where did that leave her? What did that mean for the girl stuck in a tube that would keep her alive no matter the cost?

Ellie opened her eyes, praying to a god she didn't believe in that everything would be the same. And it mostly was. There were bright white lights over her head, screens on all the walls surrounding her. It was all the same. Exactly as she had left it.

Except... Now there was a dark shadow looming over her. A shadow with long dark hair, eyes like the deepest depths of the sea, and a wide, split mouth that opened up to reveal long, sharp teeth.

"The princess finally wakes," he said, and his voice was the abyss coming to claim her.

She screamed before she could even think to draw breath.

Chapter 5

Proteus hadn't expected her eyes to be quite so strange. He had seen human eyes throughout most of his life. Humans were, in general, boring. The People of Water called them achromos, the colorless, because to them there were so few colors of human. The undine scales were every color under the rainbow, and some of them exhibited multiple colors at the same time. So he thought he had seen it all when it came to her species.

But her gaze was almost clear. Those eyes were so blue they were nearly white, clearly affected by some kind of drug or strange blip in her creation. The clones were made rather carefully, though. He'd seen how much work and money went into their lives, so he doubted anyone had made such a grievous mistake.

This must simply be how she was. Strange genetics aside, it was almost uncomfortable to look into a gaze that clear. It was like she looked through him into the soul beneath, one he wasn't all that certain he had.

They were two beings created by something much bigger than

themselves. They should never have been created, most likely. Whoever thought they should have existed had gone against the laws of nature to bring them about.

What a strange feeling to experience a sense of kinship immediately upon meeting another creature. Proteus had never felt that way before.

Her strange eyes opened even wider, wider, and then she screamed.

The sound blistered through his thoughts, pushing him away from her with an almost physical force. She had no magic or power that he could feel, but that voice of hers was ear-piercing. He couldn't think. He couldn't exist with that insanity of sound reverberating through his head.

Planting his hands on either side of his skull, he reeled away from her. His tail made it hard to flee quickly, and he couldn't see where he was going. The hatch suddenly seemed to disappear, and the sound made every bone in his body ache.

He wanted to kill her. He wanted to slam the top of her coffin down upon her head and end the sound of her voice for good. He needed her silent. He needed the quiet and the calm that had been in this room only moments before her awakening. The fear of him would shut her up, he was certain of it. But he couldn't make her fear him if he was careening away from her at the first sound of her terrified shriek.

Finally, she stopped, although it was only a small reprieve he was certain. She had likely never been witness to a monster like him. He was worse than the People of Water. Worse than she had likely ever dreamt of something that lived within the sea.

He glanced back over at the coffin that had kept her alive to find her huddled up in the corner. She had her arms wrapped around her legs, that wide, eerie gaze glued to him as she watched his movements.

Proteus recognized that look. It was the same wide-eyed stare all prey gave him before they were about to be devoured. Those eyes said she recognized a predator when she saw one, and she was not going to let him get close to her without releasing that sound of wrath once again.

"Calm," he said, although his tone spoke of his anger and the rage that still boiled within him. "Keep your mouth closed, human."

She swallowed hard, the little nodule in her neck bobbing up and down at the sound of his voice. "You speak?"

"So do you."

He stared her down, waiting until she looked away from him. He had won that little battle, but soon enough he knew she would test him. Humans couldn't help themselves. They saw a creature that didn't look like them, and they decided its presence was a challenge. Any moment now, she would pepper him with questions. She would push and prod until there was nothing but anger left in him.

His rage had always been his downfall. This delicate little thing needed a sensitive touch, and he needed this creature to do his bidding. Control like that would only come from fear or respect.

Fear was so much easier.

Baring his teeth in a snarl, he coiled his tail around himself, looping it over and over and watching as her eyes stuck on the shimmering bones she could see through his flesh. He hadn't even realized he'd been upset enough to illuminate them, but he was certain it would work to his advantage. She would be terrified of the skeletal creature from the deep that revealed himself to be more monster than man.

"Keep yourself silent while I work," he said. "I have brought you back to life only to serve. That is your only role here. The sea awaits if you do not serve me well. I will gladly feed you to the sharks that surround this place, as I am certain they are starving."

She swallowed hard again, those strange eyes watching him with a focus that made it hard for him to breathe. He hated it when people like her stared at him. Proteus knew he was unlike anything she had seen before, and that likely he was uncomfortable for her to look at as well. But she didn't have to stare.

Turning away from her, he focused instead on the task at hand. He had his accomplice, whether she wanted to help him or not, but now he needed to find the first place where he would connect Above with... Below.

He supposed that rhetoric worked. The People of Water would likely not be interested in calling it Below, as that had some implications they wouldn't agree with. But in reality, that's exactly where they were. Below the land. Below all the storms and the madness that still plagued this planet caused by people who had no right to even attempt to do what they had done.

If he could make that connection, he could get somewhere. He'd need people to cooperate with him, of course. But stepping into the role of god again would certainly help with that. If the People of Water returned to worshipping him as they were supposed to do for all these years, then he could force them to do his bidding as well.

They would evict the humans from this sea with ease. He would make certain of it. Because that had always been Proteus's life goal. His reason for being.

The ancients had created a god they knew, at some point, would bring the world together again. They had planned to destroy all that was here, and then stitch it back together the way they wished to see it. Though the plan was perhaps terrifying to most, it was the only way that it would work.

For all the future that Proteus could see, the ancients saw much further. They saw centuries into the future, they knew what would happen at the very end of time. They were guiding him and everyone else in the sea through the complicated webs and continued to react and move all the pieces that needed to move when someone did something they shouldn't.

He reached for the buttons on the control system, pushing them so that he could peer through what few systems were still online. A map unfolded on the screens before him. There were quite a few of this wealthy man's connections that were spread across the entirety of the planet.

Unfortunately, only the ones underwater were still online. The rest were either destroyed completely, or they didn't have access to enough power to broadcast any feeds. He tried to connect with a few of them that were close by, but nothing he did would convince even the droids there to awaken.

Finally, he found one that he remembered.

Long, long ago, he used to work with these humans. He remembered there was a place where they would often meet. Not just with him, but with some of the People of Water who believed in his work and what he wanted to bring about. They trusted that Proteus knew what was best for them, and they would also come with him to convene with the humans.

This place had been safe for all of them. But it was also a work of art.

If he could get the other undines there, then he could convince them that he was godly in power again. That alone would be enough to bring about their trust, if he could get them to believe it. They would convince the humans to trust him, and then… Well, then he would give them all a place to go that wasn't here. That was where the woman would come in.

"Pilot," he said, waiting until he heard the tap of the droid's claws approaching to continue. "This is where we will go. This facility needs to be turned online."

"That would be impossible." Pilot climbed onto the console and connected to it. Then it used the screens to project the status of the facility and all that needed to be turned back online.

It was a lot. There was no power, of course. The solar systems on the top of the facility had been entirely destroyed, most likely by wind. So there was no way for it to get power anymore. The droid systems were gone as well. That could have been due to a cave-in, or something else, like an animal had come in and wrecked their charging station. And then, of course, there were the actual cables and systems that connected it to the other facilities. All of it was gone.

He could go there and realize that there was nothing left in that facility but sand and dust. He could make the journey and find nothing but a tomb, and who knew what else happened up Above after all the power went out.

A plague. A war. Countless deaths—all of it had likely happened before the humans had snuffed themselves out.

Sighing, he rubbed a hand over his face. "That is the only one that will work, is it not? Look at the location. Look at the others. That facility was at the core of everything else. It should have been built in the safest place for it. No other station will bring the entire network online. We will be fixing facility after facility rather than utilizing the droids to do so. You're asking me to fix something that will take not just years, but perhaps even centuries. It is impossible without this central building being fixed."

"Sanctuary," Pilot murmured. "They called it Sanctuary."

He knew the little droid said that with the intent to make his heart squeeze. But it didn't. He cared very little what the humans had called it, or what the reasoning behind all of that was. Perhaps this was the last known bastion of humanity before they succumbed to their own folly. He cared not.

It was going to be the place where humanity started again, if he had his hands on it. But he would need to make sure that it was suitable for such a thing.

"I don't care what they called it, Pilot. All I care about is that it is fixable. Find the last known logs from that facility and tell me exactly what went wrong."

"The logs are unreadable. They must have been destroyed in some kind of solar storm. Even the backups are damaged beyond repair. The only way to know what went on there is to go and discover it for ourselves."

"That's not good enough," he snarled.

But then he froze when he heard the faint sound of feet hitting the floor. Snarling, he turned to see that the woman had frozen where she had gotten out of her pod. She held onto the edge of the metal tube, her eyes wide as she stared at him as if he were going to attack her at any moment.

"Where do you think you're going?" he asked, his voice deep and echoing in the chamber. "You are to stay where I put you."

She lifted a hand slowly, pointing toward the screens. "You missed something."

"We didn't miss anything. I have a droid. They do not make mistakes."

"They try to do their best not to make mistakes, but even

artificial intelligence is wrong sometimes." She straightened. Her body seemed to unfurl itself. She was tall for a woman, softer than most he had dealt with in his life.

Proteus was used to warriors who would battle until their last breath, but she was rounded at the hips and breasts, clearly designed to do so by the hand of a man. He'd never understand their obsession with hourglass shapes, but Proteus rarely had any intent to find anything attractive. He wasn't built to do so.

But as she slipped by, he was startled by the scent of her. Underneath all the chemicals that had kept her alive for such a long time in that pod, he could smell flowers.

It had been centuries since he'd smelled those, and even then, he wasn't given the opportunity often. Suddenly he remembered a scientist who had brought flowers into the lab and showed them to him. She'd laughed, saying she hadn't thought he would ever get the chance to see them. She'd loved the scent of daisies and wildflowers, so she brought them for him to experience.

This woman flustered him. She smelled like flowers and approached his droid with a hesitancy that made him want to snap her neck and get it over with. Already she was an odd beast that he wasn't used to.

"Here," she said quietly, pointing out a line of binary code that meant nothing to him. "This means that the droids created a separate file backup on an outside server, doesn't it?"

Pilot tapped its feet on the console a few times, not hitting buttons but almost... angrily. "I don't know how I missed that. I ran it through my language module multiple times."

"They wrote it so that another droid wouldn't notice it," she murmured. "This was meant for a human to read."

"Why would they do that?"

Proteus wanted to know the answer to the same question. "Are you suggesting the droids in that facility were hiding something from their own kind?"

"Or they were ordered to do so."

He stared at her reflection on the screens, but she wasn't looking at him. She was staring deeply into the codes as though they held the answers to the universe within those two numbers. She wanted to help, he supposed. Perhaps she thought this was an opportunity to prove her worth.

He would allow it. If she knew how to read what Pilot did not, then that would get them further in this plan of his. So be it. He'd trust her for now, because he had no reason not to trust her.

But he lifted a clawed hand and pointed it at her. "If you lie to me, or try to escape, then I will pull you apart. I'll start with your finger joints and remove pieces of your body at every junction, keeping you alive until I give you permission to die."

Why did she look so serene at his threat? She nodded and replied, "I understand. Allow me to read through these old messages, and hopefully I can provide you with a better picture of what occurred."

"Do that."

Proteus slunk to the back corner and leaned against it, unfurling his tail along the perimeter of the room to stretch it out. He'd see what this woman was made of, but he wasn't going to leave just yet.

Chapter 6

Ellie might not be the bravest person in the world, but she knew how to perform. It wasn't like Malcolm had been a kind man whenever she woke. He had been brutal too, ruthless in getting what he wanted, and he kept a blistering pace for her to learn anything. Maybe this was why he had been training her. Maybe he knew about this deep-sea creature who would eventually call upon her to... help him? She thought?

She'd been listening to what he and the droid said, and that was all she could gather from this situation. Maybe they were even still within Tau, although the sounds of burbling from the outside made her think maybe they weren't. She'd been so certain that her training had been for a purpose, so this must be it.

Listening to them bicker, however, had given her very crucial details for this situation. She'd always been good at picking up those details.

Malcolm's breath smelled funny when he was going to be overly aggressive with her. If his eyes were red, it meant he was going to leave the lab for a while and she could sneak through his drawers to peek at what it was like to live in the real world. If Steve was the only person in the room, then she was actually going to work that day, and likely work hard because he was the only one who actually challenged her.

Noticing things like that had kept her alive for a lot longer than she was likely meant to be alive for. The other clones of herself were still in their tubes, after all, and she was out here. Experiencing the world like few of them ever would.

She snuck a glance over to the shadowy corner where the monster currently reclined. He was so big. She had no idea what he was, though, because she had seen countless undines in her life and he wasn't one of them.

The undine were delicate, or at least, that's how they looked. While their species was extremely hardy, it wasn't difficult to see the beauty in them. Their thin fins moved in the water so prettily, and the framing of their features had always caught her attention. They had pretty faces, flat noses that were almost royal in appearance. They were everything she had dreamt of being. Ethereal. Otherworldly. Creatures that made people think up sonnets and tell stories about their bravery in the depths.

He was nothing like them.

His tail was thick and blocky. The fins on the end were ragged and had holes in them from years of misuse. Not to mention the ever glowing skeleton that dotted up his tail to a torso that was equally roped with muscle, but hollow with hunger. He looked like a creature that could eat for centuries and never satiate himself.

Massive hands rested beside his tail on the floor, too big for her to give them a look without becoming uncomfortable. There were extra joints in them, so his fingers were eerily long. They were the first thing she had seen when she'd woken. Those inhuman, dark hands lifted up to her face like some creature from the old classics that she'd read in the simulation.

Nosferatu, she thought. His hands belonged to a vampire.

And then there was his face. Eerily beautiful and yet wrong in the same sense. Looking at him was almost like looking at a human, but the more she looked, the more wrong he appeared. There were lines on his cheeks, as though someone had once split his mouth open, and they glowed along with his ribs and the bones in his tail. She could follow the glowing lines of his mouth down his cheeks to his neck, and that alone made her shudder with fear.

Long, dark hair pooled down at his waist, so impossibly long she was shocked it wasn't a tangled mess. But a creature like this, one who had lived in the sea for as long as he had, surely didn't need to brush his hair. He was a creature of legend. A comb didn't exist in stories like that.

Although it was hard to even see him now. Once he had gotten comfortable in that corner, he'd broken the light in the ceiling above him to plunge himself into darkness.

"Girl," the droid next to her said, summoning her attention back to the task at hand. "Read this line."

She looked over the binary code, her mind snapping back to translating. It was her favorite thing to do, really. There was an immediate feeling of accomplishment when she managed to figure out what a string of code meant. "They shut down all external power to maintain the data storage transfer."

"It doesn't say where they put it?"

"No."

The droid let out a little, angry grumble, and then the numbers were scrolling so fast there was no way she could keep up reading. It appeared to be angry that others of its own kind had tried to hide information from it. She supposed she would have been upset as well.

"Droids can express anger?" she asked before she could think about what she was saying.

"I can express anger."

"That's... odd. Isn't it?"

A dark chuckle erupted from the back of the room. "Yes, it is odd. That droid has been a menace since I picked it up. Clearly, it has a malfunction that has yet to be addressed. Are you good with droids, little human?"

"I have never been trained in droid functionality." She took a deep breath, realizing that might be the one thing to get her killed. "But I do learn fast. I suppose I could research droids and see what can be done."

The little crab droid spun around on the console, suddenly stopping what it was doing to stare up at her with eyes that should have had working screens. Instead, just one blinked on and off. "You will not experiment on me, human."

"Ellie."

"What?"

"My name is Ellie." She squared her shoulders, trying very hard not to look like she was going to faint. "My Original was Eleanor Lovelace. She was a renowned inventor throughout her life, and most of her clones were capable of the same logical processes. I was awoken by Malcolm Maximus Cornwall and continued my training throughout state of the art artificial simulation that allowed my brain, thoughts, and development to grow much faster than many of the other clones."

"You were grown in a test tube like all the others," the droid snorted.

"Pilot." Again, that dark voice threatened from the other side of the room. "Aren't you at least a little curious about her?"

"No. I am not." The droid turned back to the console and seemed to almost hiccup its annoyance before the binary code started floating across the screen again.

That was rather odd, wasn't it? She was very used to people being confused by her existence. In Tau, many people had actually seen Eleanor before. They'd spoken with her, worked beside her, so to see Ellie walking around was confusing. Eleanor herself was slightly older, much more cultured, and she knew even more than Ellie did. She was incredibly intelligent, and most people were honored to be around her.

Ellie was awkward in comparison. She didn't know how to talk to strangers, had never really been introduced to them, and had been taught her entire life to keep her head down and her eyes on the floor when anyone realized she was awake.

It was strange to even be here talking to them. Neither this creature nor the droid should want to speak with her at all. They should have ignored her just like the others, but she was starved for more of their attention.

More conversation. More chances to bring these memories back to the simulation and play them through her mind. For a few moments, she was a real person.

"So you're a clone," the creature from the corner said. "Ellie."

Her name dropped off his tongue both like a warning and a prayer. A shiver traveled down her spine at the sound of him using it. How strange it was to hear him say the vowels of her name. He caressed her through the word, even though he was all the way across the room.

"I am."

"What's that like?"

"What?" The question popped out of her before she could catch it. "I mean... I'm sorry, I don't understand the question."

"What is it like being a clone in Tau?" He leaned forward so a slash of light reflected in his eyes. The eerie glow in them reminded her she was staring at a predator. "I'm curious to hear your thoughts on that. It seems like Tau abused those clones. You were meant to be nothing more than meat."

"I was more than that. Some of us were... were..." She closed her eyes and resolved to lie. No one was going to erupt out of the shadows with him and be angry at her, but it still felt like it might happen. Malcolm wasn't here, but these people could report whatever she said to him.

"Do not lie to me," he growled.

"Being a clone is an honor. I am pleased to serve Malcolm and to learn from his great knowledge." The words had been drilled into her head from a very early age, although most wouldn't call it an early age.

She hadn't been woken as a child. She'd grown in a test tube like all the others and become conscious as an already fully formed adult. He'd kept her frozen in time, using chemicals to slow her aging so he could teach her, train her, do all the things that no one was supposed to do to a clone.

"Malcolm is dead. All of them are."

The words lifted all the hairs on her arms. Dead? No, that wasn't possible. None of them would ever die; that was the whole point of the clones. They prolonged their lives through the use of clones. Malcolm had been alive for ages...

"Who is my new master then?" she asked.

"Me." A wide grin split across his face again, his mouth impossibly wide and full of jagged, sharp teeth. "Tau has fallen. Most of your kind have been released from their pods, brought to other cities to learn how to live as real people. Some of them are still frozen. And then there is you, little Ellie. Dropped into the pit of the sea as a sacrifice to an old god who has only just awakened."

No, that was something out of a story. He was trying to scare her.

She looked over at the droid, a creature that shouldn't be able to lie. Pilot looked back up at her and then slowly nodded his entire body. "The man you speak with is Proteus, son of the ancients. Lost god of the People of Water. He has been summoned to bring about a new age in our world. You will be the one to help him. Along with myself, of course. I was the one who woke him."

Ellie noted a small bit of pride in the last bit of what he said. As though the droid wanted to remind her that she might have the attention of a literal god right now, but that didn't mean she was the one who had saved him.

She was a pawn. Someone to do work for other people when they needed work done. It was the same role she had always played.

But somehow, this felt a lot more dangerous than what she was used to.

Her nostrils flared on an inhalation. She could do this. She knew how to pander to powerful men who gave her only a few moments of life. Ellie would suck out the marrow of every opportunity she had to be alive and not in a simulation. She just had to figure out where the marrow was here.

"You want me to help you?" she asked.

"You are going to do so whether you want to or not," Proteus replied.

Son of the ancients. She had no idea what that meant. But she had already recognized that he wasn't the same as the other undine she had seen. He was more than they were. Stronger. Powerful. Different in a way she likely would never truly understand.

"Then I will help you as you wish," she replied. "How often will I be awake?"

He stared at her as though the question confused him. It took him a long time to reply, and she could see it was like pulling teeth for him to even answer. "You will be awake until the task is complete."

"Malcolm..." He tensed, and she knew already that this was a conversation she shouldn't have. "I am used to being placed back in my pod once my work has been completed."

The droid on the control system snorted. "Well get back in that pod then. It's going to take me at least a day to find all these hidden codes that I couldn't even see. Damned droids. They had to make everything hard. I don't understand why they did this!"

Damn it.

She'd been awake for such a short time. All she wanted was to explore the room a little more, maybe stay awake to watch the water that was revealed from the hatch on the floor. She'd stare at a wall if that's what they wanted to do, anything not to go back to that simulation.

But Proteus didn't argue. And if he was the one she had to listen to now, then maybe he was saying he wanted her back asleep again. She headed over to the pod, smoothing her hands over the sides like she had a million times.

The cushion was comfortable inside. Even if she wanted to lie on her side, though, the machine within the pod would turn her to the optimal position. It would hold her in place if she struggled. Ellie had lain inside for so long that the indent of her body remained. The glowing lights would turn off. It would be slightly too cold for comfort the moment she got inside, and then it would inject her with the drugs that would keep her pliant. The lights would turn off, and the simulation would turn on.

Licking her lips, she looked up at Proteus and said, "My simulation was wrong while I was in there. I believe it was damaged. Did my pod fall?"

He nodded. "You fell all the way to the deepest part of the ocean. The lava field you were resting on may have damaged some of the circuits."

"It's nightmarish in there now." He had told her not to lie, so she told him the truth. That simulation had frightened her, and the idea of going back into it was even worse. She wouldn't beg him, though.

She knew begging didn't help. No matter how prettily she did so, as Malcolm used to say.

He sighed heavily, then his gaze flicked away from her to the droid working on the code. "I do not care what you do, human. If you wish to stay awake and suffer through the mind-numbing annoyance of watching Pilot work, then you may."

"I..." She shouldn't thank him, either. But she did shut the lid of her pod and sit down on top of it. The cold top made her thighs ache, and goosebumps rose all over her skin without a blanket.

Still. This was the best she'd ever felt.

She wasn't asleep. She was here, watching a strange droid working with code and knowing a monster was at her back.

What clone could ever say they'd experienced this?

Chapter 7

It was strange to be awake. Even stranger to have companions such as a human clone and a droid who rarely seemed to stop talking. Pilot was not kind to the woman. The droid's quips were clearly meant to be cutting, but she took them all in stride. In fact, she just seemed happy to be awake and not back in that pod.

That was something he could agree with. Even being in the facility was too stifling for him after centuries of imprisonment. Proteus made a point of going out into the ocean every time he had a chance so he could breathe. This square wasn't big enough for him. He needed the entire ocean, the whole of it, to feel like he was still alive.

Swimming through the waters, free as he hadn't been in so many years, that was what mattered. Hunting through the depths, feeling the goddess of the sea guiding him toward hunting grounds that would challenge him, make him stronger, that was what he had missed most during his imprisonment. And now he could do it all and more if he wished.

Now, he had to return to the facility. The two of his companions were capable creatures, but he knew very well that they couldn't be left alone. Pilot wasn't one he trusted all that much. The droid had proven to be unhelpful so far. And the woman? She was not one that he would trust as far as she could swim.

Which wasn't very far at all. He'd seen her watching the water with fear in her pale eyes. He was quite certain she didn't know how to swim at all.

Sticking his head up into the hatch, he watched her as she moved in front of the screens. He had to compliment whoever had trained her, because she was wonderfully efficient. Her attention was always on the work in front of her, and he could see her lips moving as she read. Then she'd start typing, making sure that every single word was correct. She was quick, and she wanted to help.

What he didn't understand was why. There were a lot of reasons for her not to trust what was happening around her. Even more reasons for her to refuse to help. Perhaps it would even be safer for her in the long run to go back into that pod and pretend nothing was happening. That was the gift she could give herself.

But she wasn't doing any of that. He needed to understand her reasoning.

Pulling himself out of the water, he ignored the rush of liquid that covered the floors immediately. The drains turned on, and the loud noise interrupted any secrecy he might have once had. He didn't even wince this time, though. Perhaps he was getting used to the overabundance of sound.

She spun around, her eyes wide until she realized it was him. And even then, she didn't relax.

"You're back," she said.

"I am. Are you disappointed?" He grinned, knowing his teeth were on full display.

Proteus so enjoyed the tiny shudder that ran through her at the sight of his teeth. He'd figured out very quickly that they made her uncomfortable, and they should. He was a predator who was watching her as though the tiny bones in her hands would pick his teeth clean very easily.

She turned back to the screens. But not before he saw her shudder with shock and fear. "We've been deciphering the messages left by the droids. They are not only hiding messages in binary code that only a human can read, but said messages are a riddle. We're trying to understand what they meant, but someone went to extreme lengths to hide this place. They didn't want the power turned back on."

"And yet, we will make sure that the power is on. Or are you incapable of figuring this out?"

The last sentence was full of meaning that he knew she would hear. If she wasn't capable of it, then he would dispose of her. This was the only reason she was still alive, after all. He didn't need to keep her around for any other reason.

Her throat bobbed in a gulp before she nodded. "I believe we're working toward understanding their message."

Pilot clambered from the other side toward them, its metal legs clacking against certain keys as it went. The screens turned on to show an old video from the cavern where he wished to go. For a moment, he saw it in all its glory.

Massive tracks of water moved up and down the wall, levels and tiers of undines moving through them to head over to other rooms where they could speak with scientists and give their opinions of what they were researching. Lights glimmered from the ceiling, and there were so many tanks of creatures that were being reviewed by the greatest minds in this realm, not just the humans who had discovered them.

In the blink of an eye, he was there again. He was a towering god who had made it nearly impossible for anyone to move around him without fear. He had been the terror that kept all of it moving.

Of course, there was also the wealthy man who had kept them paid. But that man had simpered at his feet, begging for an ounce of Proteus's attention, as all the humans should have done long ago.

Now, look at what he had.

A woman in a black suit that was so plastered to her skin he could see her heart beating in her stomach. A droid that had seen better days and was so rust-covered it was a marvel it could move at all. And an abandoned facility that couldn't even turn the locations on that he needed to be turned on.

Sighing, he waved to the screens. "Yes, I have seen this before, Pilot."

"Look closer. They made sure that the videos were encrypted, but now we can see the destruction was not by time. But by choice."

Proteus crawled forward, pulling himself toward the screens so he could watch the details. And yes, the droid was right. They were turning off all the important pieces that had made that facility so great. The tiny scientists were draining the tanks, destroying all the pieces of proof that they had been working on for years. Even the specimens were incinerated.

"Why would they do that?" he murmured, lifting a claw to tap against the screen. "It makes no sense for them to destroy everything they worked so hard on."

Pilot clicked a few more buttons, and the images disappeared. "I do not know. There are more encrypted videos, but it will take me a while to break through the passwords and codes that are preventing us from seeing them."

"Do that quickly, then."

"I will need to go into stasis to do so."

"I don't care, droid."

Pilot still hesitated, though. He was looking at the woman as though waiting for her permission, or... no.

Proteus picked the droid up, hanging him in the air like he had the first time he'd met it. "Are you worried about the safety of the clone?"

"I think the two of you are dangerous to leave alone. I am not a maintenance droid. If this room is covered in blood, there is nothing I can do about it, and I need the servers to remain clean and pristine for us to continue our work." It didn't struggle this time. Limp in Proteus's hands, he had to wonder if this was a ploy.

The droid wanted all of Proteus's attention on him.

Snorting, he dropped the creature to the floor and rolled his eyes. "I have no interest in bothering her. She still has use. You have my word she will be alive when you return from your stasis, Pilot."

The droid took that as good enough. It rolled up into a ball, wheeled itself into a corner, and then appeared to become a rock while it worked on decoding all the information they would need.

The problem was that left a strange silence in the room that was as awkward as it was eerie. She had sat down in a chair that he hadn't realized was in this room. But every time she leaned closer to look at a screen, it squeaked. The sound grated on his nerves as much as the quiet. Wasn't she going to say something? Anything?

Another creak of her leaning forward, peering at the screen and ignoring him. He hated that. How could she sit there and pretend a sea monster wasn't right behind her?

"You seem to have no fear," he murmured as he headed toward his own screen. If she wanted to be so apt at ignoring him, he could do the same thing. Proteus knew how to use these computers too.

"I don't know what I would be frightened of."

"That I kill you."

Wasn't that obvious? And she had been lying. She had plenty of fear. He could smell it on her at all times, it seemed. She was an incredibly flinchy creature who seemed to always be watching him out of the corner of her eye.

She shrugged. "I suppose there's not much to fear when you're not alive. I'd like to stay here and keep experiencing everything that other people get to experience. But at the end of the day, I know what I am."

"What are you?"

"A doll. A creation that was made to serve, and if I cannot serve, then it makes sense to remove me." She shook her head, still not looking at him, but at the screen in front of her. "I've never really been alive, anyway. It's hard to mourn a death when you've never actually lived."

That was... odd. And wrong.

Frowning, he turned away from his computer and shifted his tail close enough to spin her chair. She was forced to look at him, which was clearly uncomfortable for her. Her face turned red, and she stared at him with wide, insulted eyes.

"What?" she asked. "I'm working on what you asked me to work on. If you keep distracting me, then nothing will get done."

"Why do you believe you are not alive?"

"Because I am a clone."

"You are breathing, are you not? You can feel your heart beating in your chest. I watched you come back alive from that pod, and I know you had woken up before meeting me. You have existed for a very long time, woman. That does not make you less human."

She winced at his words. "But I am still a clone. Even you admit that, great sea god that you are. I am a copy of someone who once existed. Trust me, I never forget that she was here before me."

He was at a loss for words. Someone had failed this woman thoroughly. She did not understand that even if she was a copy, that didn't make her less of a person.

"You have experienced things she did not. You are not her." He frowned, knowing that he was botching this. "You deserve to live just as much as she did. You are a person all on your own, and saying that you aren't is denying the fact that you live and breathe right now."

She stared up at him, confused by what he was saying. "I hear your words, sea god. But you are wrong."

And then she tried to turn her chair back to the screen. Dismissing him.

Him.

Proteus snarled and forced her chair back toward him so quickly that her hair flew in front of her face. Those dark strands obscured his view of her flashing eyes for a brief moment before she glared up at him. "You are preventing my work from being completed," she said.

"This feels important. What kind of god would I be if I didn't remind you how mortal you are?"

He loomed above her, reaching forward with his elongated fingers to wrap them around her tiny throat. It was so easy for him to lift her out of the chair by her neck. She weighed next to nothing in his grip, although he could tell she was a solid woman who was likely not used to someone even thinking that.

"Humans are weak," he snarled, bringing her closer to the wide open maw of his mouth. "You think because you have been living only in small spurts in this world that you are not alive? If I snap your neck, you will stop breathing. If I plunge my claws into your chest, that racing heart of yours will no longer beat. If I tear into your flesh with my teeth, you will feel pain. Trust me when I tell you, Ellie, you are very much alive. Don't ask me to prove it to you in your final moments."

As he dropped her back onto the chair, he watched her breathing hard and grabbing her throat. He'd likely made her sore with that, although he had been trying to be at least somewhat gentle.

But then, a small smile crossed her face. It was pretty. Innocent. One that he hadn't thought she would wear on her face after he had threatened to kill her.

"Thank you for reminding me that I am perhaps alive after all." Her fingers still ghosted over her neck.

It didn't feel quite right. Yes, she was agreeing to being alive, and that was progress. But he had a feeling it was in response to pain, which wasn't healthy either. He might be a terrifying god of the sea, but he wasn't heartless. Proteus had always seen the humans as weaker than him. They were creatures to pity.

She was perhaps one of the most pitiful he had ever met.

Ellie leaned back in her chair and asked, "May I return to my work?"

"If you want to." But even that didn't feel right. A strange voice in his head didn't want her to be forced to do anything. He needed her help, of course. She would do what he told her to do. But a part of him whispered that she was akin to him.

He had the sea to explore. Freedom whispered through the waves as they caressed through his gills and over his scales. He'd only had a few days out of his prison and already he felt better stretching his limbs. What did she have? A bigger box than the one she'd been in before.

"If you would like to be released from your work today, you can be." He cleared his throat. "I can work on something else while you are... resting."

Her face immediately paled. "You want me to return to my simulation?"

"No. I'm just saying if you want to do something other than this, you should." He waved a hand. "Do whatever you want."

The tension in her eased. "So you don't want me to go back to sleep?"

He gave her an odd look. "You are inconsequential to me. I do not care what you do."

The relief that flowed through her body at his words made him feel worse, somehow. But she nodded and turned back to the computer. This time, he could see she wasn't working on the same code she'd been before. She was doing something else, although he couldn't hazard a guess at what might entertain a woman like her.

At least she was keeping herself busy. The quiet clacks of her typing were better than the awkward silence of before.

Chapter 8

Ellie worked hard, even though he had told her in so few words that she didn't have to work as hard as she had been before. Both he and the droid expected perfection, and she was going to give them exactly that.

Her entire life had been spent working to be perfect. No mistakes. Making sure that any task she had been given was completed exactly as expected and within the correct timeline that had been outlined. She was good at this. She had trained her entire life for this.

The longer she was here with this droid and this sea god, the more she really believed that this was what she'd been training for. Malcolm didn't do things without reason. He wouldn't have died without ensuring that she was taken care of.

After all, he'd spent countless years with her. She knew he had looked at her as a man did a woman he loved. He'd never touched her, but she'd seen him with other clones that looked just like her. Those were the ones who were given that kind of attention. Ellie was meant for other things.

She'd never let herself think about it too much, but now that she was out of the pod, she couldn't stop thinking about it. There had been so many versions of her that Malcolm used to his own benefit. He was everywhere all the time. He'd brought out versions of Eleanor for sex, some for entertainment, some for experimentation, others to do his work.

Was that all she'd been doing? His work so he could live a life of leisure?

The more she thought about it, the more frustrating it became. Because yes, she had just been doing his work. The signs had been there; she had refused to see them. Steve had been his coworker. No wonder the man hated her so much. Malcolm had been one of the few lead scientists on the team, and he had clearly been trying to do too many things at once. So he'd trained her to take his place, to do the work that he should have been doing, so he could... what? Wake up other versions of her and go on dates they couldn't say no to?

It was all vile. Every bit of it.

But then her mind would swing around to the fact that she had been abandoned. Proteus said everyone in Tau was dead, and that clones like herself had been spread across the underwater cities. There was nowhere for her to go, because they likely hadn't factored in a lost pod in their repopulation efforts.

If she went back to them, they would put her back into stasis until they were ready for her. That much she knew for certain. No one, not even someone who had gotten away from Tau, was that different from the people within those walls. She was still a mistake, regardless of what Proteus said.

Just a number that hadn't been factored into an equation. She was certain anyone would rather ignore her existence than rewrite the entire problem.

Sighing, she leaned back in her chair and stared at the binary code she'd been struggling with. The numbers all made sense now. They were written so intentionally, it would have been hard not to understand exactly what the droids had hidden.

Sure, it was a riddle within a riddle. But she'd spent her entire life figuring out riddles exactly like this.

"Pilot?" she said, pointing to the screen. "I think I got it."

The binary code had been jumbled. The words it hid were in the wrong order, which made everything even more difficult to figure out. So she'd had to write everything down, and then figure out exactly what each sentence meant until she had it. It was simplistic what the droids had done, but only a human could figure it out.

Pilot headed over to her, clearly still a little disgruntled that he even needed a human to help him in this matter. "Well?"

She pointed to the screen. "It looks like they chose to shut down both the solar and hydro power that they used to power the facility. Once they turned those offline, they were able to ensure that no power grid could be turned back on. Nothing is broken, just… dormant. Someone has to physically step foot into that place and turn everything back on."

"But they destroyed it. I can see them breaking things in all the surveillance that I unlocked."

Ellie lifted her thumb to her mouth and started chewing on the nail. It was a terrible habit, and one that Malcolm used to swear would get her sick. "This makes it seem like the assumption was always that someone had to actually be there to turn it on, so that they couldn't control everything from another location. The logs state… I don't know. Something about destroying other facilities. Are you sure the footage is from this one and not another that they laced through the surveillance logs?"

Did Pilot... swear? He immediately turned back to the screens, and she could see him comparing the video footage to other parts of the facility.

"Would you look at that," the droid muttered. "They spliced the videos together."

Another voice interrupted them. "So we need to fix what has been broken first, and then we can turn it on remotely?"

Proteus.

She had forgotten he was coming back any second. But it didn't matter if she remembered he was returning or not. He always showed up at the worst opportune moments, startling her with his size and the amount of space he took up. He didn't care if he startled her either. Sometimes it seemed like that was his intent.

She'd had a hard time forgetting his hands around her throat, reminding her that she was alive. Even though it had been painful and perhaps terrifying to stare into his black eyes and see her own bitter end looking back at her... he'd been right.

Ellie had been told her entire life that she was only a copy of a great woman and that she wasn't needed. She didn't even exist if she peered too closely at herself.

But this sea god told her she did exist. She was breathing, she was here. That meant she had worth and value. It was more than anyone else had ever given her.

"Ellie?" Pilot asked, tapping on her hand.

"Oh," she said. "I'm sorry, what was the question?"

Proteus pulled himself out of the water, all glowing bones and scaly skin. "Do we need to fix the broken parts, and can we then turn everything on remotely?"

Right, that was the question.

"Fixing the broken parts means going to other facilities. There's a map here, and it appears those are the ones that are part of this complicated locking system. Once we fix what's been broken there, the solar power, the hydro power, the electricity from those facilities seems to power this," she replied. "We'll still need to be in the main building to turn everything on, which I realize complicates things. But it requires certain codes to be put in, and unfortunately, I don't think just anyone could put them in."

"Why is that?"

He wasn't going to like this. "The requirement is a human voice. I have to be the one, or another human, to say the code that will allow everything to turn on."

She winced as he cursed and turned toward the hatch. She fully expected him to slip back into the water, enraged at what she had said, and disappear for hours on end. He tended to do that when something went wrong.

What a refreshing change from her old life. Malcolm had merely raged in front of her. Breaking glass beakers and uncaring if she was caught in the crossfire of broken glass. Her pod would save her, he always said. And sometimes it did.

"Fine," Proteus muttered. "I will call in some help then."

"Are you sure you want to contact the People of Water?" Pilot asked. It skittered over to the hatch, almost as if it was trying to prevent him from leaving. "We are not prepared yet to make them believe that you are a god. I think we should wait."

"I'm not contacting the People of Water."

Were they talking about the undine? That must be what they called themselves. She'd always been fascinated with them, of course.

But she hadn't thought to see a live one up close.

Was he one of them? Now that she was thinking of it, he really didn't seem like he was one of them. He looked different from any of the creatures she had seen under the waves, and that was saying something.

Proteus headed into the water, dropping beneath the surface but not quite leaving. Ellie could see his head still and the dark locks of his hair that somehow looked like kelp. Then a rumble started from underneath the water until the surface looked like it was boiling. The sound was strange and low, like the keening call of a whale, that he sent out into the sea.

"What is that?" she asked.

"He's summoning someone," Pilot replied, sounding exhausted. "You might as well relax for a bit. This will take some time."

Relaxing wasn't something she knew how to do. A little confused, she walked over to her pod and hit a few buttons. In the bottom, there were survival rations that could keep her alive for a month or so. She didn't want to be a bother, after all. The liquid packets were an entire day's worth of nutrients, and she hadn't sucked one down yet.

In the simulation, there had been solid food. She'd eaten apples and all manner of delicious meats and cheeses. But here, and every time she was awake, she ate this.

Sucking on the bag, she turned to find Pilot staring at her.

"What?" she asked.

"What in the world do you have in your mouth?"

"Nutritional paste?" she said, although the words might have come across like a question.

Pilot made a sound that almost made it seem like he was disgusted. But there was no way she had disgusted a droid with what she was eating! He ate... well, she didn't think they ate. He used oil to keep himself running, so that had to be nearly just as bad.

Turning away from him, she covered her mouth so he wouldn't even get a glimpse of what she was eating. She finished swallowing right about the same time that Proteus poked his head back up out of the water. And then came the rush of the ocean as he pulled himself through the hatch.

She hated when he did that. Her feet always got wet, and the water was so icy cold it made her toes feel like they were going to fall off. Disgruntled, she sat back down in her chair and crossed her legs so her toes were at least wedged into her thighs.

"What message did you send?" she asked.

"That we needed assistance. We are at a depth that will make it hard for anyone to come here, but there are a few who can still manage these pressures."

He muttered something else, but then his gaze stared at the surface of the waves. That laser focus was unnerving. He was waiting for something, clearly, but she wasn't sure she was going to like what he had summoned.

A thud on top of the facility made her flinch. Then another, and another. The strange sounds continued all around them and reminded her that there wasn't really any safe place in the sea. Not for her, at least.

The hairs on her arms rose as the sounds continued until they were at the bottom of this floating building. She held her breath as a tentacled arm rose out of the water and stuck itself to the floor. Eight arms followed, covered with suckers, followed by two more arms with suckers on the ends, which the creature almost seemed to use like hands as the first squid pulled itself out of the water to stare up at Proteus. Its eyes were eerily human. She'd never seen eyes that looked at her with such intelligence and such hatred.

The hair on her arms stood up straight. She didn't want to anger a creature with such a sharp beak, nor was she all that interested in getting closer to them.

Ellie reached behind herself and pulled her chair farther away from the opening. Just in case.

The language Proteus started speaking was not one she was familiar with. It was strange listening to him speak. He made sounds that shouldn't be able to come out of a mortal throat, chirps and hiccups and guttural, throaty sounds.

The squid seemed to understand what he was saying, though. More tentacles looped out of the water, piling on top of others as their strange, gelatinous bodies rolled at the words. Clearly they were going to help or... do whatever it was that he had ordered them to do.

One by one, they all disappeared back into the water.

An unsettling feeling bloomed in her chest. She assumed he had asked for their help in fixing the far-off facilities, but also, she knew those buildings weren't in the sea. Squid were not creatures that were meant to leave the water.

"What did you ask them to do?" she asked.

"They will fix what is broken, at least in the water. That will give us enough time to get there ourselves so we can fix what is out of the water." Again, his grin made every hair on her body stand on end.

He looked so powerful seated there, completely confident that his choices were correct. She had never seen someone who was so sure of himself. His body was stronger too, she realized. Rippling in muscle, glowing with power that was already deep inside of his bones, she had to wonder if she had unleashed something that could not be stopped. Maybe helping him hadn't been the right choice after all.

"What do you mean when we fix the rest? I'm not an engineer. I don't know how to fix broken machinery."

"I am confident you will learn how to do so. Isn't that what your pod is for?" Proteus headed back into the water, that evil grin never budging from his face. But just before he sank beneath the surface, he turned to look at her. "You are very capable, Ellie. I do not know you, nor have I had much time to get to know you, but that much you have already proven."

He disappeared, likely heading off to help the squid. But...

She should be happy that he'd complimented her like that. She should feel better about herself. And she did, she supposed. She liked that someone saw how capable she was and how much she wanted to be seen as someone who was useful.

But it didn't feel all that good. Somehow it felt like maybe she had helped someone who didn't deserve to be helped. Like he was going to turn this world upside down, and she was part of that.

Looking at Pilot, she asked, "Do you think this is the right thing to do?"

"I am a droid, Ellie. I have been programmed to do what I have been told to do. I do not have an opinion on right or wrong." The droid headed back over to the consoles, typing in a few things that pulled up more code for it to go through. "I'm going to plan what you and Proteus will be doing once you get to the new location. You should rest."

Why was everyone always telling her to rest? She didn't want to rest. She wanted to live!

And yet, it seemed like this facility was just another prison. Still, she did not rest. She walked from one end to the other, over and over again, just to feel like she was still alive.

Chapter 9

His plan was coming together. The squid would head off and figure out what was broken. They were intelligent creatures. Even if they weren't proficient engineers, there weren't many puzzles that creatures like them couldn't figure out. He trusted them. Much more than he would sending anyone else, and that said something about the sorry state of affairs.

Proteus had no one. He had no one to fall back on, nor did he have any creatures who were really helpful. If he could speak with the People of Water, then perhaps he would have others who could assist him. The only issue with that was that the seafolk didn't remember him properly.

There were only a few creatures left in this entire sea who could help him, and they were the ones who had created him.

Proteus didn't like visiting his parents. Namely, because he'd never thought of them like that. They were his creators. The beings who had breathed life into something they created, but they certainly did not care if he survived. He was their tool to use when they desired to do so, but even then they rarely remembered that he even existed. Perhaps that was the reason he'd been locked up for all those years and they hadn't even tried to get him out.

They were very old. Everything to them was just a blip in time, unworthy of their attention. They had seen the future, they had seen the past, and they knew how fluid both were.

He remembered when he had first awoken how cold he had found them. Of course, it had taken him some time to realize that was what he had felt. He'd been raised to think their treatment of him was normal until he had seen proof that it wasn't.

Proteus had snuck away to spy on the People of Water. He'd watched a mother and her child, flicking their tails as she taught the little girl how to swim. The joy on that mother's face had burned something inside of his chest.

Proteus had desperately wanted to feel that way. He still remembered that sensation as he swam ever deeper into the sea. The ache in his heart when he had wanted to feel what it would be like to have a parent who loved him so much. Someone who was gentle as they taught him how to swim, how to laugh, how to live.

He'd come out from his hiding place as a child, wondering if the mother would be as kind to him as she was to her own. It had been the wrong thing to do.

He winced, his massive mouth splitting in a grimace as he remembered the horror on that woman's face. She'd grabbed her daughter as if he were something to be afraid of. She'd held onto her little girl and hissed at him, slapping through the water with a tail that had sent him careening away from their little family.

It was the first memory he had where he'd felt like a monster. He'd never really thought much about his looks, or where he had come from until that point. He barely even noticed that he was different from the other sea folk.

The wild swim away from that mother and her child was still burned into his memory. His gills still remembered the ache of how fast he'd been breathing, so quickly that he'd torn through the thin membranes and all he had been able to smell or taste was his own black blood.

The ancients waited for him now. He hovered above the cavern where they lived, although many who came here would not know it was a cavern. It looked more like a giant crater in the sea floor, a trap for anything that might disturb them. But Proteus had been made with better eyesight than any of the creatures who would visit his family.

He could see how the earth had been carved out of their den. He could see the faint tips of their tentacles that stretched out of the entrance. They were massive, gray beasts. Nothing about them was soft or kind or welcoming.

To others, they seemed to be giants of the sea. Terrifying and endless, they were an amalgamation of many sea creatures. Unfortunately, that made it hard for many to even guess what they looked like. Their minds simply could not fathom what they saw.

Giant, bulbous heads made up most of their bodies. They did have tails, although they were hard to see because the ancients rarely moved. Their mottled skin was gray, although varying shades for the three of them. Their eyes were small, but they did not need them to see. Of course, small to Proteus meant the eyes were the same size as the average undine. The tentacles that came out of their forms were more than an octopus or squid, so they could reach any prey that fell close enough to their den.

The ground around it was littered with bones. Skeletal remains of whales and massive sharks, even megalodon skeletons from times long past. The bones here told a story of a hunger that could never be satisfied. He had inherited that hunger.

He floated before the entrance, anxiously awaiting them to notice him. They had, he was certain. They would have smelled him from miles away if they weren't already all-knowing. They would sense that he was coming to see them. They would know that he would return to his family to know what they wished for him to do.

Proteus had always been theirs, after all. And he was ashamed to admit that he still was.

"Come inside," their voices boomed from the cavern. He knew part of the reason they'd chosen this place was because of the echo. But their voices were louder than those of any creature in the sea.

He'd gotten used to the sound of them. But now that it had been many years since he'd heard them speak, he flinched.

Perhaps that was why he was so afraid of loud noises.

Proteus corrected himself immediately. He wasn't afraid of loud noises. He merely reacted to them more strongly than other people. It was easier to believe that than the alternative.

Floating closer to the entrance, he remained still as one of the tentacles emerged from the murky darkness. It was as long and thick as he was, but surprisingly gentle as it touched him. The tentacle ran down from his torso to his tail. The suckers worked against his skin, helping to move the long, mucus-covered appendage as it went.

The ancient tasted him. He stayed still until it confirmed that he was who it knew him to be.

"Son," it whispered. "You have returned to us."

They had no names. They had no sex. They were beings who could procreate on their own, and yet, they made him together. All three of them.

Their genetics were weak. So old, they couldn't create a being who was like them. One who would take their place. Instead, they had created something new. At least, that's what they had claimed all those years ago.

He wished their intent had been clearer. The knowledge that they had wanted a child, that he hadn't just been an experiment to see if they could alter the timeline, would have been helpful in those dark times. To at least know someone wanted him. Someone cared that he had been lost for so long.

The tentacle drifted away, back into the darkness of the cavern and the silt that made it almost impossible to see the rest of them.

"I was awakened," he said quietly.

It was the only thing he could say. Seeing them was harder than he had expected.

The murk shifted, the dust settled, and finally they moved. The three creatures emerged out of the darkness, their bodies barely visible in the shadows as they pulled themselves free from the darkness and landed on the ground before him. Massive, beastly monoliths. The ancients were nearly impossible for any mind to actually comprehend. They were unending terror and inspired madness just from a glimpse.

"Our son," another said, this one's voice a little deeper than the other. "We have waited for this for centuries."

Tentacles lifted over his head, slamming down onto the ground so hard that the resulting sound was slow to come. He waited for the thunderclap to rock over him, and the wave that pushed him slightly away from them. He took it all, enduring even as the bones throughout his entire body lit up.

"You bid me to wait," he murmured, and the bitter pill of knowledge that they had known he would suffer and they did nothing to stop it made his stomach burn. "So I did. Now I am here, as you requested."

"You came back," the third whispered.

They had no gender, but he had always thought the third one had more feminine energy than the others. It was softer, more apt toward kindness and pity, but also not quite so rash. The other two were quick to threaten bloodshed. But the third always strove to find some way toward peace.

It moved a little closer to him, her tentacles not quite so loud as they braced her body while she peered down at him. "We missed you."

"Very much."

"Terribly so."

The words resounded around him, and he wished he could believe them. The ancients did not know how to miss things. Perhaps they regretted that their greatest weapon had to be put on a shelf somewhere they could not use, that he would believe. But he did not think they had it in themselves to know what missing someone felt like. Not for him. Not even for each other.

"My mission continues," he announced, his voice booming through the cavern with them. "I have discovered help already. There is a certain facility that will turn all the rest on. We can explore the world above again, and we can turn this planet back online, as the humans say."

A low rumbling echo came after his words. It was a pleased sound made by one of the males, who leaned even closer to look at him.

His massive eye was black as the deepest part of the sea. All he could see within it was his own reflection. Proteus was glowing so brightly that he was certain it hurt for the ancient to even look at him, something he was reminded of often when he was a child.

"This is good," the ancient said. "We grow weary."

"I know." Proteus knew how tired they were. Even centuries ago, they were determined to continue going forward, but that was why they had ended up here. Swimming was too hard for them. Hunting even harder. The sea folk had always taken care of them, and they must have continued to do so considering the size and health of his family.

Still, there was something different about them. Their breathing was more labored than he remembered. Their words were a little slower. And they were being far kinder than they had ever been to him before.

"We have seen the future," the feminine one said. "We know that you are the key to all of this. We were correct. You will be the one to bring about a new age in this planet. You will bring them all to a brighter future, where land and sea remain separate but still a whole. They can survive with each other without killing and maiming. Perhaps someday it will return to that, but not for a while."

The ancient to her left sighed. "The land and sea will heal each other. I can see it now. The entire planet will be able to breathe again. Old wounds can finally close in the wake of a new age."

"It will take time," the other replied. Its deep, rumbling voice spoke of hardship and many years of struggle. "It will not be easy."

"No," the feminine one replied. "But he is the start."

Proteus remained frozen where he was as her tentacle came up again and gently tapped him on the belly. "He is the one who will lead them, guide them, show them that there is more to this world. The key that will open the treasure trove of the future."

He hadn't felt this responsibility for a very long time. It had always been there, of course. He knew what his purpose was and why he had been created.

But in that coffin, he had pretended that he didn't care about them. He had told himself that they were his creators, and that they were part of his problems. They'd wanted him to hurt, and they could have saved him, but they didn't. It was why he had been so hard on them himself.

Being here, listening to their voices, he was pushed back to the time when he was a little boy. A small tadpole in a massive sea, and they were the only ones who had wanted to help him. They were the only ones who cared that he was lonely or tired. They made sure he was fed. They treated him as well as any parent could treat a child, no matter how strange they were.

Even if they were the reason he was so strange, they were still all that he had.

"It is my honor to serve you. To serve the future." He twitched his tail, bowing low to them. "I will continue my work."

"Wait." The deepest, rumbling voice stopped him when he would have continued.

He turned to look at them, really seeing how weak they were. How tired. It killed him to see them like this. They were more than this. They should have been full of energy and hatred, electrical power that should have slipped beneath his scales and made him vibrate just to be close to them.

And yet...

The feminine one sighed. "It was good to see you one last time, our son."

"One last time?" Proteus asked.

"We were waiting for your return. But that was all. Now, we can finally rest."

"Rest?" He repeated their words because he did not want to know what they meant. He couldn't hear it. "No, you cannot rest. There is so much we still need to do."

"We have had our time in the sea. The People of Water have a new god to worship." Three tentacles gently came down before him, one after the other. "All of our trust is placed in you, Proteus. Our first and only son. The future is set, which means our time has passed."

He refused to believe they were going to do this to him. He just got back. He still needed their guidance! They had to tell him what to do from here, and where to go. He couldn't read the future like they could. He'd always been able to see it, but only in spurts.

Proteus saw the same thing they did. A future that was within reach, where both land and sea had pieced themselves back together, but he didn't know how to get there.

But the ancients, the gods of the sea that had been there for a millennia, laid down instead. They all rested together, a pile of massive monoliths that would slowly feed the creatures around them.

"Stay with us," the feminine one said, her voice filled with sorrow and what sounded like relief. "Stay with us, our son."

And so he did.

He stayed there in silent vigil, counting each of their breaths until they were no more. He remained even as the crabs started to approach, and as the squid descended, to take pieces of their gods and consume them. Not a single part of him dared to move as he watched the only living creatures alive who cared even the slightest about him... die.

Then his bones burned with rage. They turned white-hot within him, casting shadows upon massive, empty eyes.

There was no one to pay for this. No one but himself.

A wail erupted from deep within his body. Grief and abandonment aching through every bit of him. He tilted his head back and screamed. It was the cry of a man who had lost everything.

Chapter 10

I'm really not sure that's the right way to do it," Ellie said. She was seated on the lip of her open pod, devouring yet another of her flavorless nutrient packets.

No one had offered to feed her here, and she was a little concerned with how many she was going through. Maybe there were other pods they could find, though. If the clones were taken out of them, wouldn't they eject the pods out into the sea? They were useless once the people who resided within were taken out. Sure, they could recode the parameters to bond with someone else. But it didn't sound like there were any more clones to put in them.

If she could find those pods, then she could easily pull the nutrient packets out of them herself. And there were other bits and bobs that would be useful. She didn't want to dismantle her own, just in case they needed to put her back in.

The chair was the only place to sit unless she sat on the floor. But that was usually damp because of Proteus. So she'd taken to sitting on her pod to stay as dry as possible.

"Of course it's the right way," Pilot argued with her.

She discovered she enjoyed annoying the droid now that she had been given leeway to live her life. Not that Proteus had said such a thing explicitly, but it did seem like he didn't mind if she was herself. And in doing so, she had discovered that it was fun to tease Pilot.

The tiny crab was very uptight. It was obsessed with rules and the right way to do things. It was disgruntled when she was anywhere near it, but mostly when she pointed out the flaws in its plan.

Of which there were many.

"I thought droids were usually smart," she said as she tossed her empty nutrient packet behind the pod and then headed over.

Pilot was working on a plan to get them into the facility that had not been in use for centuries. Unfortunately, that meant that there were a lot of rock cave-ins where the entrance used to be. Tapping on a screen that showed a pile of rubble, she asked, "Where did you get this footage?"

"It is from a surveillance drone I still have access to." A tiny foot pressed a bright red button, turning the screen off. "Don't look."

"The more rocks we pull from that, the more likely there will be another cave-in. We cannot, and certainly should never, play with that. A cave-in on the outside could cause the entire inside to be destroyed." She arched her brow. "Or do you disagree?"

"Of course I disagree! I wouldn't have suggested moving the rocks if I hadn't looked at every possible angle." All eight legs moved it in a circle until Pilot stared up at her with those flickering eyes. "You clearly have no thoughts in your head at all if you believe I would risk his life."

Well, he had her there. She didn't think he was likely to risk Proteus's life. For whatever reason, the droid was oddly loyal to the massive creature who terrified her.

She picked Pilot up from the console, turning him in her hand to look him over. "You know, I could take care of this rust for you."

"Get your hands off me! You—" Pilot blinked. "You could?"

"Do you prefer he or she?" she asked. "Just another odd question. I don't feel right thinking of you as an it."

"I prefer he. Now what were you saying about getting the rust off me?"

She walked over to her pod with him in her hand. "There's a great number of tools in this pod. Most of them are there to help keep me alive, but also many of them were with the intention of anticipating all manner of strange happenings that could occur if I were in the pod. Besides, what if something broke? It knows that it could wake me and I would be able to fix some things from inside the pod itself."

Ellie leaned over and stuck her hand into the area where she usually lay. She just had to get the right angle, and then her hands closed around a small rod. It was particularly good at dealing with rust. She supposed its purpose was to assist if the lid was ever rusted shut and she needed to get out in an emergency. Then all she'd need was a damp cloth, and she thought she could get Pilot looking brand new.

She showed the droid her tool. "The liquid inside eats away at rust, but it is sensitive to metal."

"It's not liquid," Pilot said in awe. "Those are nanites."

"I don't know what those are."

"Tiny robots, just like me. They have one programmed task for their entire existence. Amongst droids, they're the stuff of legends." He made a sound that was almost a sigh. "Of course you'd have some of those if you were from Tau."

She almost laughed when he said that. "Come on, Tau didn't have everything that everyone wanted."

"Yes, it did."

He seemed so certain that it even made her pause for a moment. "Well, then I guess I'm glad I can share it with you. No one deserves to have rust impeding their movements for centuries on end. How much of it do you think we'll need?"

"Not much at all. They should be able to do their work without either of us needing to help them."

She sprayed some of the liquid on him, and maybe it was filled with little robots like he seemed to think was in there. She still wasn't convinced that was what it was.

Holding the droid up in her hand, she watched the rust start to peel off of him like red dust floating down from his body. "Why are you able to feel things? I don't think I've ever met a droid who could."

She could tell he could feel things so powerfully that he even looked uncomfortable when she asked the question. "I..." Pilot cleared his non-existent throat. "My creator wanted me to feel emotions. He wanted me to be more human than the others."

"Why?"

"Because he thought every living being deserved to feel everything deeply."

Something in her twisted at that. She believed this scientist meant the best after what he'd done, and that was sweet. "What was his name?"

"Dr. Fairweather," the droid murmured. "He was a very sad man. His entire life. Never did tell me why."

And no one would likely ever know. But she thought about Fairweather and his sadness, and wondered if that was why he'd given this droid a personality. Perhaps he had been lonely. Perhaps he'd lost someone very dear to him. So he'd created another person to be close to.

Water flowed over her feet, ice cold and immediately making her shiver.

"Proteus," she scolded. "I thought we talked about you at least announcing yourself so I didn't—"

She froze and stopped talking the moment she saw him. There was a different kind of light in his eyes as he glared at her. An anger and a bone deep pain that she tried very hard to recognize but couldn't. Usually there was at least a person in those black eyes that she could relate to, but she couldn't do that at all today.

She stared into the eyes of the abyss. If she stared too long, she feared she would fall straight into his gaze and never be able to crawl her way back out.

Swallowing hard, she tried to back away, but her hips instead pressed against the pod. "Proteus?"

He did not reply as he rose out of the water. His fins were all on display, flared out from his face and sticking straight out. Spines rose on his arms, down his back, and his clawed hands were tense.

"Pilot," she murmured quietly. "Get in the pod."

She heard the little droid trying to move, but she wasn't going to risk its life. Instead, she hit the button to close the pod and sealed him inside. At least there, she knew he would be safe.

Proteus came out of the hatch, one hand over the other, clearly hunting her across the room. She kept her eyes on him, as any prey animal would do. She moved slowly, carefully, trying not to catch too much of his attention while also being very aware that she was his sole interest.

His gaze never wavered from her. He never looked anywhere

else. It was rather terrifying to be trapped in his gaze like that, because she wasn't entirely sure what to do about it.

"Proteus," she said again, lifting her hands to show him she didn't have any weapons. "Talk to me."

There was no talking with whatever beast that was in front of her, though. This wasn't even him. She didn't see any part of the man she knew in that gaze. All she saw was a nightmarish beast who had risen out of the murk to attack her.

"Stop," she whispered, but she already knew what was going to happen.

He lunged. Time seemed to slow as the massive bulk of this sea beast rushed toward her, and there was nowhere for her to go. She couldn't run or fight back. She was stuck exactly where she was.

He struck her with a surprising amount of weight. For one moment, she was airborne. Then Ellie's back struck the floor hard enough to force all the air out of her lungs. She lay there with him on top of her, staring up into a massive mouth full of teeth.

To her horror, his mouth split open. The sides of his mouth, the area from his chin and down his throat, dropped open to reveal rows and rows of teeth. Not just one set, not just the ones she'd seen when he smiled, but at least ten rows of sharp teeth going all the way down his throat.

She had the insane thought for a moment that it almost looked like a flower blooming until those teeth closed around her arm.

Before she remembered herself, she screamed. Ellie tilted her head back and let out a sound of pain that bounced against the walls of this strange facility in the sea. But then she remembered that pain wasn't something she was supposed to feel. She wasn't allowed to cry out like that because she wasn't really a person. Not a real one.

So instead, she ground her teeth and forced herself to get through the pain. She'd be fine. It didn't matter if he bit her arm off and ate it. There was nothing and no one who would care if she died. At least she had helped him a bit. She had figured out the binary code that would have stood in his way for a very long time.

Ellie's existence was to serve, and she had done so well. That would be her memory.

The teeth sawed through her arm, and she could feel it ripping and tearing through her flesh. Against her palm, she could feel his tongue moving against her, swallowing her blood and flesh. He intended to eat her. Eat her arm. Why would he stop at the limb, though? He was going to devour her whole, and that...

Made her sad.

She whimpered, trying hard not to make a sound. But then Pilot threw himself against the clear lid of her pod, and the loud bang seemed to be the only thing that got through to Proteus. He froze, his teeth embedded in her flesh.

Something cleared in his gaze. She suddenly saw more of him. The god who had been so haughty and yet so confident that she was a real person. She watched as he realized what he was doing, that her arm was jammed down his throat and that Pilot was locked away. That they were sitting in a pool of Ellie's blood that was growing more and more concerning.

He lurched away from her. Her arm slid out of his throat with a wet sound, flopping down at her side, completely useless. She couldn't even feel her fingers, but with that amount of blood it really wasn't surprising.

The horror on his expression was, though. His eyes had widened. His breath came in rapid pants. Proteus closed his mouth, becoming the man she knew once again.

"Ellie?" he whispered, clearly horrified by what he had done.

"It's fine," she said, trying to make it a little easier on him. "I'll be okay."

"What do I do?" Clearly he wanted to come to her, but he worried it would scare her. His hands stretched out, those long, eerie fingers stretching like shadows across the floor toward her. "What do I do to help you, Ellie?"

"It's all right." Her vision was skewed. Everything was a little blurry, and she swore she might be seeing double. "I'm just a doll. I'm sorry you broke me, but a broken doll can still be played with."

Everything in her wanted to tell him not to kill her. Even without an arm, she could still be useful. Her mind was what Malcolm had honed. She could still read the code. She could still help him figure out his plan. She could still argue with Pilot and be the person she had been learning how to be.

"Ellie, what do I do?"

Why was he repeating the same question over and over again?

She blinked, and he was leaning over her. Or no, she was lying down now. Had she fallen? That was embarrassing. She'd been hurt before, and Malcolm had been so angry that she had reacted to the injury at all. He'd told her she needed to pull it together and then put her right back in her pod to heal immediately.

Oh right. Her pod.

"The... The..." Why couldn't she talk? That was so ridiculous. She pointed to the pod with her only good hand, which was somehow also covered in blood.

He scooped her up in his arms and moved toward the pod so quickly it made her head spin. Or maybe that was the blood loss. It could have been that too.

He shoved the lid off and Pilot almost flew out of it, but laid her down gently. She almost didn't feel it when her back hit the soft cushioning within.

"Now what?" he asked, his voice clearly worried. "What do I do, Ellie?"

She tried weakly to reach for the lid. He needed to close that, or she was going to die. She wasn't entirely sure that there was a way to fix a dead body, although she was a clone. A lot of things could be done to someone like her. She hadn't tried it personally.

He seemed to understand what she needed, at least. The lid closed over her head, sealing her into the pod that would know what to do.

Already she could feel it whirring on. The strange sensation of the metal skeleton moving beneath her, shifting to prep her for surgery. A prick on the side of her neck warned that she was about to go to sleep.

Her last sight was him looming over her pod, a dark smudge with his hand on the clear surface. He looked worried.

She hadn't thought he would look so worried.

Chapter 11

Proteus stared down into the pod, horrified at what he had done. He had just been so angry. So lost in his own confusion and hatred that he'd looked at her and suddenly she was everything that had gone wrong. Ellie had become a symbol of all the humans who had destroyed his home, turned the sea to mud, and then continued to battle against the People of Water until all hope of fixing what had been broken had nearly been lost.

He hadn't even seen her. He'd seen the enemy who had turned his life upside down. He would have done the same to any sentient creature in his path.

The loss of his family had him reeling. He wasn't himself. The world felt like it had turned against him, even the sea goddess he had always worshipped. He was alone, scared, angry, all the emotions that he did not know how to deal with at all.

He was ashamed of himself for taking it out on her. That wasn't who he was. It wasn't who he had always intended to be. And yet he was the man who had hurt her. An innocent woman who had no

reason to be harmed.

Then she had been the one to comfort him.

"You are not a doll," he murmured, staring down through the clear lid as the machine put her to sleep. "And I am sorry I ever treated you as such."

She looked so peaceful as soon as whatever drug that was injected into her body started to work. He'd never be able to guess what was used, but he was pleased that she looked comfortable. In her sleep, he wondered if she had already entered the simulation. Did her mind ever get to rest? He hoped it wouldn't have put her back in that place when she had earned a long sleep. Her body and mind needed it.

Pilot climbed on top of the pod as well, staring down at the unconscious woman as the pod started to knit her skin back together. There was a strange gel-like substance currently being spread over the massive wound.

"I don't feel like I have the right to ask why," Pilot murmured. "Everything in my programming is telling me to get back to work. But there is a part of me that wants to stay right here and make sure she's put back together correctly."

"Do you have any reason to assume it is not capable?"

Pilot pointed to her arm. "Humans are very fragile, Proteus. That arm is in a worse state than you or I could guess. I think it's likely that the machine will replace it. They might have harvested a limb from another clone if we were back in Tau, but that isn't possible considering where we are."

He didn't want to believe he'd broken her beyond repair. But as they both watched, the machine pulled out what looked like a small saw and started hacking through her flesh.

Pilot tapped a few times on the lid, bringing up her vitals. "Well, at least this machine is very thorough. Her vitals are surprisingly stable for such a massive surgery."

"What does it look like?"

"Blood pressure is low, but that's due to blood loss. Her heart rate is perfectly stable, and it appears even that her oxygen levels haven't been impacted somehow." Pilot leaned down to look and then shook his body like a nod. "Ah, of course. Synthetics are being used to keep her mind believing that her arm is fine. Fascinating. It's using the chemicals in her own brain to convince her that nothing is wrong."

He didn't really know what all of that meant. If anything, it just reminded him of a time when he had watched humans experimenting on each other.

They used to be obsessed with it, at least when he had been alive. Perhaps even then they had known that there would be a time when they would not be able to live on land. The wealthy man had spent countless hours of his time and money to try to splice humans together with other creatures.

It had never worked. Not once. The human DNA that he used simply could not be melded with another creature. They were very different.

He had been focused on trying to steal what the undines came by naturally, just like many of the men and women who had lived in Tau. Proteus had watched those videos, too. He'd seen them trying their best to become the creatures who lived beneath the waves, but they had never succeeded.

The machine under his hands whirred. Even Pilot reacted with surprise as it suddenly seemed to shift. Then he watched as it removed her arm entirely, cauterized the wound, and then placed the arm in a small tray. Her arm sank into the belly of the pod, and then a drawer opened next to them. It hit him on the tail, nearly closing again before he grabbed it.

Now he was staring down at her mangled arm which was no longer attached to her body. It was so much smaller like this. The tiny fingers curled in on themselves, and her skin speckled with blood.

"What do I do with it?" he asked Pilot.

Proteus feared his eyes were wide with shock. He didn't expect to be given the limb. Should he consume it? He did after all need as much sustenance as he could get.

Pilot hit his legs on the side of the pod so hard that he was forced to look at the droid. "Drop it into the water and let the current have its way with her arm," the droid said sternly. "Do not do what you're thinking of doing. She'd never forgive you."

"Is it not a waste?"

"Other creatures will make use of it. If you are hungry, you can go track down another whale."

He supposed that was the truth. Proteus lifted it delicately and tried not to focus on how stiff it had already become before tossing it out of the hatch. He returned to the surgery that was happening before his eyes, still a little unsure of himself. This all made him feel strange. Guilty. Like he was the problem when he...

Well, he was the problem.

"How do I make it up to her?" he asked the droid. "Surely you are more knowledgeable about human interactions than I am?"

"Make up... what? Almost killing her?"

That made it sound far worse than he felt about it. After all, he had stopped before she died. Proteus tried not to show how much the thought of making such a mistake made him angry. "Injuring her."

"Tearing her arm off?"

"It was still attached when I stopped myself! Her lack of an arm is entirely the fault of the machine she's currently in." He wasn't helping his cause. "Fine. How do I apologize appropriately for losing control over myself and biting through her arm, thus making it so that she had to lose the limb because I was struggling with my own emotions?"

"Are you going to do it again?" Pilot tapped a few more times, keeping a clear eye on her vitals.

"I don't intend to."

"That's not really good enough, Proteus. You have to know that you won't harm her again or anything you say will just be a lie. She'll know it's a lie, and that will make everything even more complicated. Trust is earned, not freely given."

He watched as the machine started whirring again. Both of them stared down at the smooth sleeve it was creating next to her arm. It seemed that Pilot was right. The machine was going to remake a limb for her that easily. It was almost like it had done it before for her. At first, it seemed to work on a 3D mapping of her body that it had stored. Then it was working on building the piece while she rested.

Every now and then another needle would approach her neck, injecting her with whatever medication it thought she needed. And all the while, he kept himself calm and tried to think through what Pilot had said.

This was a droid. Proteus did not need to explain himself, his feelings, or what he was doing to this creature. After all, the little thing had been made to serve him. It was a hunk of metal.

But then he noticed that some of the rust had been peeling off of Pilot's back as they spoke. Using a single claw, he nudged more of the rust off of his droid and watched it flake onto the ground.

"Why are you peeling?" he asked.

"She sprayed something on me from the pod, because she said everyone deserved to live their life rust free." Pilot clacked a few times and muttered something about how the machine had better be watching her blood pressure a little more closely.

The droid had proven himself to be a little vain. Proteus had never even had a stray thought about the orange rust that had turned the droid another color. But now, as the silver metal of his form came through, there was a truth that Proteus had refused to even consider.

"You like her." The words were more accusation than realization.

"I don't like anyone. It's not in my programming."

"Yes, it is. Clearly. You have a soft spot for the human who took away your rust. I don't know if I find that endearing or pathetic." Proteus thought about it a bit more and then finally said, "I believe it is more endearing."

Pilot didn't respond for a while. They both watched the machine finish making the arm. It was nearly identical to her other one, even going so far as to paint veins on the insides of her wrists. Then the machine started working with the arm, turning it so the fingers moved and the wrist bent correctly. It was... odd to watch.

Whatever pod this was, it was extremely advanced. Tau clearly took the health and safety of its clones far more seriously than they did for their own people.

Pilot tapped a few more times, still keeping an eye on everything before he murmured, "I do like her. She's kind, almost to a fault. She's quick witted and rather lovely to talk to. Even though she teases me incessantly and I do believe that is a horrid trait in a person. She is smarter than any other human I've met, and she even sends me notes in binary while we're working together. These things have made my programming... difficult."

"I thought you said you weren't programmed to favor people?" he said wryly.

"I was programmed to experience more than the average droid. I like to fight against that, because I think it is easier for me not to think about how different I am. The other droids get to live a life much easier than I do. Emotions are hard to live with."

Proteus understood that feeling more than most. Look at what he had done with the difficult emotions going through him?

"I visited the ancients," he murmured, knowing that Pilot would understand what he was talking about. "They are gone."

"Gone where?"

"Gone. For good." His hands curled into fists when the droid froze. "I stayed with them until they died. Their voices will sing in the depths no longer. Our sea is without guidance, and without any gods to visit. That is why I acted the way I did."

"Are they not your progenitors?"

"They created me. They raised me. They brought me into this world, and they threatened to take me out of it more times than I could count." He rubbed the back of his neck and then shook his head. "I did not think I would miss them. I told myself I didn't miss them at all while I was locked away in that coffin."

Pilot shifted again, this time clearly looking up at him. "But you were wrong? Did you miss them?"

"Every single day I was there. I was so angry at them for leaving me, but I was lying to myself. Now that they are gone, I only wish I had more time."

Proteus watched the machine move the new arm to where her missing one was. With rather impressive precision, it started attaching the prosthetic to her body. But it didn't even look like a prosthetic. The machine was pulling out long tendrils from her body, something Pilot informed him were nerves. It connected them to the new limb so that it would work entirely like she had never lost anything at all.

Throughout the entire procedure, she never once moved or shifted. Instead, she just lay there, looking rather comfortable for all that was being done. It was shocking to know that Tau had created these clones, understanding that they would likely need to be put back into their compartments after they were hurt.

"Do you think this is the first time she's had such extensive surgery?" he asked quietly, already knowing the answer.

"No," Pilot said. "I think most of the clones have experienced surgery like this before. From what I researched, they were often harvested for limbs and organs. These pods are to keep the bodies alive for as long as possible, so more pieces can be harvested. As far as the machine is concerned, her arm was needed for another procedure."

That was disgusting. Beyond horrendous. It was barbaric to consider they were doing that to people while allowing others to live freely and comfortably.

He leaned back a bit as the pod made a hissing sound. He leapt back, trying not to get in the way any more than he already was. But then he realized that it was opening.

Pilot hopped off the top, clattering onto the floor and trying to get out of the way before the lid fell on top of him. And as they both watched, the pod opened up and allowed fresh air in.

Ellie took a deep breath, her lungs filling with air all on their own. How long had the surgery even taken? A few hours? He'd been staring at her and watching the surgery happen with Pilot for such a long time, he wasn't certain how long those breaks between talking had been. But it didn't feel like long enough for the machine to wake her.

Another metal arm lifted from inside the machine, and it sprayed some kind of white fog into her face. She breathed it in, and then those strange eyes fluttered back open. So pale they were almost entirely white, she turned her head to look at him.

"You didn't put me back in the simulation," she said. "Why didn't you?"

That ache in his chest had to be his hearts, but he didn't know why they were hurting. "I told you that I wouldn't. If you wish to go back into that simulation, it must be by your own choice."

She blinked a few times, then lifted her new arm and wrapped her hand around the side of the pod. "All right, well. I don't really wish to go back in yet."

"Shouldn't you rest?"

She gave him an odd look. "Why would I do that?"

Proteus stared at her arm and then back up into her eyes. "Because I... I..."

"Oh." She rolled her eyes and then pushed herself out of the pod. "It's not the worst thing I've seen done to a clone."

He hated that he believed her.

Chapter 12

They were treating her like glass, and she didn't like it. Ellie had always been useful. Useful made her feel important. She liked working with her hands and mind, and yet for the past three days, all Proteus and Pilot wanted her to do was rest.

They said she needed to heal after her surgery. Humans took a long time to feel better after trauma like that. Proteus was barely even coming back to the facility at all, citing that he needed to address the damaged facilities and she couldn't be helpful in those circumstances. Not with an injured arm.

She liked it when he was here and able to answer her questions, though. Without being able to ask them, she couldn't be certain that she was doing what needed to be done. Ellie was starting to feel a little untethered, and she didn't like the sensation in the slightest.

All her life, she'd been told what to do. Not having someone doing that was making her head spin.

"It's been three days," she scolded Pilot as he tried, yet again, to move her away from the console. "The least I can do is review the drone footage. I can figure out where we can head into the main facility and how to enter the building in the safest way. If you let me take control over one, then I could really look around."

"You need to rest that arm, and it's not fair for you to use it. You didn't tell me he bit off your dominant hand," he scolded, yet again.

She'd been trying to hide that for a few days now. Apparently, that was the worst thing she could have done to poor Pilot. Now he was certain everything he'd given her as an easy task had hurt her arm worse.

It seemed that neither of these men in her new life understood that it didn't matter if she'd been injured. Her pod was designed to put her back together again. She was a doll that could be played with as roughly as anyone wanted. If they wanted to rip all her limbs off, the pod would just build her new ones.

Maybe that's what she needed to make very clear to the two of them. Nothing could really hurt her, not like they were thinking. And if they would just give her a chance to prove that, then maybe they wouldn't feel so guilty about what had occurred.

She still wasn't all that certain why Proteus had entered the facility with such anger. It didn't matter why he was angry, she supposed. If he wanted her to know, he would tell her.

That's how Malcolm always ran his life. She knew only what he wanted her to know. Regardless of her own thirst for knowledge.

So the next time Proteus entered the building, she launched up from where she had been leaning against her pod. "Proteus!"

He flinched, and then seemingly lunged far across the room. Like he was afraid.

But that couldn't have been right. The god-like creature of the sea had no reason to fear her, or realistically, anything in the ocean. He was strong and large and had more weapons dotting his body than even the greatest ships of Tau. Why would he be afraid of her?

"I brought food," he said, eyeing her as if she were going to jump at him. "I realized I have not been providing any sort of sustenance for you while you were here."

"I have food," she replied.

Pilot interrupted them from his position on the console. "No, she doesn't. She's running out of those nutrient packets. It's a good thing you brought whatever it was you brought. Hopefully, it's edible."

Proteus scowled at the both of them and then lifted his hand. In it, he clutched a good handful of what looked like dead squid. "I have seen humans eating these before. I know they will not make you sick."

"Squid?" she breathed. "I have seen Malcolm eating these. I don't know how to cook them down here without ventilation, but I can make something work. I'm certain."

"Cook?" The furrows between Proteus's nude brows grew deeper. "I had forgotten humans do not eat their food raw."

"I don't know if you can eat squid raw..." She supposed she could give it a try? There were likely bacterial infections or parasites to worry about, but then again, the pod should be able to fix all those issues as well. Ellie didn't enjoy the thought of intestinal distress when she'd already been trying to be as discreet about that as possible.

Pilot didn't care if she relieved herself through the porthole, but Proteus might not like swimming through her refuse to get inside of this room.

The sound of a disappointed droid interrupted her thoughts. "If you're going to eat them, you better do it quickly. That won't be fresh forever, and that's when it'll likely hurt you. So eat up, princess."

Princess?

She stepped forward to take the squid from Proteus, only to have him rear back from her once again. He set the fresh squid on the floor and then backed away from it quickly, bunching himself up in the corner so he wouldn't disturb her.

"Why are you acting like that?" she asked, grabbing the squid and swishing them in the cold seawater one last time. She walked on this floor. He shouldn't put raw food on it and then expect her to eat it.

Proteus just stared, as he tended to do when he was trying to figure her out.

She looked at the squid instead, then. If he was going to be odd—as if he wasn't ever not odd—then she would focus on the task at hand. Eating these would likely not be a very pleasant experience, but she did need the calories.

Like Pilot had said, her food supply was running shockingly low for how short of a time she'd been here.

There wasn't any way to make the food taste better. Lifting it up a little higher, she stared at the pale, translucent body and muttered, "Down the hatch, I suppose."

Swallowing it whole felt like she had somehow done something wrong. One moment, she was fine, and the next, a gag reflex nearly had her spewing the dead squid and the rest of her nutrient packet onto the floor.

It wasn't necessarily the taste. There was an undeniably fresh quality to the squid that she knew was the correct flavor. But the texture was shocking. It was so smooth, not quite slimy, but certainly not dry. It slid down her throat and then seemed to get stuck so she couldn't keep swallowing.

It did go down, though. She managed to swallow the entirety of the disgusting creature and then tried very hard to smile through the nausea. "Delicious."

Proteus stared at her as if she'd lost her mind. Then Pilot made a clanking noise and turned his attention back to the screens. "At the very least, you should have cut it up. Swallowing it like Proteus is only going to choke you. Humans."

Right. She could have sliced the little squid into more manageable bites. That would have been a much more reasonable choice.

Ellie bit her lip. "I haven't ever had real food. Nutrient packets were all I've ever been given, so I don't really know how to eat this. It seems that there is a right and a wrong way."

The monster in the shadows held out his massive hand. The claws at the tips were still intimidating, but Ellie found it easier to hand over the other four squid he had hunted her. At least he would be able to cut it with those claws, and maybe she could slurp down smaller pieces a little easier.

Still, he remained so far from her. It was hard to even reach across the hatch to give him the squid.

"Why are you way over there?" she asked again.

He sliced a clean piece off the squid and held the strip out to her. It was much easier to manage, but still it was hard to swallow down. Almost like it was too big for her throat, even though it was such a tiny piece.

"Because I assumed you would be frightened of me." Those dark eyes were intense as he stared into her gaze. "I thought you would not wish to see me again after all that happened."

"I'm a doll, remember? They made me for whatever purpose my master sees fit." Ellie grimaced as she felt the squid slide down her sternum into her stomach, finally free from her throat. "If you wish to hurt me, you can. The pod will fix almost any injury as long as I'm still alive."

"You shouldn't have to live like that. Not in fear. It was a mistake on my part, and one that should not be so easily forgiven." He stripped another slice from the squid and held it out to her. "Chew this time, Sisu."

"My name is Ellie." She took the squid and tried to imagine what chewing would feel like. She knew what teeth were for. She'd had them her entire life and yet never really used them. They were for chewing, mashing food. She did it in the simulation, so why couldn't she do it here?

This time, she put the squid in her mouth and opened and closed her jaw. Easy enough, once she really started doing it. Her natural instincts seemed to kick in, and then when she swallowed, it was much easier for her to do so. It didn't hurt this time, and now it made sense why humans chewed.

She'd only been given nutrient packets her entire life. That was all. Liquid food meant she never had to chew, so this was an entirely new task for her, but one that was rather satisfying.

"I know your name," he replied, that deep rumbling voice filling the chamber. "Sisu is the name I give you."

She quite liked Ellie, but if he wanted to rename her, she supposed that was all right. Shrugging it off, she waited for him to continue slicing through the squid, piece by piece, until her belly was so full it felt like it was near to bursting.

Finally, she held up her hand to tell him to stop. "Thank you, Proteus, I am very full now."

"You should not thank me. It is I who should be paying penance for harming you. I will do my best to prove that you are safe with me, but perhaps you wish to be apart from me for a while yet. The plan can wait. The ocean is patient."

"No, I don't want to be the person who slows everything down." Ellie headed back over to the screens, gently brushing Pilot aside so she could pull up the drone footage. "We've found a way in, you see. A few channels that I could certainly fit through. I think even you could move through one of them, and then we could get into the Sanctuary as you have wished."

"You should be resting."

Never in her life had she felt anger. There had been a lot of disappointment, refusal to see the world as it truly was, and frustration at her master for not listening to her. But this rage that burned deep in her belly was as unfamiliar as it was enjoyable.

She spun around quickly, so she didn't slam her fist down on important equipment, but she knew her voice had a snap to it that made Proteus's eyes widen.

"I am not fragile," she argued. "I have lived my life like this for many years. I have been a clone in a pod, living in stasis and growing only as my master saw fit. I have lived a life that is not an easy one. I have been beaten, broken, abused, and torn apart by scientists. My brain was once used for a study! They took the top of my head off and poked around in there, waiting to see what part of my body reacted, and I had to be awake for all of it to tell them if it hurt or not. I am not a fragile little creature who cannot be trusted to take care of herself. If I say I am healed, Proteus, then I am healed."

The silence that followed that declaration was deafening. Perhaps she'd revealed too much. Sometimes she did that, and people were uncomfortable.

But she wanted him to know the truth. She wanted him to understand that she wasn't going to let a little lost limb make her life anything other than what it had to be.

Ellie was built for a purpose. And right now, her purpose was to help them.

It was as if he could see into her soul. Proteus had an expression that said he knew exactly what she was thinking, and how she was struggling with what it meant to be human. He could see that she needed to do something with herself to keep busy and to feel like there was a purpose for her to even be awake.

Perhaps he could even see that she needed to know she was being helpful. Otherwise she would end up back in that dream space within her pod. She feared going back to sleep and not knowing what was happening in the world.

Maybe that was why he agreed.

"All right," he said. "We will start our journey soon, then. But you will agree to do something for me first."

She swallowed, knowing that whatever he might want would be something difficult. "Anything you ask, I will make sure it is done."

"You will learn more about what it is to be human. Not through any book or screen, but through doing. You must learn how to walk through this world making your own choices, rather than waiting for someone to order you around."

"I don't know why that's—"

He interrupted her. "You will be speaking with other humans on my behalf. They must believe you are who you say you are. I do not know if they will take orders from a clone, nor do I believe they will be kind to you if they knew your origins. Someday, you will be my mouthpiece to your people, and I will not have their mistrust of you ruin this plan."

Ellie supposed that made sense. After all, if she was going to be working with her own people, she did need them to trust her.

But she wasn't entirely sure why he would be the one suggesting this plan. Shouldn't she be the one who thought about that?

Hesitantly, she asked, "How do you want me to do that while I'm stuck in here?"

"You won't be stuck in here for much longer." He took a deep breath, nostrils flaring as the bones in his body started to glow. "I will bring you through the sea. You will like it."

"Through the sea?"

"Yes."

She looked at Pilot and then back at the god before her. "So you intend to put me back into the pod after all?"

Once more, confusion crossed Proteus's features. She'd never seen him look quite so thunderstruck. "Why would I do that?"

"I cannot breathe underwater," she said slowly, impressing upon him just how dangerous this was.

But he only paused for a moment before shrugging. "Surely that is fixable?"

Chapter 13

This fragile, broken thing had been cracked and shattered far too many times. He hated knowing that he had some part in the breaking, and there was no way to fix what he had done. Proteus's dreams were filled with the moments he had lost control. He could still see the serene expression on her face, and how little she cared while he had been biting through her soft, delicate flesh. She'd stared at him, perhaps a little surprised, but not at all reacting as though something terrible was happening to her. She'd only been there with him, enduring the rage and anger that had absolutely nothing to do with her.

He'd been wrong to take it out on such a quiet creature. So very wrong. All she had done was stand in front of him, existing as she always had, and he'd been the monster who had taken advantage of her.

But how to make that up to her when she didn't care that she'd been harmed?

He'd sworn he would bring her somewhere to experience

humanity, but the reality was that he didn't know what humanity was either. After all his years of spending time with creatures like her, he had never truly understood them. They were as much an enigma to him as they were to her.

And there was also the small issue that he wasn't entirely sure how to get her out of the facility.

But he knew there were ways to breathe for her. Ways for her to experience the world at large and to know what it was to be elated, frightened, and yet still feel her heart race with a surge of adventure.

That was what he could give her. The experience that all humans desperately craved.

A life-threatening adventure to remind her that she was, in fact, alive.

He swam up to the facility knowing that now was the time for him to get to know her. He would bring her through the depths of the ocean, providing her with the safety she would need. She would trust him. Learn from him.

But the moment he popped his head up into the room, he knew something was wrong. There were diagrams on the screens now, equations and numbers that ran across every single surface. Neither Ellie nor Pilot looked at him as they poured over the details.

"What is it now?" he asked, already exhausted.

Ellie looked over her shoulder at him before pointing at the screens. "I didn't realize we were this deep in the ocean. I can't go out there without being in my pod."

"Of course you can."

"I cannot. I will quite literally explode."

He blinked. He hadn't thought about the depth and her body, but he supposed the pressures would be concerning. There were very few creatures who could survive at these depths, and no matter how much she insisted that she wasn't a fragile creature, she was. He'd need to figure out how to bring her up to the surface without killing her. Or, at the very least, how to get her to a depth that wouldn't cause her to explode, as she so eloquently explained.

"Pilot," he ordered. "It's time for you to download everything in this room. We're moving."

"Understood."

The little droid plugged himself in and started to work. All the while, Ellie stared at him with a questioning expression on her face. With her hip cocked like that and her arms crossed over her chest, she reminded him of a scientist he used to work with all those years ago. That woman had been ambitious as well, and was never afraid of the things she should have feared.

Ellie watched him with eyes that saw far too much. "What do you mean, we're moving?"

"There are other research facilities. This one lasted us only as long as it was required to. Now, we have outgrown it."

He spoke in lies, and she knew damn well that he was. Her eyes narrowed as she stared at him, clearly disappointed that he would even try to lie to her like that. But then she nodded.

"Fine. If you want to move to a facility with less use, then we will do that. But it is not me making this choice."

She turned away from him, waiting until Pilot was done downloading all the information he would need on the next leg of their journey, and then headed to her pod.

"Where are you going?" he asked.

"We're going into the deep sea. There is nothing else that can protect me from the pressure other than the pod. I will attach myself to it once more, and when we reach our next destination, you can wake me." She sounded so brave when she said that, but he could see the hesitation in her. She glanced over at him as she said it, and then he swore he heard her murmur, "I hope you wake me, at least."

This was supposed to be his apology to her. He was supposed to show her the sea, to show her all the things that might have once terrified her. He was going to prove to her that they weren't terrifying.

That he wasn't terrifying.

"Do you have to be asleep inside it?" he blurted, the words hanging between them.

He could hear his own hope, and it made him want to cringe in horror. There was no hope to be found here. Proteus was a god who could order her to do whatever he wanted. He should not care that she deserved to see more than this, and yet... he did.

He hated that he had hurt her. That was all it was. He felt guilt for the first time in his life, and that was why he wanted to prove to her that he wasn't the monster she thought him to be. Even if she said she didn't see him as a monster.

"I don't," she replied, drawing the words out. "Do you wish me to stay awake?"

"I want you to see the journey. To see the ocean as I do, and to understand all that we are protecting." That was it. He just wanted to give her another reason to help him.

She opened her mouth, closed it again, and then nodded. "All right."

Pilot hopped in with her, muttering how he wasn't going to get all his circuits rusty again all because they got it in their head that this facility wasn't good enough. The droid could complain all he wanted, but the truth was that they had outgrown this place. There weren't enough hunting grounds to provide food for Ellie. The depth would make it difficult for them to access the surface world, and they needed to be able to do that. Drones took forever to come back to their facility, and even then, sometimes the pressure or the icy cold prevented it from happening at all.

They did, in fact, need to move. He was just using it also as an excuse to sweeten her mind toward him.

As soon as the lid closed on her pod, he lifted it up into his arms. He was careful not to loom over her as he had when he'd attacked her. He was certain that memory was not one she wanted to think of while enclosed in a small space she could not easily leave. Then he turned the viewing window away from himself, so she could see where they were going.

"All right?" he asked as he squirmed his way toward the opening.

Dragging the pod seemed unnecessarily loud and would likely damage it. So, he had to figure out how to move his massive body across the floor while still holding onto something in his arms. It was no easy feat.

"We're fine," she replied. Her hand pressed against the lid, and for a frozen moment he thought she was trying to open it. But she was just stabilizing herself as it rocked back and forth.

It looked like she was standing. With her hands braced on the clear glass, and a determined expression on her face, she was a woman who was ready for anything to happen.

Even if that was the pod shattering into smithereens under the pressure of the sea.

He sent out a silent prayer as his tail hit the water and he drew her into the icy cold. Perhaps if he warned the sea goddess that Ellie would be at risk, then the sea would look favorably upon the both of them. He was, after all, her favored son.

He could feel the currents gently wrapping around him, careful even with her pod as the sea peered through the clear glass to look at Ellie. He felt deep in his bones the rightness of this moment. As though the goddess of the water approved of his choice.

"Still alive?" he asked quietly, his voice slicing through the current as he headed away from the facility.

"I'll be fine once you position me better. If you don't mind, could you flip my pod over?" He could hear the stress in her voice, and immediately did what she asked.

There was a faint thump, and then he could see what the issue had been. By turning her away from him, he'd pressed her against the lid, rather than the comfortable backing of the pod. Now that she was facing him, she was technically looking up toward a surface she could not see. Her back rested against the soft cushion that usually supported her while she slept.

He tried not to stare down at her face, knowing it would make her feel awkward. He certainly felt that way. Because every time he did happen to glance at her, she was staring up at him. Looking right at his face.

At some point, he could almost feel her gaze like a physical touch, running down his neck to his pectorals. No, between his pectorals. She was looking at the shadow of his twin hearts, revealed by the glowing lights of his rib cage. She stared straight through him, seeing the rapid heartbeats that always seemed to speed up when she was around.

"What are you looking at?" he asked as he sped them toward the surface. It would take a long time to get there, so he might as well ask.

"You. I haven't really gotten to look you over, and I figure this is as good a time as any."

"What are your thoughts, Sisu?" He couldn't stop himself from asking. He wanted to know what she thought of his body that was not just different from hers, but from any of his people's as well.

"You are unique. I've never seen an undine that looks like you." Her words trailed off at the end, growing a little quieter as though she didn't want to admit that to him. "I'm ashamed to admit I have seen many of your kind. The experiments in Tau were brutal, and none of them deserved to be pulled apart as they were. It always made me sick when I walked by them."

"Humanity has always experimented. I doubt we were the only people those scientists pulled apart." He hated it as well, but he had not been released until now. The rage and anger at what had been done to the People of Water burned hot and wild within his chest, but now there was nothing left for him to stop. "Your kind has always been a desperate people who would do anything to stay alive. That is the reality of their situation. They knew if they did not discover a new way for them to live, then they would be destroyed. Hundreds of years ago, they already knew that the end barreled toward them. They had one generation, maybe two, and then all they knew would be completely and utterly wiped out."

"That's a rather benevolent way of looking at it, I suppose."

He glanced down to see an odd expression on her face. Her eyes were narrowed, her jaw clenched as a feeling came over her.

"What is it?" he asked.

"It's just... You make it sound like they didn't have a choice. Death was the only option if they didn't do what they did, but desperation isn't an excuse for cruelty." She shook her head. "Where were you? Aren't you a god? Shouldn't you have stopped them?"

He sighed and adjusted his hold on her pod. It drew her a little farther away from him, tilting her so she couldn't look straight up into his features. "I was trapped. Imprisoned by my own people so I could not interfere with their choices. They wished to attack the humans, but I have always seen the use in collaborating with humans. I argued too hard one day, and they renounced all worship of… me. So I was stuck. Unable to help either side, no matter how much I dreamt of doing so."

"For how long?"

"Hundreds of years." Even saying it seemed as though it couldn't possibly be true. No one could survive that. But he had.

Her eyes widened even more. "Hundreds of years?"

"Far longer than I should have been trapped."

A shadow passed over him, though that was strange. He hadn't thought there was enough light to cast one. But then he realized the glow of his own body had illuminated a massive, pale form moving past them.

She went absolutely silent in the pod, as did he, as they both watched the sperm whale move past them. Its small eye barely even glanced at the sea god before it disappeared into the darkness once more. Scars dotted its sides, most around its mouth where it had fought massive squid for many years. The battles had been hard enough to leave marks.

"Wow," she whispered. "I forget how dangerous the sea is until I'm in it, and then... Well, it's hard to forget this place is terrifying when I'm just a small speck that could be killed by almost anything here."

"I would not let them kill you," he murmured. "There are few creatures brave enough to go up against me in these waters."

"Perhaps. But you would have to drop me to fight."

The spines all along his arms and back rose, lifting in deadly, poisoned points. "No, I would not."

Her eyes widened again as she looked them over. "I can see the water shimmering around those. Is that venom?"

"In a way. It paralyzes most creatures. Anything that breathes it in. It would not affect the mammals in the sea until I cut them, and then it would make it hard for them to move. They know better than to touch one such as I. If they are paralyzed, they will drift to the bottom and die long before they are able to wake." He looked down at her, trying to soften his expression that he knew must be truly wicked. "I will keep you safe, little human. You do not have to worry when you are with me."

It should have eased her mind, but instead, she just stared at him. Then her hand lifted, pressing against the glass. "I'm not sure I'd call it safe, but I don't think anything other than you could kill me now that you have me in your sights."

She was right.

He turned away from the original direction he'd planned on bringing them. If a sperm whale hunted in these waters, then it was very likely there were other creatures hunting as well.

The last thing he needed was for them to be attacked on this journey. He wanted to focus on her and nothing other than that. Distractions were unnecessary when their time together was limited.

Chapter 14

Ellie had no idea how long they traveled. For the most part, it was rather quiet. The depths of the ocean muffled all sound other than what she and Pilot made. The robot was relatively quiet, and she only heard his legs clacking together as he readjusted himself. Which meant the loudest noise was her own breathing and the thudding of her own heartbeat that echoed in her ears.

She'd seen the massive whale as they swam by. The scars on its face had terrified her, as had the intelligent look in its eyes. The whale had seen her. Not just recognizing that it was swimming past something other than empty water, but actually seen her.

The beast looked into her heart and seemed to see far more than she even knew was there. It even recognized that she had a soul, which she hadn't really thought about before.

Swimming through these waters gave her too much time to think. So she didn't. She just stared at Proteus. A god of the sea, and a monster she hadn't thought possible to exist. He glowed in the water, his bones so visible they were almost painful to look at.

She could see each one, count the ribs that decorated down his torso, although there were a few more than a human. She could see his hearts beating beneath them, the silhouette of all his organs so obvious that she found herself counting his heartbeats as though that would help calm her.

Something about being in total darkness except for him made the entire experience almost seem like it wasn't real. She was floating in nothing. She was nothing. And all that existed was him.

"I'm bringing you somewhere that will be better than the old facility. You will like it," he murmured, his voice ghosting over her pod and breaking through the thick clear glass.

"Are you bringing me to see the sun?"

"Better."

What could be better than the sun? Humans had tried for centuries underneath the waves to replicate that which they had lost. The sun was all they cared about. For years and years she remembered working with Malcolm on lightbulbs that were supposed to replicate the heat of the sun, but all of them had failed. Or at least, they had failed in what the other humans thought the sun should feel like.

She had no idea what else was worth chasing. The heat of the sun, feeling what humans had lost, it was a dream that she'd never believed would come true. What could be better than that?

She mused about the idea for a long time. There was little in this realm that could rival such an experience. Perhaps he wanted to show her one of the human settlements. The original ones were supposedly marvelous, but she didn't think they would have survived the storms. Which meant it was very likely he wasn't bringing her to one of those.

Where else could they go?

Light started to break through the water around them, although it wasn't the light she might have expected. Here she had been dreaming up beams of sunlight breaking through the surface in rays of gold. But all she got were bright white slashes, illuminating the water for merely a split second before disappearing again.

"What is that?" she asked. "The light?"

Proteus looked above him, his brow furrowing for a moment. "The sky is angry today."

A storm, then. Ellie should have known there would be many of them, but it was still terrifying to know they were right under one. She'd seen the reports from Tau's research. She knew these storms could last for days, sometimes weeks. They grew stronger and stronger out at sea, turning into monsters that would level an entire town and destroy buildings without ever slowing down.

They grew closer to a sheer ledge made of tumbled rocks. Giant stones, larger than her head, had all crammed into each other, creating a labyrinth of multicolored stones. Lightning made it easier for her to see the crevices that hid massive moray eels, each of them sneering at Proteus before disappearing into their homes.

"This is where you will find the secrets of your people," Proteus said. "The greatest secret they kept, in fact."

"Which was?"

"Me," he said quietly, but she heard the regret in his voice. "I worked side by side with them, creating so much that the humans have already forgotten. But I am certain, without question, that there is still some of our work remaining here."

Here? Wait, was this...

"Is this the main facility?" she asked, suddenly pressing her face against the pod as though that would get her even closer. "It doesn't look anything like the videos the drones sent."

"It is. Here is where all the work was done, and it is here where you will find even more knowledge. So much of it I have forgotten, but you will be able to achieve an infinite amount of progress in a short amount of time. You and Pilot, you will be the ones to discover it again."

She wasn't sure how she felt about that. It was a lot of pressure to be tasked with discovering all that humanity had lost. Even a facility like this, one where so many experiments had been held, would have hidden its secrets well.

Taking a deep breath, she pressed both her palms to the glass and searched through the massive boulders for a way inside. "How am I supposed to go in?" she asked. "The rocks..."

"There is a tunnel. One you can fit through. The drones have already shown you the footage."

She'd seen that footage, yes, and knew that she could squeeze through it. But that didn't mean she could breathe.

"Proteus, I don't know the way through well enough from that footage. I don't think I can hold my breath for that long."

Saying she didn't think she could was an understatement. She'd watched the footage from the drone. It had taken exactly six minutes and forty-two seconds to get inside that facility, and that had been with jets propelling it. Ellie didn't know how to swim, but she knew she could pull herself through the crevice with her hands. Still, it wasn't going to be quick.

No one could hold their breath that long. Maybe divers in the old days when there had been people training to do exactly what he was asking her to do. But she couldn't.

"Pilot," Proteus said, his voice stern. "You have a breathing apparatus, do you not?"

The faintest scraping sound could be heard from her feet as the droid stretched out his limbs and awakened at the sound of his name. "It has not been used for a while."

"Is it functional?"

There was a long pause before Pilot grumbled, "I suppose it must be. I wouldn't know unless we tested it out."

That wasn't good enough for Ellie. She wanted to make sure she could breathe no matter how far into that crevice they went. What if she got halfway in and all her oxygen cut out? She had to know for certain that she was going to survive.

But then she remembered that she was just a doll. This was an experiment, like all the other experiments she'd been a part of. If she didn't do this, then wasn't she failing him?

At any point, Proteus could open her pod and let the ocean swarm inside her only safe place. Even open, the pod would continue to try to heal her while she died. It would run out of energy trying to stop her from drowning.

Swallowing hard, she finally nodded. "All right. Pilot, let's give it a try."

He felt like a spider crawling up her body all the way to her face. Every footstep as he climbed her torso made her skin crawl, but she would not fall apart. This was what she had been made for. It was her duty. Her job to do what she was told to do.

The droid wrapped his legs around her face, and his body landed against her mouth. A panel in his belly opened up, and she could feel a tube pressing against her lips.

"It's mostly oxygen," Pilot said, as though that was reassuring. "Now, I'm going to close off your nose."

She had to whisper in her own mind not to panic as something pinched her nose shut. He was breathing for her, though. She could take a deep breath through her mouth, and it didn't feel all that different. She was still getting oxygen into her lungs. She could still feel them expanding.

That had to count for something.

"I only have fifteen minutes worth of breathable air before there's nothing left," Pilot said, but she had a feeling he wasn't talking to her. "Open the pod up and let's get going."

Get going? But she didn't even know the direction she was supposed to be swimming in! Hell, she didn't know how to swim!

A faint hissing noise filled her ears before Proteus ripped the door off her pod. Icy cold water rushed in, pinning her against the back for a moment before she was floating. She could feel her limbs lifting on their own, moving without her permission as the ocean held her in its grip.

She wanted to speak. Wanted to tell him that he needed to close the pod back up after she left. It was designed to handle leaks, or even something like this, as long as the seal was fixed again. It could drain the water once she wasn't inside it.

But there was no way for her to tell him to save what had kept her safe for so many years. Proteus pulled her out, holding onto her while the pod fell to the sea floor below them. It hit the ground with a dull thud, dust exploding around it as the two pieces landed far apart from each other.

Her home. Her safety.

Gone.

It felt like a hole had opened up in her chest. Sure, she hadn't been thrilled with the idea of ever going back to that unreal world that only existed in her own mind. But that had been the safe option. If the real world ever got too much, she had always had the option of returning to that place.

Now, she couldn't. The only place she could live was right here. With a monster holding her by the waist and his cold claws digging into her hips. Her reality was only what was right in front of her, and as terrifying as that was... it was also thrilling.

She looked up at him, blinking the saltwater into her eyes until she could see clearly.

"Go," he said, nudging her in the direction of the rocks.

She still didn't know where she was going. Ellie turned and looked over the rock formation, trying to remember exactly where the drone had gone.

The rocks in the footage had been very distinct. A pale white rock, visible above all the others, had set it apart from the rest. But now that she was in the water, it was harder to tell them apart.

Until she saw it.

The rock was so obvious, she wasn't sure how she hadn't noticed it sooner. Pale with striations through it, she was almost certain that the stone was part of an old building. It was crumbling apart like the rest of it, but it was so obviously different. Almost manufactured.

Breathing in deeply, she held her breath as she kicked herself toward the opening... and fell through the water all the way to the bottom of the sea.

How did people swim? She was flailing her limbs, but she wasn't moving at all. Proteus reached down, grabbed her arm, and propelled her toward the stones, where he deposited her in front of the crevice.

"You will learn to swim," he said. "But for now, get to where you can breathe."

There was air where she was going? She had to assume there was, or he wouldn't have relied on Pilot to breathe for her.

The crevice between the stones was big enough to maneuver

through. She twisted, wriggling her way through the stones until she was fully inside them. Entombed within rock.

She'd thought she would be terrified with the press of stones all around her, threatening a cave-in that could crush her between the sharp edges. But there was something comforting about this space. She trusted that the stones would remain where they were. Logic stated they'd been here for quite some time, after all. A little movement from her would not make them all tumble down.

Still, as she reached for one of the rocks to pull herself forward, she was careful not to tug too hard.

It felt good to use her body. The stones were rough against her palms, abrading the skin there and giving a texture to the environment around her. The pressure of the surrounding ocean muffled all sound. She could breathe, but only barely through Pilot, who was trying to conserve her oxygen.

Ellie had to remember the exact path the drone had gone. Otherwise she would end up stuck in this labyrinth for good. But it made her mind laser-focused on keeping her alive, ensuring that nothing went wrong. Adrenaline poured through her, making her muscles seem stronger, her mind quicker, her entire body ready to do whatever it took to get to the next rock and then...

Light.

Beams of it against the stones, even though she knew that wasn't possible. Light couldn't exist down here when the storm was raging over her head.

She pulled herself a little farther through the stones and felt the pinch of how tight they had gotten. She had to turn her body through some of them, twisting and tugging at her hips that got stuck in another section, and then she was through. The stones opened up here, not tighter, but giving her so much more space.

And there was light. Glimmering at the top of her head where the water met the air.

She had no idea how long she had been pulling herself through those stones, but she was here now. Staring at a surface that wasn't quite glassy at all. Almost as though a slight breeze ruffled it. That breeze turned the surface into glittering diamonds.

Pilot's legs moved against her face, and suddenly the droid detached from her skin. Oxygen now gone, she used her hands to pull herself up the wall of stones and lift her head out of the water.

She was assaulted with gold.

No, not gold.

Sand.

There was so much sand everywhere her eyes looked. Bright yellow and illuminated by overhead lights, there were dunes lifting over everything that might have once been the remains of humankind. Massive pillars held up the ceiling, painted in jewel tones with depictions of humans and undine alike. Carved sea creatures swam with them up the columns, to a ceiling that was entirely gold. Some parts of it had fallen now, as the gold foil was visible in massive chunks on the floor.

This room was beyond reason. Beyond understanding. It was so big, so tall, that the more she looked, the larger it seemed to get.

Ellie was used to Tau. Yes, there had been large rooms, but nothing like this. It was as if she clung to the side of a hollow mountain, and so much space made her dizzy.

"What is this place?" she asked as Pilot crawled out of the water with her. He shook water off himself before crawling up onto the sand.

"Welcome to Sanctuary, Ellie."

Chapter 15

The old paths into the Sanctuary were no longer open. Time had collapsed the tunnels, so it took him a little while to figure out how to get back inside. Eventually, Proteus grew tired of waiting and just shoved the stones out of his way. Sure, there had been a few more cave-ins that were more annoying than they were deadly to one as large as him.

The stones were easy to move. They just took time. And all the while, his mind wandered back to the little human who had been unable to swim.

She had surprised him.

But then again, many of the humans he had met couldn't swim. They were all so terrified of the ocean, uncertain when an undine would appear and drag them into the depths, so many had decided to forgo ever learning how.

He hadn't even thought about it when he ripped her out of that pod. He'd been wanting to destroy it since the first moment she'd asked him not to put her back inside of it. Yes, the healing capabilities were useful, but also very unlikely to be needed again. He'd already decided he didn't like it when she was hurt. Liked it even less when he was the one doing the hurting. Which meant he was going to keep her safe for the rest of her days.

No one would ever touch her again. Not even him.

She was the safest person on this planet now. A god of the sea himself was going to keep her safe, and no one would take her from him.

Finally, the rock wall gave way, and he entered the room that had plagued his dreams since he'd been captured. This had been where it had all started. This was where he had been so close to making a truce with the humans and learning how all of them could benefit from each other. But that had all crumbled because of greed from both sides.

This had once been a facility that would have rivaled the dreams of the gods. He remembered it being full of light and technology. All the equipment that they had struggled to make work had taken up nearly every free space. All of it was in use. All of it was used to research more and more incredible things that would have helped the ocean and the land at the same time.

Now, the equipment was gone. He poked his head out of the water to discover an empty room. The channels that used to be filled with water were still attached to the walls, at least. He would be able to move about the room once those systems were turned back online. They were little more than giant troughs that surrounded the area, but they had been useful back in the day, so he didn't dry out. The other undine who had helped him were also more likely to use those. Comfort was paramount while helping the humans.

Everything else was sand. He could see there was a small section of wall that had been blasted into the building, although it was hard to see that it was a hole at all, as the sand filled that so much it looked like it was part of the room. But he knew there hadn't been a door there, and the massive amount of sand in that area suggested that was where most of it had come from.

The wind he couldn't guess at an origin for, however. Perhaps there had been windows. He honestly did not remember.

So many of his memories had been worn away by time. But this place should have been glorious. It should have made a human heart stir with awe. These ragged remains wouldn't impress anyone.

"It's... magnificent." Ellie's voice carried through his thoughts.

Immediately he found her. She'd gotten out of the water, dripping wet in that strange black suit, and was sitting on one of the sand dunes. Granules of gold clung to her legs and arms, but she sat there with wide eyes, staring at everything around her like it was all the most beautiful things she had ever seen.

He tried to see it through her gaze, but all he could see was a ruin. This had once been a place of knowledge and learning, where so many people had flocked to try their experiments to help this world.

"There is nothing left," he murmured, trying very hard not to destroy this moment for her. "But it was once magnificent, yes."

"Once?" She finally looked at him, and he swore there was a glow in her eyes that he'd never seen before. "Do you not see where we are? This place is beautiful, Proteus."

He did see where they were. The room was beyond his saving, but her... He could see the beauty in her. With her hair slicked back from her face, she was all pointed angles and harsh features. Her cheekbones were so sharp they could cut glass, and the hollows of her cheeks would likely have made other people think her face was drawn. But her eyes were glowing, and the way she looked at all the destruction around them as though it had hope? He'd never seen anyone prettier in his life.

She was a perfect example of why he had helped her people all those years ago. What he saw as nothing but useless junk, she saw as an opportunity. Humans were ever so good at seeing refuse and making it bloom.

"Beautiful?" he repeated.

"Did you know sand was dry like this? I never knew. I mean, I'd seen it outside, of course, but Tau never had sand that we could touch inside of the city." Something wiggled in the sand in front of her, and he realized it was her toes.

She'd buried her bare feet in the sand and then done the same with her fingers. Ellie drew up fistfuls of the stuff and let it rain back down in a waterfall of colorful gold. Her gaze was pure wonder at the sight of it.

Then she scooped another handful, and he could quite literally hear the sound of her fingers striking metal. The echoing, hollow sound filled the facility they were in, and it made both of them freeze.

Metal. That meant...

"Dig it up," he said, already pulling himself out of the small area where he had been able to float. He didn't care if the sand scraped his sensitive scales, or if it tore through the membranes of his tail. Pain didn't matter. There was metal, and that meant there was so much more here than he had thought.

Breathing hard, he arrived at her side as she started to dig. She used her arms like shovels, a smart woman who knew how to move sand quickly until it was revealed.

The first console.

It wasn't much of one. Sand had done its damage, likely from the wind that had blown it in here with the force of a hurricane that had eaten away at the metal. But it was there, and they could make it work if they wanted to use it again.

He stared at Ellie. Her pupils had blown wide as she looked at what they had revealed, and then she looked back at him. There was a strangeness to her features and the way she looked, something that he had not quite been prepared for. Almost as though she was afraid of what they had found.

"This place..." she whispered, the words slow and drawn out. "What was it?"

"The same as all facilities were. A place of research and learning. Why do you look like we have just uncovered a body?"

She smoothed her hand over the top of the panel. It was rather flat and circular. Now that he was looking at it, he still didn't understand why that would scare her so much. The sand that covered it had eaten away at the smoothness, leaving behind rusted pieces that picked at her skin and left little red marks when she lifted her palm.

"This is where a test tube would go," she replied. "I have seen these my whole life. Giant glass tubes, with people hanging inside of them. The clones lived in them until we were grown enough for someone to wake us. I've even seen the undine within them. Horrible, hanging people and creatures, none of them aware of where they were. They slept without knowing how much danger they were in."

Now he understood. She had memories of a place like this.

And for the first time since meeting her, he wanted to look into her past. He could. At any point. Proteus had always looked at her as a creature beneath him. She was simplistic, a human; their futures and pasts were never worth looking at.

But with her, he wanted to see.

Sliding his hand over to hers on top of the panel, he pressed his palm against the top of her hand and pinned it to the abrasive surface. All it took was the slightest focus, and then her gaze was locked on his eyes. He knew what was happening to them, because he had given the same gift to a single bloodline who still lived beneath the waves.

Not the depthstriders, but something even more. Those jellyfish-like people had eyes that looked like a rainbow of colors. Just like his. People fell into them, unable to look away from the beauty of their gazes, but also trapped within the future that he would pull from them.

But this time, it was the past. He tumbled into her memories with her, watching as though he had been there at that very moment.

He saw her in the test tube, as she described it, although he would have called it a tank. She was suspended inside of it by some kind of liquid that looked rather thick even to the naked eye. Scientists surrounded her as she watched them.

She wasn't asleep in this memory. Her eyes were open wide with fear. There was a strange contraption around her mouth, and he recognized it was meant for breathing. No one in the room even looked at her. They were all there, of course, wandering around and doing their jobs, but they didn't care that she was terrified.

One of the women walked up to her tank, a clipboard in her hand that she didn't look up from as she hit a button on the outside of the tank. Three men approached as the liquid drained and the front of the tank opened up.

Ellie fell through it, and they caught her. It was then that Proteus realized she was much younger than she was right now. Her face was smooth and round. Her limbs were shorter and leaner. The men grabbed onto her the moment she started struggling. Some deeply embedded part of her realized that she needed to fight.

Even without ever having drawn breath before this, she knew to be afraid of men grabbing her. They all grunted at her waving limbs, and then one of them grabbed the tube that was still attached to her throat.

With a rough yank, he pulled it out of her body. It was shockingly long, having been lodged so deep inside of her body that he thought perhaps it had gone all the way into her stomach. Two tendrils pulled out, one for air and the other for food. And then she was breathing on her own.

Proteus was in her mind, so he knew that at this point she hadn't even learned how to talk yet. They had woken her many times before, but they'd never taken out the comfort of her breathing and feeding tubes. Now, she was surviving on her own.

And the only sound she knew how to make was a scream.

Pulling his hand away from hers, he forced himself to give her some space. The memory made something ache inside his chest, and he rubbed a hand over his thundering hearts.

He wanted to kill those men for her, and that was ridiculous because they were likely already dead. But there was no death good enough for what they had done. No death would ever do justice to the pain they had put her through.

He had promised himself and her that he would keep her safe. Even from her own memories.

"I can wipe them from your mind," he said, as though that might help. "I can remove all those memories until there is nothing left to scare you."

"I don't want them to be gone. I just want to be able to look at a stand like this and not be frightened that someone is going to put me in another glass tank and forget that they put me there." She swallowed hard and removed her hand from the stand. "I assume we need to clear this room out?"

"I intended to show you the beauty of this place. To give you the gift of your own history and the existence of so much human intelligence, even hundreds of years ago. I am sorry it brought back your memories of… that." He felt a little lost.

She shouldn't be afraid of his gift. He had been certain this facility would awaken the curious part of her that enjoyed seeking new things. She had been so intrigued by the drones and the cameras and all the footage that he had access to in the other facility, so he had thought this would inspire the same feeling.

Thunder rumbled overhead, so loud it seemed to shake the very foundation of the room. She flinched and drew her arms around herself, tucking her hands into her armpits and staring up at the roof.

Proteus realized that she was a very small creature that he'd placed in a very big room. She'd never been in open spaces before. Only small containment areas, tanks screwed into the ground, a pod that was barely bigger than a coffin, and limited research rooms in places that were underneath the sea so they simply could not be big.

He'd dropped her into a wide open space and told her to be comfortable with it.

Proteus was a fool to think she would be happy here, but he had hoped she would see what he did.

Breathing out a sigh, he gestured toward the sands. "Are you going to be all right here?"

"I can dig them out while you clean yourself off. The sand is hurting your scales." She turned toward her new task with a determined expression he recognized. "It will take a week, though. I'm very small, and I'm not sure where to put all the sand. But this body will learn how to perform manual labor. I'm quite certain of it."

Proteus cupped her chin, forcing her to look at him. Those eyes went wide again, pupils once more blown out. "You will be careful with yourself, and you will not harm this body any more than it already has been. But I asked you a question, Ellie. Will you be all right here?"

"I'm fine anywhere you put me."

"That is not an answer." He drew even closer, incapable of looking at anything beyond her eyes. "I do not want to put you somewhere you will not be comfortable. If you need me to move you, I will happily do so. This facility was meant to be a gift. Not a place to cause you even more fear."

Something in her expression softened, and she reached up to place her hand over his. Just the feeling of her palm against his skin was electric.

All the lights in his bones lit up again. He could see the sickly yellow and green lights illuminating her face, and how they burned through her fingers where she had her hand on him.

It was the first time she'd willingly touched him. The first time he could experience what it was like to have her hand on his skin. And oh, it made him burn.

"I will be fine here," she murmured, her voice a soothing balm to the sudden ache her touch inspired. "We can work together to clear this space out."

"Together," he repeated.

Chapter 16

Ellie had always been interested in historical relics. She'd only seen a few of them during her time in Tau, and even then they had been hard to come by. She would never forget the first time she'd been allowed to place a black disc onto a record player and listen to the tinny sound that had likely been listened to by countless people before her.

The music had been unbearable. But she had been so fascinated with the sound of it. The woman's voice was a little warbly as time had bent the record, but that didn't matter. She had been enraptured by the thought that there had been people just like her hundreds of years ago and they had still wanted to sing.

But here in Sanctuary, she was surrounded by the past.

The room was slowly revealed over the course of a few days. Proteus remained in the water where it was safest for him, and she threw sand into the hole they had arrived through. Her underwater companion had found some fabric that was still sturdy enough for him to catch most of the sand she threw down, and then he dragged it away through the rocks.

It was slow, backbreaking work. Her body hurt within an hour, but she kept moving as much as she could. Thankfully, it took Proteus more time to get rid of the sand than it did for her to scoop it into the water.

At least at first.

She uncovered what looked like a floor about a foot and a half down from the sand closest to the opening. It was an old tile floor, similar to the designs in Tau, and some small artifacts that had lingered behind. A floor lamp that had been bent in half, likely by someone stepping on it. An old access card with someone's face and name. A plastic bag full of sand with ancient words on it in a language she couldn't read. But it looked like it used to be maybe something edible.

Then, once she got to the areas where people had worked, moving the sand became nearly impossible. It was deeper in the back, closer to the hole in the wall where it had blown in. And even then, it was harder to move around all the equipment that she revealed.

Not to mention Pilot jumped to work. The little droid knew how to fix broken machines, that much was very obvious. But suddenly she had to maneuver sand around a droid that was pulling things apart to put them back together.

Proteus also had to discard the metal pieces that Pilot tossed into the water with muttered expletives. So much of what was still here wasn't useable. But there was still hope that they could put all of this together.

After four days, she had to take a break. Her back hurt so badly it was spasming even when sitting down. Her legs ached even though she didn't feel like she'd used them all that much. Not to mention her arms. Those had turned into useless noodles, so she was mostly using her chest and back to shove sand.

They had gotten maybe a quarter of the room revealed, though, and it was starting to look like the place it had once been.

She just needed a few minutes, and she'd get the broom out again. She'd found it in a metal locker that had been sticking out of the sand. It must have been a cleaning supply cabinet. Most of what remained was useless, but the bucket had proven helpful in moving sand, and the broom made it easier to get all the little granules that always seemed to spread out no matter how often she chased them.

Ellie sat down on the lip of the hole in the floor and marveled at the design. Clearly, this was no mistake that there was an entrance here. The edges were still smooth. Tile curved over the lip, so there wasn't any sharp metal to bite into her legs as she dangled them into the water.

She'd love something else to put on her body. This black suit had once been stylish, but now it clung to her skin and made her feel itchy.

Or maybe that was all the sand that was jammed into it from days on end of working in it.

Ellie started unzipping as the water rippled around her feet. Proteus was arriving soon. Those bubbles were usually the precursor to his appearing. The suit parted easily enough, and she'd just gotten one of her arms out by the time his head appeared in front of her.

His eyes went to her arm, strangely enough the one he had chewed upon, before flicking his gaze to hers. "What are you doing?"

"There is sand in my suit."

"And?"

"And I would like to get it out. It's uncomfortable. You washed the sand out of your scales. It's the same feeling for me." With one arm free, she was still so impossibly itchy. It was hard to even focus on anything other than the incessant itchiness that plagued her. Scratching at her other arm through the fabric, she finally shook her head and continued pulling it off.

It didn't matter if he looked at her anyway. They were friends. Sort of. Or he looked at her as a means to an end. Proteus didn't care if he saw her boobs or if she got into the water with him naked.

A soft sound rocked through his chest, and then air bubbles burbled up from around his chest gills. She almost thought the sound was a scoff, but then his face turned a rather interesting shade of greenish gray and he spun away from her.

"I..." He cleared his throat, and that sound happened again. "I will give you privacy."

He seemed almost ready to swim off into the rocks again, but Pilot interrupted them. "Proteus? I have a report for you."

Ellie watched his shoulders bunch even more before he blew out a long breath and seemed to resolve himself to stay. "What is it, Pilot?"

She finished stripping off the suit while Pilot spoke about all the equipment that had been repaired and what was unsalvageable. There wasn't much that was still working. Most of what had remained here had been so damaged in the storms that it was likely they were either ruined by water, sand, or time itself.

Sitting unused for two hundred years would do that to almost anything, she assumed. Pilot was quite disturbed by how much of the remaining equipment had been left to rot long before the facility was no longer in use.

Finally pulling her last leg free, she turned her back to Proteus as well and dipped into the water. She still couldn't swim, so she had to hold on to the ledge, but at least she could swish her legs around in the water and feel like the sand was moving off her skin.

But it wasn't. The damned jagged little pieces seemed to cling to her form, no matter how hard she tried to wiggle her body. The water wasn't making them get off. It was just existing with the sand. How was that even possible?

"The hologram pod seems to be working the best. The puck had to be thoroughly cleaned, but I managed." Pilot sounded pleased with himself. "The logs are very thorough, and watching them might help us determine which of the remaining equipment we wish to uncover, and perhaps decide if there are any we can ignore or remove from the facility."

"I would prefer this place to be cleared of sand entirely," Proteus said, his rumbling making the water vibrate around her.

"Unfortunately, that is unlikely. There is nothing to patch the walls with, and I've already identified multiple areas where the structure of this building is compromised. Unfortunately, even if we fixed the major damage in the wall, sand would still get in."

Proteus grunted, clearly in disapproval.

Ellie tested moving one hand off of the wall and using it to scrub at her torso. That seemed to work to remove all the spiky granules. So she leaned down a little farther and instantly lost her grip.

Her head dunked underneath the water, and she waved her arms like she'd seen others do. Kicked her legs. She even wiggled her body the way it was supposed to so she would float to the surface, but nothing seemed to work.

Then, a massive arm hooked around her waist and hauled her back up to the surface. Spluttering, she leaned back against the massive wall of muscle that was Proteus and trusted him to hold her up while she shoved her hair back from her face.

"Try not to die," he said, although his voice sounded strained.

"I still don't know how to swim."

"I will teach you soon enough."

She thought he would bring her back to the wall and allow her to cling to it. Instead, he moved her in his arms, and then his tail was between her legs. Thick and muscular, it made something deep inside her chest awaken in a way she hadn't realized it could. Her entire body felt hot. Her breathing was a little more rapid. Her heart felt like it was trying to beat its way out of her chest and between her legs...

Heat.

Indescribable heat.

Proteus sounded almost pained as he said, "I will keep you afloat. Finish your bathing, Sisu."

How was she supposed to finish bathing with a sinuous tail undulating between her legs? She hadn't even realized her body could feel like this! It was glorious, terrifying, aching, everything she had not realized a human could feel.

Pilot was still prattling on about the holograms, and she was supposed to be scrubbing herself. So that's what she did. Robotically. Trying not to move at all because she was so terrified that the feeling would get worse. Or better.

It was best not to encourage a rebellious body.

"Perhaps you should turn the hologram on," Proteus said. There was still an odd edge to his voice. Clipped and different from normal, as though he were straining himself.

Was she that heavy? She didn't think it would be a struggle for him to keep her afloat with his tail, but she really had no idea how much effort he was exerting. Maybe it wasn't easy to use his tail like this, although it sure seemed like there was enough of it.

It was his damned fluke, she realized. It was flicking in the water and that was what kept her afloat, but it was also what was twitching the thick muscles of his tail against a very sensitive part of her body.

"All done!" she announced, as if anyone cared that she was finished.

Stupidly, she jolted herself off his tail. Pushing until she was clinging onto a few of his scales and desperately grappling for the lip of the floor. She hadn't even noticed the icy temperature as she hauled herself out. All she wanted was to put that suit back on, and to ignore the feelings that had been building inside of her body.

If she ignored them, they weren't real. If she pretended that he didn't make her feel that way, then it wasn't serious.

"Oh good!" Pilot said, completely oblivious to what had just occurred. "Allow me."

She yanked her suit on while the droid clanked around wherever he was. She didn't know if Proteus was looking and shouldn't have cared. But something had awakened in her, and she almost wanted him to look. She wanted to feel the weight of his eyes on her limbs, to know if he liked what he saw.

These were beastly feelings, and they had no place in her mind. She was a clone, nothing more, nothing less. A tool to be used. She had seen the other clones servicing people before. Many of Malcolm's friends, and Malcolm himself, had their way with clones that looked identical to her. Ellie had seen them many times.

But she had one purpose. And it wasn't this.

A hologram of a woman burst to life right in front of her as she pulled the last sleeve up and over her shoulder. Letting out a little shriek, she would have fallen back into the water if Proteus hadn't planted his hand firmly on her back and shoved her through the hologram.

She staggered forward, catching herself before she fell on her face, and then reeled around to see him staring at the hologram with clear recognition in his eyes. As if that wasn't enough, the hologram appeared to be speaking directly to him.

"Proteus, if you're seeing this, I'm likely long dead." The woman was looking at the water, as though expecting that was where he would be. "The equipment is being prepped to see how long it can last, but I know your own people would never let you come back without a fight."

The hologram turned, walking straight through Ellie and toward the back corner of the facility. "This is the weakest area. We assume the storms will affect this wall first. We've moved everything to the opposite side and built as many structures behind this place as we could to strengthen the wall. It's the best we can do on such short notice."

The opposite wall had seemed to be better than the others. There was still a lot of sand over there, but it had been pushed in that direction by the wind. If they could board up the other side, or just let the sand keep clogging that wall, she could move most of the sand and uncover the equipment they'd stored on the safer side.

"But Proteus, just know that if you're back, then that's because of our research. We won't stop looking for you. I know the others have created their own little world underneath the sea, but if history has taught me anything, it's that humans will stop at nothing to control what they do not deserve." The woman brushed her hair back from her face. "I wish I were there to help you, but we both know that would be walking in the same footsteps as the others. I will welcome my death. Even earn it, if you believe what others have said about me."

The hologram smiled at where Proteus was, and something ugly burned in her chest. Maybe it was the expression on the woman's face.

Ellie wasn't all that sure. But there was a fondness there, a familiarity that made Ellie want to turn the hologram off.

He'd been trapped underneath the ocean for centuries, and no one had gone to find him. This woman, whoever she was, was claiming to be the person who had saved him. But how could they prove that? No one could ever know who had actually saved Proteus.

"She was one of the scientists who performed most of the experiments. She had a vision of creating a better world, not just for your kind, but for everyone." Proteus finally looked at Ellie. The uncomfortable expression was already gone from his face, and she had a feeling it was the other woman who had given him such ease.

Ellie should be better. She had no idea who this woman was, what she had done, or her relationship with Proteus. This jealousy was unlike her and must be in some way related to the feeling she'd experienced in the water.

Again, this was not her function. Not her job.

She swallowed her pride and said, "She must have been an impressive woman."

"She was. Then she died, and the world wept." His gaze turned in the direction of the rest of the hidden equipment. "I am ready to work whenever you are, Ellie. I am eager to discover what she left me."

An ache bloomed in her chest, but she turned her tired body toward the sand once more. Perhaps a little labor would do her good. Perhaps she could forget how horrible it had felt discovering someone else had known him first.

Chapter 17

Proteus watched Ellie working herself to the bone, and his soul recognized her need for reassurance. This was the only way she could get that. The harder she worked, the more worthy she felt of being awake. Ellie still felt so certain that she needed to earn her place beside him, even though he had tried to show her that it was unnecessary.

He knew her type. Some humans were so fearful that others did not want them, and so they were wiling to do as they were told. They worked until they fell apart, doing everything they could to prove to others their worth. And yet, their true value was in that worry.

He wanted to tell her that no one would ever question why she was with him. The amount of hard labor she had shown day in and day out proved how wondrous she was to have around. No matter what task he asked her to do, she would do it. No matter how tired she grew, she would push through. The cost to herself didn't matter.

That was bravery. That was loyalty. It was all the features of a person he would never grow tired of, because he could see how much

she cared. These were the traits of a woman dedicated to a cause.

And yet, apparently he had not shown her enough how much he appreciated her. She worked tirelessly until he had to tell her to stop.

Even then, Ellie didn't want to. She argued with him that they weren't done yet, and why should they stop when there was still sand to clear?

He did not know how to tell her that he worried for her health. She could tell him when she needed to stop. She could complain that her body hurt. None of that would change his opinion of her or lessen her value.

"Sit down," he grumbled, his voice deep and low. Perhaps a little of his anger showed as well in that statement, because the damned woman did not know when to stop moving. If he told her to sit, then she shouldn't argue with him.

Ellie glared, but her wobbling legs could not do more. Huffing out an angry breath of her own, she sat down on a pile of sand they had yet to clear. "I want to get this done, Proteus."

"And you will."

"Not if we keep stopping. I know I'm tired. I know I'm slowing down. But if we push just a bit longer, then we could finish this project and move onto the next."

Except they both knew that they couldn't. There was a lot more for them to do, and even more sand for them to shift. It was like it replicated itself, and no matter how much they got rid of, there was always more sand.

He had to give her a reason to stop.

Narrowing his gaze, Proteus looked over at Pilot, who had been working on one of the newer equipment pieces that had been revealed by the sand. It had survived where many pieces had not. Pilot was currently working on bringing it back online, since the computer system within could help them learn what had happened here, and what other parts of this system needed to be turned online. Pilot suspected this terminal controlled all the others in the room.

"Pilot," he said, waiting for the droid to look at him before he continued. "Can you replicate yourself?"

"I have that function, yes."

He glanced over at a pile of scrap metal. They'd had to ask the droid to stop throwing parts into the water since it was getting in the way of the sand removal, and now he could see good use for them. "Use these pieces and make more of yourself. Give them the directive to move the sand so Ellie can rest."

There was a moment of obvious disbelief from the droid. Replicating himself would take time and effort, Proteus knew that, but there was also the realization that the intelligence that had been stored within that droid was going to be used to give a human relief from manual labor. The sheer rage would fuel Pilot for the next few years.

Proteus tried not to smirk as he gestured for Ellie to come closer to the entrance where Proteus lurked. He had retreated back to the water after trying to help her move sand, and was only now feeling relief from the drying that had curled his scales up.

She sat down with her legs dangling into the sea, not a care in the world. He'd seen countless humans terrified of the ocean. They feared what would bite them from the depths, or if they would drown if they slipped in. This woman couldn't even swim, and yet she sat here with her legs in the water.

Perhaps that was because she'd seen death so many times. She didn't fear what waited for her beyond all the darkness.

Proteus took a moment to look at her. When did the sight of her make him so soft? He wanted to linger as he peered at her features, listening to the sound of her breathing and the quiet, steady beat of her heart. He could listen to her for ages. The sounds of her body, the whispering truth of her mind, all of it made him want to touch her.

With a flick of his tail, he coasted a little closer to her. "Are you hungry?"

She shrugged. "I suppose. I'm still getting used to eating anything that isn't liquid."

Hm. He wasn't sure what he could bring her that would replicate that liquid packet that had brought her so much comfort. He knew it likely had all the necessary vitamins and nutritional needs that would keep her alive. While he had to guess at what humans ate, he barely remembered what they had consumed years ago.

"Would you like more fish?" he asked.

She made a face, but then immediately cleared it from her expression. "That would be fine, I suppose."

"You don't like fish?"

Ellie shrugged. "I don't really know what I like. Nutritional packets have little flavor."

He ran through all the things he could think of in his head. Obviously, clams and oysters were an option, although they were a little deep for him to find those. Starfish were a delicacy, but he wasn't certain her kind ate them outright. Which meant he would need to find something else for her to feast upon, or at the very least, a way for her to cook them.

Perhaps she would like sea urchin. He had seen the humans taking out their yellow innards before and eating them. It was surprisingly briny, and usually eaten raw, so he could see her enjoying that.

"I will be back," he said, and with no preamble, he disappeared beneath the surface.

He caught her a few extra fish as well. Eating those raw hadn't seemed to bother her, and there were a few other delicacies he could find. The water weeds that had always annoyed him were edible, and the seaweed that tangled around his tail actually had a decent flavor according to some of the humans he remembered.

So he brought those up with him and then placed them all in front of her. Each one he delicately set out, even the fish, before slicing into the first one so she would eat it before it went bad.

"Try this," he said, staring at her expectantly.

She looked at him as if he'd lost his mind. "What?"

"If you do not know what you like, then we will discover what you do. Together." He gestured at the food. "Please. Take your time, but tell me what you like and dislike about each of these."

To the music of Pilot clanking behind them, creating horrific looking droids that were clearly meant to be terrifying, Ellie picked up the slice of fresh fish he had offered her.

The barracuda was one of the few fish brave enough to fight him back when he tried to get them for food. He admired them, in a way, but the fresh slices of its flesh would keep her healthy. So he didn't mind killing the beast.

Watching her place the slice of raw fish on her tongue did something to him that he hadn't expected. He liked feeding her. He liked knowing that he was the one giving her energy.

At least, until her face creased a bit. "It's... fishy."

He arched a brow. "It is a fish."

"Yes, but..." She took a deep breath and then shrugged. "I don't know. I guess I wasn't expecting it to taste like it smells."

Like it smelled? Proteus leaned forward and took a deep breath, inhaling deeply the scent of the barracuda to make sure it hadn't gone rancid. There was nothing wrong with it. And he'd even say it didn't really smell like fish either. There was a scent of the sea on it, but that was all.

"Hm," he muttered, before nudging an oyster closer to her. "Try this one then."

When she struggled to crack it open, he reached for it and expertly opened the delicacy. He personally loved oysters and knew many creatures in the ocean liked them as well. They were easy to eat, and they were plentiful. The People of Water grew them in farms, and he remembered them being abundant and so sweet with many flavors depending on where and how they were grown.

Handing it over to Ellie, he watched as she slurped it up.

There was a long pause as she seemed to think about what she thought. But she hadn't even chewed. How was she supposed to get the flavor if she didn't chew? She kept forgetting to do that with all the food he gave her.

"It's sweet and salty." She licked her lips, and he couldn't keep his eyes away from the little flicker of pink that was revealed. "I like it. Maybe not for an entire meal, but it is quite delicious."

"Do that again," he asked before he could stop himself.

"Do what?"

His eyes were so clearly on her mouth, what did she think he wanted? "Stick out your tongue."

And bless the little thing, she did so without hesitation. She stuck her tongue out and all of his gills suddenly ached with need. Her tongue was short, flat, and so pink it was startling. For all his years working with her kind, he had never realized that their tongues were pink.

He stuck out his tongue as well, showing her that his tongue was long and black. Both of them stared at each other in surprise, their eyes wide as they both looked at what was very obviously a different kind of appendage than the other had.

Then he realized how stupid they likely looked. Both of them with their tongues hanging out of their mouths.

He put his back in his mouth and cleared his throat. "Right, well. Try the next then. Urchin I've heard is very good to your people."

She sucked her tongue back in as well, and very gently picked up the black urchin he'd laid next to her. He'd already gutted the beast, leaving the remains inside that she had to scoop out with her fingers. Swallowing hard, she looked at him before looking back down at the urchin. "This?" she asked.

"Yes."

"I just..."

The yellow innards didn't look appetizing to him either, but they tasted good. "Yes," he repeated.

She didn't look excited about it, but she did scoop the gelatinous substance into her mouth and swallowed it. He watched her face go through many stages of intrigue, horror, disgust, and then a very odd expression that made him lunge away from her so he didn't get caught in the crossfire when she gagged.

Ellie managed to keep the food down, but he hadn't thought she would. Then she pressed the back of her hand to her mouth and shook her head. "No. Not that one. Never that one."

And then she let out the most ungodly sound as air expelled from her mouth and she gagged again.

Proteus leaned forward and carefully removed the urchin. Dunking it into the water, he let it fall onto the ground so she wouldn't have to look at the black spines anymore. "Noted."

Pilot skittered forward and then pointed with a single leg at the other droids he had put together rapidly. They were all terrors of droids, barely more than legs and a shovel at the front. But they would serve their function very well.

It was a good distraction as he looked them over and then grumbled, "Good job, Pilot."

"They will resume your work then if you are done staring," Pilot muttered as he headed back to the console to get power on in this facility again.

Ellie cleared her throat once more, but this time he had a feeling she was trying not to laugh. Her watering eyes sparkled as she looked at him, and he had never been so enraptured with a human before. She was so beautiful it was shocking, really. Humans weren't supposed to be beautiful. They were tools to be used, functional and interesting to look at sometimes, but certainly never so stunning.

She smiled at him, and those eyes sparkled even more. "I think we're getting called back to work."

"I am being called back to work. You should rest."

Proteus touched her leg in the water. His hand wrapped all the way around her calf, and he should have just squeezed the flesh there and left it be. But he couldn't quite force himself to remove his grip.

He couldn't even feel her skin beneath the thick hide that covered her, and yet...

"I'm not sure I've ever met a human as fascinating as you," he murmured, staring up into her eyes as though they held an answer to questions he was afraid to ask. "Why is that?"

"I'm not all that human, I suppose."

"No, you very much are human. You hold all the things that I admired about them, all wrapped up in one person. Resilience, dedication, hope, the need to use your imagination. You are the blueprint of what your kind should and could be." He lifted his wet hand and skated the backs of his claws against her cheek. A single drop of water dripped down to her chin, hanging off the pointed tip like a sparkling diamond. "If only all humans were like you, Sisu. I think I would have killed a lot less of them."

He watched her eyes widen and knew she was struggling to comprehend how she was meant to feel about that.

His words were a compliment, though. Because he did wonder if others had been like her, would he have spared them in those early days? If he had seen the value of humanity earlier, if he had seen more of it in all the people he had interacted with, perhaps the future would have been very different.

Proteus had recognized those traits too late, after all. And by then, the damage had already been done.

Chapter 18

There," Ellie said, stepping back to look at her work. She didn't have the delicate hands of an engineer. That much was painfully obvious. But the patchwork she'd done on the piece of wall would hold. "I think that's done."

Pilot scuttled over to her, the clicks of his feet on the now mostly clean tile echoing in the massive chamber. "It'll hold. It just looks horrid."

She wasn't going to argue with him about that. The welder they had found was very old, and it spat flames in fits and spurts rather than a consistent white flame like it was supposed to. That led to her having to go over the same places far too many times, and globs of metal decorated the outline of the door frame, rather than a smooth line like a professional might have done.

But it would hold. And that was good enough.

Leaning down, she scooped him up in her hand so they could head back to the new chamber they had revealed. The sand had hidden more than just this chamber. Apparently, there were other corridors where other people had lived.

"Do you think there's clothing in there?" Ellie asked, heading over to the door that kept them away from the rest of the secrets.

"Who knows? I worked on the settings to make sure we could bypass the coding that keeps it locked," Pilot said as he climbed up to her shoulder and then perched there like a metal parrot on a pirate's shoulder. "I just... I'm not sure if we should go in there."

"Why?"

"We don't know what we're going to find." Pilot paused for dramatic effect before then adding, "It was their living quarters. I don't think it would be out of the ordinary to expect there to be some dead bodies in there. I think many people remained here until the very end."

She'd never seen a dead body. That was concerning, certainly. But also, she wanted to get out of this wetsuit and into something that would be more comfortable. Something like she'd seen the other scientists wear.

A clean, pressed shirt that would hug her waist. Pants that would comfortably fit around her thighs and maybe make her legs look a little longer than they were. She wanted to feel pretty in clothing that was meant for real, living people. Not just dolls like herself.

So she stood in front of the door and asked, "Pilot, how do I open the door?"

He sighed, a strange mechanical sound, before answering, "The password I set is butterscotch cookies. That's all you'll have to say. It recognizes your voice activation."

"That's an odd password for a droid to pick."

"My creator was a fan of them."

And he had paid his respects to his creator in the only way he knew how. By keeping Fairweather alive.

She knew how important it was to droids for the living to still be living. They did that by never forgetting who had made them, long after their mortal bodies had decayed on this planet.

She patted the top of his head before saying quite loudly, "Butterscotch cookies."

The door slid open with a long hiss, revealing a room beyond that was somehow perfectly preserved. It was a living area, just like Pilot had said, although very ancient in its style.

Rather than mostly metal accents and clean lines, this place had once been filled with color. A rotting quilt was even hanging on the wall, clearly once filled with brilliant blues and yellows. A wooden table had three broken legs and leaned on its side next to it, and the chairs were just as bad. But those looked like they had been broken intentionally. Someone had been here before. They'd likely taken everything of value.

She stepped into what must be a kitchen. All the doors were ripped off the cabinets, some of them hanging on by a single hinge, but most of them had been strewn about the checkerboard black and white tile. The fridge stood open, the electricity long turned off in this room, but it didn't matter because the food inside was so ancient it was nothing more than dust on the shelves.

As she moved through the living quarters, she found a door that was still open. The bedroom beyond was in better condition than the rest of the ransacked place. That was where she found the body.

The skeleton had wasted away in the dry air. There wasn't even a hint of skin left on it, but the hands were still placed on the person's chest in an almost reverent manner that made Ellie think even the grave robbers who had come in here hadn't touched the body. There was a tablet still resting on the bed beside them.

"You said you were looking for clothing," Pilot reminded her as she reached for the tablet.

"And answers."

"But mostly clothing."

Apparently, the droid didn't like looking at dead humans. Neither did Ellie, but this wasn't much of a human anymore. The skeleton gave the room an almost holy air. Like she had stepped into a tomb rather than a bedroom.

Tapping on the tablet, she blew out a breath at the dead battery. Of course it was dead.

"Pilot? Can you connect to this?"

"Absolutely not."

"Just do it for me, please. I want to read what's on here. What if there are more schematics for the building?"

That did the trick. The droid extended a wire from beneath his crab-like body, grumbling about how disgusting it was to be connected to something that was just resting next to a dead body.

She plugged him in and the tablet burst to life. It wasn't anything about the facility, but a diary, it looked like.

"Entry 213," she read aloud. "The facility is dying, just like me. I wish there was more we could do to preserve it, but the sands have started to take the building back. I have overstayed my welcome in this wild place. Perhaps I should have gone to the sea with the others. Yet, there will always be a part of me dedicated to my work here. I am the last remaining scientist. I am determined to find the cure for living on land."

Ellie paused, her eyes darting over the words. She sank down on the bed beside the skeleton, reading as fast as she could before setting the tablet down on her lap.

"Pilot... You both said this was a research facility, didn't you?"

"Yes."

"You didn't tell me they were experimenting on humans. They wanted to make a being capable of living on land again."

Pilot climbed down her arm and then bounced onto the floor. He clearly did not like being anywhere near that body beside her. "This facility was dedicated to preserving humanity at any cost. They had seen that the undine were capable of living in the sea, but the scientists who worked here were of the mind that there was no possibility for humans to survive long term in the oceans because of the undine people."

She took a deep breath. "So they decided to experiment with other DNA? Knowing that the planet was going to get exponentially worse as the storms sucked all the moisture into themselves? They know all that would be left was a desert until the rains came every year? And then only floods."

Pilot bounced his body. "Exactly."

But if that's what Sanctuary had really been… "So what is it that Proteus is trying to do?"

"He wants to see if the scientists completed their work. And then he wants to show the undine that he is the god they remember. It will keep them in check while he learns the state of the planet. The humans must move here, regardless of safety."

Her entire world seemed to spin to a stop. "But what if the scientists succeeded? There could be people living on the surface."

"That was always the hope. Perhaps even some humans survived. Those who worked here were also building bunkers. Places for people to outlast even the worst outcomes. They were the wealthiest people, of course. Some of them split off from those who built the quadrants in the sea." Pilot bounced a little, almost like a nervous movement that he couldn't keep still.

He needed to get out of this room, but she needed her answers. "So they were experimenting on creatures like the undine? Were there any creatures even here to experiment on? Species like the undine, who were already more capable than humans?"

Pilot shook his head, his entire body in denial of what she said. "No, they weren't experimenting on other creatures. They were trying to create them."

They were trying to create new life in this cursed place. A being who could live in harsh climates like this, without fearing the storms or how a depletion of water would affect their bodies.

She scanned through the woman's diary notes again, seeing more and more horrific things popping up as she read through them. "They tried every animal they could," she muttered as she kept reading.

It seemed like they were obsessed with fixing what they thought of as broken. But humans weren't broken things. Humans just weren't meant to live on a planet that looked like this. They weren't supposed to survive massive hailstorms and hurricanes that hung over the land for months on end. None of this was ever supposed to have happened.

But the biologists here hadn't had much luck, it seemed. There were a lot of animals they tested, but human DNA was so specific, it was impossible to create beings out of it.

Pilot made a whirring noise and headed out of the room. Ellie followed him, trailing along behind with the tablet still in her hands. "What happened to their experiments? It looks like when she was alive, there were some viable ones, but they all died in infancy."

"Splices," Pilot muttered as he headed through the trashed living room. "They called them splices. Abominations of man and beast. Most of them took after the latter. Some of them were so mangled, but had the brilliant mind of a genius. Others were viable in life, but they were little more than monsters. All of them had to be put down. Over and over again."

"How do you know all this?"

He stopped in the doorway, and his little crab body curved in on itself. "I was here, Ellie. I was one of the droids who helped all of them. I saw what they created, and it was terrifying to look upon. Nothing like that could have lived long. None of them."

Ellie frowned but then spun around. "Wait, the clothing."

"I will not stay in that haunted place any longer."

"You don't have to."

She didn't care if she was alone with the body. After all, there wasn't anything left. But she intended to read every entry in the diary because no one would have left this tablet lying next to them if they didn't expect someone to read it.

Rummaging through the woman's wardrobe, Ellie found a few pieces of clothing that were, for some reason, vacuum sealed. They smelled a little odd when she ripped them open, but the pale green blouse and simple long denim skirt happened to be in perfect condition. Whoever this woman had been, she had good taste in the preservation of clothing.

Perhaps she'd known someone like Ellie would wander in here someday and really appreciate the clothes.

She stripped, changed into the outfit quickly, and then headed back into the main room. "Pilot, it seems like some of the experiments were viable. 327 and 411 seem to be the ones that they were most focused on. How do we find out more information about those beings?"

A deep voice interrupted her, rumbling like the depths of the sea. "You don't."

She startled, looking at Proteus, who had somehow entered the facility without her hearing him. "Why not?"

"They are not our current focus."

"Well, what is the current focus? You haven't told me anything about why I'm here or what I'm doing."

He tilted his head to the side. "I thought you were a doll. Not a real person. Someone for me to order around and who would do what I said without asking why?"

Those were her words, thrown right back at her. She had really said all that. But things had changed, she supposed. She'd been living outside of that pod, using her body, working with the two of them. She'd been learning how to be a real person. He'd been the one who wanted her to choose what food she liked, and now she had real clothing on. Not the same outfit she'd worn her entire life.

This was... intoxicating. Making choices. Thinking for herself. Learning and growing and changing into someone new who had her own thoughts and feelings and opinions.

Taking a deep breath, she hugged the tablet to her chest and said, "What if I want to be more than that?"

"Then I will happily support it." Proteus lifted himself out of the water, a splash of liquid flooding across the floor and clearing much of the sand that had already blown across her hard work in keeping it clean. "But we cannot focus on what these scientists were working on creating. They did not succeed."

"Are you certain of that?" She looked back at the tablet, frowning once more. "Her notes make it seem like… like… 411 might have been alive when she died. And it seemed to test high on all the aptitude tests and learning skills. I don't know if 411 was the only one of its kind."

"They only made singles of the splices. They didn't want to risk the chance for them to reproduce without knowing what genetic qualities they had." Proteus reached for the tablet and set it aside. "Right now, you and I are going to focus on convincing all those who are actually alive to worship me once more. Only then, once I know that the undine are under my thumb, will I look at what the humans did while I was gone."

She rubbed her face. "But if there are still humans in bunkers beneath the sand, surely they are still working on this plan?"

"If they are, then it is not our problem." Proteus framed her face with his hands, forcing her to look at him and ground herself in the reality that was right in front of her. "We are going to work on one thing at a time. First, we will find those whom we know will help us. We find the people who have consistently proven themselves to be on our side. We will show them that a god is amongst them once again, and that will give them the courage they need when we reach out to any who might still be alive on land. Whatever lives here, human or otherwise, will not want its resources stolen by someone who could have stayed in the sea."

"Then why are you dragging them out of the waves?" she asked.

His eyes softened. "That was always the plan, Ellie. I did not promise those ancient people who worshipped me that they would live in harmony with the humans while more and more resources from the sea were depleted. I promised that I would allow the humans to live under the sea until I could fix their home. You and your people were refugees. They were never meant to be neighbors."

Suddenly, it all made sense.

"You're going to fix Above," she whispered. "How?"

"All in due time. And if I cannot fix it, then those who remained here were supposed to find a way for their people to live here." He released her and turned his attention back to the channels above their heads where he and his people had once swum. "It is time for the humans to move out of the sea, Sisu. Once and for all."

183

Secrets of the Void

Chapter 19

His plan was going to work. Proteus was certain of that.

This room had started as nothing but the remaining trash of the humans, and now it was an impressive atrium that would take the breath away of most who entered. Sure, there were greater and more impressive areas in Alpha. But apparently, that city had been destroyed.

None of the underwater cities had channels like this. None of them allowed the People of Water to move through the walls so that they could work side by side with scientists who desperately needed their knowledge and information. Together, they could start their work anew.

He watched as Ellie finished her last bit of work. She had been coding the last few bits that would put on a show for those he intended to summon here, but apparently there was something wrong in the mapping up there. The holograms would work in their favor. Projections on the walls and throughout the area would show the humans and undine what he planned for their future. Seeing it would make them bend to his ways much easier than not.

They would also be able to try it out for themselves. He longed for the moment when he could see his own people swimming through the channels again, each of them imparting wisdom that was necessary for their human scientists to understand what it would take to do what they wanted.

If only they were so lucky. He could not wait to see what would change with these people, or how they would continue the work he had started over two hundred years ago. As long as the humans were no longer in the sea, he could finally rest.

Ellie peered up at a higher part of a channel, clearly seeing something he didn't. There were creases on her brow now as she looked up at it, and he was suddenly struck again by how intelligent this human was.

He'd met geniuses before. He'd worked with them for ages long before he had ever met her. But that expression warmed something in his chest. Perhaps the stasis in his prison had changed some chemical makeup inside of him. It wouldn't be surprising. Being alone for that long was bound to change how he saw the world.

Still, even looking at her made something in his chest heat in a way it never had before. She was so attuned to detail. She stared at the channel and then finally he saw it too. A mere drip. A small one, nothing that most people would have been concerned about, but his little Sisu noticed it and she would not let it stand.

"It's not a leak that would threaten those who are within it," he said, his voice tinged with amusement. "You can leave that alone."

"I think you're wrong. It's leaking from a seam, and I think if we added any pressure to it, the whole thing would break." Her frown deepened. "But it's all stone. I don't know how to fix stone."

Pilot chirped from where he was working on the hologram show.

"Bring some metal and weld it into the stone. All you have to do is hammer it in place, and then it'll stay there."

"Right," she muttered, already looking for a piece to do exactly that.

She shouldn't have been doing any of this. He appreciated how much she wanted to help him, but Ellie was far more delicate than most humans. She hadn't been using her body for very long. Her arms were still weak, and her legs were shaky even with the bare minimum effort.

Of course, clearing out the sand had helped. In the week and a half that they'd worked on that project, he had seen her body changing. Her muscles were slightly more defined now. She was able to continue working for a bit longer every single day. But he was concerned about how deeply she slept and the dark circles under her eyes.

She needed more rest than he did, and he feared he would run her ragged long before she was ready to stop working on her own.

Sighing, he shook his head and watched as she gathered all her supplies and climbed up one of the channels. She'd done this a few times already. Dry as a bone, the channels were mostly chutes that would eventually hold running water. Although the water would be slow moving, it helped to keep oxygen in the gills of those who floated in them.

She crouched right above the broken part, muttering under her breath. For a moment, she disappeared from his sight as she laid down to look at the damage underneath and peered at the leak before her head popped up once more.

"If I weld metal here, is it going to hurt their scales?" she asked.

He asked the pertinent questions. How thick was the metal? How high did it stick up? And they both decided she would melt the edges, first to make sure it had a good seal, and second to make sure that it didn't cut anyone when they were up there.

He listened to the sound of the crackling welder, and for a moment, time seemed to waver. Pilot tested the holograms, and Proteus stared at all the images of the scientists who once worked here. It was like he had taken a step backward.

Proteus remembered so clearly being here as they built this facility. He remembered what it was like to listen to all the engineers working, the intelligent dreamers who had wanted to make a better place for humans to live, the environmentalists who truly believed it was possible. Their voices had echoed throughout the rafters in calls for hope and discoveries that would change everything.

Their voices had gotten quieter over the years. Roadblocks, as they called them, stopped them at every turn. From politicians to the rich and famous, so many people tried to stop them from saving this planet until it was far too late. The world was part of an agenda. Saving it had to serve someone before it could be saved.

He hated how sad all the brilliant minds here had gotten every time they had been forced to stop what they were doing. Their work had gotten so close so many times, and yet then they were forced to not even use some of it. Heartbreaking, really, but he knew where it ended up.

Those in power wanted the world destroyed. Because they had thought they could control the destruction themselves.

They'd been wrong.

The welding sounds stopped, and Ellie poked her head back up with a triumphant grin on her face. All the holograms faded away as Pilot muttered about something not working, and Proteus himself was forced to come back into the present.

"Did you fix it?" he asked, trying to keep the amusement out of his voice.

"Of course I fixed it. It wasn't that hard, really." She stood, wobbling a bit precariously before catching herself. "I think it should be better now. Can we test the water again?"

"If you'd like."

Proteus kept his eyes on her as she moved down the chute. It wasn't entirely safe for someone like her. Though it wasn't all that steep, it could still be slick as the insides were worn smooth. She needed to be sure-footed and careful, and those weren't traits Ellie had. She was clumsy, and often times distracted.

Like this instant.

He watched as her foot caught on something within the chute and she tripped. Already he could see what would happen playing out. Another engineer had fallen just like this in the early days. There were two tiers for her to fall onto, just like the man had. His back had made a sickening crunch that had haunted Proteus for days on end.

Humans were so fragile. Their bodies were so easy to break.

With a whip of his tail, he propelled himself forward. Just in time, he caught her. His arms took the brunt force of her impact as she toppled over the edge of one chute and nearly killed herself on the wall of the next. The backs of his arms hit the stone hard enough to make him grunt, but it wasn't nearly hard enough to break his bones, which were so much stronger than hers.

He tucked her in closer to his chest, holding the warmth of her skin against his and breathing out a long sigh of relief.

"What were you doing?" he finally hissed. "I told you to be careful with yourself. Was that being careful?"

His eyes couldn't look at enough of her. They trailed down her throat, down the green shirt that really was far too transparent, to the denim skirt which had likely tripped her up. It was too long. He was going to tear the offensive thing at the thighs so that maybe she could walk around without tripping over herself every second.

Teeth bared, he stared down at her wide-eyed expression and waited for her to defend herself. Lately she'd been arguing with him, and he hadn't corrected her. It was healthy for her to push back at him for some things. But this? This he knew he was right about.

Instead of arguing with him, she lifted her hand and pressed her palm to his cheek. "Did you know you have freckles?" she whispered.

"I have no idea what those are."

"Little dots across your cheeks. Freckles are usually from the sun, but I highly doubt you've been in the sun that often." Her thumb ghosted over the peak of his cheekbone, and his entire body heated at the touch. "You're almost handsome, you know. If not for..."

Her words trailed off, but her fingers didn't. They smoothed over the harsh lines down his cheeks, the ones that were always there no matter how much he tried to hide that his jaw could unhinge and he could likely have swallowed her whole. He was not the same as the other undine. He'd always known that.

Humans weren't usually the type to find the sea folk handsome. The fact that she looked at him and saw anything that was possible to find pretty was a shock to his entire system.

He couldn't stop holding her. Couldn't put down the warm body that heated him right down into the depths of his ancient bones. She saw him as a man. As a creature who had been with her for so long, perhaps, but also as someone who was handsome. Someone who was kind.

Her fingers pressed against the seams of his cheeks, and he obliged her unspoken question. Proteus opened his mouth, allowing his jaw to fall open even more, his chin peeling away from the rest of his body so his mouth could open up completely and she could stare down into the depths of the many teeth that spiraled down his throat.

"You are terrifying," she whispered, but then he felt her reach inside of his mouth and gently touch the tip of a very sharp tooth. "But I don't feel fear when I look at you like this. Does that mean something is wrong with me?"

He closed his mouth so he could speak. "No, it just means you are more curious than the average human."

"I took it for granted that you've been calling me human all this time. I remember Malcolm saying that most people under the waves called humans 'achromo'." She stared at him expectantly, wanting to know why he used different words than the People of Water.

"I am not undine," he decided on saying. "I am not them, and they are not me. I am something other, just as you are something other."

She hummed low under her breath. "I suppose that makes sense. You certainly don't look like any of the undine I've seen before. And you worked with the other scientists for years here, didn't you?"

"I did."

"Maybe you picked up on more of their language than you're giving them credit for." And then... a blinding smile.

It was like staring into the sun when she was this happy. Her eyes scrunched up and her nose even wrinkled as she grinned at him. She was just happy. Happy to see him, happy to know that he was using words that she could understand. Happier than he'd ever seen her and he had no idea how to process her beauty.

He should put her down on the floor and get back into the icy cold depths. Perhaps those would cool the feelings that rioted inside of his chest that were as unfamiliar as they were tempting.

But he didn't. He couldn't force himself to release her even as his head dipped closer and closer to hers. He couldn't stop himself when he was breathing over her lips, inhaling the air she exhaled.

"Ellie," he whispered, and the sound of her name on his lips made all the spines on his back raise. "You are unlike anyone I have ever met."

"You've been gone for two hundred years. It's just because you haven't spoken to anyone in a very long time."

He met her gaze, so close that he could see little flecks of gold hidden in them. "No, it's not that."

He surged forward and kissed her. It was inevitable that they would do so. From the first moment he'd seen her as more than just a tool, he had known he would devour her lips. He'd been dying to know what she tasted like, beyond the sweet metallic flavor of her blood.

But Proteus hadn't expected the little breathy moan she let out to tempt him as thoroughly as it did. Kissing a woman like this was sacrilege. Surely she would feel violated that a mouth like what she had just inspected was touching her.

Ellie surprised him at every turn. She curved a hand around the back of his neck and drew him even closer. Pressing her torso to his, she seemed to try to crawl her way inside him with her lips and teeth and tongue.

This was the unpracticed kiss of a woman who had never done this before. She'd been denied physical pleasure for such a long time, it all came rushing to the forefront as she kissed him like a woman possessed.

He was only a man after all, so he kissed her back just as wildly.

A deep groan burned in his chest, rumbling out of his throat with all those razor sharp teeth as he consumed her. Still, there was a need in the back of his head to chew rather than just lick, but he silenced it quickly.

There would be no more pain for her. Not from him, and not from anyone else.

When he finally drew back at the loud sound of clanking from a very irate droid who was displeased with what was happening, Proteus touched his forehead to hers and breathed out a sigh.

"I do not—"

She pressed her fingers to his lips. "Don't ruin this moment with words, Proteus."

So he didn't. He just held her until he had to let her go.

Chapter 20

Ellie was alone for the first time since waking in this strange new life.

Pilot had decommissioned all the extra droids he had made. They had no use now that this place was almost entirely cleaned up, and he claimed that he didn't want them sticking around when they were just copies of himself. She didn't really blame him for that. Ellie knew what it was like to have exact replicas of who she was all around. It was rather eerie, and she couldn't imagine how strange it was for the Original of all of them.

But once only Pilot remained, he had informed her he was heading to the other facilities to check over the squid's work. They should all be online. The power seemed to be coming on in increments in this building, which meant clearly something was right. But Pilot had to make sure it was all perfect.

She'd watched him roll into the water and disappear, and a strange feeling overcame her.

This was... odd. Lonely, maybe. But also it was the first time in her life that she'd been able to stand in complete and utter silence, and not have someone else talking. Even in the distance.

At first, she wasn't sure what to do with herself. She'd gone through one of the few doors they'd left without the barricade against the sand. She'd poked her head out now that the storms had passed to see what the real world looked like.

Awe inspiring.

And terrifying.

Even standing in that doorway looking out at the vast, rolling dunes of sand, all she could think was that humans were doomed if they lived here. There wasn't life on this planet. Only the blistering sun, the intense heat that made her mouth feel dry just standing in it for a few minutes, and the endless wasteland.

From what she had read in the woman's diary, this place had once been green. Plants had dotted the land as far as the eye could see, and even more if they kept going. Trees had lived here. Ellie had only ever seen pictures of them.

But now, there was nothing. A few scraggly, skeletal remains of what might have once been trees were still standing in the distance, but even from here she could see they provided no shade.

This place couldn't host life. Not unless people went underground, which might have been the plan all along.

Maybe. She wasn't really sure. The diary hadn't given her more information other than what they were working on, which was a lot of impressive gene splicing and genetic alteration.

What a pity it hadn't worked. Maybe there would have been a very different story to tell if it had.

Ducking back into the cool facility, she shook off the feeling of heat that still clung to her arms. At least the sea was cold. She could always dunk herself in the water if she wanted to.

But as Ellie stood in the center of the room, strangely bored, all she could think about was that kiss. She'd call it a kiss, even if he didn't. They had brushed their mouths over each other, and maybe he had just been tasting her. It wouldn't be surprising for a creature like him to want to taste her one more time. He had, after all, nearly consumed her arm.

Her thoughts always ended up back at the kiss, though. No matter how many times she told herself it was foolish to think of him as anything other than a demonic creature who lived in the sea. He was more than that.

He was Proteus. A sea god who was kind to her, but also a man who had worked hard two centuries ago to try to find a way for them all to live together. He was a man who had seen all of this happen, and who was still here. Fighting for what was right.

Even if Ellie didn't know what was right.

Dropping down onto a chair they had found in the woman's chambers, she leaned back and stared at the ceiling. What would he think if he knew where her mind continually wandered?

Proteus had been the one to kiss her. She had kissed him back. Probably poorly, but that had been her first time. If he tried it again with her, she was certain she would kiss him better than before.

Ellie wanted to. She wanted to kiss him again because there was something about him that... She wasn't sure how to put it into words.

Lifting her hand, she ghosted the tips of her fingers over her lips. He had kissed her like a man possessed. No, a man frenzied. He'd wanted to kiss her for a long time, that's what that kiss said. He had been dying to kiss her for ages, and the fall had frightened him into realizing he didn't know if he would ever get the chance again.

The hunger in his touch had set her body on fire. Ellie wasn't ignorant of the idea of sex. She'd seen enough of it in Tau to know how it worked, but only with human men. She didn't even know if he had a cock. So far she hadn't seen any hint of it whatsoever, and she assumed she would have seen it by now considering all the time they spent together.

She'd seen humans doing things with more than just a cock, though. Her mind flicked back to the room full of writhing bodies that Malcolm had brought her to once. He'd been there to fish another scientist out of the fray, who was very late for an important meeting. But she had been unable to stop staring at the people who were doing deplorable, yet very exciting to watch, things.

Her hand smoothed down her neck, following the lines of her throat all the way into her shirt. The men in that room had all been so interested in the women's breasts. She mimicked what they had done with her own fingers, pressing a circle around her nipple before pinching it hard.

It wasn't as good a feeling as the women in that room seemed to think. But even the memory of them made the sensation somehow a little stronger. A little more than it had been before.

The moans filling that room had made her wonder what could feel so good. She wanted to listen to them moan like that for hours. Not just the women, but the men too. They had all been enjoying every touch, every taste.

This time, when she rolled her fingers over the tips of her breasts, the touch felt even better. It was so easy for her to imagine Proteus doing this. His long, extra jointed fingers would look like an abomination against her skin, and yet she wanted to feel him touching her like this. She wanted to feel those long fingers digging into her skin, to see his claws leaving tiny pinpricks of pain and blood in their wake.

Throwing her head back, she thought of what else she wanted him to do. There was, of course, the intriguing thought of that long black tongue. He had no idea what it had done to her to see him stick that out of his mouth and let it hang from his lips. It was so long, and clearly stronger than the average tongue of a human man.

She wanted to know what it would feel like sliding along her skin. Perhaps he would taste her belly, pressing those sharp teeth to her sensitive skin there, and she would know that at any point, he could bite into her. The threat of his strength would always make her shiver and quake with desire. Did he know that? Did he know that the thought of his touch made her clench her thighs together?

This feeling was so new. The heat that poured through her skin was hard to understand. All she knew was that she wanted to keep touching herself. She wanted to feel more of these sensations, to chase what her mind had conjured up.

Her hand smoothed down her belly and toyed with the waistline of her skirt. She had seen what the men and women were doing between their legs as well. The men were more obvious, of course. With their cocks in their hands, they hadn't seemed embarrassed at all to grab themselves and slowly pump their fists up and down over that engorged flesh.

But Ellie hadn't been able to see what the women were doing. Everything was so hidden between their legs. Now, however, she wanted to discover what it would feel like to touch herself. Just for a little while. She wanted to know if it would feel as good as the others had made it seem.

Unbuttoning the top few buttons of her skirt, she focused on the sensation of her fingers. The skin between her legs was soft and wet, so much so that it made her feel a little shivery when she touched it. But no matter what she did, the fingers weren't enough.

At least, until she thought about him. Until she imagined Proteus between her legs, his massive, unhinged jaw unfurling between her thighs so his long tongue could join her fingers.

She swore she could feel him even now. The sensation of that long, thick muscle wrapping around her calf. He would stroke his tongue higher to her thighs, but the fabric of her denim would stop him for a moment. Breathing hard, she imagined those long fingers unbuttoning the skirt, one by one. Each button would pop open, the feeling of those pops echoing throughout her entire body as he moved higher and higher.

His tongue was so warm. So slick. She could feel it leaving a trail of thick, viscous liquid as he trailed it up her thigh, but it didn't matter. She liked the feeling. She liked knowing that a monster was about to devour her whole.

And then she could feel his breath between her legs. The idea was as foreign as it was familiar that soon enough, his tongue would trace between her folds. For now, he wanted her to feel the hot air from his mouth fanning over a place she had yet to discover on her own body.

She opened her eyes, fingers still delving into the liquid heat, only to realize that she hadn't been imagining this at all.

Ellie stared down her body to see a monster between her legs. His dark eyes seemed even bigger as he met her gaze. That mouth was indeed unfurled, a strange vision of teeth that just kept going, but his long black tongue was right there. Still gently licking the crease of her thigh and so close to where her fingers were still moving.

The question in his gaze was obvious. She could ask him to stop, and he would. He would slink back into the water and let her be.

But she didn't want him to stop.

Ellie took a deep, steadying breath and then slowly moved her fingers out of the way. She wasn't getting the job done anyway. She wanted to know what he could do if he was in control.

A long, rumbling groan echoed from deep inside his chest, and then he lunged forward. His mouth was so large. Teeth clamped down above her pelvic bone, not hard enough to make her shriek, but a threat all the same that somehow heightened this interaction.

His tongue suddenly replaced her fingers, and her eyes rolled back in her head. The sensation of that powerful, muscular tongue pressing against her clit and sliding over it was almost too much. Combined with the sensation of teeth that wrapped all the way around her waist?

Ellie's mind fractured. All she could focus on was that long, hot tongue working over her most sensitive flesh. Breath sawed in and out of her lungs as he spun her higher and higher, into a place she hadn't realized existed.

Her muscles coiled. For some reason, she wrapped her legs around his head because that seemed like the only way she could ground herself. She even tried to reach down and grab onto him, but he let out another growl and put her hands on the arms of the chair.

She grabbed on as if her life depended on it. The moment she did, his tongue moved down to probe her center.

She'd known this had to be part of it. She'd seen people having sex, and knew there was something on a man that entered a woman. But she hadn't realized it would feel like this.

Warm and slick. Undulating inside of her until he let out a rumbling sound like that of a whale that ended up vibrating his tongue as he worked it further and further inside of her. The strange sensation of something foreign gave way to pure pleasure as that vibration drew her closer to the edge.

The edge of what, she had no idea. All she could do was continue to hold on to the chair and stay as still as possible because he'd clamped down harder with his teeth. If she moved at all, she'd slice herself on those sharp edges.

Ellie was completely at his mercy as he licked her from within, pistoning his tongue deeper and deeper inside of her with every stroke that made her want to scream for mercy and also beg for him to never stop.

She tried to form words, but they wouldn't come. She couldn't figure out how to tell him not to stop, but she didn't have to. He clearly wasn't going to.

And then his tongue found a spot deep inside of her that made pleasure sparkle behind her eyes. She stopped breathing as he slid past it and knew the moment he recognized her reaction. Suddenly he attacked that spot. That hot, vibrating tongue flicking quickly right where she wanted him most.

Her back bowed, her hands clamped down harder on the arms of the chair. Every muscle in her body tensed and coiled, reaching for something she feared might hurt, but then...

Bliss.

She could feel her inner muscles clenching around his tongue, milking him for something that wasn't entirely possible from a tongue like that. Her chest ached and then soothed as everything inside of her rode that wave to become liquid with relief.

She had no idea what had happened. But she'd seen people in Tau react the same way, and now she knew what it was like to come. Now she knew what a wonder it was to feel connected like this with another person.

Blinking her eyes open again, she stared down at him still between her thighs. He had withdrawn his tongue, but was still gently licking between her thighs. Soothing her through what had been her first orgasm.

Proteus seemed reluctant to let her go. But eventually he opened his jaws, pulling his teeth from her flesh where they had all bitten a little too deep. Tiny aches of pain registered, but she didn't mind them. Ellie didn't even care when droplets of blood dripped from the wounds, sliding down her torso like he'd decorated her torso in rubies.

Proteus stared at them with a strange mix of emotions in his eyes. She swore he was sad, but also immensely pleased to see those marks.

"I promised I wouldn't hurt you again," he said as his jaw closed back up. "I seem to have lied."

She reached for his face, palming it in her hand to make him look at her. "It didn't hurt. You gave me a gift, Proteus."

The grin on his face was decidedly wicked. "Trust me, Sisu. You were the one giving that gift."

Chapter 21

Proteus did not have time to be so distracted, and yet, here he was. The taste of her still lingered on his tongue. The sounds she made in the throes of passion haunted every waking and dreaming moment.

He couldn't get her out of his head. Every second of his time was spent thinking about her, and still it only seemed to be getting stronger.

The plan was the only thing he should be focusing on. Proteus knew damn well there wasn't another person in the entire ocean who could do what he could do. If he played this out correctly, then he could finally get the humans back where they belonged. He could free the People of Water from their shackles and make certain that the world returned to the way it had been before.

He could and would do this. It was his destiny, as told by the ancients, from the very first moment he was born. He was meant to bring this world back together, putting the pieces back into the whole as they were always meant to be.

And yet, here he was. Distracted by the clone of a woman who was dead, and he couldn't stop thinking about her.

Not the Original. Not the woman who had been the first. But this wonderful, distracting, honorable woman who had given him every ounce of her attention and focus since the very first moment that he'd woken her.

He had to get moving, though. He couldn't stay in here with her forever knowing that, no matter what he did, he was just going to focus on the way she tasted and the noises she made.

Proteus left both her and Pilot in Sanctuary. Both of them had been given very strict instructions, so they were ready when he returned.

Ellie was to focus on building holograms that would inspire the people he brought back with him. He trusted her to know the human mind and what would convince them that it was a good idea to leave the sea permanently.

Pilot was to stay and watch over Ellie. The droid would ground her, and help her in her task, but it was not to leave to go to another facility like it had before. That kind of behavior would end with the droid's memory bank being wiped, and he would make sure that Pilot would forget every ounce of what he had learned in all these centuries since he had been created.

The threat was perhaps an empty one. Proteus knew he needed the droid. But knowing that Ellie had been left alone specifically because Pilot had been bored made him want to strip the metal parts off of it and scream into the void that was left.

Neither was an easy task. Proteus swam up and over a mound of rocks that had once been part of a towering spire. He remembered this area so easily from when he had been a boy. There had been so much here that used to captivate him.

Once, it had been a mating ground for giant squid. They had been bigger than him, which was surprising considering he'd been massive even as a child. But now there was nothing left here. Just darkness and a wasteland.

The sea was still licking its wounds. After centuries of mistreatment, there was plenty for him to focus on here. His home was still bleeding, and he needed to pay attention to that. Not her. Not the woman he had left behind, who he knew was in safe hands.

He had to focus on the sea he was going to save and the world he left behind. It could be fixed if he could just get the humans out of the sea. Then, he would finally be doing what he had been created for.

But first, he had to convince them. Thankfully, he expected that to be easy.

For a while now, he'd been followed. He knew who was following him from the scent on the waves. This depthstrider had been trying to seek him out for ages. This was the one who had first found his tomb, although Proteus had yet to forgive the male for not trying to release him.

Fortis, he thought, was the depthstrider's name. If he remembered the ghost of his wife talking to him correctly, Fortis was almost like a human priest to his people.

He saw the future. He spoke to the gods. And now, this massive creature of the depths was about to meet one of his own gods for the very first time.

But depthstriders were smart. They knew the waves better than others, and they knew to follow whatever they were tracking at a distance. Proteus would need to draw him out. A task that might have been more difficult if Proteus himself wasn't such a strange creature to see in the ocean.

He allowed his bones to illuminate. Glowing in the darkness of the sea, he knew that no undine would be able to avoid trying to figure out what had changed in some animal that lived in their home.

Nothing else looked like him, and that curiosity could very well be the end of any depthstrider who thought they could control him. Still, Proteus swam slower through the waves and waited for Fortis to get close enough.

This specific bloodline of their species should have recognized him immediately. Proteus's parents were, after all, the ones who had given them their power.

Come to think of it, there had been one of their own who was nearly a direct descendant of the ancients like him. Perhaps that's how he would start the conversation, because Fortis would almost certainly recognize the name.

Proteus stopped, floating where he was as his bones illuminated even more. They were so bright that even he couldn't see past their light.

"Here I was seeking someone to ask if Mitera was still alive," he said, his voice booming through the ocean. "And instead I find a familiar face."

The darkness hid Fortis from his sight. The religious fanatic would likely want to remain hidden in that darkness until he was certain it was safe for him to speak with Proteus. But then his voice came from the darkness, and Proteus knew exactly where the male was hiding.

"Mitera still lives," Fortis called out from behind one of the many spires that were still standing. "But she does not speak with just anyone. Who are you?"

"You have met me before."

"I have never seen anyone like you in this sea. I have never seen you in any vision of the future either. Which means you are an anomaly, who does not deserve to be in these sacred grounds."

So at least they remembered that mating grounds were off limits to the People of Water. Somehow, Proteus doubted they remembered why this area of the sea was off limits. It was dangerous to be in the waters when the squid would attack them for being anywhere near during the mating season.

Sighing, he took a deep breath and allowed bubbles to erupt from his gills. "Do I not look like someone you have met before?"

"I would remember such a creature."

So at least Fortis could see him well enough. He would know not to attack. Proteus was too large and far too dangerous.

"You found me not so long ago," Proteus said. "I was stuck in a coffin, trapped there by your people, who no longer wished to worship their gods. And now you have found me again."

He could almost hear Fortis thinking. The male rolled the words around in his head until he finally came to the conclusion that Proteus wanted him to. They had in fact met before. Fortis had taken his words as prophecy, then, as he should have.

"The god at the bottom of the sea," Fortis murmured. "You have been released?"

"It was my time to return. I have come home and now I will guide you and your people into the next stage of your future." Proteus allowed his bones to dim just slightly, enough so that Fortis wouldn't see him as a glowing beacon in the darkness, but also be able to see the monstrous features of his face. "You are the one who will help me in all of this."

"I cannot help you much. My people have already created their own plan." A flick of his tail appeared from behind the spire. He was forgetting to hide himself, at least. That was a good sign. "They rebuild the cities. They are building a new city even as we speak. They will continue to build until they feel as though all people can live together, humans and the People of Water."

"What if I told you they could live on land again?"

The sudden silence made the sea feel heavy. But he could feel the goddess swirling around his own tail, and knew she had moved to Fortis as well. The sea herself was excited by the idea of removing the humans once and for all. She begged at Fortis's fluke, tugging on his gills and his fins until he would know that she approved of this plan.

"They could see the sun?" Fortis asked quietly. "So few of them ever have."

"But only glimpses. What if they could see it every single day?"

"The storms are too strong."

He scoffed. "The storms are strong, yes. But they are survivable with the right technology and the right homes. More than that, they can be fixed in time."

"The storms cannot be fixed. They have raged for centuries because the very earth is mad at the humans. That cannot be fixed in a generation, let alone in many." But again that tail flicked, and Proteus could see that the depthstrider was thinking about his words. "How are you going to convince the humans to go above? There is nowhere for them to go."

"What if I had a place for them to go?"

Again, that silence. But now he was reading it better. He could sense that the depthstrider was interested.

Then he moved. Fortis came out from behind the tall spire, and he was everything that Proteus had hoped he would be. A massive creature, violet because that was the ancients favorite color. Though his chest was pale, it was obvious that he was laden with muscle. Every part of his body was built as a weapon, but he would only wield it should he need to or should the sea order him to.

What a specimen. This was the kind of creature that Proteus was proud to call his. These were the men and women who would fight to the death to protect what was theirs, and who he knew would always make a choice with their people's best interest at heart.

"You seek the future," Proteus said, without preamble. He knew what a priestly man like this would be expecting. No deal would be made unless Proteus could offer proof that what he said was true.

"I can see the future on my own."

"Can you? Can you see this future that I will draw to fruition?" Proteus shrugged. "Or perhaps you are not capable of such a thing. The only way to know for certain is if I touch you. If I guide you."

Fortis must know this was a trap. He looked at Proteus as if what he offered was poison, and the depthstrider wasn't wrong. To touch a god was no easy feat, especially for their people.

"You will show me the future?" Fortis asked, clearly tense.

"I will show you all that I have always seen. What the ancients who created me tasked me to create. It is a future that was built by someone who knows what they are doing." Proteus held out his hand. "Let me show you, Fortis. Allow me to guide you."

Though Fortis still hesitated, he reached out his hand and took Proteus's. It was a mistake for him, but it was all part of Proteus's plan.

With a surge of magic that he'd been born with, Proteus launched them both into the prophecy that he had been born to fulfill. The future was one that would not be easily won. He remembered this prophecy bit by bit. He'd never seen any changes to it because it was the only prophecy that was set in stone.

The humans would return to the land. They knew how to hunt and fend for themselves, but the People of Water would still be a large part of their lives. They would trade with each other often, and in doing so, both of their peoples would prosper.

Were the humans entirely safe? No. The storm surges still threatened them, the hurricanes could still kill them, but they were working toward ending all of those things. The storms would slowly start to understand that. As the land healed and grew safer, so would the tempests that were caused by a riotous land constantly trying to find its balance once more. They needed to soothe the beast, and they could only do that if they were on the land to do so.

Their homes were shorter, squatter, and far sturdier than before. Their research would be focused on healing their land and in making their lives easier, along with living with the People of Water. He could see it now. Vast cities spread deep underground. Some of them even stretched out into the sea so they could all work together, but none of them took up too much of the water that was already angry at all of them.

But then Proteus noticed there was something different about the prophecy after all. There were shadowy pieces in the back that he had never seen before. Parts of a future that could be changed, and something that could be affected.

People? Perhaps. Maybe this was a sign that they would find more humans living on the land. Soon enough, if they were lucky, they could unlock allies who would help them far more than they would hurt. These were all good signs that he was on the right path.

They all were.

Finally he pulled away from Fortis, watching as the depthstrider seized like he'd been attacked by an electric eel. Proteus grabbed his chin, forcing the other man to look at him.

"You are lucky, friend. You met me at the right time. This pain will pass, and you will bring this information to your people. There is a facility where you will bring them and yourself, to see this future with your own eyes and not just a prophecy made by the ancients long ago. We will send the coordinates to you through one of your droids. And you will help us, Fortis. You were born to do so."

He headed off, leaving the large male to drift down to the bottom of the sea where he would wait until the venom of Proteus's prophecy finally left his body.

It was time for this plan to show movement. Proteus grew tired of waiting.

Chapter 22

Ellie still didn't understand the plan. He wanted to prove that he was a god to these people, who should have worshipped him for centuries, but they had forgotten him. She understood that part.

What she didn't understand was why anyone like him needed to prove that he was what he said he was. Just look at him. Even the undine had to realize there was something different about Proteus. Ellie had seen their kind before. She'd stared at them hanging in the tanks at Tau, and even helped take notes about dissections. She'd seen them a hundred times, if not more than that.

Proteus was not them. Just the sight of him was enough to know that, but it was even more than his looks. It was the way he moved. How he spoke. The strangeness of his gaze and the way he could see straight through her. The determination to fix what had been broken, and the dogged way he continued forward until the end.

Proteus knew what he was doing. He had been in the past, and he had lived for such a long time. Anyone who didn't believe he understood how to fix this world of theirs had to have lost a few of their marbles.

Pilot muttered under his breath, checking the last few modules he had programmed to make it even more impressive when their visitors arrived. "Are you ready?" he asked.

"As ready as I'll ever be." She was hidden behind a makeshift wall, but one that would never be seen by someone who didn't know how the shifting sands worked. The door that led into the room was hidden behind a sand dune. All she had to do was hit the right buttons to make sure that the manual process of the holograms was where it was supposed to be.

But something didn't feel right about this. It wasn't getting people to worship him in the way he deserved. This was all smoke and mirrors. Parlor tricks that entranced the mind, but meant absolutely nothing.

Shouldn't these people see him for what he was and make their choice from there? She'd always thought worshipping gods required some sort of faith. Proteus should tell them who he was, show them the old sites of worship, and let them decide on their own.

"I can see your thoughts ticking away in that head of yours," Pilot grumbled as he made one last tweak. "It's too late to back out now. We're here for a reason."

"What if he's wrong?"

"Then he's wrong." She swore there was more to what he said, though. The droid agreed with her. He'd been taking his time programming those holograms. She knew they were easy to make, even easier to summon up the old data that allowed other people's images to be used. And yet it had taken a very long time for him to prepare for this.

Narrowing her eyes, she pointed at the little crab that hopped down onto the floor with a soft bang. "You are hiding something from me. What's your real opinion?"

Pilot seemed to sigh, a real feat for a droid, and then looked at her. "You and I both were designed to follow orders, were we not?"

It was as if he'd stuck an arrow through her heart. That was the truth, what he said. She had been designed to follow orders. She'd been told her entire life to do what other people said and not to question why they wanted her to do so. She was a puppet. A doll. Someone who had never had to think for herself.

But this... She knew this was wrong. Deep in her gut, she knew that anyone who had survived this long outside of the cities, the very people who had brought down the vast and seemingly all powerful Tau, would not fall for a story like this.

They would see the holograms for what they were. They would know that they were being tricked. This would all crumble down upon their heads, and she wasn't sure there was another way to come back from it.

So she waited, as she was supposed to. But she turned on the few cameras that had survived all this time so she could watch the waters burble and churn as Proteus arrived. He pulled himself out of the water, his massive length snaking out of the opening for what seemed like an endless amount of time before he coiled himself in the center of a podium that had once held a massive cylindrical tank.

It gave him the perfect stage to lord over all the others that would come here to see the truth of the god who had summoned them. Ellie felt like she was the only one who could see him for what he really was, though. Maybe even Proteus himself didn't realize how wonderful he could be, and how much his sheer presence made others feel like they needed to bow down and worship him.

The waters stirred soon after him. He hadn't led their guests here, though. He'd sent a message.

Or rather, he'd had Pilot send a message. So, the people arriving knew that this facility was here. What they didn't know was that the facility was alive now. Breathing just like it had in the old days. A living Sanctuary, full of potential that she knew they would realize. They didn't need a god, they needed...

Hope.

Everyone alive now needed hope and to see that there was a future in this world, and in the Above. They needed proof, not someone to tell them what to do. They needed a choice.

Just like she had needed the choice for all those years.

Swallowing hard, she opened up the coding for the holograms and began to change them. Proteus would be furious. He was going to be so angry with her, and she knew that rage was something she wasn't prepared to handle. She'd seen him angry before. She'd lost her arm to him already, and now there wasn't a convenient pod to put her back together.

But she had to try. She was the only one who could understand how these people felt. Maybe Pilot could in some manner. She supposed the droid knew what it was like to be ordered around when he knew an easier way to do what he had been told to do.

Ellie glanced up to see the group of people who had arrived. There weren't nearly as many as she thought. Clearly, there was the big purple beast Proteus had spoken to before, but there were only three other undines who had arrived with him. Blue, red, and yellow, the four of them took up the entire space in that small pool.

Then she saw the others. Her fingers stilled where they had been typing in the new protocols for the holograms. Four women got out of the water. Four human women.

They all wore wetsuits, similar to what Ellie had worn when she'd first woken as well. They pulled mechanical pieces off of their faces, and their determined expressions were as terrifying as they were inspiring. One stood ahead of the others, revealed to be a redhead as she pulled the hood of her wetsuit down.

She spoke, and Ellie could hear her through the wall as her voice rang throughout the entire hall. "I do not believe in gods. Therefore, I want to know exactly what you are and why you think you can tell us what to do with ourselves."

A thrill of excitement ran through Ellie's body. This woman didn't even seem afraid as she stood up to a creature who looked like Proteus. How was she so brave? How was she so willing to protect her own, even in the face of a terrifying beast like him?

"Your people never worshipped me," Proteus replied, his voice thunderous and deep. "But your mate's people did. They have always been smarter than humans."

She knew this was when she was supposed to turn the holograms on. This was when she was supposed to turn the entire room into a futuristic madhouse that would overwhelm their senses and give Proteus the upper hand. She had no idea what his plan was going forward from that. Likely, he had some harebrained idea that he would overpower them in some way.

Instead, she rushed through the last bits of the new protocol. She timed it so she had a few moments to speak, and then left her post.

"What are you doing?" Pilot whispered quietly at her as she headed toward the door.

She wasn't all that sure. For the first time in her life, Ellie didn't have a plan or someone else telling her what to do. All she could do was go with her gut. She grabbed a folder where she'd been gathering her own research on the way out. The sharp plastic edges bit into her chest where she pressed it into her sternum.

Letting the door swing open, she stepped out into the room with the rest of them.

So many eyes swung in her direction, but it was the eyes of the other women that she was most interested in. The redhead stood in the front still, tall, and muscular. Beside her was a pretty blonde, a rounder woman with glasses and short cropped hair, and then a monolith behind the other two. The last woman was massive and stood heads taller than Ellie had ever seen a person stand except... except...

"You," the tall woman said. "You're awfully familiar."

Ellie pressed a hand to her chest. "I believe my Original may have been, yes. But I am not who you think I am."

The tall woman pushed to the forefront of the crowd, and Ellie remembered people like her. They had been guards, personal guards of the Originals, and genetically altered to be the best at their job that they could be. They were impressive warriors, but they had been trained to be like that.

The woman might have stalked all the way up to her if Proteus's tail hadn't lashed out, catching her in the chest and throwing her back into the water. It didn't escape Ellie's notice that the purple undine was the one to reach for her as she fell.

"No one touches her!" Proteus hissed, but then he turned on her, rage burning in his eyes as he hissed, "What are you doing?"

"Preventing you from making a mistake." Ellie clutched the folder to her chest, holding on to it with as much courage as she could muster. Her voice shook as she addressed the newcomers. "I know that I look like someone not to trust. Part of you recognizes that, and I'm sorry for what history has painted my face to be. But I am certain that you are here for a reason. Just like I am."

The silence that rang out after her words made her heart ache. Still, she plunged forward. This was the right way to do this. She was certain of that.

The holograms blinked to life. They weren't moving though, not like Proteus wanted. They were static images of what this room had once been. Frozen undine in the channels above them. Scientists leaned over the edges as they showed their work to the deep sea creatures who advised them. The tanks were similar to those in Tau, but they didn't house undine or monstrous, torn apart bodies. They were filled with small corals and fish that swam around them.

The facility was elegant, bright, and full of life. "We used to work together," she breathed. "This isn't programmed. This is a snapshot of what once was. Centuries ago when humans and undine worked together to fix what had been broken. Everyone here knew what was rapidly approaching, and everyone was trying to stop it."

With an angry sound, the tall woman yanked herself out of the water. "I know the past. I saw what our people did. No one was trying to stop it."

"Some tried!" Ellie insisted. "Perhaps that wasn't the people in charge who were trying to change the future, but there were still people fighting until the bitter end."

She held out the folder for the tall redhead to take, and she did without hesitation.

Ellie couldn't help but say, "There were people fighting even after the end, it seems. People who were more knowledgeable than any of us. They were trying to reverse the damage and what had been done to our world. People who left a legacy that only we can continue."

There it was. Her soul knew it. Her heart knew it.

The answer.

Words bubbled out of her lips. "I know it feels like you have overcome immeasurable battles. You have fought a war. You have defeated the corrupt people who destroyed all that we had. It is too much to ask you to do more, but that is why you are here. We can fix this. And wouldn't it be a shame if we didn't even try?"

The redhead frowned as she opened the binder. "What is this?"

"Notes from the scientists who worked here. They were trying to reverse the damage, like I said. There are many other projects as well that are... well, no scientist thus far seems to be entirely ethical in how they dealt with the end of our planet as we knew it, but still. So much knowledge is in this book. And I believe if we were to combine our efforts then—"

"This is not what we are doing." Proteus's voice interrupted her, and every word dripped with rage. "They will take orders from me. They will learn through doing."

"You cannot ask them to trust you blindly!" Ellie had never shouted before. But it felt good to be angry like this. To challenge him when she had never done so before.

He stared at her, his mouth slightly open and those dark eyes flashing. "What did you say?"

"You have to give them the choice, Proteus. They have to know everything that you're asking of them, and they have to choose for themselves." She was clutching her hands so tightly her nails were digging into her skin. The pain grounded her. "We cannot order anyone to help us because then the help isn't genuine. They need to see hope in this future, just like you and I do. They have to choose this for themselves."

Then she turned to the other people, avoiding catching the gazes of the other women and instead looking at the undines. "I know you have spent so much time creating a world where undine and humans could live together in some sort of peace, but what if you could finally send them back to the surface?"

The blue one pulled himself out of the water, glaring at her. "That's not possible."

"What if it were?"

"I will not entertain any fool's errand—"

"Arges." The redhead turned toward him, the binder almost limp in her hand. "She's not lying."

The connection between the two of them was undeniable. It was almost electric the way they stared at each other, emotions palpable as their thoughts seemed to connect. As though they could read each others minds.

The redhead turned to her. "Where did you get this?"

"Here."

"In this facility?"

"In the back rooms. There were some people who stayed here, even after the storms drove everyone under the water. People who continued their work throughout all of it until they died." Ellie swallowed hard. "There is more, I believe. I'm just not capable of finding it all."

"And you want us to help you? Why?"

Ellie looked at Proteus, but he merely gestured for her to continue. So she bit her lip before replying, "Because it would help you more than me. This is our world, but I'm... I'm not really part of it."

She met each of their gazes, holding them until the redhead nodded. "We need some time to talk. We'll be back." Then she held up the binder and shook it. "I'm taking this with me."

"I thought you might."

The group placed the binder in what she assumed was a waterproof bag and then headed back into the ocean. Leaving Ellie alone with a very, very angry god and the silence that burned around him.

225

Chapter 23

He waited for them to leave, seething but not wanting them to realize. Proteus wasn't even sure if he was angry because she had defied him, or because he knew she was right.

Ellie had been alive in this era, and he had not been. Why he hadn't thought to even ask her opinion about this plan was one of his own failings, a reminder that even as a god, he was not flawless. She was the one who would have given him the direction that he desperately needed. She could have poked holes in his plan, and yet... Perhaps she did not feel comfortable doing so.

It was complicated to acknowledge that he had failed her. But the weight of this responsibility was his alone to bear. He wanted this world to go back to the way it was meant to be, and he did not have the ability to do that without others helping him.

Ellie understood that. She saw through his decisions, and she helped him get to where he needed to go, that was an honor. It was wondrous that she would even think to interrupt so that he didn't royally fuck this up.

But she was terrified of him. As the others slipped into the water and disappeared, he could see that Ellie wouldn't even look at him. She kept wringing her hands, pressing them so hard against her sternum that he feared she would hurt herself. She looked everywhere but at him. The water. The sand. The ceiling that was still lit up from a sun that would soon disappear as another storm barreled toward them.

She feared he would be angry with her. But he wasn't angry with the woman who had saved his plan. He was angry with himself.

"Come here," he ground out through teeth that ached as he clenched them so hard.

"My pod is at the bottom of the sea," she whispered, still not looking at him. "I feel as though I should remind you of that."

"Why would you—" And then he understood.

Proteus stiffened. Every part of his body wanted to scream at the knowledge that she wasn't just frightened of him. She thought he would harm her again. Hadn't he been trying to prove that harming her had shamed him beyond reckoning? Never again.

"I wouldn't," he said, his voice low with emotion. "I gave you my word."

"What does the word of a god mean? The world ended. People starved. The gods did nothing." She swallowed. "After all I have seen, it's hard to imagine that gods even exist. I believe the people who just left feel the same."

"I suppose you are right." He uncoiled his tail, the bones already glowing with emotion as he hooked his fluke around her back. Ellie looked a little uncomfortable, shifting as if she wanted to make space. There was nowhere in this room where she could escape. He was too large.

Proteus reeled her into him until she bumped into his chest. Her hands planted firmly against his warm skin, and she stared down at the sight of her pale fingers against his strangely colored flesh.

The bones there glowed, too. He knew it relaxed her to watch his hearts beat in alternating thuds that calmed her mind.

"Listen to me, Sisu. I promised you that I would never harm you again, but I promised myself that I would never allow someone else to harm you either. I am in your debt." He laid one of his massive hands over hers, the long digits covering up her fingers. "I should have asked you about this long before now. You see the world in ways I do not, Ellie. I should have known better than to believe I would know all."

Finally, she looked up at him. As though his words had made her come alive, those bright eyes blinked up at him in shock. "What?"

"I am not angry at you. But I must admit I felt a great deal of fear when you walked out of that room. If they wished to claim you as their own, they certainly could. You are human. They will want you to be with the humans and I..." Proteus breathed out a long hiss. It wheezed out through the holes in his cheeks and down his throat, as though his entire body rebelled at the fear that rioted through him. "I do not wish for you to leave my side."

"That wouldn't be their choice. They don't get to tell me where to go or how I live my life." Her tiny hand came up, pressing against his cheek. "I... I think I'd rather stay with you. Here. I want to explore all there is to see in this world, and you're the only one who can give me that."

"The humans will be here. Above. And there is so much more here for you to discover without me."

"No. I don't want to know what there will be. I want to know what once was." She smiled, and that soft expression nearly broke his heart.

"You're the only one who can give me that, I believe."

A low rumble started in his chest. He wanted to keep this woman far more than what was healthy. He hadn't hoarded things since he was very young. Proteus had learned a long time ago that keeping living things was only disappointing. He didn't die. They did. He was the one who was left behind, wishing that he had never given them a piece of himself.

And yet... This woman made it impossible not to want to keep her. She looked at him with those wide, bright eyes, and he would do anything for her. To prove that he was worthy of even an ounce of her attention.

Breathing out, he shook his head and looked back at the water where the others had disappeared. "How long do you think it will take before they come back?"

"Long enough."

He looked back at her to see the heat in her eyes. The same heat that mimicked the lust that burned deep inside his body. He froze where he was, watching as she cupped his jaw and drew his face closer to hers.

A kiss, Proteus realized. It was still a strange choice for someone like him. His lips were far too wide, and he could have bitten her face clean off if he had wanted to. But she was gentle as she pressed her little mouth against his.

She was warm and soft. Every part of her kiss was everything that he was not. Kind, sweet, tasting like virtue and something broken that was his fault. The shattering of innocence, he thought. The corruption of a virginal spirit tasted sweeter than wine.

When she drew back, they were both breathing hard. He wasn't sure what to say after a gift like that. She didn't have to touch him. She didn't have to give up her fear of him, either. He knew what he was. A monster. A being who was made as a weapon to carve out the end of the world and rebuild it in the image of the ancients. But she saw him as so much more than that.

Like she could read his mind, Ellie traced her fingers along the lines of his cheeks and said, "You're not all bad, Proteus. Not all good either. But neither makes me think less of you."

He shook his head. "Ah, little human. You never cease to amaze me."

He brought her back to the room where they had worked on the holograms. He set her down in there with Pilot, ignoring the droid who had gone against all his programming when he allowed her to change what he'd been ordered to do. And then they waited.

Ellie busied herself looking through another binder she had found hidden underneath the bed with the body still on it. Proteus remained where he had been before. With his gaze trained on the water, waiting for any hint that the others were returning.

Because he needed them. They had impressed him when he had peered through Fortis's memories. These were the kind of heroes who could continue his work without Proteus having to force them to do so. They were so similar to the scientists who had once worked here, but with purer hearts and minds.

Their intent was to help. Always. It wasn't to push themselves toward greatness or to make a name for themselves in the history books. In fact, likely no one would remember the small team of people who considered themselves a family, but who had saved the entire world.

Finally, the water rippled again.

"Ellie?" he called out. "They return."

He could hear her sprinting through the room and following him into the atrium as the first male's head crested the surface. Proteus had been surprised to find that the largest male wasn't the one who controlled them. Fortis should have been the leader, or perhaps the massive red one. But no, it was the blue undine.

This time, it was just the blue male and the redhead. She crawled out of the water the moment her mate released her, pulling at the contraption on her face and immediately yanking the hood down. She'd clearly done this a few times.

"So," the woman said. "I might as well tell you my name is Mira. This binder has a lot of interesting things in it."

"Yes, it does."

"So you believe these scientists were onto something? You think that the Above is not only inhabitable, but could be saved so that these facilities aren't the only place where we can survive?" Mira's expression twisted. "I have to admit, it's hard for any of us to believe. We've all been under the sea for such a long time, but those of us with mates have seen the surface. We know how dangerous it is and what the storms are like. Not to mention the lack of water."

"I have seen it for myself," he replied.

"Have you? Have you seen the ice storms that can flay your skin right off because the shards are so sharp? Have you seen the hurricanes that reshape the coastline every single month? Have you seen the flooding, the dangers to people like us? I don't mean to be rude, but I need you to understand that this is not a planet that has had humans on the surface in over two hundred years. The world has not healed itself."

"Because no one was helping it heal." Proteus slithered down from the podium, landing on the ground and ignoring the warning hiss of her mate in the water. He loomed over the woman, waiting for her to cower in fear but ridiculously pleased when she did not. "What do I look like to you?"

"You aren't one of the People of Water, that's for damn sure. You don't even call them by their preferred name." She looked him over, her eyes seeing all the details of his body, right down to the tentacles at his hips. "You're an amalgamation of all the creatures in the sea and yet not at the same time. I have never seen anything like you before."

"No. I imagine you wouldn't have. The ancients were the ones who created me, many years ago."

That was when the male in the water spoke. "I have heard the ancient stories of a son, but we always thought they were false."

"They were not false. They were of me." He was pleased that some of the stories had survived all these years. "But it seems your people have forgotten my ways."

"That son was imprisoned by my people."

A twinge of anger burst in his chest. Proteus had thought he would be more understanding about this, but come to find out, two hundred years of imprisonment had given him a bit of a chip on his shoulder. "Your people imprisoned me because they did not like the idea of working with the humans. When it was discovered that I, their god, had been conspiring with mortal scientists to help save this planet, your people overreacted. They threw me into that coffin and sank me to the bottom of the sea. Forever awake. Forever alive. Trapped while knowing that I could only inhale and exhale but move no more than that."

Rage burned through every word. The truth hurt, he could tell. The undine before him flinched. "The stories claim you were a monstrous being who wished nothing more than to hurt those who did not worship him."

"Many things can be true at the same time," he muttered, before turning back to Mira. "If your people are interested in helping, then I would like some of them to set up here. I know that likely will not be yourself, or perhaps any of those we met before. But there is much knowledge here, and this facility has sustained itself throughout the storms."

"We can arrange that."

"If any of them step out of line, I trust you all know that I will drown them before feasting upon their bodies."

There was a long pause of silence. Mira's nose wrinkled. "Feasting upon their bodies seems a little much, don't you think?"

"It will not sustain me for long, that much is true. But they are easier to catch than a whale." He bared his teeth, allowing his mouth to split open a bit. He had the thorough pleasure of seeing her eyes widen in horror. "I consume much to maintain a long life."

She swallowed and backed toward her mate. "I will be in touch then. Your droid seems to already have a connection to our base."

"It does. There are a few remaining facilities needed to bring Sanctuary online. I will need your people to go there as well."

Mira nodded. "Then we will talk through the droid. A small team of people will volunteer to come here and... research as well."

"Good." He was still smiling at her, certain that he was making her uncomfortable. "We will look forward to your message."

The other two headed out again, but not before he heard the long, suffering sigh that Ellie let out. He turned to look at her, exasperation making him want to follow the others into the sea as well.

"What?" he asked.

"You could have been nicer."

"Nicer? I was very nice. I didn't eat any of their limbs. I didn't threaten them even once. They were allowed to leave without any arguments or fights." He frowned at her. "I was very nice. I didn't expect him to prove himself to me, and many of his people used to do that. I battled any male who was within my presence."

"Maybe that's why they didn't like you back then," she muttered, heading over to the water and peering down into the depths to make sure they were actually gone.

"They feared me. They weren't meant to like me."

"They might not have locked you up if they had liked you."

Anyone else would have ended up in the ocean or his belly for saying something like that. Proteus snarled at her, baring his teeth even though he knew she was right.

"Go prepare the room for visitors," he muttered as he crawled toward the water. "I am drying out."

"I'll prepare for as many as I can," she cheerfully replied. Then dragged her finger down his back where he knew his skin was already getting paper thin. "Huh. You are getting dry."

Snarling once more over his shoulder, he slipped into the water to get a break from the tiny demon who now seemed to run his entire life.

Chapter 24

There was freedom in knowing she could disagree with him. Ellie wasn't sure what the feeling was in her chest, but she was thoroughly and wonderfully relieved that she could speak her mind without fearing his anger.

She trialed it ever since she'd gone against his wishes and walked into that room with all the other people there. First, she told him she didn't want a particular fish for dinner. He'd been busy, and the only thing he could find were herring, which he brought to her in a fistful. She didn't like herring and told him as such.

Of course, anxiety bubbled up in her chest the moment she did. She waited for an argument. For rage to burst forth from his chest as he yelled at her that he'd been taking care of her for so long, and what was she offering him? But none of that happened.

He just looked down at the herring, sighed, and then nodded. As though he had known she would say that. Proteus disappeared back into the sea for a while before returning with squid, which had become one of her favorites.

Another time she told him that she wasn't quite ready for bed. He'd ordered her to get some sleep so that she would be ready in the morning, but she wanted to watch a few more of the holograms. Instead of picking her up and putting her to bed, he'd nodded solemnly and resolved to stay awake a little while longer with her. If she wanted to research more, then he would do the same.

The freedom it gave her was staggering. She hadn't realized she could tell anyone how she felt. She hadn't realized how easy it would be to just say "no". And life continued on without anyone being angry at her.

What a strange feeling it was.

But now, Proteus had been gone for a while, and she'd been left to her own devices. Ellie had seen countless of the holograms, freezing them in time so that she could wander through them. It was so easy to walk through all the images of what this place had once been, to peer into the past. The glory days really were remarkable.

So much of their equipment was taken for granted. She'd seen marvelous things done with machines that could perform surgeries on their own, but also create. Her pod had been very similar, but that was the most expensive equipment in Tau. Not just anyone was allowed to use it, but it seemed like the machines here had been freely used for centuries.

The people here had been so intelligent. They used their minds without hesitation, and they made every hair on her body stand up on end when she watched them do it.

There was only one thing left to do. Push her limits just a little more.

She stood in front of one of the exits, taking a deep breath. She didn't hear the wind howling outside, nor could she hear the crackle of thunder. Sand wasn't blowing into the doorway, and as far as she could tell, there wasn't any ice falling outside. Which meant, if she was going to do this, then the perfect moment had arrived.

"It'll be fine," she muttered. "Everything will be fine."

"Ellie," Pilot said as he stood beside her. "This is a very stupid idea."

"Yes. It is." But she had to see it for herself. She couldn't stay in this place, or even honestly allow others to stay here, without leaving it. She had to know what it would be like to not just poke her head out the door, but actually try and exist where the sun could touch her.

Steeling herself with a steady breath one more time, she opened the door and walked outside.

The heat was the first thing she noticed. How could anyone not? It blasted her in the face, nearly pushing her back into the opening that she'd just left. Brutal, blistering heat made sweat slick her body. She'd never experienced heat like this anywhere else and had no idea how anything could survive it.

Ellie tried to breathe through her mouth, but it was like she was trying to breathe water. The air was so heavy out here. It made her lungs seize, trying desperately to suck in more air, but she couldn't no matter how fast she breathed.

Not to mention the weight. Maybe it was just that it was so overwhelmingly hot, but her body felt heavier as she stepped out onto the golden sand.

She'd seen this sand countless times inside. Ellie had played with it, letting it run through her fingers and fall in a waterfall down onto the ground. But when she touched it out here, the sand was so hot it burned her fingertips.

Hissing out a breath, she backed toward the building. How could anyone live out here? How could there ever be any hope at all that they would return to this place?

At least it was cool inside the facility. For the first time, she noticed the vents where there was icy air pouring out. Her eyes clung to the insulation that was one of the few things left remaining in this building and suddenly she was grateful for it.

Gasping as she was overcome with dizziness, she sat down on the much cooler sands and stared out the still open door.

"You're alive then," Proteus's voice interrupted her thoughts. He was still in the water, watching her with those dark eyes that saw far too much. "Did your little experiment go well?"

"How are you expecting us to survive out there?" she asked, shaking her head in disbelief. "It's so hot. Everything is so warm it feels like it would melt the flesh right off my bones."

"Some people might think that it's possible. I've seen humans die in heat less than that." He pulled himself out of the water, sliding across the floor toward her. With him came a rush of icy ocean water that pooled around her feet and gave her some sense of relief. "But no human would be out in the heat like you just were. It's dangerous, for one. You'll have to adjust. When the sun is at its peak, humans cannot be outside. The facilities were meant to protect you from the heat."

She swallowed hard. "I'm just not... not certain how it will be possible for any of us. You know? It just feels like it's futile."

"Perhaps. But with the plan the other scientist laid out, and with your own people working on it, I believe we could make the environment more habitable for all of you with a few tweaks of the plan. The world is malleable. It is not something that exists only in one way, shape, or form. And yes. It will take a lifetime to fix, perhaps even generations of your people before you'll see the difference." His hand came down on hers on the floor. "But you will see a difference. The world will ease. The heat will become easier for you to withstand. And what has been broken will be fixed."

She nodded. "I know in practice it makes sense, but I just... I still don't see how we're going to do it."

"You don't?" He nudged her with his shoulder. "Do you really not see how it's possible?"

She took some time to think about it. There was a lot that could be done, but most of it was almost impossible from where they were.

"The land is uninhabitable. We can't grow things out there." She waved her hand at the door.

"No, you cannot."

She thought even harder, almost breathless with the work of it all. "So we'd have to start with the sea. With the coral reefs. Rehabilitating what we can to make sure that the colder sea could perhaps slow down some of the storms that are brewing on it."

"Correct. And once that is done?"

She blew out a breath. "Then we can focus on the land. There are pockets of areas less affected, perhaps areas around mountains with natural shelter from the storms. Focusing there would give us a chance to grow more trees, more barriers, and create pockets where the earth itself could start to heal and spread out from there."

"Smarter and smarter every day." He nudged her with his shoulder. "That is precisely what we're going to do. But that is a lot of work. Humanity has long thought it could rage against the planet, forcing it to do what they wanted, but a planet is not like that. It does not bend to human whims. It cannot be told what to do. The best it can do is take what it has been given, and create from there. That was the downfall of humanity long ago, and it is a downfall that we will avoid once again."

"Are you certain we even can?" Ellie looked up into Proteus's concerned expression.

He blew out a long sigh and then shrugged. "We have to try, do we not?"

There was a part of her that saw this as a failing mission. Now that she had seen and experienced the madness that was just outside her door, she wasn't as confident as she had been before. But another part of her, the stronger part, knew that it wanted to try. The very least she could do was give it her all.

Taking a deep, steadying breath, she nodded before standing. "Right. Well, we have the rooms all set up and prepared for those who are coming here. And we're ready to research whenever we can. Most of the equipment is unsalvageable, but we have the blueprints. From what you told me, Mira and the others are quite resourceful when it comes to building, well, anything. So they should be able to replicate what has been lost."

He reached for her, grabbing her hand in his and tugging her closer to him. "Ellie..."

She wouldn't ever know what he was going to say to her. Holograms flickered to life around them, and Pilot came careening out of the back room.

"Look!" the droid shouted. "Look at what I found!"

Ellie held her breath as the hologram that flickered to life in front of them was... her. Literally her.

There wasn't a single strand of hair that didn't look out of place. From her eyes, her lips, to the button of her nose, all of it was Ellie. But she didn't recognize the weight of responsibility that dragged the woman's shoulders down, or the way the bags under her eyes darkened her entire face.

"Whoever finds this message, I apologize." The woman before her ran a hand through her short, cropped hair, just like Ellie wore it. "For everything. For the world. For the cities below the sea that should never have existed. For the future that is so murky now, I can't even hazard a guess at what it will end up being."

The woman looked over her shoulder, toward the room where they'd found the body. "For my love. If we had gone with the others, she would have survived that sickness."

"Is this..." Ellie stepped up to the hologram, running her fingers through the sparkling edges.

"Your Original," Proteus murmured, but his brows were furrowed in confusion. "She shouldn't have been here, though."

The hologram backed up and sat down on a chair that was no longer there. She leaned forward, cupping her head in her hands as she sighed once more. "It all went wrong. Everything. We are doing our absolute best, but I don't think it's fixable. What we started is what will end this world. But I want people to know that I... I tried to change it."

She blew out a laugh. "I don't know why I'm even recording this. I know they already have my clone ready to go underwater with the others. She's got all my memories, mannerisms, looks just like me. Maybe I'm the clone, for all I know. They just refused to bring me with them, and for good reason. I'd tell the others the truth. There is no coming back from what we've done."

The hologram looked up, and the horror in her eyes was hard to look away from. "This message has absolutely no purpose other than to assuage my own guilt. I know that. You all know that. Why I'm even recording this..."

And then it stopped. Just like that.

Suddenly the image of herself was gone, and Ellie remained standing there, shocked at what she had seen.

"Well," Proteus said. "That was interesting."

Pilot clicked his legs on the floor and then headed back toward the other room. "Sorry, I didn't watch it before I played it. Guess I should have."

Even so, Ellie found she couldn't move. She stared at the spot where the hologram had once been. As though if she looked hard enough, she could see where the other woman had once sat and bring her back. Some part of her wanted to look her fill. What would it be like if she could see the other woman again?

Did she have the same quirks that Ellie had? Did she bite the inside of her lip when she was nervous, or wrap a strand of hair around her finger over and over again when she was thinking? There were so many features that looked just like hers...

"Ellie?" Proteus asked. "Why are you still standing there?"

"I never had a mother," Ellie whispered. "Not even a mother figure. But seeing her makes me wish I had."

"You are more than just a copy of her, you know."

For the first time in her life, Ellie agreed. "I know. I am so much more than the woman they cloned me from, but I guess there is a part of me who wishes I could at least talk to her."

His hand came down on her shoulder, squeezing tightly. "It sounds like you grew up rather similarly to her, at least. You will continue her work, Sisu, and I cannot imagine a greater way to get to know her."

She couldn't either. The notes she had been reading, maybe they were written in her mother's hand. Maybe she could know the woman who had come before her a little better through the scientific discoveries she had made before she died.

It wasn't much reassurance, but it was something. It was more than any other clone might get.

The other Originals were monsters in Tau. They were the ones who still thought what they had done was right. They were pleased with themselves. Proud of what they had built.

They turned their faces away from the monstrous things they had done, only to look at the light. But that was no way to live.

Monsters lived in the dark, after all, and those people had been surrounded by the dark their entire lives.

Ellie ran a hand through her hair, catching the movement as one that mimicked what the hologram had done. She had to stop doing that. She couldn't watch any more of that hologram lest she end up copying the Original of herself.

"I need some time to think," she whispered. "I'll... I'll go double check that everything is ready for our guests."

She disappeared into the back room, suddenly feeling like she didn't know herself all that well after all.

Chapter 25

Proteus made sure he was present for every human scientist, engineer, and research assistant that arrived at Sanctuary. He wanted them to see who was presiding over them, and to ensure that they would not do anything foolish. But the longer he was there, the more overwhelmed he became.

Hundreds of years in a coffin hadn't made it easy for him to be around so many people. It was hard for him to pick out voices, considering how many of them were talking all at the same time. The humans never stopped talking, either.

They were so awed when they got out of the water like silver fish, their wetsuits clinging to their bodies as they pulled themselves onto the floor and then walked around what should have been a museum. Everything here was ancient. Everything was part of their history.

Their wide eyes pleased him as they stared up at the massive ceiling all those stories above them.

Of course, the first few groups were rather unlucky, and they arrived during a terrible storm. The sound of the ice and rain on the roof barely made them flinch, but the rumbling thunder that shook the walls made a few of them drop to the floor before they realized they were safe. A few awkward chuckles followed, but he could see how nervous they all were. They didn't know how to live here without feeling like they were under constant threat.

Good. They were.

Proteus needed them all to know that this wasn't a vacation. They weren't here because it was safe or that it was even a good idea to be here. There were so many things that could kill them on land, and they knew so very little about where they were. Above, as they called it, had changed a lot since the last time humans were here. Proteus had no idea what nightmares awaited them.

Ellie had asked him to gather food, and he was amenable to it. So many mouths to feed was going to be a problem. Sure, they had brought their own resources. A sight which had delighted Ellie, as she hadn't been able to eat many fresh vegetables, and the guests came with a whole host of them.

Proteus didn't want any of them to complain that they weren't being fed while they were here. The last thing he needed was for that coalition of undine and humans to decide the surface wasn't viable after all. It was their choice to help, but it was his choice to keep them here.

At least tuna were hardy. Those fish seemed to survive through the greatest downfall of the planet, and he could find them easily enough. Proteus came across a school of them that was so massive even he took one for himself. Usually, he didn't eat prey unless it was large enough to sustain him for some time, and these were sizeable enough to curb his never-ending hunger.

Proteus unhinged his jaw and feasted before killing two more and bringing them to the humans.

As he surfaced, he was surprised to see that there was one of the undine here as well. The male made the waters reek with his interest in whomever he was talking to. Undine and their mates. Their stench would turn his insides out, and he had already eaten for the day.

With a massive tuna in each hand, there wasn't much room for him to maneuver around the other male. But he did so, taking up far more space than he needed to when he finally crested the water. Shaking the water from his head, he glared at the massive green male.

"What are you doing here?" he grumbled as he slapped the fish up onto the floor. "At least make yourself useful and gut these."

The male looked at him with surprise in his dark eyes before letting out a little laugh. "I suppose I could do that. When you surround yourself with intellectual women, it's hard not to get distracted, I fear."

Intellectual women? He had counted four females among the humans that arrived. There had been five men with them, although most of those men were seemingly there as support. One of them was clearly a cook, and another was there only to record what went on. He'd told Proteus that four times as he inched by the massive god of the sea.

So, four females and three males who were useful, he had decided then. If one of those women were intellectual, then that was good enough to start their projects.

But his gaze slid over, and he did not see a stranger. Instead, what he saw was... Ellie.

She stood beside the water in new clothing. It had been made out of crudely created fabric, clearly an attempt by the humans in this group to replicate something like cotton. Still, it was pretty. Dyed a lovely shade of green, just like the color of the male in the water. It hugged tight to her hips, showing off how long her legs were. The dress made his mouth water.

And apparently it made the other undine interested as well. Suddenly all he could think about was the scent of lust that had clogged his nose as he came up through the stones.

He saw red.

Proteus grabbed the undine by the gills along his ribs. The hiss of pain was the only sound the other male could make as Proteus lifted him out of the water. His hands slid into the gills easily, feeling the bones of the male's ribs resting in his palms and the wet heat of his breaths. All of it wasn't enough. He wanted blood to smear down his arm, and to hear the rattling gasp of a dying undine that was flattened beneath his touch.

"Proteus!" Ellie shouted. "Put him down!"

He had no intention of doing that. He would not put the male down when he had been lurking, leering, looming above Ellie like he had any right whatsoever to do that. This male encroached upon what was Proteus's.

Even if he was uncertain that he was worthy to keep Ellie with him for all eternity, he knew damn well this male wasn't.

The undine flopped in his grip, writhing and wriggling just like the tuna had done before he killed them too. "Release me," he wheezed, his breath reedy now that he was out of the water. "I beg you! I beg of you, god of the sea. Spare my life."

For a moment, Proteus remembered how it had once been. He saw so many other undine in his grasp, just like this one. He had killed them too, even after they'd begged. He had seen the oceans turn black as night while they still cried out for his mercy. But he had no mercy to give them. Never had.

They were tools to be used. Tools that would listen to him or not, and if they didn't, then he would replace them with tools that would. This newer generation would learn. Proteus had proven time and time again that the death of a few undine was the greatest way to get the others to listen to him.

But then he heard her. The quiet sound of a sob. And when he glanced in Ellie's direction, all he could see were her hands pressed against her mouth as she stared at him and the grip he had on the male in his hand.

"Please," she whispered. "We've worked so hard to get here."

Grunting, he looked once more at the pained expression on the male's face. Leaning close, he growled, "Now all I can smell is your fear."

Dropping the undine into the water, he climbed out and headed toward Ellie. She backed away from him, those eyes wide once more. But he didn't think it was terror in her eyes. She knew better than to fear him now. But there was something in her that recognized a predator when she saw one.

"Proteus?" she asked, breathless and stumbling. "What are you doing?"

He didn't have it in him to say a single word. There were no words that would fall from his tongue for what she had encouraged. She should have known to stay away from the other undine who came here.

Males looked at her, and they wanted her. That was all he knew. Because the moment he had seen her, frosted inside her pod, a gift from the sea itself, he knew damn well that he would think of nothing but her for a while yet.

He backed her farther away, ignoring the murmured questions from so many people who watched what he was doing.

"Should we intervene?" someone asked, a male voice that made Proteus snarl in response.

"Nope," a woman replied. "Sorry, clone. Not my problem."

That made him snarl too, but for an entirely different reason. Ellie was so much more than a clone. She was a thinking, living, breathing person with thoughts of her own. She was impressive and kind, and she had seen more in him than anyone else ever had. Not even his parents.

Creators.

Ancients.

Memories burst in his skull of all the times he had been here. Of how long it had taken him to convince the humans that he wasn't a monster, and even then, so few of them believed him. The scientists here had wanted to get rid of him at first. They saw him as the abomination he was.

But not Ellie. She had never once cowered away from him, and for that, he would always reward her.

Her spine hit a wall, but he now remembered that wasn't a wall at all. It had once been something else.

Proteus lifted a hand and hit the emergency button over her head. No one would know that's what it was. The flat panel didn't want to be depressed, likely from sand caught in it. But eventually it gave, and she tumbled into a new room.

He followed her.

The darkness surrounding them was nearly oppressive. It was warmer here, too. He had a feeling some part of the building had torn off, perhaps the roof above their heads. He didn't look. Instead, he crawled on top of her as the door behind them sealed.

He didn't need light to see her. Proteus could smell her, and that's all that mattered. She was within his grasp. So easy for him to pin down beneath him and devour whole.

But no, that wasn't what he was doing. His mind was all scrambled even as little, icy pricks attacked his spine.

Growling, he shook himself, freeing the little daggers that had been thrown at him. Had one of the humans followed them? Were they trying to protect her from him? Such was an honorable choice, but it would lead to their demise.

Snarling once again, he shook himself and turned to look at the door. But it was sealed. No one had trailed after them, and even as he scanned the remnants of the room, he found there wasn't another living soul here with them.

Only sand. Mounds and mounds of sand.

Small hands framed his face, forcing him to look down at the woman he had pinned. All of his focus suddenly turned to her. Like a predator who had found the prey he had been searching ages for, he filled his lungs with her scent. Every detail of the room disappeared, his entire focus narrowing until there was only her.

The way her dark hair fanned out on the silver sand. The way her pupils had blown out because she couldn't see in darkness like this, but he could. He could see every detail of her body, how she moved with such grace as she blindly touched his features. There wasn't even the slightest scent of fear in the air as she traced the outlines of his lips, up to the slits of his cheeks, down his throat where there were even more teeth waiting for her to find.

"It's okay," she whispered, and he thought maybe she had been saying that for a while now. "It's okay. It's just the rain."

The rain?

Oh, the little daggers. The sharp pricks were hail. Although this hail was formed more like shards of ice, raining down on his back and tried to burrow its way underneath his scales.

A flashing memory burned through his mind once more. A human who had stepped out into one of these storms. Proteus had begged him not to, telling the man that it was foolish even to test it. But he'd gone anyway, and the ice shards had stripped the flesh from his bones so quickly he hadn't even been able to scream.

Wincing, he pulled her more completely underneath him. "You are not safe," he murmured as he coiled his body around her more.

"And whose fault is that?"

"Mine," he muttered, looping his tail over her and making sure that not even a hint of her skin could be touched by the ice.

"We could go back inside."

"No." They couldn't. Because that male was there with his wandering eyes and his scent that screamed he wanted to touch her, taste her, learn her just like he had.

And a part of him feared that she would rather bind herself to a normal undine, one with pretty hair and eyes that reflected the light. Not someone like him.

An abomination.

Her hands feathered over his chest, gently tracing the outline of his ribs and following the hollows there. "We can stay for a few more minutes, if you'd like. But would you care to tell me what made you so angry?"

"He wanted you."

"And?"

He huffed out a breath. "And I won't stand for it."

"Why?"

He couldn't tell her why. Proteus refused to debase himself like that when she knew why he felt the way he did. Ellie knew how much he thought of her, and how strong his feelings were. She knew...

She didn't, he realized. How could she know any of those things if he had never told her?

He took a deep breath, expanding his ribs and preparing to tell her every bit of what had made him so angry. But then he felt her press a kiss over one of his thundering hearts, and he froze. She did it again, and again, peppering little kisses along his skin as she made her way from one heart to the other. Like she could feel the beat pressing against her lips.

"Better?" she asked, the word so quiet he almost didn't hear them.

"Better," he agreed, coiling around her a little tighter. "But don't stop."

She didn't, not for a little while. Not until his heartbeats slowed and until reason returned to his mind.

He was in danger from this woman, Proteus realized. Far more danger than he could ever have anticipated.

Chapter 26

Ellie hadn't ever expected Proteus to be so... clingy wasn't the right word, but it was the one that kept popping up in her head. He didn't like it when she talked to anyone other than him. He didn't like that her attention had to wander from him to all the others. The amount of times she'd had to calm him down in just two days was getting a little embarrassing.

For him, not for her. It was rather thrilling to know that she was the only one who could control this massive sea god, who was always one split second away from killing everyone and anyone who stood between her and him.

It probably wasn't normal to feel like that.

In fact, she knew it wasn't. She was supposed to be kind and thoughtful and guide their visitors through living here, and yet most of her attention was on Proteus as he learned how to share.

And that was what it was. At the core of his objections and disappointment in everything that was happening, was that he didn't want to share her. He wanted all of her attention for himself.

Eventually, on the second day, she asked him to go hunting again. He'd put up an argument, but they were already running out of meat. Most of the people here had actually brought items with them to grow food. But food didn't grow quickly, even with grow lights. So they would need supplemental nourishment.

Apparently, the undine who had come with them was the hunter who should have provided additional meat. But he had quickly been chased out of the sea god's lair, and Ellie had a sneaky suspicion even further than that. Proteus had muttered a few times about the stench that lingered long after the undine male had left.

"Please," she said, putting her hand on his arm and squeezing. "We have to make sure they stay, Proteus."

Which was a feat in itself. Proteus certainly did not make that job easy for her.

The humans weren't terrified of him, per say. But they were wary. They knew they were here to help, and no matter how hard helping was, they all had the same goal in mind. Saving the land so that they could use it.

Unfortunately, that was much easier said than done.

Proteus finally gave in, but his hand lingered on her ankle for a moment too long. "What do you wish then, Sisu?"

She twisted her lips to the side, trying to think of what food would be far enough away that it would take him a while to find it. "The tuna was tasty."

"Then tuna you shall have." He glared at the humans behind her, even though no one was paying attention to them. Or if they were, they were pretending very well that they weren't. "Take care of her, all of you. I expect her to be in one piece when I get back."

He sank under the water, disappearing without leaving even a ripple behind. Ellie found herself smiling at the place he'd left, like the dolt she was. It wasn't a good thing that he was so possessive of her. It should worry her.

But it didn't. Because she knew he was dealing with some strange emotions related to her.

She was doing the same.

As she turned, she caught the gaze of an engineer who was working on rebuilding what they thought might be a replicator. It would not give them more food, but it was definitely going to help with the computer parts they would need for many other pieces.

The engineer seemed to wince when she realized Ellie's eyes were on her, and then her gaze went right back to her work.

Ellie vaguely recognized that woman more than the others, and that was because the engineer had taken up a bunk next to Ellie. She had dirty blonde hair that leaned more toward the brown side, and muscular forearms. Her entire body was muscular, in fact. Far more than the man who worked with her, but that engineer was still a wiry kind of strong.

"What is it?" Ellie asked, but no one said a word back to her.

They all kept their gaze on their projects, ignoring that there was another person in the room with them at all. It was as if they were frightened of her. Like...

"Oh," she whispered.

They didn't want to talk to her if it was going to make Proteus angry. They'd already seen him attack one of the undine. A massive male like that was uniquely capable of surviving an attack, but a human certainly wouldn't.

No one wanted to take the risk of even talking to her, because it was likely that Proteus would have some kind of unreasonable reaction.

This was a byproduct of his behavior that she hadn't anticipated.

Maybe it was one she should have thought of. After all, she'd been there watching with them.

But she knew Proteus better than anyone else in this room. She knew he worried for her safety, not that he was trying to make it harder for her to live here.

"I'll just..." She pointed at the room where they were all sharing their quarters. "If anyone needs me."

Ellie doubted anyone would. They all worked well together, clearly having done projects like this before. The two engineers, a man and a woman, both worked together seamlessly, moving from piece to piece like clockwork. The others were just as talented, all but one woman having another person to assist them.

The solo woman seemed to be the one pouring over the notes they'd found. She'd unlocked a section of the records in one of the computers and spent her days making notes after reading through them. Apparently, she was some kind of genius, but she hadn't said a word to Ellie since arriving.

None of them had. They'd all introduced themselves too quickly for her to catch their names, and they stuck to themselves. If she asked a question, they were quick to answer, but that was the only interaction she had with them.

Walking into the living quarters was suddenly stifling. All of their things filled the room. They'd moved the body of the woman who had died in here, dumping it outside like it didn't even deserve a burial at sea.

She'd overheard them talking about the "unsanitary conditions" and mentioning it was strange any human would live in quarters like these without trying to make it a home.

She had. She just... didn't know what a home looked like.

Her heart started hurting. It squeezed in her chest, thundering harder and then rapidly slowing down, making it hard for her to even breathe without worrying what was wrong with her. But being in here? It wasn't helping. Of that much she was certain.

Ellie headed back out into the antechamber, looking for the only person in this room who would always talk to her, no matter what Proteus was doing.

Pilot was on top of one of the computers, plugged into the mainframe as he did some other task asked by a person who shouldn't have mattered as much as her. Or at least... No, her thoughts were all scrambled.

They mattered. They mattered a great deal. Every single person here was doing work that she never could have done on her own, and it wasn't fair of her to even suggest that they weren't. To even think of them as anything other than the intelligent people they were was cruel.

"Sorry," she muttered as she grabbed Pilot and unhooked him from the computer. "I need to borrow him for a few minutes."

"Hey!" the woman who was seated below him complained, but Ellie didn't have it in her to care right now. Tonight she would worry about whether or not they all hated her. Right now, she needed a friend.

Even if that friend was a droid who was programmed to agree with her.

She headed out into the other room that Proteus had revealed. She was lucky it wasn't hailing. At least today, a storm only loomed on the horizon, ominous clouds overhead making it seem like being out here was a bad idea, but there wasn't any rain just yet.

"Unhand me!" Pilot grumbled, his legs moving so quickly that he almost sliced her skin until she put him down. "I have work to do."

"I know. I only..." She started pacing in front of him. "I think everyone in there dislikes being around me."

"They don't have any opinion of you whatsoever. They are afraid of Proteus. Is that what you want to hear?" Pilot inched toward the door, wanting to open it and return to his work.

"Pilot, please." Ellie dropped onto her knees, so tired she could barely stand. "I just need a friend."

The droid waffled between what he wanted to do and what was the right thing to do. Heaving a mechanical sigh, he folded his legs beneath him and settled onto the sand to look at her. "What is it that you're afraid of? Does it matter if they like you?"

"Well, a bit. I'm living with them now, aren't I?"

"You are. But that doesn't mean they have any right to your time. If you don't like them, then who cares if they like you? You've won." He seemed a little proud of himself for that statement.

"Liking and not liking someone isn't about winning."

"Isn't it? Most of life is about winning."

"Pilot..." She should talk to a person about this and not a droid. "I want them to like me. I want to talk to them, and speak with other people like me."

The door hissed open, and a woman walked through. The engineer who had been looking at her, in fact. "Droid, go back to your work."

Ellie wanted to protest that he was supposed to stay with her. She needed him, even if this conversation wasn't going as well as she had hoped. But Pilot ran out the door so fast, she didn't get a moment to say a word.

She sighed, looking down at her hands in her lap. "I suppose I should head back in as well."

"They don't see you as a person," the engineer blurted.

The words hung between them. Not a person. Never had been. That was the issue, not Proteus. The problem with all the other people here was that she wasn't an actual human, and they could tell.

"Oh," she murmured. "I suppose that makes sense."

"It doesn't, actually. A clone isn't anything like the Original. I know that because I work with a lot of them." The woman crouched in the sand. "My name is Quinn. Nice to meet you, Ellie."

Quinn. She remembered the name now that it was said. When they'd all introduced themselves, Ellie had said it was a pretty name. One of the other engineers had snorted and said people in their roles didn't need pretty names, they just needed to be good at their jobs.

Licking her lips, she tried to start a conversation that she hoped might go somewhere. "You work with clones like me?"

"Not the same kind, obviously. Whoever your Original was, I haven't seen a clone that looks like you. But that could have all sorts of reasons. I helped wake up the first crew that came to Beta." Quinn shrugged. "The whole ordeal was traumatizing. For them, for me, for everyone involved and probably generations to come. We were told that your people would be like children. You wouldn't know what was happening when you woke, and that you'd have to be taught how to speak, how to eat, maybe even how to breathe."

Ellie winced. "No one knew that the Originals were waking us up?"

"The only person left alive from Tau was Alexia. I believe you met her when the others first arrived."

Ellie only gave her a blank stare. She knew Mira because the redhead had introduced herself. She didn't know any of the others who had shown up here.

Quinn held a hand over her head. "She's real tall."

"Ah, yes, she reacted like she knew me."

"She probably knew your Original. Worked with them all, as far as I know."

Ellie nodded. So she'd been right that Alexia was one of the personal guards of the Originals. Changed and manipulated like the clones were. "It's awful that you had to be there during that process. Waking is never all that comfortable, and I remember... Well, some of the clones screamed a lot."

"Most of them did, actually. I don't think there was a single one in Beta that didn't." Quinn shrugged. "Listen, I'm just letting you know not to take it personally. Most folks who had to deal with the clones weren't the ones in fancy offices like a lot of the people out there. The other engineer, his name's Tim. He's also dealt with folks like you before. You can talk to him."

She nodded. "I just..."

Quinn waited. Patiently. It didn't feel like she was rushing Ellie's thoughts or that she was pressuring her to finish the conversation so she could get back to work. It just felt like two people talking about their day.

And that's what Ellie settled on. "I haven't ever felt like I belonged anywhere. When I was awake in Tau, it was because they wanted me to work. They trained me to be the person they wanted, and now that I've been given this second chance, I just want to feel like maybe I have friends. Or not even friends, but people who see me as more than a tool. People who recognize that I'm a person, too."

"You are a person."

"Very few people see that." She blinked up at Quinn. "Even now, you're saying the rest of them still see me as a clone. Which I am. I recognize that. But... Well, I hope that maybe someday they'll look at me and just see Ellie."

Quinn seemed to freeze. Her face turned very red all of a sudden, and she stood abruptly. "I'll talk to them."

"Oh, that wasn't what I was asking—"

"I'll talk to them," Quinn repeated firmly. "Just give it some time, yeah? It'll take time."

Ellie watched her walk out of the room and listened as the door hissed shut behind her. It was a start, she supposed. At least someone had spoken to her as if she were real.

The beginnings of hope blossomed in her chest. She wanted to believe that these people might talk to her a bit more. They didn't have to be her friends, just like she had told Quinn. But maybe they would share a little of their own lives. Just about their day or about what their days were like in their cities. She wanted them to acknowledge that she was alive, and maybe helpful if they gave her a task to complete outside of her own duties.

Ellie just wanted a life. A normal human life. And they were the only ones who could give that to her.

Chapter 27

The others weren't accepting of her. He wasn't sure why, but he could see it every time he came back to the facility. That was his only complaint about the newcomers, however. They were quick to discover many new and helpful things that were otherwise hidden in Sanctuary.

Of course, Proteus had no question that his companions would have found them, eventually. Both Ellie and Pilot were capable. But would they have discovered all of this so soon? It seemed unlikely. The future was barreling towards them now, and that should have made them all happy.

Instead, all he saw were the scientists and engineers getting more serious. They avoided Ellie's presence as if she had some kind of disease that one of them could catch if they weren't careful. He didn't understand it. It made his skin crawl.

They had no idea how special she was. How quickly her mind worked. Or even how deeply compassion was embedded beneath her skin. They didn't even care.

So he decided if they weren't going to make use of his beautiful, wonderful, and talented human, then he was going to take her out on his own for a while. She deserved that.

Grumbling under his breath, he rose out of the water and watched her as she crossed the room. She had an armful of metal that had already stained her pretty arms with rust, and he didn't like that either.

A low growl rumbled from his chest, churning the surrounding water before he could stop himself. All the humans froze, staring at him with expressions of fear until he stopped.

All right. Maybe he was partly the problem here. He needed to control his reactions. She was working, and that was what he had brought her here for, after all.

"Ellie," he said, his voice a cracking summons in the air. "You are with me today."

She nodded, depositing the metal where it was likely supposed to go before heading over to him. "What would you like me to do, Proteus?"

"You'll swim with me."

"Oh." She blinked a few times and then said, "So you want Pilot to come with us as well?"

No, he didn't want the droid to come with them. That cretin would ruin all the sweet moments he had planned and likely make the water icy cold with his disdain. Proteus had no interest in a cock blocking droid tainting this moment for him.

"Absolutely not," he snarled. "The droid stays here."

Again, she looked at him like he had lost his mind. Quietly, Ellie said, "I still can't breathe underwater, Proteus."

Another woman walked up beside her. The engineer was someone he had seen around Ellie a few times. Her dirty blonde hair made her stand out amongst the others, mostly because she was so strong. Broad shoulders and muscular arms that were revealed by her sleeveless shirt made her appear far more capable than the others. She wore an engineer's uniform she must have found in the back, but the one-piece suit didn't fit her. Thus, the arms being ripped off.

"He hasn't breathed for you yet?" the woman asked. "It's eerie, but they can do it just fine. All they do is stick a tentacle in your neck. A quick prick and suddenly you're breathing underwater."

"Who are you?" he grumbled.

"Quinn. Be nice to me, or I won't be as nice to your friend here." Quinn pointed at Ellie and then flashed him a grin. "Go ahead with the tentacle. I've watched it enough times to not let it make me too sick."

He didn't like where this was going. Ellie was already heading toward him, and this wasn't going to work the way either of them thought. "I do not have one of those," he said.

Now everyone was listening. He could sense it. Even the man in the back, who had been making a racket while he hammered together some contraption, was suddenly hammering much more quietly.

He could have heard a pin drop, and that said something for how loud this room had been until he admitted that.

"What?" he hissed. "I'm clearly not an undine. They have always been resilient, and when they discovered the use of that tentacle, it was proven that humans and undine were compatible with each other. I am neither human nor undine."

Quinn just stared. But then he felt her gaze trailing up and down his body, looking him over with fresh eyes before she blew out a long breath. "Ah. Well. That's fine, you can take my rebreather."

The two women disappeared into the back for far too long. He was already antsy, and having to wait for Ellie to return was somehow even worse.

What if she didn't like where he was bringing her? He doubted that she wouldn't like it. Ellie, so far, had been very easy to impress. She liked the ocean. She liked seeing new things. He was going to combine both loves and show her something only in the water and new.

But still, something ugly slithered inside his chest. He hadn't felt doubt like this in such a long time, and shouldn't that say something about him? She weakened him. She made him question his own abilities. She...

Was heart-stoppingly beautiful.

He had to make sure his jaw didn't drop as she walked back into the room wearing a wetsuit with one of the metal devices over her mouth. But his eyes lingered on the curves of her form, and how she moved with such innate grace.

Her long legs were on display so all could see them. The slight roundness of her stomach made his eyes linger on the softness there, but then he could only look at the plushness of her breasts and swallow as his mouth watered. He'd tasted her, and now all he wanted to do was rip that wetsuit in half so he could feast upon her again.

Maybe she knew his thoughts. Her cheeks turned bright red as she met his hungry gaze and then gestured at the device on her mouth. There was a muffled sound of her talking, but it was hard to hear her this far away.

"What is that?" he asked, suspicion blooming in his chest. He needed a lot more information before he'd take her into the deep sea wearing that. What if it didn't work?

The engineer swaggering next to Ellie replied. "Rebreather. One of

Mira's creations. It's a newer version, so it'll last longer. Her idea was to create a way to breathe underwater like fish do, a filtration system for oxygen essentially. If you look on the side, you can see the canisters of nitrogen and... You don't need to know all that. I'm getting in the weeds. It'll let her breathe by filtering out what she needs through the water itself. That's all you need to know." Quinn clapped a hand to Ellie's back. "Have fun. We'll all be slaving away here while you're gone."

"Should I stay?" Ellie asked, and he heard that loud and clear.

"No," he replied for the rest of them, and then held his arms out for her.

She came to him like a woman in a myth. All the world faded away as her hips swayed and she sauntered toward him. Did she know how enraptured he was with her? Did she know that she had woven a spell around him and that somehow she was all that he could think of?

She likely didn't. And that was part of her charm, he supposed.

Proteus took her waist in his hands and lifted her into the water with ease. She barely weighed anything to him, but nothing weighed much when one was as big as he was.

They sank into the water, and once beneath the surface he could breathe again. He pointed for her to go the way she had before so that he could meet her through the rocks. The other way just wasn't safe enough for her. Yes, there was more space, but the rocks were questionable. A cave-in around an undine was something they could all manage. But her? She would die in a cave-in.

Flicking his tail, he moved through his side speedily so he could be on the other side of the rocks once she pulled herself through. And again, he was just stunned by her. With her hair spreading around her face, the short dark hair looking like ink, he was shocked at how well she seemed to be adapting here.

Without a word, he wrapped his arms around her and started the journey. It would take a while, but he was a massive beast. Proteus could move faster than most undine could imagine in the water, and he intended to use every bit of his body to get them there with time to spare.

He wanted her to enjoy it for as long as she could, because the seas were calmer today. Almost as though the goddess herself knew that he wanted to show someone something special.

She didn't say a word until they approached the underwater monolith. It was rather impressive to see from this distance. A mountain that had been sunk beneath the waves.

"What is that?" she asked.

"An old volcano," he replied. "It erupted many years ago, and the center has worn back down. The rising tides allowed water to get into the center, but it has hidden the interior from the greatest anger of the waves."

"I'm not really sure what you're about to show me."

"The last living coral reef," he murmured before heading that way. Already he could see it. The coral that clung to the stones, and the schools of fish that decorated it.

This reef had clung to life for years, managing better than he'd expected. Giant brain corals were still there, some of them hundreds of years old. The branching coral had mostly broken in the storms, but deep in the center many of them were still safe.

"The waves break around the reef," he said as he released her from his grip. "And that saves much of the coral from death in the storms. As angry as the sea could get, she always protected this place. Now, I show it to you."

"I... I don't know what to say."

"Explore," he replied with a soft smile. "Say nothing and explore, Sisu."

She turned away from him and glided through the water. At least, she tried to. She kicked off his body and managed for a little while before she sank again.

He'd forgotten she didn't know how to swim. Here he was, choosing the best day he could for her in the sunlight that speared through the coral, and he'd forgotten the most important detail.

Proteus hooked an arm underneath her waist and approached the surface. Flexing a bit, he turned his tail into a float that she could grip onto. He took her hands and made sure she was holding his scales with a solid grip.

"Hold on," he said. "I will keep you on the surface."

She nodded, clearly shocked at what was occurring, but did that matter? He couldn't go too far over the reef himself. There wasn't enough space above the coral for a creature of his size. But he could stretch his tail over it and hold her there.

The rebreather allowed her to watch every tiny fish that darted past them without worrying about lifting her head out of the water. The goggles on her face had yet to fog up either, so he knew she could see all the most incredible parts of this reef.

The tiny fish had always been his favorite. He liked the black and white ones. Striped and quick, they lived a little deeper than the others. They spiraled around the two of them, clearly curious at what new creatures had joined them.

Then there were the needlefish. Long and pointed, they had serrated teeth within their pointed snouts that were sharp enough to break her flesh. But they hovered near the surface in a school, watching the two of them with beady eyes until they all darted away as one.

Ellie touched her fingers to her ears a couple of times, and he thought for a moment there was water in them before he realized she was hearing the reef itself. The crackles and pops of the coral moving made her watch it a little more closely.

He floated her toward some of the larger, colorful parrotfish that were integral to keeping this reef alive. One of them crunched on a coral piece, and he saw Ellie touch her ears again.

Laughing, he pointed out the large creature where the sound was coming from. "A parrotfish," he explained. "They are part of a large ecosystem that helps this entire place work."

But her eyes weren't on the big fish. She was watching a tiny, neon blue and purple fish cleaning a massive clam. The little fish rubbed its side against the massive clam, and the bigger creature slammed shut with a surprisingly loud crack. But not before he had seen the delicate blue insides that were dotted with glittering white like stars.

Then she pointed behind him, and he turned to look at an eagle ray that swam past them. It almost looked like it was flying through the water. Each wing moved with such grace, with its long pointed tail trailing behind it. The black body was dotted with white spots, very similar to the clam before it disappeared through the waves into the darkness of the sea beyond.

They spent hours there, watching the sea move as the tides ebbed and flowed. This was his favorite place to rest. Always had been. And when the sea had told him that it was still safe, that he could still come here, he'd known he had to show it to her.

"This is what you want to rebuild?" she asked, her voice still muffled by the metal device on her face.

Proteus nodded solemnly. "It's what we all need to see rebuilt. The sea needs this to live. Your people need it to survive as well."

She looked at him, and for a moment he thought her goggles had a leak in them. Until he realized she was actually crying. Tears slid down her cheeks within those goggles and had pooled at the bottom. "This is beautiful, Proteus. Everything here is so healthy, so... alive."

"That's all the sea wants. That's all this planet needs. More life and beauty." He reached out and brushed a tangled strand of hair behind her ear. "I'm glad I could share this with you."

"There's so many colors."

He chuckled. "Yes, the sea knows how to put on a show of colors, that much is certain."

She shook her head, and bubbles erupted from her rebreather like she was laughing. "I don't think I've ever seen so many colors in my life. How long can we stay?"

Proteus estimated they'd already been here for a few hours, but when he lifted his head out of the water, all he could see was the hurricane barreling toward them. "Not long now. But I did want to show you one more thing."

"You have another gift?" she asked, her voice filled with awe. "What did I do to get spoiled today?"

You exist, he wanted to say. You exist, and you see me as someone more than a monster.

Instead, he grinned and reeled her closer to him so he could gather her up in his arms. "There's an old human temple here. It's been sunk into the sea for years, but I think you'll like to see it."

Chapter 28

Ellie still had no idea what she had done to be given gifts like this. Truly, it was the most incredible thing she had ever seen in her life. Being able to float above the fish, watching them dart around each other, had made her rethink everything.

Sure, it had only been one experience. And she'd seen fish before. Malcolm, the scientist who worked with her in Tau, loved to look at the fish he kept in tanks in his office. She'd watch them swim around for ages until he yelled at her that she had work to do. But that wasn't the same as seeing them in their natural environment.

Somehow, watching them live in this world made her feel like they were more than just pets. They were real, impressive creatures who had so much personality. They darted around each other, clearly getting into little spats and arguments, but then heading back to their homes.

Every fish on this reef seemed to know its place in the world. They all had jobs and had relationships with other fish that they knew or recognized from daily life. They lived in such a way that it was very obvious they were all a functioning part of a whole.

So when Proteus said he wanted to show her more, she wasn't going to say no. How could she?

"A place of worship?" she asked as they darted through the water.

They were so close to the surface, she could see when the rain reached them. The water above her head went from wavelike patterns to holes made by the rain that drilled into it. She was so enthralled by the texture that she didn't notice when they'd arrived until Proteus laughed in her ear.

"Come on, Sisu," he said with another chuckle. "I think you'll like this better than the rain."

A flash of lightning illuminated the sunken building. It was impressive, with columns easily three stories tall that were still white as bone. It looked like buildings she'd seen in old myths and legends. The kind of building where gods would be worshipped, and statues would be built that were ten men tall. But as Proteus headed inside, she realized that it was quite modern.

A door had been sealed long ago, and as Proteus entered a pattern of complicated numbers, it slid open with a rush of air bubbles that made it hard for her to see anything at all. She threw an arm up, trying to keep her rebreather in place while Proteus forced the two of them into the airspace.

The door must have sealed behind them, because they were tossed into a space that suddenly had air.

She blinked a few times underneath her goggles, trying to reconcile the fact that she had just been in the ocean, but was now very much in a space that almost felt like it was... heated.

Proteus had gathered her in his arms, making sure that she wasn't ever thrown too far or injured. But now she was lying on top of a god, while realizing that the floor beneath him was entirely gold. Not just gold in color, but the metal that reflected the expression of shock on her own face.

She lifted her head, staring at the wealth surrounding them. Everything in here was coated in gold. The floor, the ceiling, the walls. All of it. They were inside a gold box, essentially, with very few items left.

But she could see there were areas where more feet had tarnished the gold. Smudges were still in certain areas where people had likely knelt to worship the god of the sun. There were benches against the far wall, all of them equally coated in what she could only assume was gold leaf. But those benches looked old.

The walls were mostly left bare, plain, reflecting the people who were within the temple rather than having any murals or artwork that depicted the god itself. Except one wall was entirely glass.

She stared out into the sea, knowing that this likely wasn't what the people who were here before her had looked at. A massive drop off plummeted from the base of the windows, leaving her staring into an abyss, while what the previous worshippers must have seen was the surface of the sea itself. They must have stared into the glittering light of the sun reflected upon the waves that made this whole room glow.

The more she stared into that dark void, the more nervous she became. It felt like something was staring back at her. Something she could not see.

Proteus rolled onto his stomach, helping her stand as he did so and then bracing himself on his arms to look out the window with her.

"Ah," he murmured. "So it's still alive."

"What is still alive?"

But then she saw it. The tentacles that were waving in the sea. She hadn't noticed them because her mind skittered away from the possibility that something like that was real. It couldn't be real. She wasn't looking at a real life sea monster that was sunken into the bottom of the abyss, just waiting for unfortunate prey.

"Your people used to call it the kraken," Proteus murmured as his arms came around her. He'd coiled his tail beneath him like a snake, using the weight of his lower body to allow him to almost sit up straight.

Her back hit his chest as his words rushed over her. "A kraken?" she murmured. "Like..."

"It's a species of squid. Usually only in the deep sea, but as the water levels rose, they came to the surface more often." He pointed with a long finger, and she followed the way his claw traced the outline of the tentacles so far out to sea. "Its prey moved closer to the surface, and so did the beast."

"You know it?"

"In a sense. It's an animal, not a mythical creature. It cannot speak or converse in the way you are assuming, but yes. I have interacted with it, and I know that it will not harm me if I swim past." He tightened his grip on her. "We swam past it to get here. I was surprised you didn't see it."

A spark of fear ignited in her chest. "You took me right past a monster like that?"

"Monster seems like a harsh word."

She spun, slamming her palm against his chest. "You swam right past a kraken, which I have heard of, by the way, and you thought I would be okay with that?"

"I didn't ask if you were okay. And you didn't see it."

His hands were warm on her waist. He didn't seem to care in the slightest that she was hitting him with her tiny fists. In fact, if she had to guess, she thought he might enjoy that she was striking him.

But that grin made it hard to focus on anything other than the man in front of her. Even though she knew there was a terrifying sea creature in the water right behind her, and some part of her mind wanted to focus on that, the rest of her wanted to look at him.

When had he stopped being scary to her? This god had nearly chewed her arm off right in front of her. He'd attacked her in a fit of rage, and yet, now she could only remember the good things he had done. How gentle he was. How much he wanted to make sure she was fed. And how angry he got whenever she wasn't treated right.

Things had changed between them.

Her hands slapped him one more time, but this time her palms lingered on his arm. The undine that she had seen before were all cold, but he was burning up. Like a furnace, he heated her palms.

The muscles of his chest were so intriguing. They were flat, like a human's, but so pronounced. She could feel the power in him, and the way that each muscle fiber twitched when her fingers played over them.

Ellie dragged her fingers lower. The rough bumps of his abs created hills and valleys that were so... intriguing. She had never looked at a man's body and wondered much about it at all. Humans were simply human. She had never been created for pleasure or to be interested in it, but he had woken something in her that made every part of her want to explore.

"What you did to me a week ago," she whispered, her voice a little rough at the thought of his tongue and his touch. "I can't stop thinking about it."

He hummed low under his breath. She could feel the gills along his ribs moving with that breath, the softness of them sliding through her fingers as she traced her touch around his torso.

Proteus said nothing else, so she kept talking as she explored the soft filaments of his gills. "It made me think, is there a way I can give you the same experience? It hardly feels fair that I could take all that from you and you got nothing in return."

"We both have struggled to find pleasure in these forms," he murmured, his gaze like a brand on her. "I am uncertain I am even capable of such things."

"You've never?"

"Never."

Her gaze flicked up to his, surprise written across every feature of her face. "You've never?"

So many implications were in those words, but she was thoroughly surprised. People had worshipped him. He was a god. Surely there had been at least a few moments where he had indulged in pleasure.

But he hadn't, she realized. He didn't even know if he could.

She supposed there was a chance here for her to show him.

She knew he liked it when she kissed his chest, so she figured she would start there. Ellie pressed kisses to his skin, laving her tongue over his muscles to taste the salt that lingered there. She allowed him to pull her onto him, not even realizing that he had drawn her down onto his chest so that they were both lying down until she could fully relax on him.

Every kiss felt right. It made her body warm, her skin tingle, and she could so easily feel that wondrous sensation that he had woken in her a week ago.

Pleasure, she reminded herself. Lust. There were words for this, even if she wasn't very good at remembering them. She would soon, though. Already her skin was both too hot and too tight.

Her hands danced down his sides, trying to listen to the soft sounds he made when he liked what she was doing. But it wasn't entirely the same noises that she had made. He wasn't necessarily making sounds of pleasure, but of comfort and relaxation.

But when she licked in between his abs, she swore there was a hiss of breath he made that was different from the others. Glancing up, she saw the same expression on his face that he had when he'd seen her walk out in the wetsuit. That was what she wanted. The heat in his gaze, the need that seemed to burn up from inside of him.

He had it in him. She was certain of it. He just hadn't ever been given the gift of discovering the pleasure that could make him see stars.

Leaning up, she straddled him as she pulled the zipper down from her wetsuit. The expression he had was of a man who coveted the creature above him, and she thought perhaps her body would be enough to intrigue him.

The zipper moved, inch by inch, revealing miles of her flesh until her breasts were free. Her nipples tightened as the air hit them. His gaze never moved from her chest, and those dark eyes seemed to darken even further.

His hip fins were mostly tentacles along the edges, but she had never seen them move like they did right now. They were usually limp, like the fins on a regular undine, unless he was swimming of course. But right now they reached for her, all those little suckers flaring as though he wanted... wanted...

"Oh," she whispered. "You want to touch me."

"Dreadfully so," he murmured.

She grabbed onto his fins and brought them up to her exposed skin. With a groan, her head fell back as she felt a hundred tiny mouths latch onto her skin. His tentacles played across her breasts, many of them wrapping around her skin, layering around each other.

His head tilted back as well, and the sound he made was one of pure rapture.

"You taste so good," he murmured. That long tongue came out to lick his lips, and she realized he could actually taste through the suckers of his tentacles.

This was easily the strangest interaction she'd ever had with another living being, and she could not suffer it ending any time soon.

One of his tentacles pushed at the zipper of her wetsuit, sliding down her belly and delving between her legs. It suctioned onto her clit with what seemed like almost impossible accuracy, but she couldn't think much after that.

She was so wet. So needy. Ellie rocked against his hip bones, making little sounds that were both embarrassing and needy. This wasn't about her, though. It wasn't meant to be about her.

It was meant to be about... about...

Ellie slid her hips back again, and her bottom came up against something hard behind her. Something hard and impossibly large.

Her eyes nearly bulged out of her head as she realized he did, in fact, have a cock. He could get hard, and therefore, he could most certainly experience pleasure.

But then it was hard to think again because another tentacle slithered between her legs, and this one seemed a little thicker than the other. She could tell what he wanted. He wanted to plunge inside her, to delve into the wet depths of her body and make her forget that she had a point to all of this.

Well, two things could be true at the same time.

With a wicked grin, she stood. She hoped it wasn't hurting him for her heels to dig into his tail, but he didn't look like he was in any state to complain as she pulled her wetsuit off.

His gaze followed every movement, devouring every inch of skin revealed until she turned around. His hands came up to frame her hips, holding onto her and bringing her down so that he could watch every movement of his tentacles as they attacked her slit once more.

But now she was facing his cocks. Plural.

Now she could stare at the monumental challenge before her, both of them glistening in the golden light of the room. As one of his tentacles slipped inside of her, the feeling both foreign and immensely welcome, she let out a little groan.

"These will be difficult," she murmured, knowing that she had only watched someone get fucked before, but had never experienced that herself. She had seen many people naked in her life, though. And she knew damn well what he had was larger than any that she would ever see again.

Still, she leaned forward and licked the closest one from base to tip, and grinned when he arched into her. A challenge, yes, but worth every second of it.

Chapter 29

Proteus had lived for centuries. He had seen cities built and fall, watched the world end and start anew. He had fought with krakens, massive sharks, and had argued with the ancients themselves. He was a god of the sea and had thought he had seen every part of what life could offer.

He had never experienced the blistering heat he felt after she licked his cock.

The world tilted. Shifted. Suddenly it wasn't just what pain he could bring or what madness he could inflict. A world opened up that was just him and her. Doing this until they both couldn't anymore or until they died.

His hips arched toward her, as though his body knew what to do while his mind did not. It was a good thing that there was some semblance of nature to this, because if he was left to his own devices, he thought his mind might fracture and he'd freeze.

Ellie's tiny lips wrapped around the tip of his cock. The softness of her tongue swirled around the head, tasting him as his tentacles tasted her.

Loops of his hip tentacles had wrapped around her. Latching her onto him, forcing her to remain where he wanted her as they worked through her folds as though they were made to do so. His body was a foreign creature. He allowed it to continue only because he wasn't sure how to stop it. Or if he even wanted to.

A low vibration rocked through his cock as she hummed. The sensation was unlike anything he had ever suffered before.

"You taste like saltwater," she whispered, laving her tongue down the side of his cock and then grasping the second with both of her hands.

She tasted like the end of all things. Like ruination and an awakening that he could not stop. He wanted to devour her whole. Already he could feel his jaw unhinging, and his throat opening up as though his body wanted to swallow her. But no, it wouldn't. He wouldn't. He knew damn well that no part of him wanted to hurt her.

So he was not all that surprised when instinct had him curving up, using all of his abdominal muscles that he had spent centuries building so that he could feast upon her flesh while she worked on his as well.

His tongue slid up the inside of her leg, catching a few drips of heaven that had leaked out of her. And then he plunged his tongue into her depths.

He listened to the music of her moans. Tried to focus beyond the sudden suction and friction as she started to pump her hands up and down his cocks. There was no thought, only feeling. Knowing that she was here. He was here. They were together, and that something like this couldn't end so soon.

But Proteus had never done this before. He hadn't even realized that his body could produce the cocks that she now used to her own devices. All of this came to an end far sooner than he wished it to. His hips jerked again, and suddenly he couldn't think. Couldn't breathe.

Thunderous pleasure, aching need, all of it struck him at the same time. He was suddenly slammed with what felt like the best and worst experience of his life.

He came hard. Probably too hard. He wasn't truly paying attention when she reared back from him and then moaned again as apparently his tentacles started rioting against her skin because they too experienced a sensation that they had never once indulged in before. His entire form seemed to seize until sudden, wondrous relaxation turned all the muscles of his body to liquid.

Ellie gave a moan of her own, the sound alerting him that, thankfully, his tentacles had done their job right and she, too, had enjoyed this experience.

Limply, he moved his arms. Gently turning her so that her head could rest against his chest while he played with the strands of her drying hair. How strange it was, not even to think about someone attacking them.

He couldn't even if he tried. All of his thoughts were of her. This woman who had brought light and life into his life, even as he desperately attempted to destroy much of what she valued. She'd played along with his game, and then she'd turned him inside out.

Still breathing hard, he glanced down to see that her hair was nearly dry already. The silken strands clung to his fingers and claws, holding on as though even that part of her body wanted to cling to him as well.

He'd let her. He'd let her hold him for the rest of her life. Proteus would consider himself a lucky man if that were the case.

She stirred against his chest, her breath fanning over his overheated flesh. "You're always so warm."

That's what she had to say? After what they had done?

He chuckled, the sound reverberating through his chest. Then he tried to reply, saying something along the lines of, "Not many sea creatures are warm," only to realize that his mouth was still open.

Not just his jaw, but the entirety of it. All of his teeth were still bared, his throat was completely exposed to the world. She was lying against him, knowing that this beast with a throat full of teeth had yet to close his damn mouth.

He used his free hand to put himself back together. The body that he was stuck in fought against him. Apparently it wished to air out the teeth that had closed upon her hips once again. He could smell the metallic scent of her blood in the air, and it infuriated him that he had been so careless.

But she didn't complain. Of course she didn't. Ellie never complained about anything.

She just sighed and snuggled her face into his neck once his mouth was completely closed, and Proteus realized he had never felt more whole than he did right now. With her snuggled into him, he felt like the god so many had called him for so many years.

This was where he was supposed to be. This was where his life had been leading him.

All those centuries of pain. All that torment. All the years hidden in that coffin deep within the sea, all of it had been worth it to bring him to this moment, here and now, with her.

Breathing in her warm scent, he relaxed against the floor and allowed his eyes to close. When was the last time he'd slept? He couldn't even remember. He knew that he didn't need that much sleep. Perhaps he had never slept in his life. But right now, he was so relaxed that he felt like he could rest. Even for a few moments.

Proteus didn't know how long he had been out. All he knew was that he woke to her shifting on top of him. The smooth weight of her thigh slid across his belly, and her arm tightened around his ribs where she'd been holding him all night. Her face nuzzled closer to his neck, and he swore she inhaled his scent before another sigh blew across his chest.

"Proteus?" she asked, her voice a quiet rasp of sleep. "Are you awake?"

"I am now."

"How long have we been sleeping?"

He rubbed a hand up and down her back, arching his neck to look out the window. The storm had passed, and that usually took hours. But he couldn't hazard a guess to answer her question.

There was almost no light left in the temple. He thought perhaps that was a lack of sun. The building seemed to mimic what time of day it was outside, at least the few times he'd been here. Which meant it must be nighttime, or nearly that.

"I think it's the evening," he murmured, his fingers finding knots in her back and slowly working them out.

"Should we be getting back?"

"They'll be fine on their own."

And in truth, they would. It made him a little angry that they didn't need her, because he found himself needing her a bit more every day. But they would continue the work without Proteus or Ellie being there to watch over them.

"All right," she whispered. She wriggled a bit closer to him and shivered. "It's colder in here now, isn't it?"

He wouldn't know. The icy depths of the sea made any temperature warmer for him than it was for her.

Proteus drew his massive fluke up over her like a blanket, checking to be sure it was completely dry before laying it over her body. She tucked the edges in around herself, making a happy little moan as the heat of his body rushed over her form.

"You feel like velvet," she said with another happy sound. "So soft when you're dry."

Proteus swallowed. "What we did... You enjoyed it?"

"Just like the first time."

"Good."

An awkward silence settled between them. They hadn't even had sex, and he found himself not knowing what to say to her. Proteus feared that if he opened his mouth, he would start spouting off things that he couldn't believe he would say.

Like asking her to stay with him forever.

Telling her that she was as much a part of his soul as his own body.

Whispering that he never wanted another woman in his life after knowing her.

She leaned up, bracing her arms on his chest and staring down into his eyes. He almost didn't pay attention to what she was saying. Her hair was sticking out at all angles, and there were dark circles under her eyes. But she had never looked more beautiful than she did at this moment. Even if she should rub her eyes to get the crusties out of them.

"What?" he asked, realizing she was looking down at him with expectation.

"Oh, you weren't listening."

"No, I—" he brushed a strand of her hair out of her eyes, merely as an excuse to touch her cheek. "I wasn't."

Those cheeks burned a deep, dark red that was so adorable. She couldn't seem to even look at him before she glanced away and then whispered, "It's strange waking up with you like this. I think I like it."

"If we could do this every day, what would life look like?" He wanted to know. He wanted to crawl inside her head and know exactly what she dreamt of.

She shook her head with a small smile. "We'd wake up like this and go on some adventure. Perhaps you'd show me another coral reef or... you could introduce me to the sharks."

"Sharks aren't very friendly."

"Oh, well what about other animals?"

"Dolphins are curious. Manta rays would be my choice, though. They're eighteen feet long, and they seem to fly through the water. Sometimes they're hunting, so they're busy and they will ignore you. But other times they're playful. They want to swim up to you and then dart upwards, but it's like they're dancing with you. They'll do it for hours until they grow bored with you and move on to the next journey."

"That sounds lovely." Her eyes were full of wonder, and he swore he could see the picture he'd painted in her gaze. "Then what? We'd play with the mantas and then..."

"Well, you'd be hungry."

"Of course. And the only way you'd know how to feed me would be to raid an old human settlement. Because you know without question that I don't like eating raw food and I prefer the slop, as you call it." Ellie laughed at her own joke, and he couldn't help but laugh with her.

She dropped back down onto his chest, curling up against his skin like it was the most natural thing on the planet to do. He held her close to him. Listened to the sound of her heart beating so steadily, so sure. And he knew from this moment on, everything was going to change.

He would do anything to keep her by his side, no matter what.

As Proteus tilted his head back, he stared at the ceiling. There were etchings in the gold there. He didn't think Ellie had noticed, or she would have brought it up. But there were serpents and gods who mated with them. Creatures from the minds of the humans who had worshipped here.

It had been a temple of fanatics. He'd avoided those who had worshipped the sun god in the end. They were the ones who had unfortunately thought the rising temperatures of the world were a blessing from gods who thought the humans could take it. Or that they would become creatures that could manage the heat.

They'd been wrong, of course. And they had died like the rest of them.

His gaze turned instead to the sea. The cold, endless sea that had survived the chaos of the world above. He could see the kraken as it waited for prey to come near it, and the shadows of the water as night fell above. He swore there was another shadow nearer to them, something that was vaguely familiar. But then it darted away.

Such a thing must have been a figment of his imagination. No one knew they were here. No one but him and her.

Gathering Ellie a little closer to his body, he breathed in her scent once more before squeezing her tightly. "There's more I wanted you to see here. It wasn't meant to be all pleasure, you know."

"I thought you said this was a gift?"

"Ah, I can give you a gift and then want something in return, can I not?"

She stuck out her tongue and blew air at him. The strange expression made him laugh, even as he helped her stand up. "Come on now, Sisu. What's an adventure without a discovery?"

"And what discovery is that?"

"Get dressed and I will show you. This facility used to be so much more than just a temple. The people who were here kept a close eye on the surface. I think it's important for us to be able to do the same."

He rolled onto his belly, watching as she pulled the wetsuit back on. It was a slow process, and she continued to make these little grunting noises that made his chest ache with how cute they were. She was struggling to get it on, but he didn't offer to help. Instead, he watched as the angles of her struggle showed him parts of her body that he hadn't seen yet.

The power of her abs as she arched into it. The shape of her shoulders as she tugged on the tense fabric. The column of her throat as she swept her hair out of the way so she could zip up the rest of the suit.

All of these were details he burned into his memory, so he would never forget a single one of them.

And when she was finished, he asked, "Ready?"

"Ready. What other adventures do you have to show me?"

Chapter 30

Ellie should have known he wasn't going to bring her somewhere just to enjoy themselves. But it had been nice while it lasted. She'd liked lying on top of him, listening to his breath as he slept. She'd pretended to sleep with him, maybe even dozed off a little herself. But she hadn't been able to sleep completely.

Not while the most remarkable thing happened to her. Seeing Proteus at ease, relaxed, trusting her not to harm him while he rested? It was a gift she would treasure for the rest of her life.

She'd watched his eyes move underneath the lids as he dreamt, trying to guess what she thought he might be watching or doing. Perhaps he was swimming through the waves, scheming some other plot. Maybe he was fighting the kraken off. Trying to keep her safe in a glorious battle between two ancient gods.

But no, she liked to think he was dreaming of what they had done. That the taste of her was still on his tongue, and that his mind was going back through all the pleasure she had given him.

Even now, as she walked through the room trying to find the panel he had told her about, all she could think about was the pleasure they had found in each other. She hadn't even realized it would feel like that. No wonder so many people in Tau had chased it for hours on end. She would have too if she had known it would feel so good.

"This panel?" she asked, finally seeing a small square in the wall that looked like what he had said. It was etched there, almost as if someone didn't want anyone to find it other than the person who had made it.

She bent down, looking it over before planting her hand against it and giving it one firm press.

The panel shifted into the wall and then turned around to reveal a touch screen on the other side. "Seems high-tech considering what you said this place used to be," she muttered.

Once the panel turned on, the controls were pretty easy. She just had to enter a few additional coding pieces to bypass the password she didn't know, and replace a few of the wires in the back that were easy enough to reach. And then voila. She was in.

Proteus shifted closer to her, dragging himself across the floor so he could look as well. "This whole wall should be screens, if you can pull them all up. The permissions are lost on me, though. I don't remember what was required to—"

She'd already tried out a code, and the panels were all rotating around. Exactly as he said they would.

There were likely thirty screens on the wall. Many of them flickered on and off, and a majority remained black. But they were there.

"How did you do that?" he asked, but his eyes remained glued to the screens.

"They're the same functions that Tau used. I had a feeling the passwords might be the same." She shrugged. "Maybe they knew about this place."

"If they did, then the people who ruled your old city knew more than they told anyone. How many of these screens are active?"

Running a few diagnostics took time, but soon enough, she had a report. "It looks like five of the cameras are still online. The rest are either non functional, that looks like thirteen, and a few of them are fixable but they need software upgrades. It looks like they used to use..." No, that couldn't be right. She leaned closer to the screen as if that would make the coding change. "Huh."

Proteus's gaze was like a physical touch. "I don't like that sound."

"It's just... Well, I'd swear it says they used drones to fix the old cameras. But there's no way they could have used drones. What could fly in weather like that?"

Nothing but silence answered her question. She looked up, confused at the expression of anger on Proteus's face. He should be happy, shouldn't he? At least they had five cameras that were in working order. And wasn't that the whole point of all this?

She felt all the blood drain out of her face as she realized that yes. Yes, this had been the whole point of it. Of all of it.

"The facility you first brought me to," she whispered. "You said there were supposed to be cameras there, but you needed the mainframe to be online."

"I did." He still wasn't looking at her.

"So the building where the other humans are, that's where the mainframe is. Now that it's online, and people are actively bringing it online more, we could come here. This is where all the cameras have always been."

"It has." He glanced down at her, his expression shifting just slightly when he realized she was looking at him with disappointment. "What? What is it?"

"Has all of this been about..." She gestured at the screens.

"Of course."

"But what about me?"

He blinked at her, clearly not understanding the question. "What do you mean, what about you?"

"I just... I thought some of this was maybe about finding out where I was from. The people who created all of this. Saving the planet. There are a hundred things you told me, but now it seems to all be about surveillance and... and..." She gestured at the screens again. "This."

"We have to see the surface. We have to know what is going on there so that we can bring the humans Above. That has always been what this is about."

She knew that. He'd told her that before. Ellie had just hoped maybe it was a bit more than that.

He was still staring at her, seeing that his words weren't getting through to her at all. "What? Why are you looking at me like that? You always knew the entire point of every move I have made was to bring humans back to the land. I want them out of the water. All of them."

Her shoulders slumped. "I thought that maybe there was more to all this. Maybe you wanted to save the world. Maybe you wanted everyone to see you as a savior, not just a god. But look at it, Proteus. Nothing we show them from these cameras will convince them to leave the water."

She looked at the five that were still online, and all she could think was that there was nothing there. Just sand. Dust. Heat. No one could live out there. She'd stepped out onto the sands herself and knew that blistering heat would sear the flesh off someone's bones.

But at night, it looked even worse. The cold would set in quickly. She remembered how frigid it was in that kind of cold, and how there wasn't anything at all that could warm her. Ellie had walked out there only once at night, just to try it, and the temperatures made her breath frost in front of her face. How could anyone survive out there?

"Wait..." she whispered, pointing at the top right screen. "Is that... Is something moving on the sands?"

Proteus leaned up, using his hand on the wall to brace himself as he stretched out his tail. He was right in front of the screen, watching it with true interest. "Not on the sands. In them."

"Lift me up."

"Ellie, you don't have to see it."

"Now, Proteus."

He sighed and picked her up. She brought the tablet with her so she could control the angle of the camera as they both stared at the sand. There clearly was something inside that dune. It tunneled through the granules, moving with a speed that was almost hard for the camera to keep up with.

"Something is alive out there?" she whispered in shock. "How is that even possible?"

Proteus said nothing, staring even harder until finally, the sands parted to reveal a terrifying monster.

She thought it might be an undine on first inspection. But then she realized how wrong she had been. Though it was human-like in the top half, the bottom half was clearly that of a snake. It lifted onto its tail, turning its head to look around. And then she saw a massive, long tongue flick out of its mouth. Tasting the air like snakes did.

It was hard to see the creature through this camera. The darkness made it difficult to make out exact features, not to mention it was very far away from the camera now. But that was a living creature, one who looked almost similar to a human, at least on the top half.

"Oh my god," she whispered. "The notes in the facility about them experimenting on people and splicing genetics with animals. They succeeded."

The horror of it ran through her. It meant that there were things alive Above. That all the horrible experiments those people had been doing, they'd taken root.

Had some poor woman been forced to carry a serpentine child inside of her womb? Had she been in the same room where Ellie had slept, praying that death would take her long before she gave birth to some monstrosity? Or had they created these beings in a test tube just like Ellie? Were they born cold and terrified of where they were, with no one to love them? No one to tell them that they weren't entirely unnatural after all.

The figure on the sands suddenly snapped its head around, looking at something neither Ellie nor Proteus could see. It dropped down, slithering as though hunting. Not like an undine, then. It didn't need to drag themselves. Its tail was strong enough to propel them through the sands but also keep them upright and moving.

Her breath caught in her lungs as the creature disappeared from their sight.

"So," Proteus said, sounding almost breathless. "They actually did it."

"I don't know how to feel about that."

"It complicates the plan."

"You're thinking about the plan right now? Of course it complicates the plan! There are people living Above! Just like there were people living underneath the waves." She struggled in his arms until he finally set her down. Her mind whirled with what this meant. "We can't go Above. They don't want us there. No one wants us."

"Ellie—"

"It's just as I feared. There are so many people who need hope, Proteus. Being able to go Above, no matter how dangerous, could give them that hope. People like me. Clones who were woken up and now have to deal with all the backlash from people who don't understand who they are, or don't care to even see them as people. This was a chance. But there are people already there."

She couldn't breathe. Her heart thundered in her chest, far too fast for that to be normal, and here she was, trying to clutch at the strings of her own hope.

If she could help other people like herself, then she wasn't entirely a failure. If she could give other people a chance to live a life on the land, to see the sun, to explore the lands that they had been denied for centuries, then maybe that made her more than a clone.

Hands framed her face. Claws reached the top of her head, clacking as they bumped into each other. She focused on the face in front of her. The worried god who stared into her eyes with a gaze that was so big she couldn't look anywhere else.

"Breathe, Ellie," he said. And then he did it himself. Making her watch him as he inhaled, and then exhaled.

She mimicked what he did. Dragging air into her lungs that were begging for more air far too fast, and then slowly letting it out even though it made sparks dance in front of her vision. She did it over and over again until finally her body gave her some small bit of relief. She could think. She could reason.

This didn't mean the end of the plan. It just made things more complicated. Like he had said.

"What do we do?" she whispered. "I don't think anyone is going to be convinced to go up there if there is already a known threat. Humans have spent centuries fighting the undine. Essentially, this means that we're taking them out of one place and putting them right back into the same issues that they just fixed. Now… now we're making them start at the beginning."

He pressed their foreheads together with a sigh. "Ellie, I have rarely ordered you to do anything. I would argue that I have impressed upon you that it is important to me that you learn how to make choices for yourself, and that I honor those choices."

"I know."

"I'm ordering you now to say nothing of what we have seen here. Not to anyone. The humans can never find out that there are people living Above already. They need to continue this work, and they need to move out of the sea. That is my will. That was the will of the ancients before they passed. This future must come to be."

It felt wrong what he was asking her to do. He wanted her to lie. To lie to so many people while knowing that she might be putting them in danger.

"What if the people who live on the sands hunt them down?" she asked. "What if we can't even build safe places to live because of them?"

"We will make sure that doesn't happen. We will keep them safe as we watch over them all. Do you hear me? We will use the drones. Pilot will get the blueprints for the flying ones. We will use those as our weapons. We will keep everyone safe, and they will never know what we have seen here."

No, this was wrong. This was taking people's lives and putting them willingly at risk. They couldn't do this.

But she didn't have much of a choice. For all that Proteus had been kind to her, reminding her that he wanted her to become her own person and how he wanted her to make her own choices, she could hear the finality in his tone now.

He wouldn't let her tell people. He needed her to be trustworthy in this, and if she wasn't...

Blowing out a breath, she nodded. "I won't say a word. But I don't think this is smart, Proteus. I think they need to know so they can prepare for whatever that is."

Her gaze strayed back to the screen. There wasn't anything there anymore. No snake creature. Just the trail it had left in the sands and even the sight of that made her skin crawl.

The undine were one thing. They were creatures of the sea. They made sense.

Whatever lived Above? A creature like that was unnatural.

Chapter 31

Proteus could feel the disturbance between them. He'd told Ellie to focus on downloading all the data she could from this facility. Most of it would be useless, but if they could return easily and access the feeds, or access the feeds in the other facility, then it would be much easier for all of them.

He didn't enjoy returning to this haunted place. He swore that he could still hear the voices of those who had once worshipped here. The low humming used to drive him crazy, and he swore their spirits still sang through the waves.

Now, he waited for her to finish her work while watching the screens. He hadn't told her that the suspicious new species had returned.

Whatever it was, it was long, although not as long as an undine. Proteus paid particular attention to its body, trying to understand what the differences between this new beast and their underwater counterparts. It was strange to see that there was another being capable of adapting to this world.

The two males he could see—at least, he assumed they were males—were tall where they stood. He even tried to mimic their poses but found that he couldn't. How they were standing like that, he would not understand. Their bodies were made differently. Their tails, although it seemed impossible, were stronger than those of an undine.

With broad, flat chests, they looked very similar to the People of Water. But there were no gills marking their ribs, only the dotting of scales that disappeared into their tails. Those scales looked different from the ones on their tails as well. Almost as though they wore armor. When one turned, he could see that the scales went up their spines, protecting the area there that was susceptible to attack. He couldn't tell if that was hair or a snake hood on top of their heads. The image was too small.

They seemed to converse, although they mostly spoke with their hands. The gestures were almost familiar in a way, as though if he stared long enough he could understand what they were saying.

None of it mattered. He would not tell the humans about the creatures that lived Above, nor was he interested in it pausing his plans. The humans would leave the water. He would foist them upon this new species, who had yet to see them.

They were intricately linked, after all. These creatures might not understand how linked they were just yet, but they were. The snake-like beings had come from the humans, and it seemed to him that the humans were more likely to be their problem than his.

"Proteus?" Ellie asked, her voice soft with questions.

He turned to her, softening his expression as he knew he had been staring at the screens as though he wanted to break them. "What is it, Sisu?"

She pointed at the screen he'd been glaring at. "I don't think they're going to let us go into their world. We're going to have to tell someone. To talk to them. To let them know that maybe... maybe they can learn from us just as we learned from the undine."

"Do you remember what you read in that book?" he asked. "The journal from the scientist?"

"I know they were trying to splice human and animal genetics so they could create life. Obviously, they succeeded."

"But the journals never said they did. You read it to me. You said that all they created were more monsters. And that as far as those geneticists were concerned, none of the species they created retained human thought. They were creating beasts, not men. What makes you think those creatures are even capable of speech?"

He lied.

To her.

Something dark and ugly twisted in his chest because she didn't deserve that. Ellie had given him everything and more. She had always worked with him, not against him. Never once had she betrayed his trust or who she was. She had proven time and time again that she was valuable in his plans. In his life.

Lying to her about this betrayed the trust they had been building. And he knew it. She did too.

She stared at him with those pretty, pretty eyes, and he knew that she recognized what he was doing. Maybe she had seen the same thing he'd seen. Maybe she could tell that they were conversing with their hands as well. But all she could do was stare at him. Those pretty eyes boring into his soul as they willed him to admit that he knew more than what he was telling her.

But he couldn't. Not to her. Not to anyone. This plan had to go exactly as he wanted it to go.

Those creatures in the sands were an issue. They were a wrinkle in his carefully cultivated blueprint, which he had spent the latter part of two hundred years figuring out. He was the only one who knew how to save this planet, and he was damn well going to do it.

Even if that meant he had to lie to her.

That truth sat in his stomach, uncomfortable and bubbling as though he had eaten too much rotting meat. Gruffly, he reached out a hand for her to take. "We have to get going," he said. "I apologize, Sisu. It's a hard life being bound to me."

"Bound?" she said with a soft smile, but it was one that didn't reach her eyes. "Am I bound to you, Proteus?"

He thought so. He willed it to be so. She was the only one he would admit to wanting to keep alive, and he fully intended for her to be by his side until the day he had to let her go.

Solemnly nodding, he drew her against his chest and pressed her to his hearts. There, at least, he knew she was alive. He could keep her with him, even if he was a lying, devious fool.

He made sure her mask was on tightly before drawing her into the water. Proteus still didn't trust the breathing apparatus, so he took a moment at the surface, skimming below it, to make sure that she could breathe.

Apparently, she shared the same concern. It was almost as though she were holding her breath before she finally forced an inhalation. When it worked, she gave him a thumbs up, and he sank deeper into the waves.

They headed back toward the facility where the others waited for them. He knew this was one of the last moments they had alone together, and he refused to waste it. Not when the awkward silence between them made him feel even worse for what he had done. She knew. He knew. And he wanted to fix what he could.

"Do you know why I call you Sisu?" he asked quietly, his voice a low murmur as he propelled them through the water.

The kraken let out a low moan behind them, and he could hear the sounds of an old ship shifting underneath its weight. The great beast sounded as if it was warning him not to give so much away. That she didn't deserve to know the nickname he had given her so early.

"I don't."

"Names like this are an old tradition among the People of Water. They have given names, with a meaning that is always the hope for the child. But then, those who know them, really know them, give them another name. It is that name they are called by only those who..." He almost said those who loved them.

Because if he was even capable of the emotion, that was how he felt about her.

She had proven to be a light in his darkness, and he wasn't sure how to verbalize that. He wanted to tell her that he did, indeed, love her. That his broken, torn apart soul had seen something in her that made him want to stay a little longer.

It wasn't a feeling he was used to. Or a feeling that he wanted to admit just yet.

So instead, he shook his head to clear the thoughts away and continued speaking. "Sisu is a word for someone who endures. It's quiet strength, grace under pressure, a determination to continue no matter how hard it gets. It is what I saw in you from that very first moment when you looked up at me after I had destroyed your arm, and you told me you had survived worse. You are all of these things and more, Ellie. Far more than you give yourself credit for."

She sucked in a long breath, and bubbles obscured his vision. For a moment, he thought he had insulted her, but then she reached up and pressed her hands to either side of his face.

Proteus allowed her to turn in his arms, so that they were looking each other in the eyes as she said, "You have the ability to be so sweet. As crushing as you can be, as horrible and tempestuous and maddening, you somehow reach inside my soul and piece back together all the things you break. I don't know how you do that."

He drew her closer so he could press their foreheads together. "Because I desperately wish to keep you," he whispered. "The thought of losing you is almost..."

Proteus didn't know how to verbalize it. He was a fool. An idiot. She needed to hear the words out of his mouth, and he needed to tell her how she turned all of his world to starlight.

Swallowing hard, he tried to do his best. "When I was a young boy, first created, first learning how to swim in this seemingly unending sea, I remember being in a certain area of the ocean for a while. It was where it was safe to swim, but I snuck out. In the middle of the night, I ended up in the middle of a storm-worn sea. But there was a small area of calm. So small that the currents still plucked at my tail, but in that center, there was nothing but stillness. That is how I feel when you are with me, Sisu. I can only see you and the knowledge that we will continue forward. No matter what."

Bubbles erupted again, but this time they surrounded his face and hers. He could feel them tickling the underside of his chin, almost making him laugh with the sheer joy of it all.

Her in his arms. The sea finally bent to his will. His plan nearly perfect.

All of this would take time. He knew that. But he could live for centuries more to make sure that the humans did exactly what he wanted them to do. No matter what, he would keep her, he realized. She would stay with him, and together... Together they would do whatever they wanted. They would rule this sea, and they would make everything theirs. For good.

But when had anything good ever happened to him?

Proteus felt the first strike against his side with a strange sense of déjà vu. There was a spot of pain, delayed as it was because his mind raced to keep up with what had happened. Another in his tail. Then a third. A fourth.

Blood bloomed in the water. He had forgotten that his blood even looked like that. A strange crimson mix of red and black, a combination of what should not be. He stared at the plumes that obscured his vision of her and felt his hearts racing.

His first thought was fear that she had gotten hurt. He held her a little harder, hearing her soft sound of pain as he crushed her against him a little too tightly.

"Are you hurt?" he asked, his tone frantic. "Ellie!"

But then something hit his arms as well. Two somethings that were stronger than he could fight against. Something was in the water. Something that turned his mind a little foggy, and he couldn't quite focus on what needed to be done.

It was a mistake to loosen his grip on her. But she made that soft sound again, that sound of pain as though he was hurting her, and he'd promised that he would stop doing that.

The moment his arms relaxed even slightly, she was ripped away from him. More bubbles exploded out of her, and he swore he heard her scream. It enraged him.

Fire burned in his chest with a fury that his attackers could never have anticipated. Screaming a feral roar, he wrenched an arm out of the grip of one and reached for whatever had pierced through his tail.

His hand came away with a harpoon coated in some kind of venom. The shimmering liquid glimmered in the meager light of the sea. A crack of thunder rumbled overhead, lightning illuminating the entire scene before him.

The blood that bloomed around him had hidden the undine that surrounded him. In the stark white light, he could see their forms. Massive males, each of them. Scarred from years of battle, one with a metallic arm that was still holding onto Proteus's.

And in the distance, another undine had an arm wrapped around Ellie's waist as she struggled to get free of them.

Again he roared, but the poison worked fast. Suddenly he wasn't here. He was back in time when the undine had imprisoned him, and when he had been so certain that they would never betray him.

He would get them to work with the humans. Their future wouldn't be one of ruination and despair.

But then the undine had attacked. They'd used the same poison, he remembered. The cold sensation of death crept up his tail the same way it had then. The whispering words of the ancients in his ear, screaming at him to struggle, to fight, to not let them destroy all that he had worked on for so many years.

His free arm was grabbed again. A purple and white face, one with markings of black tears down his cheeks, appeared through the blood.

Calmly, the depthstrider grabbed onto the harpoon in his hand and plunged it back into his tail. "Only for a while," the depthstrider said. "Not forever this time."

But he was already sinking. Sinking deeper and deeper into the cold sea that always welcomed him with her embrace. She whispered in his ear that she would keep him safe, but he burned with hate. The undine had betrayed him again.

"Don't you know?" he said through numb lips. "Killing your gods never lasts long."

"We're not killing you," the one missing an arm snarled. "We're just getting you out of the way until we get the truth."

What truth? He'd told them everything. He'd given them every single thing they could hope for, and yet they were still betraying him. Still killing him. Still stripping away all that made him who he was.

"Here is good," the depthstrider said. "It'll take him a while to wake up, and by then, we'll be gone."

The one missing an arm looked down at him, and the others released their hold. He was drifting, floating above an abyss, glaring into the eyes of this male who held him by one arm.

The red undine allowed him to dangle for a while, and then said, "He'll hunt us to the ends of the sea to get her back. It's what I would do, after all."

Then he dropped Proteus into the void.

Chapter 32

Ellie fought as hard as she could, but there was no point in doing so. The undine who had his arm around her waist wasn't going to let her get away, and she knew damn well it wasn't possible for her to fight him. Still, it made her feel a little better to struggle against his grip. She kicked out at him, trying to catch him in the sensitive parts of his tail. And when that didn't work, she jammed her elbows back toward his gills.

Unfortunately, all that did was get a grunt out of him.

She stared helplessly back at Proteus, seeing the others dragging him away from her. These were undine she recognized. The red one had been at the facility. She remembered him so well because he had been missing an arm at the time.

No longer. That metal arm was stronger than any flesh could be. He dragged Proteus through the water with an ease that shouldn't have been possible.

"Where are you taking me?" she asked, her eyes locked on the group that was still swimming far away from her.

"Back where we are from," the undine finally said. And that was the last thing he said for the rest of the journey.

Halfway through it, he paused. It was then that she realized he had a pouch over his shoulder. He rummaged through it, holding her by the back of her wetsuit as though she weighed absolutely nothing. She hung limp over the abyss, praying to any god that would listen that he wouldn't drop her and assume she could swim.

Thankfully, he did not do that. But he did pull a fistful of what looked like eels out of the bag and started rubbing them all up and down her body. Ellie shrieked, struggling once more as he mashed the eels against her suit and essentially turned them into pulverized meat.

"What are you doing?" she yelled, twisting and turning because at least that felt like she was trying to get away from him.

He didn't reply. Instead, the big blue beast flipped her over in his grip so he was holding her by the ankle. Upside down now, she was glad to have the face mask to breathe because she was certain she would have gotten saltwater all up her nose, and that certainly would have made her drown.

Eventually, she gave up hope of struggling and just hung there. Allowing him to rub the mashed up eels all over her body before he nodded. "Good enough."

And then he dropped her.

She tried to swim. She really did. She kicked her feet and her arms desperately, trying to do the same movements she had seen countless people do in her life, but none of it got her anywhere. Maybe, for a few moments, she floated. She could feel that something had changed, but then there was a tug of the current against her body and she was sinking once more.

At least, until a new arm wrapped around her waist and hauled her through the water.

With a shocked sound, she looked down to see a yellow arm around her this time. She looked at the undine with wide eyes, trying to understand what was happening to her and why she was being passed off to yet another captor.

"The scent will make it harder for him to track you," he said. This one grinned as if this entire situation was one big adventure that he was just happy to be part of. "And now Arges will head off to lead him in the other direction. Do you know how hard it was to get him to agree to be the bait? He likes to control everything, but he's the third biggest after Fortis and Daios. And obviously they had to be the ones to get Proteus put down in the sea."

She made a choked sound at the last bit. Put down? Had they killed him?

This undine looked her over and rolled his eyes. "Not like he's dead. He's a god. I don't think anything can kill him, and if it can, it's not going to be a little pufferfish poison. Or a lot, as it was. Took us weeks to get that much, you know."

The breath she'd sucked in all came rushing out as one. At least this one seemed a little more inclined to speak with her.

"Where are we going?"

"Home," he replied. "You're going to meet the girls, and I'm just going to drop you off. Don't worry, not much longer now."

Not much longer felt like ages passed. There was nothing in the sea he dragged her through. No creatures, no light, just the never ending darkness that he apparently knew how to get through. Until the water turned lighter blue, and then a city appeared in front of her.

It wasn't much of a city, she'd admit. But there were many domed buildings. She counted at least thirty as they swam by. Not to mention the homes of the undines that were... well, more than she'd expected.

At first, all Ellie noticed were the spiraling stones that marked the sand far below them. But then there were things that looked like corals, dead corals now that she had seen live ones, but they were definitely coral built upon each other. Making it so that the homes were twisting tunnels. Now that she'd seen one, it was easier to pick them out. Some of them even had undine in them.

One she could see a huge tail hanging out of it, and a plume of dust then erupted around the tail as though they were digging something out inside. From another, a small child darted out while his mother rushed after him.

There was a riot of color here. All the undine turned the blue and yellow sea into rainbows. It was beautiful, remarkable, and, honestly, like something out of a fairytale. She might have been more impressed if she hadn't been kidnapped.

The yellow undine brought her to a central location and deposited her outside. Then he gestured for her to go up into what was very clearly a moon pool above their heads. "Go on."

Ellie sank down onto the sand and stared up. With a kick of her legs, she tried. But the water didn't work with her and no matter how hard she propelled herself, she sank right back to where she started.

"I'm sorry," she whispered, trying again. "I'm sorry, I'm really trying."

Clawed hands grabbed onto her waist. And instead of the judgement she had expected, his expression remained soft. "I didn't know you couldn't swim. You could have asked, you know."

With a gentle push, he brought her up to the surface and held onto her waist until she'd grabbed onto the edge. Only then did she feel his hands leave her sides and then the water movement of him darting off somewhere else. Likely to keep Proteus off the scent of this place.

More hands grabbed onto her. This time, though, they were hands that were decidedly more human.

"Finally," the grunted words were angry as she was pulled out of the water and left on the floor unceremoniously. "Took them long enough. Now the clock starts ticking."

"Alexia." The scolding tones were from another person, but Ellie was so caught up trying to get the damn rebreather off her face, she couldn't hazard a guess at who spoke. "Really. You could be a little more delicate about it."

"I have never been accused of being delicate."

"You could give it a try. You catch more bees with honey."

"Bees have been extinct for years, Anya."

Finally, Ellie got the rebreather off and then ripped off her fogging goggles as well. She tore a good chunk of her hair out with the movement, and that left her wincing until she could finally see who surrounded her. The people who were revealed surprised her though.

It was just two women. Two women she definitely recognized.

"You?" she said, confused. "But... but you were the ones who sent people to the facility to work with us."

Alexia crouched down in front of her, all bulging muscles that made Ellie want to cower back in fear. She wore a loose fitting white shirt that revealed even more powerful pectoral muscles, and pants that highlighted just how thick her thighs were. "And you've been lying to us."

The air was all sucked out of her lungs. She had no idea what to say to that because yes, she had. She'd been lying a lot, and so had Proteus, and she wasn't sure what lie they were talking about.

But now was the time when she could finally come clean. She could tell them everything, just like she believed they should have from the very beginning. Doing so would make Proteus angry with her, though.

"Lying about what?" Ellie tried, but she could hear how bad the words were on her tongue.

Anya sighed, and that was when Ellie looked over at the pretty blonde woman. She wore a white dress with pretty lace on the edges. The short sleeves showed off her arms and the pearls that dripped all along her wrists. There was even a pearl bracelet around one of her legs. She had a droid attached to her face, with a screen over one eye. But the expression on her face was one of disappointment.

They knew. Of course they knew.

Alexia sighed and reached out a big hand for her to take. "Come on, Ellie. Get up. We'll show you what we've discovered in that facility of yours, and you can tell me exactly what you think we need to know."

She didn't want to do this. But Ellie didn't think she had a choice in the matter.

Grabbing Alexia's hand, she allowed the big woman to help her up and followed them into a separate room. This dome was a marvel. It was hard for her not to stare at the arching metal and the huge glass panels that held the sea at bay. They were surprisingly close to the surface here. Close enough that she could see a storm leaving as they walked through a long tunnel toward another room.

Ellie reached out and touched the glass where kelp waved on the other side. It was so clear it felt like she could reach out and touch the seagrass.

The other room seemed to be a meeting area of sorts. Most of the furniture had clearly been repaired in some way. But everything in the sea had to have been waterlogged at some point. Some of the seats were ones she recognized from Tau. The clean, modern aesthetic was mashed together with what looked like utilitarian pieces, perhaps from Beta, and then others that looked like they had been handmade here.

Ellie took a seat on one of the chairs from Tau and waited.

Alexia and Anya sat down as well, both of them looking a little uncomfortable. It was Anya who finally spoke, thankfully.

"The information we have discovered at your facility is all very helpful. We believe that Proteus is right. We should be able to fix what has been broken and perhaps move some people Above. At least into that facility, and if we can discover others, then that will allow us to move even more people onto the land. However." Anya paused and took a deep breath. "It's him that concerns us. That's why we brought you here."

"Rather dramatically," Ellie replied, surprising herself. She hadn't thought she had it in her to talk back like that.

Anya smiled. "Very dramatically, one might argue. We knew Proteus wouldn't allow you to come here if we asked him, not without his supervision. And you seem to be the person who knows the most. A good amount of information in that facility is categorized as classified, and it is locked behind walls that very few are able to get past. Certainly not someone we have here. That concerned us."

"It's just information from separate research done at the facility," she tried to lie.

"Information that your droid has functions placed to hide. That makes us think it's not unrelated research." Anya leaned forward, bracing her elbows on her knees. "Proteus is clearly hiding something from us. Considering the old legends about him, we have good reason for our concern. I think you understand that. He wants us out of the sea as fast as possible, but we want to limit the deaths along the way. So you are here to tell us the truth."

A part of her didn't want to tell them anything about Proteus.

Another part of her wanted to tell them everything. Anya was saying what Ellie had wanted to hear Proteus tell her. That he wanted to minimize death. That he would take her concerns seriously about the creatures who were already living Above.

She opened her mouth and then snapped it shut. "I don't think I should tell you anything without Proteus."

"I told you," Alexia grumbled. "There is a reintegration program for a reason. The clones need support. They need therapy. They need to be reassured regularly that they can go against whatever they were trained if they were woken up. Clearly Ellie had been used, perhaps even abused, and she will not be interested in helping us unless Proteus tells her to do so."

A spark of anger burned in her chest. "I told him to talk to you all! I told him he should tell you everything, and he said he would respect that."

Alexia's laser sharp gaze turned to her. "Prove me wrong, then. Prove that you have a mind of your own. If you want to tell us, if you think we need to know, then you should do so. Regardless of what Proteus might want."

"I don't want to anger him either," Ellie whispered. "He's done so much for me."

It was more than just that, though. They didn't understand the connection that had bloomed between them. Seeing him dragged away from her, it didn't make her want to trust these people.

It made her angry.

So angry that she wanted to lie to them. She wanted to go along with Proteus's plan and allow the humans to return Above without realizing there were creatures already there. Not to tell them that most of the facilities were ruins, and to let them find out on their own that the scientists who had been left there were experimenting on more than just animals, but people too.

But deep down, that wasn't who Ellie was. She wasn't the person who could allow innocent people to walk into the unknown without giving them all the protection she could.

She was a good person. She would do the right thing, even if it made her angry to give these people the truth when they had done nothing to earn it.

Opening her mouth, she started at the beginning. "I don't think Proteus ever wanted me, really. He said the sea led him to my pod, but I think it was just luck."

The whole story came out. How she'd woken in that other facility, with Pilot and Proteus looming over her. How she'd been trained for her entire life to be useful, to seek out a master, and that she'd thought she'd been helping. But the more she helped with his plan, the more she realized he would do anything to get the humans out of the sea, and that he didn't care about the threats to them along the way. He was rushing through everything.

And then she told them about what she had read in that woman's journal. In her Original's journal. What she had seen in the sands with the cameras that Proteus hadn't been telling any of them about. And how nervous it all made her.

She purged the story from her soul, knowing that he would be so, so angry at her.

Chapter 33

Ellie hadn't thought that telling the truth would hurt so much. She'd tried her best to tell the story as accurately as she could remember it, but at the end she still felt like she had done something irreparably wrong.

It didn't matter that Anya thanked her profusely. The words, "You might have saved a lot of people, Ellie. Thank you for telling us," was a small consolation prize for what she knew Proteus would say.

She had gone against everything that he had told her to do. It was a direct order. He'd made it very clear that he didn't want any of the humans to know about the cameras or the creatures. He hadn't even wanted them to know what the real reason for the facility was. He wanted them out of the sea, and any lie they had to tell to get that to happen, he was happy to tell.

Had she ruined everything? Their time in that golden temple made her feel like they had built something special between the two of them. There might have been a future if she hadn't screwed up by telling the humans what he hadn't wanted them to know.

Anya had taken notes. It wasn't like Ellie could say she'd made it all up. She'd told them too much in far too much detail.

Alexia stood, cracking her neck from side to side before jerking a hand toward another exit from the room. "Come on, Ellie."

"Wait," Anya said, tapping her pen on the tablet she held in her hand. "I have a few questions. While she's here, we might be able to get through a couple of the encryptions that have been stopping us from accessing more documents. If you don't mind, Ellie, could you perhaps help us with—"

"No." The harsh snap of Alexia's voice was firm, and it was very clear she would not accept any arguments. "Ellie is going to rest. We have a day or two before Proteus finds us here, and the others are preparing for that. She needs to sleep."

Without even looking at the other woman, Alexia grabbed Ellie's arm and hauled her out of the room. They headed down another glass hallway, this one decorated with silver fish that darted over the top and then disappeared on the other side. Ellie tried to focus on those, but all she could think about was how her guts felt like they were twisted inside of her.

She'd done something terribly wrong. And there wasn't any chance for her to crawl her way out of that. Proteus would never speak to her again.

Humans thought of her as a monster. That had been clear with the others working in the facility. They didn't even want to be around her. So where did that leave Ellie?

The one person who had treated her like a person would be so angry with her, she wouldn't be surprised if he just ate her and was done with it. If he spared her life, he wasn't going to stick around and talk to her. Which meant Pilot would leave with him.

Then she was stuck here. With people who thought she was little more than a droid herself. No one wanted to be her friend. No one talked to her. They'd just order her around, and she'd be forced back into the same role she'd been in before.

Doll.

Not even real.

Tears burned in her eyes as Alexia brought her to a room that was furnished with a pretty bed. It had a lovely quilt on top of it, clearly made with loving hands. The amount of colors and textures and patterns on it were obviously not even meant to go together. They were only there to be riotous and colorful. There was a workbench in the corner with all kinds of gears and scraps of metal, and then paintings on the wall. All kinds of paintings of undine, the sea, fish, and a sky that the artist had likely never seen before.

"You can sleep here," Alexia said. "I doubt Mira is coming home anytime soon."

In a daze, she sat down on the edge of the bed and tried to ground herself. The quilt was soft underneath her fingers, at least. It felt good to rub her fingers over the edges.

Her heart was thundering so hard in her chest. Every pound sounded like Proteus's voice, telling her not to say a word to the humans. She should try to control her breathing. Or at least try to drink some water. But every time she even tried to count her breaths, all she could think of was one word that kept repeating over and over in her head.

Betrayal. Betrayal. Betrayal.

Alexia pressed a button on the wall. A door hissed closed, leaving the two of them trapped inside the room together.

Ellie stared up at her, wondering if maybe now was the time that she was going to die. After all, she'd told them everything she knew. Her usefulness was entirely and utterly gone. She had no reason to be kept alive in the plan moving forward.

But Alexia leaned against the wall and crossed her arms over her chest. "What is going through that head? I can see your thoughts running over your face."

"It's all right. You don't have to ask me if I'm okay."

"I'm not asking if you're okay. I'm telling you to speak to me. Get through all those thoughts. You have to talk them out, or they're going to fester." She lifted a hand and waggled her fingers. "Come on."

That anger bubbled in Ellie's chest again. She didn't owe this woman anything. She didn't want to tell Alexia all of her deepest and darkest secrets.

An ugly side of her soul awakened, and the words that came out were cutting and harmful. "You don't have to take care of me just because I look like an Original. I'm not one of them."

"Why would I want to care for an Original?"

"I know what you are." Ellie couldn't stop herself. The venom kept pouring out of her mouth. "You were designed to take care of people like me. But I don't need you to take care of me."

"Maybe that is part of why I feel the way I do about the clones, or maybe it's because I'm just like you." Alexia took a few steps into the room, taking up so much space with the sheer size of her body. "Did that ever occur to you? Neither of us is the original of ourselves. I am the seventh generation of Alexia, and there was an eighth that I killed myself. So when I knew the clones were going to be woken in the other cities, I knew I had to take care of them. Because I remember what it was like. Waking up out of that tank, hitting the cold floor, no one caring in the slightest that I was terrified and alone."

Ellie shuddered. The same memories ran deep in her own mind. She hated them. Hated what had been done to all of them.

Alexia crouched in front of her, her knees on the well worn rug. "You feel like you betrayed him. Is that it?"

Miserable, she nodded. It wasn't the same as admitting it. Not really. Not if she didn't say the words.

"You didn't. You're allowed to have your own thoughts, and you looked at the situation with critical eyes. No one can say you didn't think about what you were telling us. Do you know how few people would even remember that much detail?" Alexia slowly reached forward.

Ellie watched the woman's hand approaching hers and had the thought that she should stop her. She shouldn't be manipulated by the thought of a calming touch, but she was. She very much was.

She wanted to know what it was like to have a friend. A friend who wasn't a droid. A friend who could grab her hand and tell her that everything was going to be all right.

Blowing out a breath, she met Alexia and laced their fingers together. They stayed like that for a little while. Ellie felt as though she was clinging onto this monolith of a woman who had certainly never been afraid in her entire life.

"You did the right thing," Alexia said. "No matter how hard it felt like it was to do. Creatures like him... If I've learned anything about the people who live underneath the water, it's that they have a hard time seeing past what they want. He sees a future for his people, and I don't think he's wrong about it. He knows how much destruction humanity has brought. He has seen what we can do, and if he's anything like Fortis, then he has seen what we will do. And he wants to stop it."

"But what if he's right?" Ellie whispered. "What if he was correct and the only way to bring that future to fruition is by not letting any of us know what is to come? Or what is out there?"

"We will all still see the sun." The firm statement echoed throughout the room like a vow. "Some humans might stay below the waves, but I'll be honest. Things are getting tighter. Food. Space. All of it is getting harder and harder for the rest of us. That's why we were so suspicious when Proteus showed up. We need this more than you or he will ever understand."

And maybe that was a blessing in disguise. It sounded like the humans in the cities didn't have a choice. They had to move out, or overpopulation would kill them all.

"How much time do you all have?" she asked.

"Another generation," Alexia replied. "Maybe. Now that there are only two cities surviving, and one of them is mostly still a prison city, there isn't a lot of room. Beta wasn't big to begin with. We can house some people here, but not as many as we'd like. Space is a luxury that none of us have when we can't breathe in water."

Ellie rolled it over in her mind. She realized two things at once.

Proteus was wrong.

And humanity had no choice but to go Above.

She nodded a few times, her thoughts telling the story that neither side had told each other. Proteus wanted them gone, with good reason, so he hadn't told them the entire truth. But Alexia and her people had been desperate. So they hadn't told him that they needed this to be true, because if they did, then maybe he would take this as an opportunity to punish them.

All of it was so jumbled and such a mess. But she also wasn't confident that either side would tell each other the truth if they were put in the same room together. So much animosity ran between them that it would be hard for either side to trust the other.

Scratching the back of her neck, she said, "I see there are a lot of problems. We all need each other, though."

"Yes, we do." Alexia nodded towards the bed. "Why don't you lie down?"

"I'd like to keep talking, if we could."

Something happened in Alexia's eyes. An emotion that Ellie couldn't name, but one that softened the hard woman's expression. It was like a mother realizing that a child of hers finally wanted to speak with her again.

Alexia braced a hand on the floor and then lowered herself onto it. She pressed her back against the bedframe, staring at the door as though keeping watch over Ellie. "I can keep talking to you. But why don't you lie down, still? There's going to be a lot more questions tomorrow, and we'd like to get as much information as we can before Proteus gets here. I'm sure he's going to take you away from us again."

"He might not." She lay down on the surprisingly comfortable bed, dragging the pillow closer to her. That also was so soft it was like she was lying on a cloud. "He can be reasonable."

"None of them are particularly reasonable when it comes to their mates," Alexia said with a snort. "And he's got his sights set on you."

"He just likes me."

"Does he, now? What does a sea god like about a clone?"

Ellie took her time thinking over the answer. For some reason, she wanted to tell Alexia the right story. "Well, for one, he said that he likes how smart I am."

"That's a good reason to like a person."

"Oh, and he thinks that I'm very resilient." She was quite proud of that. "He calls me Sisu. He said that's because I show grace under adversity."

"It's a good name," Alexia said. "Fortis gifted me Virago. It means a war-like woman."

Ellie wrinkled her nose. "I'm not sure that's a compliment."

"For me? It absolutely is." Alexia chuckled, and even that sound had so much power in it that it was hard to deny that the name fit her. "Now, what else do you want to talk about? I can tell you everything I know about the People of Water, but I don't think the man you've got wrapped around your finger is exactly that."

"He's not. Not really." Then common sense stopped her tongue. "I'm not sure we should keep talking about him. Can you tell me more about the cities?"

She'd say too much, and then Proteus would really be angry at her. If she blurted out all of his secrets or weaknesses, then he'd likely bring her right back to that kraken and tell it that he'd brought the creature a tiny snack.

Alexia did something with her hands, and suddenly the lights dimmed in the room. One moment they were on and the next, it was only the meager light from the blue sea around them. It turned the entire room into a secret place, as though everything they said wasn't real, anyway.

Dreamy already, Ellie felt her eyes closing as Alexia spoke about Beta.

She said that the remaining city was still impressive. It was where most of the engineers had lived, but no one from Tau other than the clones had survived. There were quite a few refugees from Alpha. Apparently, that city had also been destroyed.

She drifted off to sleep thinking about all these different people smashed together in a city that wasn't built for them. People who wore pretty dresses and jewels dripping down their arms, mingling with those who were soot covered and still working hard to keep a city running while it was slowly wheezing. And then clones. People like her. Trying to pass themselves off as twins, when they knew they were so much more than that. They were people who had been forgotten. People who were hoping for another chance at life.

Sleep claimed her as Alexia started telling her about Tau. How she had grown up there too, and that there had been beauty in the cold metal.

Just as much as there had been cruelty.

Chapter 34

She woke hours later, in the darkest part of the night, uncertain of where she was. A strange clicking sound had woken her. Something that she knew wasn't the quiet sounds of Alexia, who had fallen asleep next to the bed.

Ellie wasn't a very deep sleeper. She was always waking up at some sound, from shifts in Proteus's breathing, to a rumble of thunder overhead. But then she heard the sound again, and she knew it wasn't a natural noise in this room. The slight tapping was too rhythmic.

Finally, rolling onto her back after scanning the entire room for anything out of the ordinary, she almost screamed when she saw the crab-like creature on the glass above her.

Clapping her hands over her mouth, she froze as she waited for Alexia to wake up. But maybe the big woman could use some rest too, because she only shifted a bit before falling back into a deep slumber. Ellie waited for her breathing to even out before she took her hands off her mouth and glared up at Pilot.

The little droid pointed with a leg, clearly indicating for Ellie to leave the room.

The door was loud, though. The hissing sound was bound to wake someone up. She gestured with her hands, trying to show that it was a manual door that would be loud. Again, Pilot pointed at it. This time, he did so with a little more sass than was necessary.

Grumbling under her breath, she eased out of the bed and stepped over Alexia. The other woman didn't wake up, not even when she pressed the button and the door hissed open. Maybe it wasn't as loud as she remembered, but it still made her flinch and freeze.

Alexia snorted in her sleep and threw an arm over her eyes. Clearly, the light from the hallway was too bright.

A softness burned in Ellie's chest. In another life, perhaps, she would have met Alexia under very different circumstances. They might have spoken more regularly, and maybe even Alexia would have helped Ellie not be such a people pleaser. They'd have become fast friends. She was certain of that.

But maybe every clone felt that way when they met the giant of a woman.

More taps sounded from above her head as Pilot led her somewhere in this labyrinth of a domed city. She followed along from hallway to hallway, tip toeing through what looked like a kitchen, then into a garden that was so lush it was almost mind boggling to see. Ellie got a little distracted in there before Pilot led her into a workshop.

This was the messiest place she'd seen in this small city thus far. Scraps of metal, large and small, were littered all over the floor. There were bolts and hammers, tools strewn about in a way that she was certain wasn't smart to store that way.

But she could also see there was a moon pool in this room. Hopefully, this wouldn't wake anyone up.

Ellie walked over to the button and hit it, wincing as the grinding sound of metal filled the room. No one shouted, and no one came running in, so she assumed that meant the bedrooms were far away from this area. Which made sense, considering how much noise was likely generated in this room.

Pilot came in from the bottom, shaking himself off and letting out a disgruntled noise. "Do you know how long it took me to get here?"

"Really not that long. Considering I've only been here for a day." She leaned against the wall, crossing her arms over her chest and looking him over. "Why are you here?"

"Because you've been kidnapped!" He flicked a leg at her. "You are ungrateful to be saved."

"How did you even know I'd be here?"

She wouldn't put it past the droid to know what everyone in the sea was doing. He conferred with the drones that had been all over the ocean floor, throughout the waves, and even the ones that had ventured out onto the land. Still, his arrival was rather perfect.

"The humans were all talking about it as soon as you left," Pilot replied. He clambered over one of the metal pieces near her, seemingly to get enough height to look her over. "They must have believed I was a droid that could only follow orders. They packed up almost as soon as you were gone. Took everything they could in the facility, and quite a few pieces of equipment they had been fixing. Thieves."

She tried very hard not to laugh at that. "Well, they did fix them."

"That doesn't give them the right to raid Sanctuary for anything useful! It all needs to stay there, so we have a centralized location to control the land inhabitants. That was always the plan, and Proteus is always right." Grumbling under his breath, Pilot reached out a single leg and gently moved a strand of her hair to the side.

He was looking at her neck, she realized. The droid even let out a little beam of light to scan her from head to toe, making sure that she wasn't injured. "They haven't harmed you, I see."

"I'm fine, Pilot."

"You never know what humans are going to do. They experiment on everything they can get their hands on. And you are a very interesting specimen, Miss Ellie."

Tears burned in her eyes. "I think that might be the nicest thing you've ever said to me, Pilot."

"Don't get emotional. Come on now. I can breathe for you, and there's probably enough oxygen to get us on land. From there, I can guide you back to the facility."

"Land?" Ellie repeated. "I can't travel on land."

"Sure, you can. It won't be entirely safe, but I can keep breathing for you, and there are plenty of caves. If we can keep to those, then we should be able to survive. You might not get back in one piece, but you'll get back. No time to waste."

Droids. They didn't understand that her parts weren't as replaceable as his. Although she supposed she'd already replaced an arm. The experience might have confused him a little.

She took a step back from Pilot, readying herself to prepare him for the fact that she couldn't leave, but another voice interrupted before she could.

"Droid," Alexia said, her tall shadow entering the room long before she did. "She'll be staying here. Just what kind of protocol did they install in you to be able to travel this far?"

"Uh..." A gear whirred in Pilot's body. "I'll be taking the girl."

"No, you will both stay here, and you will submit to a full inspection." Alexia's arms were crossed as she paused in the doorway.

"What kind of droid even are you?"

Something popped out of Pilot. A string, Ellie realized, until it crackled in the air with a sound of electricity so loud that it made her cover her ears. Not a string, then. A weapon. Had Pilot had that all along?

It almost reached Alexia, but the big woman stepped aside before it could latch onto her and likely kill her with the amount of power surging through that thing. In one smooth movement, the old guard stooped down, grabbed a metal scrap that looked about the size of a plate, and flung it at Pilot.

The droid wasn't meant for battle. It slammed into him and pinned him to the wall. His legs gave one more angry twitch before it looked like all his electronics turned off.

"Pilot!" she gasped, running to the wall and trying to yank the metal out of it. But she couldn't. She wasn't strong enough to pull it out of him, and he was just hanging there. Limp.

"He's fine," Alexia said. "It takes a lot more than that to kill a droid. I'll have Mira take a look at him, or Ace, I suppose. She's off in Beta right now, but I'm sure Maketes would take any excuse to go get her and bring her back here. He hates it when she's gone for too long."

Ellie whirled around, balling her hands into fists. "You killed him."

"I told you, he's going to be fine."

"He was my friend."

Alexia's expression softened. There it was again, that one emotion that Ellie hadn't been able to name. But this time she could tell it was pity.

And that made her stomach churn. She lifted a hand, pointing at the other woman. "Don't look at me like that. He was a friend."

"Droids are complicated. I'm sure he considers you a friend too, but they aren't like people. Killing them requires a lot more effort than a metal scrap through him. Wires can be replaced. Hard drives are a bit trickier, but even those can be recovered. He's going to be fine, Ellie. But we can't have him taking you out of here before Proteus returns. That sea god will kill us all if you aren't here, and we don't know where you are."

The doors opened behind Alexia, and two other droids came in. One looked like a little box on wheels. The other, a strange spider-like creation with a glass body. She thought the latter might have been the one attached to Anya's head. The two of them froze, and then eyes popped out of the top of the box.

"Ah, perfect," Alexia said. "Byte and Bitsy will take care of him. In the meantime, will you come with me? We just got word that Proteus has already woken up. Looks like you aren't going to be helping us as much as we hoped, but we were wondering if you wouldn't mind bypassing the firewalls and getting us into the mainframe of Sanctuary? That way, we can look over the rest of the experimental documentation. Yeah?"

Her mind was spinning. Too many details all flew at her at the same time. Proteus was coming? She was thrilled to hear that. He was alive, and she could breathe a little easier. But Pilot was right there, and the droids were clearly doing something to pull his remains from behind the metal stuck in the wall. And they wanted her to do even more, when Alexia had killed her best friend.

But she had been so kind last night. The two of them had talked about so many things, and Alexia had seemed like she could be a friend as well.

Overwhelmed, she allowed herself to be led from the room into another. There were more people now. A man with glasses, a woman with a shaved head, and a few others she recognized who had been working at the facility. There were a lot of them, and none of them even looked at her as Alexia sat her down and put a tablet in her hands.

"Here," Alexia said, leaning over her and taking up all the oxygen in the room. "This is the coding all our best are struggling with. It looks like someone designed it in Tau, and unfortunately, we don't have a lot of great minds left from Tau. Just you. Now we can break through this. There are many people here with a lot of knowledge. But it sure would be a lot faster if you could do it for us."

She was breathing too hard. Even Ellie could hear her breath as though it were sawing in and out of her lungs. It was foolish how nervous she was. These people hadn't hurt her. But everyone was rushing her.

Mira marched into the room like a soldier, a rebreather in her hands. Her red hair stood up in all directions, and the black shirt she wore billowed around her body as it was tucked into the tightest black pants Ellie had ever seen. "Time's up. He's almost here."

"She can do this," Alexia replied.

"We don't have time for whatever coding you need her to do. She needs to be in the water now for all our sakes."

Alexia's hand came down on her shoulder and squeezed. "I believe in her, Mira."

Those words sparked a fire in her chest. Because she could do this. She had done worse in much shorter amounts of time. "Do you have a... a..."

Ellie was waggling her fingers in the air as if she were typing and someone had already brought her a keyboard. The man with the glasses hooked it up to the tablet that Alexia held in front of her as Ellie let the code flow out of her. It was a language that Tau had created, after all. She knew how to read this. She was probably one of the few people left alive who could.

She let all of her worries drop out of her head. This was her last gift to them. This was the last bit of help she would give the humans so they could prepare. A single generation was left in Beta. That's all the time they had. She would give them everything she could to prepare them.

And next, she would take on a sea god because he was going to be furious with her.

"Done," she said, lifting her hands up like she was on a timer, and the team in the room whisked away the tablet. Mira placed the rebreather over her face, and she was jerked in the direction of a moon pool.

Everything was happening so fast that she almost couldn't see straight, but then Alexia framed her face with her big hands and made Ellie focus on her and not the people running through the room.

"You stay safe," Alexia said. "You hear me? That creature out there doesn't get to tell you how to live your life, or what is right or wrong. You've got a good head on these shoulders. You can choose for yourself."

"I can't swim," Ellie whimpered.

Again, pity darkened Alexia's expression before she took a deep breath. "Your man's out there, sweetheart. You won't have to."

Cold metal touched the inside of her wrist. A knife? Why did Alexia have a knife against her wrist? The metal pressed down hard enough to part the flesh, a strange stinging sensation as red bloomed down her forearm. Not enough to kill, just enough to really hurt. And then Alexia planted a hand in the center of Ellie's chest and shoved her out into the water.

The icy cold stole her breath for a moment before she remembered that she could breathe with the device attached to her face. Sucking in a deep, startled breath, she stared up at the dome that was slowly disappearing. Blood streamed from her arm, like a red ribbon reaching up for the dome that was getting farther and farther away.

A cliff's edge, Ellie realized. The rock rushed up in front of her, but not close enough for her to touch or grab onto. That dome had been over a steep drop off and she was slowly sinking beyond it.

They'd killed her.

She'd told them that she couldn't swim. Even the stinging ache of her wounded arm wasn't helping her gain enough adrenaline to try to swim harder, faster. They'd thrown her over the edge because she wasn't useful any longer.

Until a long, echoing snarl made the water around her shake. She could feel the sound of his anger and rage as he barreled toward her. A dark creature illuminated the entire sea with his skeleton glowing so brightly it almost hurt to look at him.

And then...

Impact.

Chapter 35

He was death.

He was destruction.

He was ruination.

Proteus had never been so angry in his entire life. He'd been imprisoned before. The undine had attacked him all those years ago, making it very clear that they wished he was dead. But even then he had understood their actions. He had forgotten those reasons while imprisoned. Hatred had eventually festered as it always would with enough time to think about the actions of others.

But he had never cared about anything so much that it hurt to lose it. As he watched that undine swim away with the one person who had ever truly mattered in his life, he knew he was going to make them all suffer.

It didn't take him long to track down the blue undine. The male had holed himself up, though, perhaps the best way to keep himself out of Proteus's reach. The stones that he had wriggled through made it impossible for him to be reached. Even for someone who had arms as long as Proteus.

He had tried. For hours. He had pounded his body against the stones, raging against the currents that tried to pull him away from the male. He would tear him limb from limb, bathing the sea in the blood of the fool who thought to take her from him.

But his rage had changed as the sea finally showed him what she wished for him to see. There was another scent on the water. Another scent that was important.

While the blue undine smelled like Ellie, it was faint. He wasn't keeping her in those stones with him, and so Proteus had moved on. The acrid scent of dead eel had originally repelled him, but now he understood the trick for what it was. And though the male screamed for him to return, Proteus focused on the scent that still lingered in the water.

Few could track like he could. Partly it was the scent, and the other part came down to the powers that the ancients had given him. The ability to know what had come before pulsed through the water, highlighting the image of a yellow finned bastard who had taken Ellie next.

He'd found that one at another outpost, although the yellow one wasn't nearly as smart as the other. He'd been trying to get out of the water to hide in what looked more like a bubble than an outpost. It was a foolish choice.

Proteus clawed through his fluke, rendering him nearly useless until he healed, which would take a very long time.

With a curved claw, he'd hooked his fingers through the gills of the chuckling male, forcing him to stop laughing for a second and look Proteus in the eyes. "Where did you put her?" he said, his tone almost bored.

"Inside the outpost." The male had coughed, looking at the bubble behind him. "Release me and I'll get her for you."

"She's not there. You will tell me where she is." He twisted his claw, digging into sensitive soft gills. "Or I will kill you."

The male didn't want to say, and that told Proteus more than he knew. With a flick of his wrist, he dropped the male into the sea and started off toward the town he knew the mortals had built. They wanted it to stay a secret, but Proteus knew everything that happened in these waters. They'd brought her to their den, it seemed.

That was a foolish choice.

They should have known that he would find them. Proteus was the god of the sea, so even if he hadn't known where the town was, the sea itself would have told him, eventually. He would get what he wanted, or he would tear down the world around him.

The moment he'd seen the domed city, he had known something was wrong. The journey had given his mind time enough to clear, and he knew without a doubt the humans would do something stupid. They would take one look at him, and they would risk her life to control him.

If he wasn't careful, he was going to lose her. They would always sacrifice another before they would themselves.

His hearts were nearly beating out of his chest as he barreled toward the town. He intended to strike one of the main buildings. They would be so focused on stopping the leakage, trying to control what they were losing, that they wouldn't notice him gathering Ellie up. He knew once she saw him, she would try to get to him. They were connected, she and him. They were one being, one breath.

But then he scented her blood in the water.

It was as if someone had struck him in the hearts. Had they

killed her? His Ellie? They wouldn't dare. They had to know that if they had done that, he would destroy them all.

His stomach twisted. His hearts ached. He felt as if someone had plunged a hand into his chest and grabbed onto the organs.

She was hurt. And he hadn't stopped it from happening.

He turned direction toward the scent and just barely caught sight of her body. It was dark, so there was very little light in the water to guide him, but he would have seen her from an even greater distance.

She floated into the void, her arm outstretched toward the people who had thrown her into the water hoping to appease him. He would not forget this. He would return to this place, and he would tear it all to the sands. They would never be able to use this town again. All of these useless scum could return to their main city that was overrun with humans. They could rot in there for all he cared.

No longer would he be kind or lenient toward humankind. They would stay where he put them. No outposts. No freedom. They would leave his waters for good and leave both him and those he loved alone.

He reached her before the void claimed her. He had known that he would, but the terror was hard to shake. The fear that she would sink beyond his reach and he wouldn't catch her before the pressure had crushed her.

Proteus wrapped an arm around her waist and dragged her into him. The soft weight of her, held to his chest even as the current tried to pluck her from his grip. He was an immovable force in this sea. And she clung to him like she knew it.

He heard her soft gasp, bubbles erupting from her mask as her limbs curled around his waist. Proteus knew, knew without a doubt, that she had been waiting for him to save her. The way her hands grabbed onto him, not a single mark of fear in her touch, healed some part of his soul that had been blistered since she'd been taken from him.

"Proteus," she whispered. "You came."

"I hope you weren't waiting long."

He glanced up at the dome where she had fallen, and some part of him whispered, "Finish this". He could put her on the ledge, knowing that even the currents wouldn't dare take her from him. Then he could raze the entire place to the ground. Just as he had planned. He would use all of his massive body, the strength that should terrify those within, and kill everyone inside. He would drown them. Any who had rebreathers like her, he would hunt them down and rip it from their faces.

Their deaths would calm him. The sounds of their screams would ease the ache in his chest that told him he had somehow failed.

But then she pressed her hands to his thundering hearts, one for each of them, and he glanced down to see those big eyes watching him. By the gods, she was pretty. So innocent. So delicate.

So much kinder than he could ever dream of being.

"Take me away from here," she whispered. "Please."

"Where do you wish to go, Sisu?" He had to know the answer. Did she wish to return to her human city? Did even a few moments with those of her own kind convince her that perhaps she wished for a life that he could not give her?

"Somewhere they can't find us."

He could see a shadow of doubt in her gaze. The way she looked back at the town for a mere moment, before all her attention was once more on him. A small part of her didn't want to leave these people behind, but a large part of her did. It was a battle she would likely fight for the rest of her life.

He ran his hands down her back, scooping the backs of her thighs so she would wrap her legs around him and he could be sure that she was secure. Then he turned away from the domes and headed out into the sea.

The pace he set for himself was brutal. Even he could feel his muscles burning as he launched himself through the currents and fought against any trail that the sea wished for him to follow. He knew where he was going. He knew exactly where they would be safe.

The place was old. Hidden. It had been one of the first caverns he had found as a child, and it was one of the few places where he knew none of the undine would follow them. Because it wasn't entirely underwater.

It took a while for him to get there, but he didn't mind how long the journey took because she was cuddled up to him. Her tiny feet had found purchase above his fins. And while there were no holds for her feet, the tentacles on his hips had wrapped around her toes to make sure that she felt more secure. It was as if his body worked on its own, holding her even while the rest of him worked to bring her to safety.

He felt out of control. No one had ever been so daring as to steal something important from him. He'd never lost something as dear to him as her, and he was feeling all sorts of emotions that he'd never experienced before.

A large part of him wanted to crawl inside her. He didn't know what that meant, only that he wanted to cling to her until there was no him or her, but just the two of them existing in a way he did not understand. Another part of him threatened that he should consume her. Then no one else but him could have her, and he would always have part of her inside of him no matter how far she went.

But that was the animalistic side of him. A creature who had never truly seen reason, and one he rarely listened to these days. That side of him knew only how to hurt others. It lashed out when it was feeling uncomfortable or raw, as he was now.

He curled his arms around her a little tighter. He had promised that no one would ever hurt her again. Not him, not the humans, no one. And already she had bled.

Proteus curved a bit, his tail still propelling them through the waters at a speed that would have been hard for anyone else to follow. But he needed to see her arm. Gently, ever so gently, he ran his palm down her arm to hold her wrist up so that he could see it.

The water pressed back against her so powerfully, she wouldn't have been able to hold her arm up on her own. It might have been a little uncomfortable for her to hold it as he was. But he had to see. He had to know that she wasn't going to bleed out in his arms while he brought her to safety.

The cut was shallow. Thankfully, the saltwater of the sea had washed it clean long before this moment, but he could see there was still a faint line of red that was prevented from clotting because of the surrounding water.

A flash of fear seared through him. If he didn't get her to safety fast enough, she could bleed out. She could die and there was nothing he could do to stop it. He'd thought she would be all right with the humans. They wanted to get back at him. They wanted to show him that they were truly in control, and that was all.

He had been so wrong about them. They didn't care about others of their own kind. All they cared about was... whatever they had wanted. He truly didn't know.

"Not long now," he told her, praying to all the remaining gods of the sea that they would listen to their son.

He would not lose her. Even though the scent of her blood was beautiful and blooming in his gills. Even though part of him wanted to devour every inch of her skin just to savor that taste for a moment longer.

Urgency pushed him even faster until finally he reached the hidden cavern that the humans had long ago forgotten. It was another one of theirs, after all. A cavern that had once been used in worship as well.

Those who had worshipped here had known the sea was a goddess. They brought her gifts from this place which had once been full of boats. They would load the wooden ships with flowers, hundreds of petals and colors that would eventually sink into the waves. Every ship had a hole in it. Just enough to allow it to head out from the dock and out to sea.

Once the goddess accepted their sacrifice, it would sink. Filling the waves with flowers that would then float back to the shore.

He still remembered them wearing those flowers in their hair, telling everyone they had been blessed by the sea.

It was a stupid ritual. But even then, humans loved to pollute the waves while justifying it was for beauty.

The docks had long ago rotted, but the sides of the cavern were carved out beautifully. Smooth sides and stairs that lifted out of the water onto a platform that led toward the sands beyond. Centuries ago it had led to the garden where they grew all the flowers that were gifts to the goddess. But now, it would only serve as a safe place for them to rest for a little while.

He helped her to the stairs, which were slick with algae and covered with barnacles. Proteus made sure to help her place her feet safely, so she could pick and choose the right steps to place her feet so they wouldn't also get cut.

He dragged himself up after her onto the smooth surface where hundreds of feet had walked. He lay there next to her, watching her chest rise and fall as she ripped the rebreather off her face and set it down on the ground next to her goggles.

She turned her face to look at him, and that's all she did. Just look. He could feel her gaze tracing his features. From his brows, down his nose, to the lines on his cheeks, and down to his lips.

He'd never wanted to kiss her more. But a splash of color caught his attention before he could.

Leaning over her, Proteus plucked the single red bloom that had somehow grown in this dark, dank place. As he did so, as if the gods had heard him, a beam of light illuminated the massive cave.

He tucked the hardy sea rose behind her ear, gently following the curve of it with his claws. "There," he murmured. "Now it's where it belongs."

"The flower?"

"A rose cannot rival your beauty, but I like to see it try."

He caught her as she lunged at him, and their lips crashed together in a kiss that was nearly painful.

Chapter 36

Ellie didn't think about all the reasons this should make her feel even more guilty. She had betrayed him. She'd gone against everything he had told her to do, and thus was the worst person on the planet.

But this wonderful, marvelous, and terrifying man had tucked a flower behind her ear because he said she was pretty with it there.

Her heart couldn't take it. That poor, strangled organ in her chest had been so misused throughout her entire life. To have someone look at her and tell her they wanted her made every part of her glow.

Proteus might be angry at her as soon as he learned the truth, but she was not going to waste the few moments she had with him. She refused.

So, she kissed him. She threw her arms around his neck and kissed him with every fiber of want and need and desire that had been burning in her for far too long. It didn't matter that he was an immortal god who would outlive her for many, many years. It didn't matter that the world was coming down around their ears, and most of it was his fault.

It didn't matter that there were far too many secrets and lies standing between them.

Right now, it was just him and her, and the need that burned between them.

She parted his lips with her tongue, feeling him arch up into her as she did so. Perhaps it was the taste of her. The burst of flavor that always happened when they kissed. She wasn't sure what made him react like she'd electrocuted him, but Ellie wasn't going to complain when his arms suddenly came around her in a vise-like spasm.

He groaned into her kiss, the splits along his mouth already opening, like he wanted to devour her whole if he could. She knew that was part of himself that he fought against. A large part of him wanted to consume her.

At the thought, she let out a little moan of her own and straddled his waist. All she could think about was the last time he'd been between her thighs. He'd eaten her like he had been a man starving. For her touch. Her taste. For her slickness to coat his throat so thoroughly that he would never forget the taste of her.

She was untried. Untested. Before him, Ellie had thought sex was something that others did but not something she could ever enjoy. And he'd never enjoyed his body like this either. Yet, there was a feral, little monster inside of her that knew what it wanted, and it was tired of waiting for either of them to take the opportunity.

Apparently, he felt the same. As she rocked on top of him, finding a ridge on his scales that felt so good, he grabbed onto her hips. Those massive claws dug into her skin, but the pricks of pain only heightened her senses as he rocked her a little more firmly against him. He pressed her down onto that ridge of scales, ripping his mouth from hers as his neck arched back.

She stared at the muscles there. Watching the seam that could split move as though he wanted to allow his entire mouth to fall open.

She knew the feeling. A burning ache spread between her thighs, embarrassingly wet as she ground down on him.

Planting her hands on his stomach, she looked down at where she rocked. His scales were different here. Slightly parted if she looked hard enough, as though there was a seam.

Was this where...?

Curiosity got the better of her. Though she was already breathing hard, she couldn't stop herself from exploring his body as he had not allowed her to. Where had his cocks come from? Obviously, she'd seen them. She'd had them in her mouth as well.

But she didn't remember exactly where they'd poked through from his tail. On one of the movements where he lifted her just slightly, readying her to bring her back down hard onto his body, she shifted her weight to come down behind the slit in his scales. And then she feathered her fingers over the seam.

The groan he made was downright sinful.

She did it again. Again. Her fingers followed the surprisingly soft, slick skin on either side of the scales until he just... popped out. Suddenly his cocks were right in front of her again, and they were every bit as massive as she remembered. Intimidating, they looked like they were as large as her forearm, if a little narrower.

A foolish voice in her head told her to put her arm up against them, but then he arched up. The hot look in his eyes had returned, and his voice was ragged as he said, "Forgive me, Sisu."

She was about to ask what she needed to forgive him for when he dragged his claws down her back. From shoulders to hip, he destroyed her wetsuit. Tore it right down the back. Then he grabbed the ragged tear and ripped it off her body.

One moment she was clothed, and the next, the top half of her wetsuit was completely gone. He'd torn the neoprene as if it were as thin as paper.

Jaw hanging open, she stared down at herself before looking back to him to see him watching her like a starving man. He stared at her revealed skin, panting and nearly drooling.

"I do not know what you need from me," he murmured. "I fear I might harm you if I do all that I wish."

She took his hands, shaking out the remaining neoprene that still clung to his fingers, and planted them on her hips. "You won't hurt me, Proteus. I am certain of that. Touch as you wish."

It was like she'd unleashed an animal. He lunged for her, his jaw unhinging as his tongue licked the space between her breasts. She was pressed back against his tail, which had come up to give her something to lie against. She tilted her head back, eyes closed as she found herself enveloped by him. He was so big, so long, that it was easy for his tail to loop around her waist, holding her in place as his tongue coiled around one of her breasts.

He toyed with the peak, watching her with an intensity she could feel. Every sucked in breath, every ragged moan, all of it spurred him on.

He played with her breasts for a maddening amount of time. Clearly he enjoyed the sounds she made as he teased her, but then his claws were tearing at the legs of her suit. He pulled them off her far too easily. In the blink of an eye, she was nude, reclining against scales that were so warm she swore they were leaving branded marks against her.

Claws dug into her hips, forcing her to open them so his tongue could slip between her folds. White hot heat speared through her at the touch of his tentacles as well. He didn't need his claws or his fingers to spread her wide, to spear her with his tongue while his tentacles found her clit and sucked.

Ellie fractured into a thousand pieces. She was a galaxy of stars, so many pieces of herself thrown out into the universe, and he was the only thing holding her together. Her legs were shaking on either side of him. Her hips ached from being spread so wide, and still he wasn't stopping.

The groaning sound he made as he licked up every drop of her orgasm had her reaching for him.

He was new to this too, she remembered. He knew what they had done before, and he knew that there was pleasure to be found in touching. But she wouldn't be surprised if he didn't know the last bit that she intended to do with him.

Spreading her hands, she reached between her legs to frame his face. But she had forgotten that his mouth was completely open, and sharp teeth pricked her fingers before she could warn him what she was doing.

Ellie felt the warmth of her blood sliding between her fingers, and she wasn't prepared for the groan that came out of him when he tasted her blood on his tongue.

He tried to flinch back from her, but she caught him.

She watched with fascination as his mouth closed. The muscles contracted, sealing the lower part of his throat while his jaw seemed to hang unhinged for a moment longer.

Ellie spread her blood on the seam at his throat, knowing that he would taste it. The seam there worked in a swallow. A flash of need burned in his eyes.

"Lie back," she whispered. "Lie back for me and trust me."

He clearly hesitated. But then a shadow crossed his eyes, and he touched a single claw to her chest. Right over her heartbeat. "I have always trusted you, Ellie. Always."

It must have taken a lot for him to lie back and just look at her. He wasn't a creature used to giving someone the upper hand. Not that she could have hurt him if she had wanted to. Ellie was so weak and so small, perched on top of him as she was.

She reached between them and palmed one of his cocks. He arched into her, bucking into her fist so his already slick cock would slide through her fingers. She knew he liked that. The tension, the tightness, but she had a feeling it would be much better once it was inside of her.

Guiding the tapered head to her core, she took a deep breath and exhaled as the tip slowly penetrated her.

"Wait," he said, nearly sitting up but lying back down when she slapped a hand to his chest. "What are you doing?"

She didn't have the words for it. The pressure, the fullness, it was unlike anything she had experienced before. She thought she liked it. She'd always heard that the first time someone did this, it might be a little painful. But all she felt was pleasure. Slick wetness. Need.

So much need.

She braced both of her hands on his chest and bore down. Pressing him deeper inside of her. Moving until she could feel more and more of him.

His eyes rolled back in his head. Proteus slammed his hand down on the rocks, and his claws gouged furrows into the stones beneath them. Every muscle in his body tightened as she took him as deeply as she could. Which admittedly wasn't that far.

There was a lot of him, and she was only one woman.

Reaching between them, she gripped him in her hand and drew all the way back up. There was a pinch of pain, but not enough to stop her. The slow glide. The heat of him. The thickness of his cock made her feel like she was going insane.

Every time she did it, it felt better. The tension inside her built again. Coiling tighter and tighter as she used him in whatever way she wanted.

Then, she finally glanced up at him again to see him watching her with awe.

"Okay?" she asked, breathless as she started a pace that made it hard for either of them to speak.

"Don't stop."

"I wasn't going to." She ended the words with a moan that echoed throughout the chamber as she spasmed on top of him.

She was so close. Back to the point where there could be some kind of magic that happened between them. She just had to push a little harder, needed something else.

His tail came up behind her again, pressing against her back and coaxing her to lean backward. And then, those hip fins. His tentacles came around her, a web of suckers that latched onto her torso. Many of them lashed across her breasts, wrapping around her nipples with delicious suction. More delved between her legs, wrapping around his cock, her fingers, and her clit. Their grip made moving difficult, but then she ground down on him as she had when they started, and sparks burst behind her eyes.

"Oh," she whispered as his stomach flexed beneath her free hand.

Suddenly he was right there. His face was in front of hers, his breath fanning across her lips.

He kissed her. Consumed her. His tongue mimicked the movements she made on his cock as she rocked back and forth on top of him until everything exploded.

She tensed so hard on him, spasming around his cock as her body came harder than she ever had before. She forgot how to breathe. How to think. She could only shake with pleasure that seared through her entire body.

And then he was coming too, the guttural sound of his pleasure muffled by her lips and tongue.

She could feel him. The pressure of all his cum pulsed inside of her, gushing out over her fingers because there just wasn't enough space to keep it all in. Spilling between them in a glimmering, kaleidoscope of colors that caught the light.

Breathing hard, she leaned back against his tail, her fingers still wrapped around his cock.

There was wetness on her back too. Slick where he must have come from his other cock as well. She'd have to explore that at some time. Ellie was a little embarrassed to admit she wasn't so creative as to know what to do with two of them. She'd only seen a few rooms full of people, and even if there were two men with one woman, she hadn't really looked that closely to see how that all worked.

Memories like that didn't matter right now, though. There was something about him that had changed as he looked at her. Something that made her want to bite him. To kiss him. To start all of this over again.

He looked at her like she was some kind of goddess that had come down from the sky to give him this gift.

Proteus cupped the back of her neck, giving her a slow kiss that made her slide down a little further onto his cock, somehow still hard inside of her. She whimpered into his mouth until he finally released her.

His grip on her neck tightened just a bit. "What was that?"

"I believe it's called sex."

"A man could get lost in that," he muttered, dragging his lips down her neck. His tongue darted out, chasing a drop of sweat that rolled between her breasts. "How many times can we do that?"

"As many times as you want."

"Good, because I have some theories."

"Theories?" She gasped as he rocked into her, somehow sliding even deeper inside of her.

"Theories," he repeated. His tentacles shifted a little, giving them just enough room for him to thrust up into her a little deeper before drawing back.

The friction was almost too much. She was still so sensitive, and he was just so big.

They didn't get up from that exact spot for a little while. But at some point, she would always remember that he had taken the flower out of her hair and put it somewhere safe. So she'd have it for later, he said.

This man would forever be her undoing, she feared.

Chapter 37

A very long time later, Proteus lay on his side watching her sleep. He had been perhaps a little too rough with her. They were both new to this pleasure, and the last time he'd tasted her there had been a distinct metallic flavor of blood. He should have stopped then, but Ellie had convinced him to go one more time. He was big enough to stop her, but he didn't have the willpower to do so.

She was so damn convincing when she wanted to be.

Eventually they had both grown tired, and no matter how much they wanted to keep going, sleep had claimed them. Or at least, it had claimed her.

Proteus had stayed up to watch her. This immensely wonderful woman who had stepped into his life was forever a strange and odd creature. He liked watching her sleep anyway. The way her eyes twitched beneath her lids when she was dreaming, or how she breathed slowly but still curled into him when she wanted him to be beside her. And she always expected him to be there.

He had gotten up only once. His scales had dried out, so he needed to soak them before they got flaky and itchy. She'd made a sound that had him freezing halfway into the water. Needy and light, it had been the sound of someone who was searching for him.

Fool woman. He was a monster. A terrifying beast of the sea and someone who could easily harm her beyond any reason.

But she still wanted to hold him. She wanted to grab onto his arm and snuggle into his chest as she slept. It calmed her. Made it easier for her to breathe and... Well, if that was all it took.

Ellie didn't seem to mind that he was damp when he joined her again. She tucked herself back into his grip and breathed out a long, relaxed sigh. As though she hadn't been able to sleep well without him.

How wonderful it was to be so adored.

Finally, as the sun broke through the clouds after a strangely calm and clear night, she opened her eyes to catch him staring at her. For a while, they just looked at each other. He watched the emotions dance across her features.

Relaxation. Calm. Joy that he was looking at her and, in turn, she could look at him. But then her features fell into something that looked like sadness and guilt.

"What is it?" he asked. He reached a hand up, toying with her chin until he made her look at him. "I know that expression. What is wrong, Sisu?"

She opened her mouth, closed it, and then seemed to think better of what she was going to say. "I don't want to ruin this perfect bubble we're in. I want to stay like this forever, Proteus. Just you, me, and the sea."

"You know we can't."

"I do." She took a deep breath. "They suspected that we were lying to them. They had seen some of the documents that Pilot had locked away from them. If I didn't tell them the whole truth, they were going to walk."

It wasn't all of it. He could tell. "What do you mean, they were going to walk? The trap was set perfectly. The option for the humans to return Above is one that no one else could ever give them. I was gifting them their home."

"But they could tell we were lying," she insisted. "They don't want to return to the surface without knowing everything."

Anger burned already in his chest, but he was careful to make sure that anger wasn't aimed at her. She had been taken from him. Kidnapped. They might have even tortured the information out of her, and he had to know the whole story. "What did they do to you? I know you, Ellie. You wouldn't have told them everything without them threatening you. Did they harm you?"

Proteus lifted her arm, looking at the thin scab still on her wrist. He had seen every inch of her body, and he did not see more marks like this. But they could have injected her with something. They could have electrocuted her. He had seen their kind torturing others before. There were a lot of options for pain that left no marks.

"I did the right thing," she whispered. This time, he felt her hand trembling in his grip. "I told them willingly, Proteus. They needed to know everything before they went to the surface."

Carefully, ever so carefully, he put her arm down. Proteus could feel himself getting angrier. The gills along his ribs flared wide, and he wanted... He wanted to hurt something.

His hearts could not believe that she would betray him like this. She didn't have it in her. His woman had always listened to him. If she had disagreed with him, she would have told him so.

Space. He needed to put space between them or he would do something he regretted.

Moving closer to the water, he took a deep, steadying breath. "Why would you do that?"

"I told you, it was the right thing to do."

"And now everything is ruined," he hissed. He stared at her as she sat up, wrapping her arms around her legs. "If they know there is danger on the surface, they won't leave. The sea will continue to fester with their pestilence that they spread through every inch of my homeland. The humans need to get out of my sea or I will kill them all and remove the sickness at its source, Ellie."

"They cannot go home if they don't understand the dangers. We have to prepare them."

"They will not return to the land because they destroyed it! It is a symbol of their shame!" he shouted. The words bounced all along the cavern, echoing back to them as though the gods themselves shared his belief.

He knew the truth. These humans wouldn't want to see the ruination of their planet. They didn't want to face their wrongs, because doing so required them to admit that they were wrong.

She shook her head. "They're still going along with it."

He scoffed. "You cannot know that. They will only return to Sanctuary to gut it for all the information it is worth, and then they will back out of the plan."

Perhaps it was his tone that made her angry as well. He rarely yelled at her like this, and when he did, it made her react as well.

Usually, he appreciated that she stood up and started yelling back. Even now, he enjoyed the redness of her cheeks and the hard clip of her tones as she gestured at him wildly.

"You should trust me!" she shouted back, her voice clipped and angry. "You should know that I have done all the research I needed to make this decision. I didn't tell them just because they asked. I looked over the whole situation before I agreed."

"And what did you discover? That they were sad and mistreated and you wanted to make them feel better?"

"Ugh!" She threw her hands in the air. "This is exactly what she said you would do. She warned me to stick to my choice, and that I would need to be strong to deal with you. Apparently, she saw right through you faster than I did."

That did it. No one else knew him better than she did, and the fact that someone else had wriggled their way into her head and told her how to think made him even angrier.

Proteus pulled himself back out of the water, dragging his body toward her with an angry growl. "How dare you take the word of someone else over me? How long have I taken care of you? How long have I proven that I will listen to your opinions if you just tell me!"

"You never listen to me! You just pretend and then do what you want anyway—"

"I have been trying, Ellie! I have tried for—"

"You aren't trying at all! You are pretending to try. That's not the same thing!"

He growled even deeper, the sound echoing through the chamber once more. "As if you listen to me when I speak—"

"I always listen to you—"

"You could have ruined everything!"

She planted her hands on his chest and shoved. It didn't do anything, of course. He was far too big for her to move, but it at least startled him into silence. Long enough for her to shout words he had never considered.

"They don't have a choice, Proteus!" She said the words right in his face, forcing him to hear every single one of them. "They're dying. All of them. The city, the people, the clones. Everyone. They don't have a choice. They have to move Above if they can. The city is overpopulated."

What she said seemed to vibrate around him. Surely that wasn't the truth. He couldn't have overlooked something as simple as overpopulation.

But then he must have. He had seen how packed Beta was when he had looked at it in passing. He hadn't even swum by the other city that was still running, because why would he? The humans needed to leave, and that was all that mattered. He could trick them. Lie, cheat, steal, until they were out of his sea for good and then he could bar them from ever returning.

Every part of him had been so convinced that he knew what he was doing, he'd never suspected that they wouldn't be able to make another choice.

"They're choking themselves," he murmured. "Too many of them are in that city, and they don't have enough food, do they?"

"No. They don't have enough resources, and they are outpacing what they can sustain. There are only two cities left, and even if they put rules on children, the clones have added another problem entirely." She rubbed her arms, a sudden chill raising all the bumps on her skin. "That's why the other scientists were so hesitant to have me around."

"What do you mean?"

"The clones aren't children. They aren't adding anything to the population other than stagnant genes. Beta has been very particular about who is allowed to marry who, and while some of my kind are new blood, they can't just keep adding in the same genetics over and over again. Food is scarce. They want the food to be going to real people. People who have been born to those who have survived under the sea for so long."

Not people like her.

People who were clones of another, someone who had already lived and affected the world in some way or another.

No wonder the humans had no interest in talking to her. He could see it through their eyes. She was like all the other clones. Stealing part of their lives. Their jobs. The food. Not even a real person, at the end of the day, because she had no parents at all.

Something in him snapped at that. He drew her into his arms, holding her against his chest even though he was still very angry at her. She should have talked to him. Told him all of what she was feeling long before this.

But he'd be damned if she thought she was lesser than the people who lived in the city.

"You deserve all that they have and more," he said into her hair. "You are not less than them because you were born in the way that you were. You deserve a life, to take up space, to be who you were meant to be. They do not get to tell you that you are worth less than they are."

"But what if I am?"

He drew back and gave her a little shake. "You are not. A single drop of your blood has more bravery and kindness than any of those people who would judge you for something so foolish as the lack of parents. You are a person, just like they are, Ellie. Repeat it to me."

She gulped. "I am a person."

"Say it again."

"I'm a person, and it doesn't matter what they think of me." A small smile touched her lips. "And you are still very mad at me."

"I am."

"Why?"

He breathed out a long, low sigh. "Because you should have told me. Because I let you get taken from me, and I know you were scared. Even though you have done all the things I feared you might do, I still think very highly of you. I wish I could be angry and decide I want nothing to do with you, but I cannot do that. Because you are you, and I am me, and I fear we were meant to be tied together like this. Gloriously angry at each other for the rest of eternity."

Ellie shifted in his grip, her hands reaching up to trace the hard outline of his lips. He was still very angry. He wanted to nip her fingers to punish her a little more.

But she was so gentle as she touched his mouth. Gentle as she whispered, "I think that's called love, Proteus."

"No," he snarled, finally giving in and nipping her fingers. But it was a soft bite, more meant to startle than to hurt. "You insult those feelings by calling it something so small as love."

"Love is the biggest feeling a person can have."

"It is not. There are unnamed feelings. Feelings of a soul who has found their other half. Feelings of knowing that you are with the person the very universe guided you to. You are that person for me, Ellie. You are more than just a love, because love can fade. What I feel for you is as permanent and endless as the sea."

She softened against his chest with every word, drawn closer and closer to him until she finally let out a sigh and kissed him again.

He was still angry with her. Furious, even. But his plans hadn't gone awry after all. She had merely cemented that the humans would do what they said, and they would make sure that no matter what happened, the People of Water would soon be the only ones left in the sea.

Taking a deep breath, he wrapped his arms around her and tightened his grip until she let out a little squeak. "I will find you food. We will rest here for a while longer before we return. I think it's long past time I had an honest conversation with the people in that dome, and perhaps we will show them all that we know."

"Really?" she asked, leaning back to look him in the eyes. "Do you mean it?"

"I do." He traced her jaw before releasing her. "Sometimes you are right, Sisu. Even if it infuriates me."

And then he headed back into the water before he did something stupid. Like sinking back into her arms for more hours on end, just because he found her to be so thoroughly captivating.

Chapter 38

Ellie watched him leave, and she was alone in this massive cavern. But the longer she sat here, the more she started to wonder about the place.

It wasn't hot, strangely enough. She had a feeling that had to do with the ocean surrounding it, and how much of that water was still very cold. The cave seemed to have been both naturally carved out of the cliff side by the waves themselves, and then clearly helped with tools made by humans. She could see some of the carvings that had been left behind, but worn away by time.

Walking along the edge of the waves, she trailed her fingers along the walls. So many people had been here for years on end, it seemed. She placed her hands where theirs must have gone. For a moment, it almost felt like she could hear them.

The voices of people long ago. They still lived here, like ghosts. All the people who had spent countless years worshipping, walking the same path she did, running their hands along the same walls and perhaps even wondering at those who had come before.

Humans were perhaps doomed to wonder about the past more than they thought about the future.

She followed the lines all the way to the back of the cave. There was a small path there, leading into the wall of the cliff and who knew where else. She glanced over her shoulder to see a storm rolling in. It wasn't a big one, just enough to stir the waves so that they were taller as they entered this space. The whitecaps crested and spat foam up onto the same spot where she and Proteus had been sleeping.

A small spark of fear bloomed in her chest. What if this cavern flooded during high tide? She had no idea how long Proteus and she had been here, but she doubted it was long enough to see a true high tide. Perhaps it was smarter for her to follow this path, just to see if there was another place where she would be safe.

She convinced herself quickly. Ellie stepped onto the stones and into the darkness beyond. It was, after all, just a staircase. She kept her hands on the walls on either side of herself, making sure she would know if there was a room on one side or if the walls suddenly dropped off. There wasn't any light to guide her, so she had to use her hands to see.

But this was only a path. One that led out of the heart of this small mountain and into the world beyond.

Ellie lifted her arm up to her eyes at the first spear of sunlight that hit her. It was hard to see beyond it. Her eyes had adjusted to the darkness, and she had to wait a while until the bright white light revealed something other than painful sparks.

The remnants of a garden unfurled before her. Though everything was dead, it wasn't hard to see what it had once been. The beds were broken by time. They had once been wooden, it seemed, and most of that wood had rotted. Earth spilled out of them. At some point, moss and some other types of plants had grown between the stone paths under her feet, leading her to more broken garden beds. Brambles were all that survived now. Massive brambles that were covered in thorns.

She had to walk carefully, considering she was still nude. The thorns would tear at her skin and leave red lines that would make it very obvious she had gone exploring, but she wanted to know more about where she was.

The sun hadn't risen too high on the horizon yet, but she realized she was in some kind of canyon. So perhaps it never got as hot as she thought out here. The air was cool on her skin, but not so cold that she was shivering.

The brambles covered most of the area closest to the cave. Almost hiding the sight of it from anyone who came into this canyon. But as she moved past them, it opened up into a much larger space.

There were tiles on the ground. She looked down at her feet, slowly moving in a circle as she traced the design that someone had left here with obvious care. It was a massive sun, she realized.

Bright yellow tiles still held their color. The circular center had long ago broken, but the spindly waves that rotated around it were still very easily seen. They shone in the sunlight. Glistening with color.

She smiled down at it, wondering who the artist was who had created this in a canyon of all places.

Ellie looked up, seeing how high the walls were that surrounded her. They were easily bigger than any space she'd ever been in before. She got dizzy looking all the way up there, imagining what it must be like to live that high. Or even to look down.

She had to brace herself against a wall with a laugh. There was no way she could stand on the edge of that cliff and look down. Staring into an abyss was one thing. Water held her up then, and she at least would feel the salt pushing back on her, even if she couldn't swim. But gravity would take her swiftly at the top of this canyon.

There were small, sparse plants dotting all up and down this area. But then...

"Is that green?" she whispered to herself. Taking another hesitant step forward.

Her feet sank into sand. It appeared there was only dirt very close to the mouth of the cave, but she was so curious to see what was green.

A voice in her head screamed to go back to the sea. She was safe there. Safer than anywhere else, because she knew Proteus would return. And there were actual people living here in the sand. She had to be careful. If she wasn't, then maybe she would see one of those snake people for herself. And what would she do then?

They were hunters, that much she was certain. Only the hardiest of people could survive out in the sands like they did.

And they wouldn't like seeing her here.

But the hint of greenery, the whisper that there was life here that she could feel and touch and see... It made her too curious.

Her footsteps were nearly silent on the sand. No one would know she was here. Glancing behind her nervously, she noted that she didn't even leave footprints behind. It was like any hint of where she had been was swallowed up by the desert.

No one would know she was here. She could explore for just a little while longer.

False bravery settled in her chest, and she kept walking. Every step made her feel a little safer. Every breath brought her a little closer to the bright green plant that was hanging on the wall.

She finally reached it, peering at the strangeness of it. It was bright green. That much she hadn't made up. Tiny spines covered the entirety. She carefully touched a finger to one, and it pricked her skin immediately.

"Ouch," she muttered, bringing her finger to her mouth to suck at the blood that welled there.

What kind of plant was covered in spikes? How strange.

She looked it over, trying to see how it was attached to the wall. The base was rather bulbous, and it appeared to be attached by a rather large circular... bubble, she supposed. It certainly looked clear enough. She reached down for one of the many sticks on the ground and prodded it.

Strangely, it leaked.

Clear fluid.

"Huh," she muttered, her brow furrowing.

Something slithered in the ground at her feet. Ellie froze, watching the sand mound over a very small creature that poked its head out of the sand.

It looked sort of like a mouse. They'd had a mouse problem in Tau for years. More years than she'd been alive. But she remembered the tiny, little creatures with whiskers just like this one. The mice in Tau had been soft, though, covered in a velvety fur that she had enjoyed petting very much until someone caught her and killed the little creature. This one had no fur.

Leathery and smooth, it darted out of the sand and attacked the plant.

She shrieked and stumbled away from both the plant and the mouse. It was only the size of her middle finger, but the mouse... thing attacked with such violence it was startling. Not a single drop of liquid was wasted once the creature got to it, though. She watched it drink every drop that it could, clawed hands violently tearing at the plant that seemed to be healing itself even as the mouse drank.

It continued sucking down the liquid until it was so fat that she thought it might have to roll back underneath the sands. How strange. Its belly bulged with...

"Water," she whispered.

Water was so rare in this desert that just the scent of it summoned creatures. Ones like the mouse, who were probably genetically capable of smelling it.

But if the scientists were creating humans that were spliced with animal DNA, then surely... surely they had started on other creatures first? Was this mouse proof of that?

Maybe this new version of their world was filled with creatures they wouldn't ever understand. Maybe everything here wasn't what they knew at all.

As she watched the mouse drunkenly cross the sand, a thought occurred that she should grab it. Bring it back to the others in the domes. Maybe they would know what to do with it and be able to test to see if there was anything interesting about it. Like genes that shouldn't be there.

Perhaps it was just a mouse, and there was nothing strange about it at all. But the more she looked at it, the stranger the creature seemed to be. This wasn't an ordinary mouse, and proof of that might be helpful.

Then reality reminded her that she was being foolish. Of course she couldn't bring it back. The domes were underwater, and she had no idea how far away they were. This mouse wouldn't survive the trip, even if she had some kind of oxygen cage to bring it in.

She crouched down, watching it burrow into the sand and said, "I wish I had proof you aren't what you are supposed to be."

Her words were too loud. The discovery of something new had made her forget that she was supposed to be wary of her surroundings. At the sound of her voice, a low growl moved through the canyon on the breeze. She might not have heard it at all if it wasn't so silent where she was.

Her blood went cold. Ellie slowly lifted her head to see the creature that had frozen in the mouth of the canyon. It looked almost like a dog. She'd seen pictures of them in Tau and knew they stood on four legs, had a tail, and a canine looking muzzle for a face. Some of that was accurate with this creature.

But it had six legs. With hands instead of paws.

The beast lifted its head, sniffing the air with eyes that almost appeared sightless. Or burned out of its skull. It also had no fur, although she could definitely see there were some scales on its body.

Then it curled its lip, revealing rows upon rows of teeth.

"Oh, fuck."

She turned and bolted back the way she had come. Perhaps not the smartest move. She had read once that dogs loved to chase things, not that she ever had an opportunity to meet one.

A howl erupted into the air, and she moved her body even faster. There was so much space here. She had never been able to run as freely as she could right now. Running inside the cities was on a small track with a ceiling very close to her head. There wasn't the endless, vast nature that there was here.

It felt as if she was moving in slow motion. The sand grabbed at her feet, slowing her down and tripping her as she made it to the sun mosaic on the ground. How had she gotten this far from the cave?

Hot breath touched her legs as she scrambled to her feet, and she heard the sound of its jaws clamping shut where her leg had just been.

Ellie ducked into the brambles, not caring that they tore at her bare skin. All she knew was that the scent of her blood made the animal even more enraged. Its snarls rang in her ears as she tore herself free and ran down the stairs.

She almost tripped. Almost killed herself falling down the long stairs that would lead down to the sea. She kept her hands on the walls, trying to take the stairs as quickly as she could without breaking her neck.

"Come on," she said as she bounded down them two at a time. "You're fine. You're fine."

But she wasn't. The beast behind her had freed itself from the brambles, and she could hear it rushing after her.

Finally, she broke free into the cavern with the sea. She ran straight for the stairs toward the water. Who cared if she couldn't swim? She'd rather die drowning than in the jaws of some animal that would take its sweet time eating her.

She turned to see the beast falling down the last bit of the stairs and landing on the hard stones. It stood, shaking its head, and then its gaze was back on her.

"Shit," she hissed, backing away with her hands raised. "Good doggie. Nice doggie."

It was neither. She didn't make it to the sea before it leapt at her, all teeth flashing and hands reaching out for her.

Clawed fingers caught it long before it could touch her. Proteus emerged from the sea like the god he was, all rage and flashing teeth himself as he brought the creature to the ground and eviscerated it.

The attack was over in seconds. She stood there, hands shaking and her entire body quivering as she stared at the animal that lay dead at her feet. Whatever it was, whatever monster those scientists had made, it was nothing like anything she might have seen before.

Proteus dunked himself in the water again. She thought he was maybe leaving her again, which made fear spike in her chest again. But then she realized he was washing the blood off of himself with quick, efficient movements before he reached for her.

She collapsed against him the moment she could, her eyes still locked on the body that was slowly surrounded by a pool of bright red blood.

"Here," Proteus said. "I had gotten you this wetsuit while I was gone. There's a sunken city around here too, but... We go. We go now, Ellie."

She had never agreed with him more.

Chapter 39

Proteus had never expected himself to go back to the domes without an explicit plan to destroy their homes for good. He still wanted to tear into them, and ripping through every single person there would satisfy some ugly part of him that longed for vengeance.

He had proven that he was worthy of worship. But the undine here didn't care if he was worthy or not. They weren't going to do it.

And that was a strange feeling. Proteus's entire life had been framed around the fact that he was the son of gods. He could see the future just like the depthstriders, if he wished. He had simply stopped using that ability since he... he...

He looked down at the sleeping human in his arms and he realized he'd stopped using it since he'd met her.

Proteus didn't want to see the future anymore. It had always been vague anyway, but he enjoyed knowing that he knew nothing about his future with her. He didn't want to ruin these quiet moments.

Like right now. With her resting in his arms, exhausted, in an ill-fitting wetsuit that had clearly been designed for a man. Yet she was still the most beautiful woman he had ever seen.

What would it have been like if he had ruined the moment where she had taken him into her body, shocking him, but also opening up his world to a whole new kind of pleasure? No, that would have been foolish to ruin that.

She made him enjoy the spontaneity of life. She made him want to keep trying to see and find new things, because he had never done that before.

He wanted to live, Proteus realized. Not as a god worshipped by all who met him, but as a regular man with the woman he loved.

The undine knew he was approaching the domes long before he reached them. He would have been disappointed if they hadn't. They were all warriors, hardened by years of fighting against the humans. They, at the very least, should know when there was someone in their waters.

The red one was the first to approach. He still wore that metal arm, and flexed it at his side as though he prepared for a fight.

"You are not welcome here," he boomed, his voice carrying across the waters.

As expected, it was far too loud. Proteus nearly scolded him but then was far too busy trying to manage the flailing woman who was bound and determined to heave herself out of his arms.

"Drop her," the red undine snarled. "If that's what it takes to get you to pay attention to me."

"She can't swim," he replied, glaring at the other male as Ellie finally settled in his arms. "By all the gods of the sea, woman, settle down."

She did so, but pressed her hands to her ears. "I can feel his voice vibrating through the water, Proteus. And now, you as well. Both of you quiet down."

For a moment, he swore this wasn't the first time the red undine had been told that. All his lights illuminated at once, tiny dots that sparkled like red stars before he coughed through his rib gills and they all turned back off.

When he spoke again, the words were much quieter. "My apologies. I often forget that human ears are so delicate."

Proteus glared at him, ready to scold the much younger male, but he didn't have to. Ellie already pointed at him and said, "Aren't you the one married to Anya?"

Saying the name was like lightning had struck the male. All the lights burst into radiance again, illuminating the water around him until even the plankton had a red glow to it. "That is my mate, yes."

"She's nice," Ellie said. "Hard of hearing?"

"Completely."

"Interesting. She was very helpful when I was in your home, and very pretty."

By all the gods of the sea, Ellie learned quickly. Proteus was shocked to see how the dangerous male in front of them preened at her words. His fins even fluttered at the compliments she lavished upon his mate.

"She is strong and capable," the male said. "I have seen her through much hardship. She is a warrior, far more than I."

"I don't doubt that. Would you mind bringing us to see her again? Proteus has come around to the whole plan, but I would like to chat with everyone else." She looked up at him, asking permission for likely the first time since he'd met her. "Do you mind?"

"I do not, Sisu. If you wish to see the others, then that is what we will do." He shifted her in his arms, holding her a little more tightly as he turned a glare to the other male. "I am not here to fight."

The lights all went out at his words, but the red male gave him a stiff nod.

He followed the undine and wondered when his life had turned to this. Proteus was born to be worshipped. A god among smaller males, those who would see him as a creation of the ancients. And now? Now he was following another male like he had been summoned.

This tiny woman in his arms sure had changed a lot.

They approached the domes, and he was pleased to see that the undine had armed themselves. So, they weren't planning on allowing him to just enter their lives without a fight. Good. They should have guessed that he would be furious with them for the trick they had played.

He bared his teeth at the first wave of them that all floated in front of their home, spears in their hands and armor on their bodies. He didn't remember the undine ever wearing armor, at least not when he'd been around two hundred years ago. These metal plates would keep them safer from his claws, but nothing would stop him from dragging them into the abyss if he wished.

A few of their grips changed on their spears as he swam past them, preparing for the moment when he would change his mind and fly at them in a rage.

Fools. All of them.

But then that blue bastard appeared, and it took everything in Proteus to not toss Ellie onto the ground so that he could attack the male who had taken her from him.

The blue undine before him lifted his hands for peace. "I didn't have a choice in the matter, and you know it. You didn't give us an opportunity to speak with you."

"I am a god. I do not have to speak to any of my supplicants." If he had been above water, he would have spat after the words. It was an insult that he was even here.

But Ellie placed her hand on his chest, and he looked down at her, finding peace and steadiness in her gaze. "I'm going to talk with the other humans. Perhaps you should fix what has been broken here."

"Nothing has been broken."

"Proteus." She shifted in his arms, lifting her hands to cup his face and leaning closer so no one else could hear her. Her voice was so quiet, even he had to strain to listen. "You have a choice. Do you wish to remain a god, and thus alone, forever? Or do you want to start a new life now? With them. With family and friends and a future that is more than you sitting in a temple all alone?"

He thought about her words as she kicked away from him. A few undine reached to help her, their touch tentative and their gazes on him. Perhaps they knew that anyone who touched her ran the risk of his wrath. But he nodded, and one of the females, a pretty one with a bright lavender tail, tugged her toward the dome with a soft push that helped Ellie float toward the others of her own kind.

That left him in the water with all the other undine. They didn't seem thrilled that he was here. He wouldn't have been either.

Holding his arms out at his sides, he tried to show them that he had no weapons on him. But they could see the massive spines that extended out of his elbows, currently flat against his arms. They likely knew there were more on his spine, and that he had enough poison in his body to put them all to sleep this instant, and then he could do whatever he wanted with them.

Tilting his head to the side, he shrugged at the blue and red undine before him. "So what are you going to do with me now?"

"Not worship you, that's for damn sure," the blue one replied.

"What is your name?"

"Arges."

"Who are you here?"

"I help lead."

Proteus nodded. "So you are the one I need to speak with then."

More undine came from the back of the domes. Apparently they had been preparing for him from all angles, but these were a few he recognized. The purple depthstrider, Fortis, had helped him start all this. He wondered if the male regretted that. And of course, the yellow male he had nearly killed.

Proteus grinned at the last one. "How are your gills?"

"Better."

But he winced as he said it, like taking that deep inhalation was a little more painful than he wanted to let on. The yellow one certainly didn't want to admit any weakness with all these oafs surrounding him.

Grunting, Proteus shook his head. "You know the green algae that grows in the warmer areas? Gets stuck on coral if you can find any skeletal remains of a reef."

"Yes." The yellow undine tilted his head to the side, obviously confused about where this conversation was heading.

"Put it in your gills. It will help."

There was a moment of stunned silence as everyone just... stared at him. Like he'd lost his mind. Or perhaps as though they had lost theirs. Surely they hadn't heard him correctly. Surely he wasn't giving advice on how to heal them.

The frown on Arges's face deepened. "We have never used that algae for healing."

"No, you haven't. It was considered a holy substance long ago, and even though it could heal, it was only used in dire circumstances. But it is abundant and very easy to find. You likely haven't heard of it because so many did not wish to use it because they were afraid the goddess of the sea would smite them." He snorted. "Even my parents, the ancients, went along with it. They thought it was funny."

More silence. More stares. Likely because they were all realizing how much of their life had been manipulated by creatures they revered. And he called them his parents.

The red undine snorted. "Arges, do you hear that?"

"I did, Daios."

"And all this time we'd been thinking it was poisonous." He scratched the back of his neck with a metal hand. "Perhaps there is some use to this man who calls himself a god."

Fix this, Ellie's voice whispered in his mind. You can choose right now to be something else.

Somebody else, he supposed. He had been created just like her, he realized. The searing thought burned through him. She was a clone. A doll, like she said. And here he had been, telling her that she was so much more than that.

Maybe he was more than the ancients's tool. Maybe he was meant to have a life and a future and a family, just like she said.

He coughed through his gills, clearing them out of sediment that had built on them for far too long. And then he said, "Perhaps I have no interest in being a god any longer. I have lived a long life. Longer than most could ever dream of. This world no longer needs a god to rule it, but it does need a group of people who see the future and plan accordingly. I would like to be part of that."

Arges snorted. "By ruling over us? We have no interest in a king."

"By living among you. By learning what you know and teaching you what I know. By being part of this world, rather than only seeing it as a thing to be... manipulated."

He knew they wouldn't believe him. Not immediately. But he had to try.

For her.

For him.

For a future that neither of them had ever had much say in, but one that he hoped to see come to fruition.

He took a deep breath, the gills along his ribs hurting. "It is a start to tell you what I know. About the algae. The places where you can hunt that are still fruitful. The areas of this sea that are hidden from your sight, but that I can still feel. I will help you in whatever way you ask of me. I renounce my godhood, however, because I have no wish to be a god any longer."

Fortis swam closer to him, flicking his tail with annoyance as he headed toward Proteus. "You'll have to excuse me when I say I need to prove that."

Ah, so the priestly one wanted to peer inside his head. To prove once and for all that the god before them wasn't lying. He was truly blessed by the gods if he was capable of such gifts.

Proteus nodded. He even held his hands behind his back, so there was no threat when Fortis planted a hand on his chest.

The depthstrider glowed. Bright dots spiraled up and down his body, flickering with the power that ran through him. The lights were pretty, but Proteus liked to think his were prettier as his body reacted to the sensation of another person's mind scratching against his.

The priest would find no lies. Only exhaustion as Proteus finally released the last tie he had to his parents, and perhaps to the sea itself. He had fought for hundreds of years to scramble back to the person he had once been, but he was so tired of that person.

For once, he wanted to rest. Of course he wanted to help them, but his purpose had always been to see the People of Water get the best life they could get. That was all.

Fortis hummed low under his breath. "What is this I see about warning us? Something to do with Above?"

"That is a conversation for all of us. For the undine and for the humans. Because it's..." He sighed. "Complicated. Everything in regards to the humans is complicated."

And for the first time in his life, he felt a comaraderie with the People of Water. There were quite a few of them around him who shared a look with each other, all of them agreeing that their mates, their humans, were a complicated bunch.

He chuckled and flicked his tail to head toward the dome, where he knew Ellie waited for him. "If you're done with all this, perhaps we should join them so we can tell you all everything we know."

The males followed him without complaint, and Proteus wondered if they would ever be comfortable around him.

He supposed it didn't matter. In the end, all he needed was her.

Chapter 40

Ellie floated up into the dome, helped by a very lovely female undine who was quite possibly the prettiest one she'd seen yet. Her lavender color was exquisite, and the way she had braided her hair so intricately made Ellie want to try it herself. Those braids were wrapped around each other in a way that looked like flowers that danced down her back.

With a soft smile, Ellie pulled herself out of the water and sat on the edge of the moon pool. Once she got the rebreather off her head, tearing out even more strands of hair in the process, she exhaled and said, "I really need to learn how to swim."

"Considering we live underwater, yes, you do." Anya's voice interrupted her with a soft laugh.

Ellie looked over to see that the room was full of four women. Alexia and Mira she knew, along with Anya, and the last must be Ace. The shorter woman stood off to the side, glasses perched on her nose, and a small robot in her hands.

"Hi," Ace said. "I don't think we've officially met."

"Not quite, but it's nice to meet you."

The droid in Ace's hands suddenly spasmed. It wriggled out of the woman's hands, dropped onto the floor, and headed toward Ellie with a quick movement.

"Enough pleasantries! Did you bring him here or not?" That was Pilot's voice, certainly. But it wasn't his body.

No more was the droid in the body of a crab. This was more like... well, a lobster, the more she looked at it. His body was significantly longer, although he still had quite a few legs. They were less spider-like and more centipede-like as he headed across the floor toward her.

Ellie picked him up with a delighted laugh, looking into the eyes that were still projected through a glass panel on his face. "Look at you! All new."

"I don't like it," Pilot grumbled.

Ace sighed, the sound filling up the room with exasperation. "I told you, Pilot. You'll learn how to use the new body just fine. It's just algorithms crossing. Soon enough, your directive will forget that you used to be in a different form."

He was all right. Ellie had been so certain that he'd died, and that there was nothing she could do to get him back. She snuggled him close and pressed a kiss to the top of his droid head. She didn't even know if droids could feel a kiss like that, but he certainly spluttered enough for her to think he could.

Setting him down on the ground, she patted his head a couple of times for good measure. "I did bring him. He'll be showing up soon, I'm sure."

"You should have run," Pilot muttered. "Left me here to my own devices. I would have escaped in my own time."

She smiled at him, but then looked up at the other women in the room. They were clearly holding themselves back, trying their best to give her a moment for their reunion before they all flooded her with questions.

"I think you already saw most of what I did in the files," Ellie finally said. "But there's more. There's so much more."

"There always is," Alexia replied. And then she gave her a little secret smile that felt like it was just for the two of them. "I'm glad you listened, Ellie. It seems like you figured it all out on your own, after all."

"More than that." She stood out of the water, shaking some drops from her fingers and shaking her head when Mira offered her a towel.

She told them everything else, then. About the creatures she had seen on the screens, and that she was certain Above was actually inhabited. Then she told them about the mouse she had seen, the strange dog creature that had chased her. All of them were wrong and certainly not what they had seen in the history books.

Somewhere in her stories, likely around the dog, the other undine showed up.

Arges hauled himself out of the water, sliding across the floor toward Mira and wrapping his tail around her. Maketes did the same, although he hauled Ace across his tail like that was where she was meant to be. Her cheeks turned bright red, but she leaned into him.

They'd done that a hundred times before, Ellie realized. The other two were looking at their mates intently. Daios clearly checked Anya over for any harm. And Fortis looked at Alexia like he worshipped the ground she walked on.

Finally, her gaze flicked to Proteus, and everything in her froze. Because the expression on his face was so soft. She'd never seen him look at anything like that before. He had been waiting to catch her gaze, so that all the love he felt for her could shine through his eyes.

Biting her lip, she tried to hide her grin before continuing on to tell them every detail.

The undine males who had joined them had a lot of questions about that massive dog thing that could have killed her. Proteus answered most of the questions about that. After all, he'd been a lot closer than her. And they all started guessing what these creatures meant.

Their words and theories started overlapping. They were all speaking at the same time, their thoughts and expectations of Above growing more outlandish by the minute. She could tell that Alexia was going to argue against their going up there at all. Surprisingly, it was Anya, sweet, quiet Anya, who was arguing the most adamantly that they should go Above, regardless of the danger.

Finally, it was Proteus who got them all to stop talking.

The sharp, whip crack of his voice lashed through the dome. "You don't have a choice! To save your people, you must go Above."

They all turned to stare at him, and at least it seemed Proteus now understood why.

"I will help you as much as I can, but I think we all know that there is no guessing what has survived up there. I would hazard a guess that the last decade of experiments that went on in that facility would shock all of us. We can discover as much as we can, but in the end, there is nothing we can do to change what we will find out there. There must be weapons developed, facilities fortified. And then we can move forward."

More quiet, until Alexia spoke next. "I can oversee the weapons construction. Tau had plenty of those, and they weren't all aimed at killing the People of Water. Plenty of those can be used in a physical fight, and if we arm enough people... Well, it doesn't matter. I'll start training soldiers. Many clones have already shown interest in it."

Anya nodded, her gaze far away as though she were reading something on the screen of the droid attached to her head. "I think the records from the experiments give me a good start in guessing what we might encounter up there. I'll start pulling together diagrams and assess with Daios where these creatures might be weakest."

"Droids will be helpful," Mira said. She nodded over at Ace. "The two of us can get them going. We'll need flying droids, probably for the first time."

The others continued to talk about all their plans, moving seamlessly together. They were a team, but more than that, they were a family. Ellie watched them all bicker together. But none of the arguments had any bite. None of the insults seemed to stick. They ribbed each other and joked about who would be best at doing the jobs.

Alexia pushed off the wall, coming toward Ellie with clear intent in her gaze. "And you? What are you going to do to help us, Ellie?"

Everyone quieted a bit, looking over at her. But Ellie was looking at Proteus.

It was as if he'd already read her mind. She could tell that he wasn't pleased with what she was going to say, but nodded at her anyway.

She swallowed and said, "I'd like to lead the expeditions heading to the other facilities. I just... I want to know what's out there. I want to see the world and to know what we're bringing people into. And then... Well, once we get a stable place to live, I think I'd like to stay in Sanctuary. I can be close to Proteus, and welcome people to the land as they arrive. I think I'd be good at that."

Alexia grinned. Pride turned her expression a little warmer than before. "I think that's a great idea. You know, most of the people who have volunteered to go Above are clones. Just like you. They all saw it as a chance for a new life, to start somewhere no one knows who they are or where they came from. I think you'd be the perfect person to welcome them."

As the others started talking again, more plans bursting through the air, Ellie felt something inside of her click into place. A puzzle piece that she had been missing, maybe. Or perhaps a reason for being that she hadn't had before.

Quietly, she moved through the crowd of people and walked over to the water's edge.

There wasn't any privacy in this room. But when Proteus flicked his tail and came closer to her, it felt like they were the only two left in the room. She sat down on the edge, and he braced his arms on either side of her body.

With a gentleness only she got to see, he pressed a kiss to her forehead and asked, "Happy?"

"I think so. Are you?"

He nodded. "There is a future for us here, Sisu. Not an easy future, but I don't think either of us would like a happy ending handed to us, all wrapped up as you humans dream of."

"No," she replied with a soft laugh. "I don't think either of us would like that. We need a purpose."

He nodded toward the others. She knew he was saying something, but all she could focus on was the strong line of his jaw and the hard look in his eyes. A muscle on his jaw jumped, and she wondered what happened to it when he fully opened his mouth like she'd seen him do so many times. Was that muscle one of the ones that helped peel his mouth open like a flower?

He looked back at her, and a hint of amusement made her blush. "Did you hear me, Sisu?"

"No."

"What were you thinking?"

"Just about you." She brushed her fingers over the lines of his cheeks and then sighed. "Right. What were you saying?"

"I was telling you that I don't think any of this is going to be easy. A long road awaits all of us, but I do think we'll get there in your lifetime." He curled his fingers close to her hips, his claws grazing her wetsuit. "And that I'm not sure they're going to need us for a little while yet. You and I could perhaps explore ahead of them. There are a lot of facilities out there, and we could be the ones to see if they're safe."

"What about the mutant dogs?" she asked.

"Those aren't dogs."

"What would you call them, then?"

"Just mutations. I think that's good enough." Proteus tilted his head to the side. "What is it with humans and incessantly needing to name things? You've seen it. Surely that is enough."

"Proteus, you're going to be around humans a lot more. I think you need to stop asking questions about us and understand that you aren't going to understand us."

He rolled his eyes. "That is because logic is never part of what you do."

"Sometimes it's just a feeling." She looped her arms around his neck. "I think I proved that to you very well, not that long ago. Didn't I?"

She swore the water was suddenly much, much warmer. Proteus leaned closer to her, his gaze locked on her lips. And she knew he was thinking about her mouth wrapped around his cock, her fingers toying with his slit, all the things that had made him make that lovely groaning noise that she still thought about when she was daydreaming.

"All right, you two," Alexia said, her voice breaking Ellie out of her daydream. "If you want to start ahead of us, that might actually be a good idea."

Ellie cleared her throat and leaned around Proteus to look at the other women. "Do you have a preference of which direction we go in?"

It was Anya who replied, but she was still looking into the glass of her droid, not at anyone else in the room. "Actually, yes. I can send some coordinates to your droid. There are a lot of facilities listed in these documents, areas they used as testing sites. If we can convert one of those into a livable space, that's the best opportunity until we can determine how difficult it will be to build Above."

Proteus snorted. "I imagine you'll find it far easier than building underneath the waves."

"Maybe." Mira patted Arges's chest. "But it will be a lot more difficult to build without the help of the People of Water. You're all a lot stronger than any human I know. That'll take some figuring."

Once again, they all devolved into trying to figure out the logistics of building on land, rather than in the water. Clearly the topic was of great interest, and everyone was thoroughly excited by the idea. Even the undine in the room were talking about all that it would take, and how they could prepare the humans to pick up significantly heavier items.

She watched all of it with amusement. At least they were excited about something. Ellie was just happy to have helped them all in some way.

Then her attention turned back to Proteus, and he had eyes only for her. He wasn't looking at the others in the room. She wasn't even certain he was listening to their conversation anymore.

He stared at her. His gaze moved from her eyes, to her nose, to her mouth. And then back up again. He took in every inch of her like a man obsessed.

"What do you think?" he asked quietly.

"About what?"

"Do you want to go on an adventure together?" He quirked a brow that he didn't have, but she knew the expression was meant to tempt her.

Ellie realized she no longer had to question why she wanted to do something with him. She got to do it whenever she wanted.

Reaching for her rebreather, she slid it over her mouth even though she knew the whole contraption was going to rip out her hair. Then she gestured for Pilot to join them. The little lobster once crab, clambered onto her arm and then clung onto her shoulder.

"I am very ready for that," she said, the words muffled through the rebreather.

As they both dove beneath the waves, she knew she'd never been more ready for anything in her life.

Chapter 41

Wiping blood off what was arguably an electric sword always made her a little nervous. Ellie checked for the fourth time that she had in fact removed the electrical pulses from the device before deciding she'd leave the blood on it a little longer.

It wasn't like the giant sloth creature had acid blood. That was reserved for nearly every single reptilian creature on this planet, now. Why? She had no idea. That sort of question was better asked of Anya, or Mira, or any of the others that were regularly cataloguing the creatures that people like Ellie caught on their recording devices.

"Oh, shit," she muttered, reaching up to stop the recording from the sunglasses she wore.

This was her tenth facility she cleared out. Most of them on her own, although some she had to call in backup for. The first three were an absolute disaster. She'd almost died so many times, Proteus had nearly decided they would not do this anymore.

He'd scolded her up and down, telling her she wasn't cut out for this kind of work if she couldn't take care of herself. And he was right. She hadn't been. She should have focused more on keeping herself alive, but instead, she'd been so focused on not killing the creatures that inhabited this place.

Those feelings were a waste, she was coming to realize. She'd thought this world had very limited creatures on it. That every time she killed one of them, she was taking away from the natural order of things. Whatever survived on this desert planet deserved to live. She had come out of the ocean, where life was seemingly much easier for the sea creatures than it was for those who lived on land.

She had been wrong.

Very, very wrong.

Or, well, they all had been really. They believed that this planet had been dying, while it had actually been thriving. At least some creatures had been thriving. Ellie still didn't know what to call half of them, but they were here. In abundance.

This facility had, unluckily, been one of the more troublesome to clear. But it was filled with smaller creatures for the most part. Some of them almost looked like cats, but they were the standard, leathery creatures that were covered in scars. The cat creatures were her favorite because they weren't usually aggressive. They hissed and spat at her, but they were quick to run out into the sun the moment they realized their home had other people in it.

All she had to do with those was trail them, and then make sure she closed off where they left. Usually some smaller hole in the wall.

But then the sloth creature? That was one she hadn't seen before. It had come up to her waist, like a small bear mixed with some kind of mole, with long claws and very slow movements. She almost felt bad killing it, since it seemed like it wasn't interested in fighting her.

At least until it woke up. She'd just gotten her sword up in time to kill the beast.

"One of these days," she muttered on her way back to the water entrance. "I'm going to get myself a gun."

"I've already argued for that," Proteus said where he waited for her in the water.

His gaze slid over her entire body, taking stock of whether or not she was still alive. Every time she returned, he did this.

Dutifully, she walked over to him and stood there for his inspection. He noticed the slightest scrape on her jaw, feathering his touch over it as though he would only make it hurt worse if he pressed the pad of his finger there.

Then, as he did every time, his fingers grabbed the front zipper of her wetsuit. His eyes burned as he stared into hers, the backs of his knuckles dragging between her breasts, and then down her belly.

"Did you clear the entire facility?" Proteus asked.

"Of course I did," she replied, already breathless and knowing where this was going.

"Are you sure?"

She nodded, allowing him to push her back until she was seated at the edge of the water with her legs spread around him. They'd both been scolded by Alexia for destroying too many wetsuits. The old guard told them she knew damn well what was happening and why they were getting torn. No one was scraping on rocks that much, and even with Ellie fighting the creatures in these facilities, no one else was losing so many wetsuits.

So, Proteus was careful as he dragged the tight material down her shoulders, to her hips, and then down off of her legs.

Then he looked her over, his gaze devouring her as his stare trailed down to her breasts. He loved all of her body, but he loved those the most. He was so fascinated with them, and she didn't mind at all when he wanted to lavish attention on her chest for hours on end. The man knew how to torture her, but she also knew he wasn't going to take his time.

He never could after she cleared a facility like this. He worried about her for far too long because she could die any moment that she was out of his sight.

Proteus trailed his lips up her leg, a relieved breath traveling ahead of him as he slowly made his way up. He always inspected them like he were expecting there to be a bite wound there. Just waiting for him to find.

"All in one piece," she murmured as he reached her thighs.

"For how long?" he asked, his mouth already opening far too wide.

Ellie watched as he allowed it to split open completely, widening farther and farther until it unfurled like a flower.

He attacked her. His tongue unerringly found her core with a speed that should have been terrifying, but she already knew he would not hurt her. She arched into him, caring very little that the tiny teeth that covered the petals of his mouth and down his throat would dig into her skin.

She already had so many scars around her hips. They were almost like tattoos at this point. Silver marks of how much he loved her, and how readily he wanted to please her.

Because he did.

Oh, Proteus pleased her every single day.

To anyone who saw them, they likely would have thought another monster had caught a human and was slowly eating them. With her arms thrown over her head, her hair spread out on the floor, and with her pale back arched as it was, she probably looked a sight. And then there was him. This hulking behemoth of a sea monster was undine and yet not. With his mouth spread between her legs, his throat worked as he swallowed.

But he loved the taste of her. He lapped at her until she was dripping. Until she was so slick she could hear it.

That massive tongue plunged inside of her, working through her folds and then starting a pace she knew he would soon mimic. Her cries grew louder, filling the facility with the sounds of her pleasure.

She shattered. Far too quickly, as she always did. Fast and so hard it made her legs shake even as he rode with her through it. He always did that. Always wanted to feel every single tremble, every lingering pulse before he finally withdrew his tongue.

And then, only then did he loom over her.

When they'd first started this, he would close up his mouth long before she could see him. He didn't want to ruin the moment, he'd said. But she had told him time and time again, she loved every part of him. Even the monstrous parts.

Now, there was a beast on top of her. His mouth was split wide, both pieces glistening in the meager light. Thunder rumbled over them, and all she could see were teeth that could close over her skull at any minute.

The thrill of that hummed through her even as the head of his massive cock slotted between her legs. It still took work. Time. Effort for him to ease his way inside of her, and she loved every single minute of it.

Gasping, she reached between her legs to help him. The head of him was easy. She'd taken him so many times now, she knew what it was like to guide that slick head inside and to feel the burn of a stretch that always happened. But then there was more of him. The thickness of his cock only got thicker the closer they were to the base.

She took the lower one, so the top one could slide over her clit and give that friction she'd come to love.

He slid back out, plunging in deeper with a thrust that made her see stars. Proteus knew how far to go before it became actual pain. They'd practiced so many times now, he could have done it in his sleep to know exactly how far he could push her.

She released her grip on the cock inside her and instead clutched the one that wasn't. He loved it when she gripped him like this, holding onto the top cock and pressing it down hard against her belly. He worked inside of her and out, listening for the sound of her panting to know when to speed up and when to slow down.

Looking up, she felt her own jaw drop open in pleasure at the sight of her monster.

The light played across his shoulders, massive and bunched muscles that moved with every thrust. The way he licked his teeth, and the drool that gathered there because she knew he was dying to taste her.

Then the tentacles.

Ah, those damn hip tentacles got her every time. She always knew when he was close because they would wrap around her. He tasted her with them too, she knew, but they were so damn good at sucking. They latched onto her breasts, her clit, even his own cock. They helped her hold on to his cock that wasn't inside of her, pressing harder, so hard she thought it would hurt him if she tightened her fist even a little more.

He groaned, and the sound vibrated through her.

His pace stuttered, staggering with pleasure. He was close. He always was when he did that.

But she wanted a few more minutes. Time for lingering glances so she could remember this moment for all her days to come. The monster above her, inside her, all of it was so picturesque that she didn't want to forget a single second of what they were doing.

The tentacles roped beneath her, prodding at the other entrance to her body that they were slowly starting to explore. As it writhed inside her, she couldn't stop herself.

Ellie came hard again, clenching around him as her pussy milked him for all it was worth.

That was all it took. He exploded, the sound of his pleasure so loud it made her ears ring. But she loved that too. She loved how loud he was, and how unashamed he had become at taking his pleasure when he hadn't even realized it was a reality for him to do.

She could feel every spray of his come, every rope of it that splashed through her insides and leaked out in a gush that simply could not be contained.

They were both breathing hard as they spiraled down from their pleasure. His mouth sealed back up again, as it always had to so he could speak, but then he looked down at her and chuckled.

He did that a lot lately. The sound was rusty, and sometimes it changed a bit, like he wasn't all that certain if it was the right sound at all. But every time she saw it for what it was.

A blessing.

A gift.

She reached up and wrapped her arms around his neck, tugging him tightly into her embrace and wrapping her legs around him as much as she could. He was so big, he could never actually lie down on top of her. But she appreciated that he pretended for her, dropping some of his weight onto her chest as they both came back to earth.

His lips pressed against her hair, the kiss chaste compared to what they had just done. "Was it hard this time?"

"No, not at all. But I got a new creature on camera." She tapped her sunglasses, which were somehow still on her head, and then realized that she had not, in fact, turned the camera off. "I really need to get better at confirming the camera is off. Now I'll have to go through the footage and delete it."

Proteus leaned back, a gleam in his eye that she recognized. "Or we could keep that footage."

"And do what with it?"

"Watch it. Together."

The heat between her legs started to build again. But then she shook her head. "It's just my perspective. All you would see is yourself."

He arched a brow.

"Well, well, well. It appears the god still wants to feel important," she replied with a laugh. "You want to watch yourself?"

"I was worshipped for years by others. If I wish to still give myself that treatment, you can say nothing about it." He leaned down and nipped her ear, only to growl into it, "Besides, don't you want to watch it all again?"

She shuddered beneath him.

Ellie absolutely wanted to watch that footage over again while having sex with him. Or maybe she'd ask him to be behind her next time. They could both watch while he slowly plunged inside her, grinding down like he'd made her do the first time.

They both needed to stop thinking about this, or they were never going to leave this facility.

"For later," she replied, licking her lips and staring up at him.

"You've made me insatiable, Proteus. I don't know if I'll ever be able to forgive you for that."

He scoffed. "Ah, this is my fault? You're the one who jumps on me any chance you get. Don't think I don't see you watching me. You're supposed to be paying attention in those briefing meetings, and all you do is stare at me."

"Because you're staring at me!"

His gaze heated as he looked down at her. "Of course I am, Ellie. I'm always looking at you."

Her cheeks burned bright red. They had a place to go. They were supposed to return to the domes and give all the information they'd discovered. This facility actually looked viable for life, and most of the rooms were still intact. Even some of the furniture. She should tell them all as soon as possible, so they could start moving people in here like they had at the other two facilities she found that were in as good a state.

But he'd mentioned watching her and... well, she didn't mind when he did that.

Ellie shifted away from him, her hands playing down her body. "Do you want to look at me right now?"

Oh, she loved the expression on his face. Proteus reached down to palm his cocks in one hand, nearly twisting them together as he nodded. "Whatever you want, Sisu. Always."

Chapter 42

4 years later

Proteus guided many of the clones toward the new facility, his massive body clearing the way in case anything might attack them. It wouldn't, but many of the clones felt better having someone of his size watching over them. Most of them had never even been in the ocean. At least not like this.

The undine that surrounded them, breathed for them, were still terrifying to many humans that still lived in the cities. They agreed to come to this place because they would have a better chance at life, but it was still all very new to them. The sea. The undine. The city they were soon going to be living in.

The facilities were ready for them. And this one in particular was better set up than the rest. The team of people who were at the head of this entire operation had learned from every single settlement.

These clones were going to the third settlement in the four years it had taken them to ready themselves. The facilities weren't huge. They weren't cities. That much was certain. But fifty people away from Beta was a start.

This was the first area that was entirely set up with the clones. Of course they would have support from many others, and they wouldn't be isolated by any means. But it was their home, and no one else's.

Ellie waited for them. He crested the water first, making sure she was standing there with a grin on her face and two thumbs up to tell him that she'd gone through the entire place with her team multiple times. Nothing was coming in or out. They were safe here.

Maybe for the first time in their lives.

If there was ever a facility he was going to like, it was this one. The main area they came into was surrounded by pretty green tile that almost looked like they were stepping onto a meadow. Ellie had gotten Mira to send over a bunch of absolutely useless plants, and even salvaged a few from right outside of the building to turn the entire area into greenery.

She could only do that because the main atrium here still had a glass ceiling. Somehow, after all the rain and hail and storms, the glass had survived. And today it was wonderfully sunny, if a bit warm, for the clones to walk into their new home.

He gestured to the undine, and they all brought the humans up with them. The tentacles attached at their necks were still disgusting to him, but at least he no longer felt woozy when he watched an undine detach from the people they were carrying.

"Welcome!" Ellie said to every single person she helped out of the water.

A long line of people stood beside her. One of them handed out towels. Another person had a guidebook to give the newcomers once they were dry. The next person would grab the hand of the person, and any family or friends if they wished, and bring them on a tour of the facility. This one was smaller than the others, but it didn't need to be big.

He waited until the last person was handed off to their guide, and then swam close to the edge of the water. "I have a surprise for you."

"For me?" Ellie said, pressing a hand to her chest. "What surprise would that be?"

Proteus already had his hand in the water, gesturing for someone to come up last.

Ellie enjoyed traveling with him. There was a part of her that yearned for adventure more than the average human, and he loved that about her. But their travels brought her away from all the other humans. Yes, she got to welcome people into their new homes, and that often made her feel good. But nothing compared to seeing her actual friends.

A bright mass of red hair appeared before Mira crested the water. She pulled her rebreather off immediately, a bright grin on her face as she yanked herself out of the water with ease.

Ellie laughed, shocked to see Mira so far away from the domes. "What are you doing here? Did you swim with Proteus?"

Mira shook her head. "No, you know I have my own ride in the ocean."

"Then why are you wearing the re—" Ellie lost everything she might have said when Arges came out of the water too.

Cradled in his arms was the smallest little girl. Even Proteus felt a certain way when he looked at that head of dark hair. She was so pretty. Those big black eyes were unnatural in a human face and blinked up at Ellie. Then, she reached out her chubby arms with a gurgling noise she exclusively made every time she saw her aunt.

Ellie reached for the child with a squeal that almost matched the little girl's.

Avaia was the very first human and undine hybrid. She looked more human than undine, in Proteus's opinion. She had two legs. Two arms. One heart, which was thoroughly disappointing. Her dark hair curled when it was dry, but it was rarely dry. Her father mostly tried to keep her in the water so she could learn to use her gills.

Yes, gills.

Though she didn't have any on her ribs, the little girl did have gills on her neck. She wasn't very good at using them, though. Learning how to go from air to water had been trying. Obviously, she needed to be on land with her mother to be cared for, as Avaia was far more similar to humans than undine in that way.

She'd even had a live birth, not inside of a purse. The process had been horrific, but Proteus had to be there because Ellie had insisted on being there.

He still heard Mira's screams in his sleep sometimes. It terrified him.

But Mira was alive, and so was Avaia, and now everyone was in love with the child. Even him. Proteus could admit that the little girl had wriggled her way into his heart just like she had everyone else's.

Mostly when she did this. Because Avaia loved Ellie, and that was something he could agree with the child on.

"Why are you here?" Ellie cooed, picking her up and swinging her into her arms. "You should be at home in bed, tiny one!"

Avaia didn't speak yet, maybe something to do with not having the same genetics as everyone else, but she watched Ellie's mouth like she understood every word.

Mira laughed at the question. "We thought we would come visit her favorite auntie. It's time to get out into the world more, don't you think?"

The two women launched into a conversation about babies, something that Proteus was very much not interested in, but then he realized Arges was looking at him. The blue undine threw an arm over his shoulders and gestured at the vision in front of them.

"I never thought my life would look this good," he said. "Did you?"

Those dead organs inside his chest thudded hard against his ribs. "No, I didn't. But we are so damn lucky to have found them."

423

Follow me on socials or Amazon to keep your eye out for the next book!

Thank you

Holy shit, I think this series is complete.

Like actually complete.

I know I wasn't that nice at the end of Call of the Fathoms, telling you guys it was over, but even then I knew it wasn't. There was one more story to tell, I just didn't know how to get there.

This series has changed my life. The amount of wonderful readers who have found me, and who I have found, that came from double-dicked mermen is just… It still floors me.

I cannot tell you how much your support means. For a very rural girl from Maine, it's still a bit of a shock to know that you are reading my books.

That my life has been forever changed because of you.

Thank you, from the very bottom of my heart, for loving the Deep Waters series. For finding excitement and adoration in the arms of a merman.

You make the little girl in me who was always asking people if they wanted to play mermaids in the pool, and always getting shut down, feel less alone.

Sending so so many hugs and kisses.

Emma.

About the Author

Emma Hamm is a small town girl on a blueberry field in Maine. She writes stories that remind her of home, of fairytales, and of myths and legends that make her mind wander.

She can be found by the fireplace with a cup of tea and her seven cats dipping their paws into the water without her knowing.

For more updates, join my newsletter!
www.emmahamm.com

www.ingramcontent.com/pod-product-compliance
Lightning Source LLC
Chambersburg PA
CBHW020052310726
48970CB00007B/2522